Adam Kennedy is a novelist of remarkable versatility whose previous novels range from the highly successful thriller *The Domino Principle*, which inspired the international hit movie of the same name, to *In A Far Country*, an enthralling family drama set in the 1960s. His most recent titles include the Bradshaw Trilogy: *No Place To Cry*, *The Fires Of Summer* and *All Dreams Denied*, and *Love Left Over* – a collection of bitter-sweet love stories. He lives in Connecticut with his wife, Susan.

Passion Never Knows

The Kincaid Trilogy
Volume One

Adam Kennedy

KNIGHT

First published in 1990
by HEADLINE BOOK PUBLISHING PLC

First published in paperback in 1991
by HEADLINE BOOK PUBLISHING PLC

This edition published 2003 by
Knight an imprint of The Caxton Publishing Group

10 9 8 7 6 5 4 3

ISBN 1 86019 6462

Printed and bound in Great Britain by
Mackays of Chatham Ltd, Chatham, Kent

Caxton Publishing Group
20 Bloomsbury Street
London
WC1B 3QA

For David and Evelyn
Who have always wished me well

BOOK ONE

The inner life is the only life . . .
everything else is ballet.

Millard Hofer

When the arbitrary is made to seem
inevitable, the result is art.

Estéban Mojada

• CHAPTER 1 •

1

How hard it is to tell the simple truth. Columns of figures. Totalling sums. That sort of thing. Isolating objects and characteristics. Seeing them for what they are. Getting the smells correct, the textures and temperatures. Marking clearly the flavours and the seasons. Getting it right.

Consider Roy Kincaid, for example. Not a remarkable man. Not a physical specimen. Medium. Medium everything, one might conclude. Average. Not tall or broad or specifically agile. None of these. A straight back. Not twisted or deformed in any way but not a beautiful man, certainly. A used-up look about him, his face a topographical record of where he'd been and what he'd seen. But nothing striking or memorable about it. Apart from his nose, with a scar-welt across it and a broken bone inside, apart from that and his jungle-cat eyes, grey-green with a squint, secret slits that gave away nothing, sleepy eyes that permitted no examination of what might lie behind them, the eyes of a tracker or an outlaw; aside from those things – the damaged nose and the dangerous eyes – his face did not attract attention, did not lead people who saw him in the street either to draw near or to step aside.

Men like Kincaid seem destined for oilfields, construction sites, or docks where ships are loaded. They recognize themselves in these surroundings. They see their

3

counterparts there. These men live and drink and work and carouse together, fight over women, punish each other with their fists. And for the most part they end up where they started, their bodies ravaged by tobacco and whisky and hard work, their early dreams long since forgotten.

We are seldom curious about such men. Like the poor, they're always with us and never in short supply. Although they do much of the world's work, when they leave that world little notice is taken of their absence. No one solicits their opinions when they're living. Few people mourn when they die. An ordinary man, we seem to believe, is ordinary by choice and is best left to his ordinariness. Even the man's wife and children often share this belief.

Consider now, if you will, a young woman named Sophie Cranston Black, a true child of privilege. Well bred, well educated, and conspicuously well served by the generations of her family who had preceded her, who had left her a legacy of good bones, gentle instincts, and thousands of acres of real property. From the day of her birth, her destiny seemed to gleam and sparkle and advertise its splendour.

Whereas men like Kincaid, or men who *seem* to be like Kincaid, abound in every country, women like Sophie Black are rare indeed. And not simply because they have money and breeding – money and breeding produce deformity and eccentricity and perversion more often than they produce true quality. If Sophie, for example, had inherited the flaws of her father, Major Cranston, no miracle of environment or upbringing could have rescued her from the paranoia which was his principal trait. Through good fortune, however, not only was she able to spend a great deal of her childhood away from her father, she also, at the instant of genetic explosion that conceived her, took nearly all of her physical and emotional ingredients from the Wiswell strain, her mother's family.

Each disappointment in her father's life, whether real or imagined, seemed to further intensify and crystallize his flaws; each unpleasantness that Sophie suffered seemed to ennoble her in some way. Her first ten years, for example, were spent in India at various military installations, and it was a life she secretly detested. But the survival process created a core of self-reliance inside her that was enduring and remarkable.

At the age of twenty Sophie was a widow with two small children. At first her parents and her close friends assumed she would not marry again. But by the time she was twenty-five, people began to arrange dinners and luncheons and picnics and tea dances with a single purpose in their minds, to introduce Sophie to a proper gentleman who would be a suitable companion and perhaps a future husband for her. She was charming and gracious to all these candidates and was actually quite fond of two or three of them. But the fondness remained simply that: *fondness*. Those who had hoped or expected that it would become something else gave up at last and began searching for another promising gentleman to invite to dinner.

Twelve years after her husband's death, however, when she was thirty-two, Sophie found the man she wanted. He was not presented to her by her family or her neighbours. They did not know him. If they had known him or had met him somewhere it would never have occurred to them to introduce him to Sophie. When some of them did meet him at last, when they understood that the man she had chosen was Roy Kincaid, the news was hard for them either to believe or accept. Only Sophie understood her choice and she cared nothing at all for the opinions of other people.

5

In London, in the winter of 1932, many men who couldn't find work went into the streets of the city. To beg, to sell fruit from rucksacks they carried on their shoulders, to kneel on the cold pavement and polish the boots of strangers.

The pavement artists increased in number, too, though not in quality. Many streets in the West End were decorated underfoot with great chalk pictures of biblical scenes or Devon landscapes, tin cups at the borders waiting for contributions. And the professional buskers who had worked in Shaftesbury Avenue and St Martin's Lane for thirty years, many of whom were as familiar to theatre patrons as the actors on the stages of the Garrick or the Haymarket, found their open-air performing areas crowded by newcomers: jugglers, weight-lifters, and tumblers, many of them dangerously unskilled.

Two such newcomers began to perform nightly outside the Duke of York's theatre. One man, a dwarf, walked about on his hands, turned cartwheels, and performed physical feats that only dwarfs can manage. His partner, a wiry young man wearing what seemed to be seaman's togs, a black cape over his shoulders and holding a heavy iron sceptre, stood bare-headed, legs spread, and recited long passages from *Henry the Fifth*, *Richard the Second*, and *Coriolanus*, and the poems of John Donne and Tennyson, all in a strong and clear voice. Neither man smiled or made an effort to ingratiate himself with the people who gathered round. The dwarf seemed tireless in his acrobatics and the young man reciting appeared to have an endless repertoire of poetry and soliloquies. The dwarf's cap lay upside down on the pavement but neither man referred to it or expressed gratitude when people dropped coins into it.

By early springtime, the young man with the sceptre had begun to attract attention beyond the kerbside. In newspaper interviews both Donald Wolfit and Leon Quartermaine praised his voice and his elocution. And the *Observer* critic, in damning a production of *A Winter's Tale*, said, 'The best reading of Shakespeare I heard last evening came from a busker just outside the theatre.' Appearing unaware or unimpressed by the attention they were getting, the dwarf and his unsmiling partner carried on with their work, divided the proceeds each night, and went their separate ways.

One night in April, however, quite late, the theatres dark and the pavements nearly empty, as the young man with the sceptre walked off towards Trafalgar Square, a gentleman near his own age approached him and said, 'Sorry to bother you, but aren't you the chap who does the poetry readings outside the Duke of York's?'

'The show's over for tonight, mate.'

'I know that. My name's Evan Tagg. I do occasional pieces for the *Daily Telegraph*. I thought perhaps I'd write something about you.'

The young man in seaman's clothes had continued walking towards Trafalgar Square, Tagg just beside him. 'Why would you want to do that, I wonder?'

'People are talking about you. They seem to appreciate what you're doing. We've seen a few mentions in other papers already. I thought we might have a chat one day soon, then I could do a longer piece about you. Take a picture perhaps.'

'Not much to tell about me. I'm out here trying to scrape a few shillings together. Just like these other sorry bastards up and down the streets.'

'Not quite the same, Mr . . . I don't know your name.'

'No reason why you should. I don't know your name, either.'

'Tagg. Evan Tagg. I told you a moment ago.'

'My name's Kincaid.' He stopped walking. 'So you're collecting a bit of money to write about us poor blokes showing our asses in the street. Good for you. But what's in it for me?'

'I can't pay you if that's what you mean.'

'Why not?'

'Because newspapers don't operate that way. But if we print the article you should benefit from it.'

Kincaid shook his head. 'Means nothing to me, seeing my name in print.'

'If people read about you, perhaps they'll come to see you. You and your partner will take in more money.'

'My partner's gone off. I've got no bloody partner. He got himself a ship. Leaving for Canada day after tomorrow. And I've got a line on something myself. Next week. A good ship's hard to come by these times.'

The following week the features editor of the *Telegraph* rang up Tagg at his flat in Gordon Square. 'What became of the piece on the busker? The Shakespeare chap?'

'Told me he was leaving England. Shipping out this week.'

'He's still here. Saw him outside the Globe last night. My wife wanted to adopt him. Loves his voice.'

'I'll look him up,' Tagg said. 'Soon as I'm back from Manchester.'

Ten days later, eleven-thirty at night, Tagg and Kincaid sat in a booth on the upstairs floor of the King James pub on Great Windmill Street.

'What happened to your ship?' Tagg said.

'It can bloody well sink as far as I'm concerned. The first mate wanted a pay-off so I told him to get stuffed. There's a hundred seamen for every berth just now and no good news in sight. So I'm stuck here. High and dry.'

'Any luck on the street?'

8

Kincaid shook his head. 'All the bastards ask me is what happened to the dwarf.'

Tagg signalled to the waiter for two more pints. 'Maybe your luck will change,' he said to Kincaid. 'After we publish this piece about you we'll see what happens.'

3

Two days later Tagg sat with Alan Winkler in the *Daily Telegraph* offices.

'If you don't like the piece,' Tagg said, 'give it back to me. I'll sell it to the *Daily Mail*.'

'I like it. I didn't mean that. Fascinating stuff. But some of it's hard to swallow. Are you sure he wasn't having you on?'

'Can't guarantee it. You know that. But if it's not true, he's rehearsed it well. I doubled back and threw him some trick questions but he didn't contradict himself.'

'So what we have here is a chap with a photographic memory?'

Tagg nodded. 'He took one look at my article in a copy of today's paper that I showed him and started quoting it back at me half an hour later. Letter perfect. He's got a mind like a blotter. Soaks up everything.'

'And besides that, he's a mimic. Is that the word for it?'

'When he's talking to you one to one, relaxed and drinking beer the way he and I were doing, there's no doubt he's an Australian. The accent, the lingo, all of it. But he can switch into Mayfair English any time he wants to. Or make you think you're talking to an American who just got off the boat. After we'd talked for ten minutes he started answering me in my own voice. Sounded exactly like me.'

'He says he learned all this in prison?'

'Didn't learn it there exactly. Just discovered what he was capable of. Worked in a prison library in Massachusetts with a retired academic from Boston who'd put his brother-in-law to sleep with a fire shovel. The old gent took a shine to Kincaid apparently, started him reading the classics, taught him how to speak properly, and little by little they found out what he could do.'

'Is he smart?'

'Hard to say. He's quick. And shrewd. And he has a lot of information in his head. That passes for intelligence in Whitehall, so it should work for him.'

'But he wants to be an actor . . . is that it?'

'Not so far as I could tell. I don't know what he wants. Maybe he doesn't want anything. Maybe he's just trying to hang on. It seems that's what he's always done.'

4

Except for the war years, from 1916 to 1918, when he was posted to a military hospital in Surrey, Major Cranston spent his entire career in India. In 1897, when he was thirty-two, he married Margaret Wiswell and, in 1901, Sophie, their only child, was born. In 1911, after the death of Margaret's mother, she and Sophie returned to her family home in Northumberland. Until 1918, when he was mustered out, they saw the Major only during his home leaves.

In India, the Cranstons lived an insular life. Depending on the season and Major Cranston's duties, they were quartered in Simla, or Calcutta, or Delhi. In whatever place they found themselves the quality of life was that of a cloistered residential island with the British Club at centre. Sophie's school classes, the parties she attended, the tennis and cricket matches, were very like the ones she would experience when she returned to their home country. Her playmates, her classmates, and the friends she made as she grew up were facsimiles of herself. They had common backgrounds and common aspirations. Like thoroughbred horses, they received identical training and learned the same rules of the course.

Sophie differed from the young people she grew up with, however, in one key respect. She appeared to have known always the things the others were being taught. She had balance. It seemed she had been born with it. She was eager to learn. She tried always to excel. She showed no taste for conflict, no instinct for rebellion. 'Too bad she's not a boy,' her father said. 'She'd make a damned fine soldier. Knows how to take orders.'

Does this seem to be the portrait of a meek and docile creature, slipping quietly from room to room, using only the back stairs, never speaking above a whisper? If so, then that picture is both inaccurate and incomplete. Although her demeanour suggested that she was willing to conform, there was a crispness to her movements, a level of energy and, surprisingly, a sensual stillness at times that gave one pause, that caused one to wonder if everything about lovely Sophie was in fact what it seemed to be.

As she grew up, when people listed the great beauties of her country Sophie's name was not always mentioned. But it was mentioned sometimes. A few people believed that her beauty was rare and unmatched, particularly their neighbour, Angus Bradshaw, an old and wise gentleman who said, 'When she's thirty, she'll be the most beautiful woman in England. When these other little pigeons with their yellow hair and cornflower eyes have gone to fat and bloated cheeks they'll look at Sophie and bite their lips.'

Sophie first met Toby Black when she came home to Northumberland from India. She was eleven years old and he was sixteen. She thought he was beautiful and flawless. He didn't notice her at all.

Later, however, when she was just seventeen and he was an infantry lieutenant scheduled to leave soon for Belgium, his perceptions of her were quite different. Without the consent of her father, who was now stationed in Surrey, but with the total approval of her mother, Sophie and Toby were quietly married.

Thirteen months later her daughter, Sarah, was born. The following year she gave birth to a son who was christened Trevor. At that time Toby was in hospital in Bristol, had been there, except for occasional home leaves, for more than a year. Recovering nicely, his doctors said, from serious shrapnel wounds he had suffered in the second battle of the Marne.

Major Cranston, who had been returned to civilian life by now and had drifted uneasily home to Wiswell Towers, assured his daughter that Toby was in good hands at St Agnes hospital. 'General Swift's in charge there. I've known him since Sandhurst. An excellent chap and a fine surgeon. I rang him up last Thursday, we had a good chat, and he told me they'll have Toby put right in no time. Medicine's a precise science, you know. Every human body is a laboratory. So when a man like Harry Swift takes charge the pieces fall quickly into place.'

When Toby died on the operating table three weeks later, Major Cranston's approval of his son-in-law was almost instantly withdrawn. That approval had been granted solely in recognition of his status as a fellow officer or so it seemed. The Major's belated acceptance of his daughter's marriage had been a sort of appendage to the military approval. Although Bill Cranston had never faced an enemy soldier or fired a weapon in combat, he saw himself as a battle-scarred defender of the Crown. Toby's falling on a battlefield in France, therefore, had gained him admittance to an honoured place alongside Lord Jellicoe, Douglas Haig, General Allenby, and Cranston himself.

By dying, however, Toby, in Cranston's eyes, lost stature. The Major, who sensed betrayal in every corner, seemed to feel that some injustice had been done to *him*. Although his son-in-law had not been a hero, he had been, indisputably, a war victim, and his wounds, to Cranston, had come to be *family* wounds. Whereas a wounded soldier in the family was an inexhaustible subject, a stimulant to imagination, to reminiscence, to personal association, a dead soldier, on the other hand, struck a single musical note that no one was eager to hear a second time.

Still smarting from what he felt had been an early and undeserved termination to his own career, Cranston had through Toby Black found a new, if temporary, connection with the military world. But as he stood at attention in full uniform, watching his son-in-law's coffin disappear inside the Wiswell family crypt, the Major felt cheated. That new identity had been taken from him. He felt anonymous suddenly, an unidentifiable figure in a grey line of mourners.

Throughout the funeral preparations and the funeral itself, however, Cranston functioned as an exemplary commander, handling procurement and distribution as smoothly as he had supervised the kitchen and public rooms of the British Club in Delhi. Quiet authority and thorough preparation. A solid presence in the war room. Members of Toby Black's family who had never met Major Cranston before were impressed by his control of the situation, both the supply side and the emotional side. Although he seemed rooted wherever he stood in his splendid uniform, there was no escaping the fact that signals were being sent out at all times. Like a florid and bulky control tower he had found a way, it seemed, to communicate with all corners of the great house.

Even his wife and daughter, who knew him for what he was as well as for what he was not, even they had brief flashes of admiration for his behaviour. When they heard him say – and he said it often during those unhappy days – 'I've lost a son,' they came to believe, they almost came to believe, that he was expressing his true feelings.

After the burial there was a period of calm, a musical rest, as though silence and kindness had been ordained, as though the healing process was what mattered most now, as though nothing else really mattered at all. At Wiswell Towers, the staff, under the supervision of Mr John Trout, always functioned flawlessly. Now, in this mourning period, they behaved as though it was possible to improve on perfection. Exceptional meals were served with exceptional grace. Triumphant wines were brought up from the cellars. Not a whisper, not a murmur was heard from the kitchens or the pantry. No laughter below stairs, no voices raised in anger.

In the garages the chauffeurs redoubled their normal efforts. The motors of the family cars purred almost soundlessly. The paint and the steel and the glass shone and sparkled. The interiors were dusted and waxed.

The horses in the stables were trimmed and groomed, their tails braided, their hoofs polished. The tack was thoroughly oiled and burnished. Even the dogs were bathed and clipped and given extra scraps from the stableboys' plates. It was as though kindness had just been discovered and defined, in that place, at those moments, and everyone was eager to learn it, to explore it, to extend it to its furthest boundaries.

Sorrow must be given its proper undisturbed niche, everyone seemed to be saying. Loss must be given its day. Everyday concerns must neither disrupt nor diminish it. The natural flowing rhythm of sadness must be respected. It must be allowed to diminish in its own time, at its own speed.

While Sophie and her mother welcomed this quiet and orderly extension of the mourning period, the Major resented it. It all seemed strangely amorphous to him. Without structure or chain of command. It had a life of its own which disturbed him. He began to feel restless and neglected. He spent more time than usual with his whisky decanters and his cue stick.

6

Sophie, wearing wide-legged black trousers and a knee-length Chinese silk kimono, sat by a large bow window in her London house overlooking Green Park. Evan Tagg sat in a deep chair facing her.

'I can't believe what you're telling me,' she said. 'I thought your article in the *Telegraph* was a send-up. And the more you tell me about this chap . . . what's his name again?'

'Roy Kincaid.'

'The more I hear, the less I'm able to believe.' She laughed. 'It's all too Alice-in-Wonderland to be true, isn't it? Do you really believe him?'

'No reason why I shouldn't,' Evan said. 'One thing I've learned from journalism: everything is bizarre. Lots of odd things going on out there. Strange dreams. Secret vices. Twisted minds. If I tried to put those people in my

15

plays the way they truly are, if I described the things they think and the things they do, the whole bloody story would fall apart. No credibility. *The Guardian* would say, "Mr Tagg has allowed his sense of fantasy to devour his sense of reality."'

'You must admit it, Ev, it's a difficult proposition. Here we have a remarkably ordinary man . . .'

'I thought you were saying he's too extraordinary to be believed.'

'That's my point. We have this ordinary-looking chap . . .'

'I didn't know you'd seen him,' Evan said.

'I'll admit I haven't studied him. But when I saw his photograph with your article, I realized I had seen him once with the Blakemores, when we were seeing Ralph Richardson and Hardwicke at the Globe. And another evening when I went with Uncle Howard to see Madeleine Carroll and Reggie Gardiner in *Pleasure Cruise*. Howard had read what Donald Wolfit said about Kincaid so he particularly wanted to see him. But since we were late for our performance we could only watch for a moment.'

'And what did you think?'

'Ordinary-looking fellow, I thought. As I said. But Howard was quite taken with him. Thought his voice was extraordinary.'

'Do you agree?'

'Unusual voice. No doubt about it. But it seemed to have been stolen from another body. I decided he was a trained actor down on his luck. A fugitive from Birmingham rep perhaps.'

'What a cynic you are! Why are you so certain he isn't exactly what he says he is?'

'Impossible,' she said. 'Nobody is simply what he says he is. Or what he thinks he is.'

'I am.'

16

'Oh, dear Lord, how we deceive ourselves. You, my dear, under that laconic exterior, are the most complex creature imaginable. I've known you for more than twenty years. In all that time I've had an opportunity to catalogue your quirks and convolutions.'

'I think you're trying to compliment me,' Evan said. 'Making me sound more interesting than I am.'

'I didn't say you were interesting. I said you're complex and strange. You may also be unknowable. But I haven't reached that conclusion yet.'

He smiled and poured wine into their glasses. 'If I'm so fascinating, why don't theatre managers discover that quality in my plays?'

She slowly sipped her wine. Then, 'Are you quite certain you want me to answer that?'

'I may regret it but yes, I do want you to answer.'

'The answer is simple. Because you are not in your plays. They're a *mélange* of Maugham and Ivor Novello. There's nothing wrong with that, of course. They're fine craftsmen and you've been learning your craft. But they're not you and you're not them. When you decide to write about something you know, something that matters to you in your own life, then people will notice. You'll be wildly successful and I'll have to queue up to get a ticket for your plays.'

Evan shook his head. 'I'm not interested in self-revelation. You know that. I don't like to see pain and torment when I go to the theatre. I want to entertain people, not enlighten them.'

'I know that's what you think you want, but you'll get over it. All of us struggle to hide what we really feel. But an artist can't do that. Not if he's serious. He has to be willing to show everything. Naked to the world. Look at Noel Coward. Why do you think people flock to see his plays? Not just because he's clever. They love him

17

because he's always in love. He's willing to be hurt and willing to admit it. While the rest of us are busy hiding our scars he's busy writing about his vulnerability. "Time may lie heavy between but what has been is past forgetting." Everybody knows that. That's what heartbreak is all about. It happens to all of us but it takes an artist to chisel it in stone, to make it clear and final and permanent.'

When Evan didn't say anything she said, 'I've hurt your feelings, haven't I?'

'No. I was just thinking that you should be the writer, not me.'

'Not a chance, my darling. I have a smattering of intelligence, boundless energy, and emotion to burn but there's nothing original or profound about me. I'm a consumer, not a creator.'

'Nonsense,' he said. 'When you were sixteen you were keen to be an actress.'

'Of course. Because I was sixteen and madly in love with myself. By becoming an actress I could demonstrate to the world how splendid I was. Or so I thought.'

'And then came Toby.'

'Correct.'

'And the theatre lost a lovely actress.'

'Not at all. I knew nothing whatsoever, you see, about the work of acting. I just loved to dress up and be taken to the theatre. I saw some connection, I'm sure, between my entrance into the stalls and the entrance of an actress from the wings to centre stage. I'm a social creature, Ev, you know that, a herd animal. Can't bear to be by myself. So of course I was attracted to the theatre. What better life? An actor is always with other actors, either rehearsing or playing. Or so it seemed to me. And when they're not at work they're dining together, or drinking, or having mad love affairs. In my innocence I thought it was an

18

ideal choice for me. Now of course I realize it's a profession that demands stamina and discipline and the ability to absorb punishment and humiliation. I have none of those qualities. I was brought up in a benevolent cocoon. I've never had to struggle and I never shall.'

'But you'll continue to make grand entrances into the foyers of theatres.'

'Of course,' she said, holding her wine glass up to the light. 'My theatrical ambitions are confined to such performances. No one can surpass me there.'

7

When he was eleven years old Evan said to his father, 'When I grow up, when I've made a great deal of money and have a fine home of my own, I'm going to marry Sophie.'

'You mustn't say things like that,' Arthur Tagg said.

'Why not? It's what I expect to do.'

'Mind what I say, young man. I never want to hear anything of that sort from you again.'

'But I don't see . . .'

'Not another word. You and I will discuss this in our rooms this evening after tea.'

When they sat that evening in their apartment on the top floor of the Cranston home, Arthur Tagg said, 'Now . . . let's have our little talk.' He settled deeper in his chair. 'I'm sorry if I spoke sharply to you today. But I was surprised to hear the things you said. Did I hurt your feelings?'

'No, sir.'

'I'm glad. But I apologize all the same. There's just the two of us in our little family so it's important that we be kind to each other. You understand that, don't you?'

'Yes, sir.'

Arthur leaned forward in his chair, elbows on his knees, and laced his fingers together. 'We've lived here for almost two years now. Ever since we came back to England from New York. It wasn't "coming back" for you, of course. Since you were born in America and your mother is an American you'll have your choice of citizenship later on. But as we discussed on the ship, you may remember, England is my home, my only home, and I hope you will also come to feel that you belong here.'

'I want to be wherever you are,' Evan said.

'I know that and it pleases me. But I hope you also like the life here in England.'

'Yes, sir. I do.'

'Good. I'm glad.' He put his hand on Evan's shoulder. 'We're quite fortunate, you know. I was fortunate to be taken on here as Sophie's tutor and drawing teacher, and we are both fortunate indeed to be able to live in such comfortable surroundings. Wiswell Towers is one of the fine old homes in this county. Some say the very finest. And because Mrs Cranston is such a generous woman we have been invited to share her home. Almost as though we were family members. You noticed, I'm sure, that I used the word *almost*. Although every effort has been made to make us feel at ease and at home here, it is important for us to remember, you and I, that we are, in fact, guests. Less than guests in a sense, because I am, as you know, a salaried employee. Required to supply certain educational and instructional services, and subject to dismissal if these services are not satisfactory to Mrs Cranston. You're aware of all this, of course.'

'Yes, sir.'

'Now for something you may not know. When I accepted this position, I fully expected that I would have to find a public school for you, somewhere in this area,

20

probably in Carlisle. Mrs Cranston knew that I had a son who lived with me and was my sole charge, but there was no suggestion made, and none expected, that you would be able to live here. I was surprised and gratified, therefore, when you and I arrived, to learn that you were to stay with me in these apartments and be tutored by me along with the Cranstons' daughter. Since Sophie had missed a year of school when she was ill in India and since you're just one year younger than she is, it was easy for me to plan a curriculum that would benefit both of you at the same time. You've been able to study together and learn together.'

'Yes, sir.'

'You are an only child, of course, and so is Sophie. I believe it has been good for both of you to be in the company of another young person. Am I right about that?'

'Yes, sir.'

'However – and this is the major point I'm making – in this atmosphere of hospitality and warmth it's important that we remember our place. Like Mr Trout and Mrs Whitson, we are here at the pleasure of the Cranstons.'

'But we don't live in the staff quarters,' Evan said. 'Sophie and I don't play with the staff children.'

'That's true, you don't. But just because certain lines are not drawn doesn't mean that those lines don't exist. Do you follow me?'

'I'm not sure I do.'

'What is it you don't understand?'

'I like Mrs Cranston and she likes me. She treats me the same as she treats Sophie. As if she were my mother. And Sophie told me she likes you better than she does her father. She doesn't like him at all. She said she wished that you and her mother could be married.'

'You mustn't pay attention to such remarks. And you

21

mustn't repeat them. Sophie's still a young girl and she says foolish things sometimes. It's important for you to remember that feelings are not facts. Can you remember that?'

'Yes, sir.'

'Let me put it to you another way. We are on a different level from the Cranstons. Financially and socially. That's a fact. We're in England now, not America. America pretends to be a classless society. Americans tell themselves that everyone is equal. England makes no such pretence.'

'You mean Sophie and I are not equal?'

'Look around you and you'll see the answer to that. All this will belong to Sophie one day. This home, these lands, the house in London. Everything the Wiswells have accumulated in three centuries.'

'So it's all about money, then. That's all that matters?'

His father smiled. 'No, it's not just that. You come from a decent, respected family. The Taggs have lived in Salisbury for many generations. Your grandfather and his father were merchants, honest, hard-working shopkeepers. There's nothing in our background to be ashamed of. I had a fine classical education. My father saw to that. Had I stayed in England and taken advantage of the teaching opportunity I was offered at St Joseph's, I would be firmly established now in an academic career. But . . . I made other choices.'

'You went to America.'

'That's correct. I followed your mother to America and we were married.'

'Are you sorry you didn't stay here in England?' Evan said.

'No, of course not. I didn't mean that. I was simply pointing out that in some areas of our lives we have choices. In other areas we do not. Each of us is born into

22

a particular class. With rare exceptions we remain in that class throughout our lives. The Cranstons are landed people. They belong to a certain class. So do the Wiswells, Mrs Cranston's family. Just as their friends and neighbours – the Blacks, the Bicks, the Causeys, and the Bradshaws – do.'

'So they're better than us,' Evan said. 'That's what you're saying?'

'No. I'm saying they're different from us. And we are different from them.'

'Sophie treats me like a brother. She tells me everything she thinks.'

'All the same you are not her brother. You are her schoolmate, the son of her tutor. Already you see that she goes to parties you are not invited to. Before long she'll go to still more balls and outings that you can not attend. And when she marries she'll marry a young man of her own class, someone whose family lives in a great house very much like this one.'

After a moment Evan said, 'Did you and my mother come from the same class?'

'Your mother's an American. As I said, things are different there.'

'But what if she'd been English? What if in every other way she was exactly the same as she is now, or as she was when you met her, would you have been from the same class?'

'No.'

'Then you wouldn't have married each other. Is that right?'

'I can't answer that question,' Arthur said.

'I think you would have got married anyway.'

'Perhaps we would have. But it would have been a mistake.'

23

'Is that why you're not together now? Because you came from different classes?'

'I can't answer that either.'

'Sophie says people get divorced because they're incompatible. Were you and my mother incompatible?'

For a long moment Arthur didn't answer. At last he said, 'When you're a bit older you'll realize that some situations can be clearly analysed and explained, others cannot.'

'What about the scientific method? That's what you've been teaching us.'

Arthur smiled. 'It works well in scientific matters. Human behaviour comes under a separate heading.'

'I don't understand that.'

'Most of us don't understand it. It's just something we have to accept.'

'Like the class system?'

'Exactly.'

8

Two weeks after his article about Kincaid appeared in the *Telegraph*, Evan went to the south of France to do a piece about American expatriates who were still living there or who had drifted back after the stock market crash in 1929. While he was in St Tropez, staying at the Palais d'Or, he had a letter from Sophie.

You rascal. I'm being rained on every day here in London while you are strolling that beautiful esplanade *en plein soleil*, sipping the tantalizing wines of Provence, and offering yourself to the tender young women of the area. And why not? But how I envy you.

Interesting news. I know you are a playwright and

not a journalist. And even if you were a full-time journalist you would write interesting and creative feature stories, as you do now, rather than report the news events of the day. But if you were here and if you were a *news* reporter you would be writing an interesting London story just now.

Your busker, Roy Kincaid, has been arrested and charged with aggravated assault and robbery. On Irving Street, last Tuesday, just after midnight, a crowd of people saw him beating a man and taking money from him. When the police came, Kincaid said it was *his* money, that the man had stolen it from *him*. When Kincaid tried to take it back the man threatened him with a knife and Kincaid knocked him unconscious. At least that was Kincaid's story. The other man, whose name is Slate, was taken to hospital. When police questioned him later he said the money was his, that he'd earned it helping a drayman on Marylebone High Street. He said the knife belonged to Kincaid, not to him. So Kincaid was detained by the police. A dozen people had seen him punching Slate but no one, it seemed, had seen Slate snitch Kincaid's money in front of the Duke of York's. One newspaper report referred to the article you wrote, saying that Kincaid had been in prison in Australia and America. The police knew about that too, so it doesn't look too promising, I'm afraid, for our mysterious busker.

For the remaining days that Evan spent in France his time was fully occupied. Interviewing people, reading old correspondence and newspaper cuttings, making notes, talking on the telephone. But the letter Sophie had written about Kincaid stayed fresh in his mind. He told himself he was not surprised by what had happened but all the same it disturbed him. The thought of Kincaid being sent to prison again, being buried, becoming anonymous, upset him and continued to upset him. The suspicion that his article might have prejudiced the authorities against Kincaid was doubly unsettling.

9

Three weeks went by before Evan returned to London. The train from Dover got him into the city just before midnight. At ten the following morning he was in Alan Winkler's office. 'Before we get into the expatriate material,' Evan said, 'tell me what you know about Kincaid.'

Winkler smiled. 'We don't have to worry about that chappie. He's become a bloody folk hero. At least in Bloomsbury.'

'What do you mean? I had a letter from Sophie and she said he was locked up for assault and likely to stay there.'

'Then she didn't tell you the complete story.'

'There was no place she could write to me. I've been on the move since I left St Tropez.'

'It's the damnedest thing I ever heard of. Sophie was right. He was in jail and things looked rotten for him. Then one of our young men, Geoffrey Cling, did some research on Slate, the chap Kincaid put in hospital. It turned out that Slate came from Liverpool not long ago. He's been in jail there for half of his adult life. Pickpocket, sneak-thief, wife-beater – the Liverpool police have quite a sheet on him. Those revelations started a bit of murmuring here and there in London. Then Cling asked the police if Kincaid had any money on him apart from what Slate claimed had been stolen from *him*. The police said no. So Cling wrote another piece asking what had become of the money Kincaid had taken working the street that night. More murmuring. Finally Cling flushed out the cleaners at the Duke of York's theatre: two old ladies and a poor undernourished lad who lives with his mum in a basement room on Tooley Street. At first they were stone-deaf and mute, all three of them, but when Cling took the boy off by himself and bought him a decent meal and a glass of cider, he told him he'd seen the whole thing as he was coming to work after the theatre closed. He said a man scooped up Kincaid's money in the kerchief he'd laid out on the pavement and ran off down St Martin's Lane with Kincaid right behind him. Cling took the boy to the nearest police station, where he told his story again. Next morning we had it in the paper.'

'Did they let Kincaid off then?'

Winkler shook his head. 'A police spokesman said the assault charge was still pending, no matter who the money belonged to. He said Kincaid would have to stay where he was till his case could be brought before the courts. He implied that Kincaid's police record made him a public threat in any case.'

'So he's still locked up?'

'Oh, no. Not at all. As soon as the papers published that police announcement the fun really began. Do you know a woman named Rosamund Barwick?'

'I've read about her.'

Winkler nodded. 'Rich and feisty and seventy-five years old. Has a house on Russell Square that looks like an annexe to the British Museum. During the war the chaps in Whitehall said they were up against two adversaries – the Germans and Rosamund Barwick. They whipped the Germans but Barwick never surrendered. She's a social-ist, an anarchist, and a royalist. Her political stance can change at a moment's notice. You never know from one day to the next where she's liable to attack you. And once she starts she comes at you from all sides. The day after the police announced they were keeping Kincaid in custody all hell broke loose. There were two hundred students with signs outside Number Ten and three hundred more outside Scotland Yard with banners reading, "ARREST US. WE'RE AS GUILTY AS KINCAID." And at the same time Barwick was in the Lord Mayor's office along with Leonard Woolf, Vanessa Bell, Duncan Grant, Clive Bell, and Aldous Huxley, demanding that Kincaid be released. Late that afternoon in the House of Lords, Sir Harold Toth stood up and reviewed Kincaid's situation in detail. Then he gave a blistering indictment of the entire affair.' Winkler shuffled through some clippings on his desk. 'I think I have it here. I saved it for you. Yes, here it is. I'll read it to you.

'"What an embarrassment to our city, to our country, when a young man from one of our sister nations is locked away and threatened with imprisonment because he vigorously defended himself and his property against a street thief. Surely our police have better things to do. Surely our government has more humane ways to deal with the unfortunate and the unemployed. I hereby charge the proper officials to deal with this young Australian, Roy Kincaid, in a just and decent manner. The time has come for us to show our homeless and hungry citizens that their leaders have neither forsaken nor forgotten them."

'What do you think of that?' Winkler said.

'Did Barwick arrange that too?'

'Not according to her. She maintains that every time she strikes it is actually just a spontaneous action by concerned citizens. But nobody's fooled. She never takes credit. She just demands results.'

'Did she get them?'

Winkler nodded. 'There's a rumour that a petition demanding Kincaid's release had been prepared and signed by several hundred poets, playwrights, artists and theatre people. We were told it would go to all London papers, to Downing Street and to the Palace. We never received it so I assume the rumour alone was enough to get the job done. The following day Kincaid was released. The next morning, the *Times* printed a sarcastic letter from Barwick saying that he had been placed in her custody because she was known to be a trained police-woman and a firm advocate of law and order. She went on to say that if he was convicted of any future crime she had promised the police as well as the Prime Minister that she herself would serve the sentence.'

'So where is Kincaid now?'

'According to Clegg he's living in a cushy flat above her coach house. How would you like to talk to him again and do a wrap-up on the whole story?'

Evan didn't answer for a moment. When he did, he said, 'I don't think so, Alan. I think we should let him alone.'

10

Not long after his return to London from France, Evan came home late one afternoon and found Kincaid waiting for him. 'Remember me?' he said. 'Roy Kincaid.'

'Of course. I understand you've had quite an adventure since I saw you last.'

'An adventure for the bloody police maybe. Not for me. They wanted to stick me in a hole somewhere and seal it up with cement.'

'But they turned you loose instead.'

'Maybe they did and maybe they didn't. I don't know what the hell is going on. That's why I want to talk to you. I need somebody to explain a few things.'

'I doubt if I can help you. I've been out of the country for several weeks and I don't know . . .'

'Don't brush me off. You're a decent bloke. I know you don't owe me anything but I've got nobody else to talk to.'

'What about Mrs Barwick? I understand she took you in.'

'That's right. She took me in all right. I mean, I'm living there. Plenty to eat and a few pounds in my pocket but I've never laid eyes on old lady Barwick.'

'What do you mean?'

'I mean, I've never met her and never talked to her. That's why I need to talk to you. To get some matters straightened out in my head.'

'Like I said . . .'

'You can help me. I'd bet on it. If you can't help me, nobody can.'

Tagg looked at his watch. 'I have a meeting at the Stafford Hotel in half an hour. I just came home to pick up some papers. But I'll meet you tomorrow if you like.'

'Later tonight would suit me better.'

'Can't do it. How about tomorrow morning? There's a coffee-house just here at the corner in Endsleigh Place. I'll see you there at nine. We'll have some breakfast.'

The following day, as they sat at a small table next to the window in the crowded coffee-house, Kincaid was wearing the same seaman's togs he'd worn the day before and every other time Evan had seen him. 'It's like I told you yesterday,' he said. 'I've never seen her, never talked to her.'

'Didn't she get you released from jail?'

'That's what they tell me. But she didn't show up there herself. Sent her chauffeur, a bloke named Upshaw, and her solicitor, an old bird who looks like a judge. Everybody bows and scrapes and kisses his bum.'

'What's his name?'

'Tremaine or Tremont or something like that.'

'Sir Charles Tremont.'

'That's right. The police inspector told me to go with Tremont and he would tell me what was expected of me. So that's what I did.'

'What did he tell you?'

'He said this woman, Rosie Barwick, and some other people had gone to a lot of trouble to get me released, so now it was up to me to behave myself and stay out of the soup.'

'What did you say to that?'

'Nothing. I just nodded my head. I was glad to be out of that bloody cell. I wasn't about to get testy with the man who fixed it, especially a man like him. He had on a pair of cuff-buttons that cost more than a six-room house in Australia.'

'Did he tell you how long you'd be staying with Mrs Barwick?'

'Not a word about that. But he gave me the impression that it was some kind of probation. I got the feeling that if somebody picked up the telephone I could be locked up again in a jiffy. Tremont said it might not be a great idea for me to cruise around too much at night. "Stay out of Soho," he said. Little hints like that. Like sending me off to my first day in school. I guess you know how much I like that kind of treatment. But I kept my mouth shut because, like I said, I'm glad to be out. So what I need to know is who is this Barwick woman and what's her game? I mean, what's she up to? Is she running some new kind of jail?'

'You're not locked in, are you?'

'Not with a key. But there's always somebody hanging around. The chauffeur or the butler or one of the maids. They keep bringing me stuff. Three meals a day they carry in and it's damned good food. But I get the feeling that if somebody shows up with a tray and I'm not sitting there with my tongue hanging out waiting to eat, an alarm will go off in Scotland Yard and fourteen bobbies will hit the streets looking for me. What do you think?'

'I think you don't know when you're well off. These are high-level people you're dealing with. They don't take prisoners, or hold hostages, or kidnap men off the street.'

'You mean they're just being nice to me? Why would anybody decide to do that?'

'A few people decided the police weren't treating you right and they did something about it. And from what I can tell, the one who did the most was Mrs Barwick.'

'But what does she want from me? I read in the paper that she's an old lady.'

'Maybe she doesn't want anything. But if she does I imagine she'll let you know about it.'

'You said you don't know her but you must know something about her. Is she crazy or just rich?'

'She's rich and she may be a bit crazy but she's very bright all the same and she's not afraid of anybody or anything. She and her friends are renegade intellectuals. All of them are successful and respected in their fields. They've been a literary and intellectual force in England since 1910, or before. They feel free to contradict or ridicule any person or any idea. They accept nothing on reputation or face value. They're also supposed to have some original ideas about marriage and some unusual sexual notions, but I can't vouch for that. In any case I'm sure you can take care of yourself since most of the group are old enough to be your grandparents.'

32

Rosamund Barwick sat in a wing-back chair in her library, a glass of whisky on the table beside her and a cork-tipped Turkish cigarette held loosely between her third and fourth fingers. Kincaid sat in a chair facing her.

'I expect you have a number of questions to ask me,' she said, 'but first let me explain myself in some detail. Question and answer sessions are a dreary form of dialogue so by the time I finish speaking one hopes that most of your questions will have been answered. Now, moving right along: I arranged to have you released from police custody because I felt you were being treated unfairly both by the authorities and by yourself. You have been wasted, my dear young man. Part of it is your own doing and part of it is not. In any case we must correct the situation because the thing I abhor most intensely is waste. But what shall we do about it? What will I do? First off, I tell you, I have an instinct about you. It struck me the first time I heard you speaking one evening in St Martin's Lane. You see, I believe you have the potential to be some sort of public person, a person who can draw people to him. I'm not certain yet what that potential might lead to, but if we are patient with each other I assure you I will find out. I know you're not a musician, or a poet, or a painter. That much my intuition has already told me. Self-discipline is not your forte. Nor is solitary work. What you have, your most obvious attribute, is a strange and unusual voice. Almost ugly, in the way that modern painting can be ugly, but at the same time beautiful. You also have presence. God-given. *Presence*. You don't know what I mean when I say that word but it doesn't matter. It's there. You needn't think about it. Better if you don't. Courage. You have that too. It takes a great supply of courage to recite passages from

Shakespeare outside theatres where England's finest actors appear and speak those same lines. What I'm saying is this: there's a bright light somewhere inside you, Cocky, and I intend to find it. I have many idiotic but important friends, you see. Because I am a wicked and relentless old person and because I amuse them, they do as I say. So we will take you under our wings, use our imaginations, and suddenly some pleasant things will begin to happen for you. I guarantee it. We'll see that you're dressed properly, some money will begin to come your way, and bit by bit you'll feel yourself transformed. And the transformation will be all yours, accomplished by you. No more busker's life for you. We'll have you reading a bit of verse at one of our poetry evenings and important people will see you there. The London journals have already noticed you, so that's a step forward. You only have to do what you have already been seen to do. What you have, my dear, cannot be taught. All you require is careful presentation. And you will have that. We'll see that you're properly presented. We will also protect you from lecherous widows and the odd married adventuress. And we'll watch carefully for whatever may turn up that can be used to your advantage. If you question my motives, and many people have done that, if you suspect that I myself might be lusting after you, I assure you that I had satisfied my hunger for slim young men by the time I was sixty-five. Now I am well past seventy, full of vigour and high spirits, but too old to undress with pride even by candle-light. So I take my pleasure in other activities. Have you understood me so far?'

'Yes, I have.'

'I'm sure you have. I don't know you at all, of course. I have no idea what your dreams are, what you *want*. But whatever it is I can help you get it, not as a fairy

34

godmother but as a benevolent witch. And my first piece of witch's advice is this: the thing you want most must be kept a secret. Don't tell anyone. Not even me. And when it's offered to you at last, turn it down. When it's offered a second time, turn it down again. When you finally accept it, do so as if the precious thing you're accepting has no value. If you seem to want nothing, everything will come to you. Stay inside your own skin. Keep your most intense desires in there with you. If you do that, if you can manage that, there's nothing you might want that you won't have. Does all this sound perverse to you? If it does, it's because the world is truly a perverse place, inhabited by perverse creatures. Once you know that and accept it, your struggles will be over. Misery comes from unrealistic expectations, from believing that love and kindness are the answers to everything. The things you really need will come from strangers. No one suffers more when we succeed than our friends do.'

12

When Arthur Tagg left Chicago and brought his son back to England he believed, he had at last forced himself to believe, that he would never see his wife again, that he would never hear from her, and that she would not hear from him. It had to be that way. It was the only way. He didn't hate her. He couldn't manage that. Nor did he still love her. He had simply replaced his joy and passion and tenderness with a cold white stillness. Enclosed it and buried it, dealt with it for the last time. Or so he told himself.

The thing that had been most painful, however, the sudden incompleteness, could not be so easily disposed of. Since it was in itself and by definition a nothingness, he couldn't hide it, or bury it, or even locate it. It simply appeared when it chose to, moved around him in small circles and stifled him as it always had. At last he sat down one evening and did what he had promised himself he would never do.

Amy

I never expected to write to you but I'm doing it. It will probably make no sense to you but I have some need to complete the circle. No matter. It makes sense to me. At least at this moment it makes sense.

Through all my childhood and youth I thought that heart-break was a word invented by poets to describe a feeling that was in fact non-existent. It never occurred to me that loving someone could alter a person's character, foul one's dreams, and change straight lines into circles. I had survived, when I was just a boy, the death of my mother and my sister. I knew the meaning of sadness. But the notion that love gone sour could make a wreckage out of everything that was important to me and put me in stasis from then on was foreign to me, almost laughable. I had persuaded myself that a man could be brought down only by a failure of character. No other person, no outside event, could do it. Only internal collapse. Then I met you. And from that moment I altered all my earlier beliefs and convictions, and to a large degree, altered myself.

If there had been a gradual disintegration of what we had together, or what I thought we had, perhaps the final result would have been less chaotic. But as it was, the last night I spent with you was like a glorious reprise of all the other splendid days and nights we had together.

The next afternoon when I came home from work,

there was the letter you had written to me. A nightmare letter filled with unbelievable information. We were not legally married, you said. You'd been married since you were sixteen to a man named Brock who left you a few months after the wedding and disappeared.

Several months later, you remember, because you were pretty and because your father had taught you to speak fluent French, you were chosen to be one of the hostesses in the American section of the Paris Exposition. When I met you there we told each other it was a glorious trick of fate, that we had both left our homes for one purpose, so we could find each other in Paris. When it was time for you to go home I left my teaching position and followed you back to Chicago.

Would you have gone through the charade of marrying me if you hadn't discovered you were pregnant? Surely not. That part, however, I can understand. I can almost forgive it. During those two years we were together in Chicago nothing could have pulled me away from you. If you had told me about Brock we'd have found a way to work it out. Divorce. Annulment. Some solution would have presented itself. In my eyes there were no flaws in the one-bedroom-with-kitchen-and-bath world we had put together. Nothing could have tarnished, or damaged, or destroyed it. I fully believed that and some part of me still believes it. As long as we were together, you and I and our son, we were indestructible. Then suddenly, in the time it took me to read your letter that afternoon, it all came unstuck.

Still I refused to accept it. I hired people to find you, but you were not to be found. Each time you were located you had already moved on. Your old friends, our friends, either knew nothing or they were unwilling to tell me what they knew. So I waited. I'm ashamed to admit how long I waited. But I was almost happy for all that time. Because I had convinced myself that one day I'd open the door and you'd be standing there. I needed to believe that and I did believe it. When I finally stopped believing it, I packed up, sold what I couldn't pack, and brought Evan back to England.

Ever since I left America, I've tried to make some sense of it all. And I think I've made progress. I can see how you must have felt when Brock left you. I can begin to understand how things happened the way they did between us. When you knew you were pregnant we had to get married. We couldn't have done that if you'd told me you were already married.

I suppose I can understand, too, how you felt when Brock came to Chicago. He was your husband, you still loved him, and you wanted to be with him. I don't like to think about that but there's no getting round it.

What I will never understand is how that wonderful two years happened for us. Were you pretending all that time? You couldn't have been. But perhaps you were. Maybe that's the answer. Maybe it's as simple as that.

But how could you leave Evan with the neighbours, walk down the stairs, disappear, and never see him again? How in hell does anybody do that? If I hated you, that would be the reason. But I don't hate you. Just because it ended badly doesn't mean that everything that went before is spoiled. Not for me.

When I came back here I planned to find a decent woman and marry again. I wanted Evan to have a mother. But I never found that woman. Perhaps I never really looked.

The joke is on me. I still feel married to you. There doesn't seem to be anything I can do about that. You'll see my return address on the envelope but this letter does not require an answer.

Arthur

As soon as he finished the letter, he read it through, folded it, and put it into an envelope addressed to the last place the detectives had told him Amy was living. He drove into Hexham then and dropped the letter into the box outside the post office.

As he lay in bed that night he was exhilarated by what he had done. He had finally put into concrete language the thoughts he'd kept to himself for such a long time. After telling himself that he would never be in touch with her again he had made an effort, at last, to establish contact. He felt positive about it. He felt that something good might come of it after all.

When he woke up the next morning, however, the first thing he saw was the ink-stand beside his bed. He knew at once that he'd made a terrible mistake. He dressed quickly, left the house, and drove to Hexham. The postal clerk was eager to help him but unable to. 'The postal lorry from Newcastle is waiting when we arrive in the morning. We open the outside letter-box, hand over the mail, and the driver is on his way again in a matter of minutes.'

'Is there any way I could intercept the letter if I drove into Newcastle?'

'I'm afraid not, sir. It will be postmarked and sorted while it's still on the lorry. As soon as it's unloaded at the central post office it will be off to its destination.'

As he drove home Arthur felt drained and humiliated. He had a clear image in his mind of Amy in her night-dress, laughing and reading his letter to a man. That image stayed with him for many weeks. At last, however, after more than three months, his letter came back. On the outside was marked 'No such person at this address. Return to sender.' But this was written with a pen, not stamped with purple post-office ink. And the envelope looked as if it might have been opened, then resealed.

When he took the letter out of the envelope he did not read it. But just before he burned it on the grate he noticed a brown spot, like a coffee stain, on the first page.

13

'You haven't been paying secret visits to my daughter have you?' Sophie said. She and Evan were having their weekly luncheon at Escorial, a restaurant in Arlington Street a few minutes walk from Sophie's house.

Evan shook his head. 'She's too old for me. How old is she now?'

'Thirteen her last birthday. And the wine is starting to bubble.'

'Too old. I specialize in twelve-year-old Indonesian girls.'

'All the same I think Sarah has a new curiosity about you. For months she's been trying to decide between Gary Cooper – she's seen *Farewell to Arms* four times – and that naked chap who plays Tarzan . . . what's his name?'

'Weismuller.'

'That's it. Johnny Weismuller. But for the past week or so she's been moping around the house singing "Mood Indigo" and asking questions about you.'

'What sort of questions?'

'She's asked half a dozen times how old you are. And I think she's fascinated by the fact that your mother's an American.'

'Who told her that?'

'I did. A long time ago. It's not a secret, is it?'

'Not as far as I'm concerned. But you've noticed my father doesn't announce it very often.'

'He doesn't announce anything. When he's not teaching

he scarcely speaks. But he's a Taurus so that's to be expected.'

'And what am I? You keep telling me but I forget.'

'Scorpio. A dreaded Scorpio. Emotional excess. Cool on the outside, boiling inside. Your sting is sometimes fatal.'

'You don't believe all that foolishness, do you?'

'I believe anything that makes me feel good about myself. If some stupid astrologer tells me I'm valuable and wonderful, I'm perfectly willing to accept it. Many perfectly nice animals survive on whatever they find in the street.'

'You're a real thinker. What else did Sarah ask about me?'

'She can't understand why you're not married. I think it disappoints her in some way.'

'Did you tell her that you're the only woman I care about? That I keep waiting for you to propose to me.'

'No, I didn't. Because I never lie to her. Besides, she knows that half the young beauties in London are on your menu. She did ask me if you and I had ever had a yen for each other.'

'What did you tell her?'

'I told her I had for you but you hadn't for me.'

'Not true,' he said.

'Of course it's true. We've discussed it. Several times.'

'When you were about to marry Toby we had a long talk about that. I recall it very clearly. You said I was your best friend, that I always would be, that we had something that was better than any marriage could be.'

'I meant it. I still believe that.'

'Did you tell Sarah that?'

'No. She'd think I was daft. She's not interested in male-female relationships that don't feature bare skin and heavy breathing.'

41

'Most people aren't,' he said. 'Except old folks and religious fanatics.'

She sipped from her wine-glass. Then, 'You had an odd expression on your face just now. When you mentioned Toby.'

'I admired Toby. A good chap.'

'But . . .'

'But nothing.'

'You're holding something back,' she said. 'I know you.'

'Not really.'

'Tell the truth.'

'It's nothing world-shaking,' he said. 'But I've always wondered why we had that conversation when you were about to marry Toby, instead of before. It wasn't as though you chose him over me. You chose Toby after Hugh Causey.'

'Are you trying to hurt my feelings?'

'Not at all. We can drop the subject right there if you like.'

'You've never mentioned Hugh's name to me before.'

He smiled. 'That should tell you something.'

'I don't want to talk about him.'

'Then we won't.'

They sat quietly for a few minutes. She looked out of the window beside their table. Finally she said, 'I've changed my mind.'

'Not a requirement.'

'I know it. But now that it's come up I don't want to leave it hanging. You and I have never done that and I don't want to start now.' She lit a cigarette and sat up straight in her chair. 'You know how close my mother and I are. Margaret and I can discuss anything. But I've never been able to talk to her about Hugh and she's never asked me to. It's just that I can't explain him and what happened. Not even to myself. I was a baby, of course. Sixteen. But it wasn't just that. I mean he didn't take advantage of me. I wasn't raped or seduced. I was a willing participant. That's why Sarah has been so much on my mind lately. She's very much like I was. Part of her feels like a woman and part of her feels like a child. Her life right now is ten per cent reality and ninety per cent fantasy. But I had an additional complication that she doesn't have. I was living in the same house with you. All our talk about being brother and sister didn't mean much to me when I was fifteen or sixteen. You know how I feel about you, how we'll always feel about each other, but just then my body was sending me messages that didn't originate in my brain. Or even pass through there. I know you must have felt the same way about me but we also knew what your father had said to you about me and about us. That we were schoolmates and nothing more, that we had no possible future together. Since he's your father you took that more seriously than I did, however. I used to lie awake at night thinking about you, wishing things could be different between us, trying to think of something I could say to you that would counteract what your father had said. I kept thinking something would happen, that we'd be alone somewhere, swimming, or boating, or riding on the moors, and we'd suddenly look at each other, like a scene from Jane Eyre, and the world would collapse round us. But nothing did happen. Then suddenly Hugh came on the scene. I'd known him all my life, his mother is Margaret's best friend, but he'd always seemed surly and dangerous to me. He had a bad reputation. Drinking too much, wrecking motors, and doing embarrassing things at parties. But when he asked me to ride out and meet him one morning I did it. I didn't hesitate. I think I knew what would happen but I went anyway. And it happened. There's something tortured

43

and cruel about Hugh. I'd never been exposed to cruelty and I suppose that's what I fell in love with. No one had ever hurt me before. I'd been taught that love was all kindness and tenderness. But Hugh turned that full round. He lied to me and disappointed me and tormented me. It was agony but I called it love. It only lasted, of course, for as long as Hugh was amused. When it ended, when he wouldn't answer my letters or meet me or talk to me at parties, I felt like an abandoned slut. I married the first man who was nice to me. I married Toby. Even then, the day I told you what I was going to do, I was still reaching out to you, hoping you'd say something that would stop me, or bring me to my senses, but you didn't. I was insane, of course. I was too young to get married and God knows you were too young to talk me out of it. Does all this surprise you?'

'No.'

'I didn't think it would. The good part is that now I'm an old broken-down widow of thirty-two, you're a wild young bachelor of thirty-one, and you're still my closest friend. So maybe things worked out the best way for us.'

'Maybe they did.'

'You don't sound convinced.'

'I'm convinced. Trust me.'

When they left the restaurant later, as he walked along with her to her house, she said, 'Why do I have an uneasy feeling?'

'I don't know.'

'I think you do. I'm thinking it might have been better if we hadn't had that conversation.'

'Why would you think that?'

'I'm not sure. Just a feeling I have that some things are better left unsaid.'

'Most things are better left unsaid.'

'That's what I mean,' she said.

'Don't worry about it. You didn't tell me anything I didn't already know. And even if you had, it wouldn't matter. You and I are indestructible.'

'I hope so.' She linked her arm in his. 'I count on it.'

• CHAPTER 2 •

1

Major Cranston had never felt comfortable with Arthur Tagg, with either the necessity for such a man or the man himself. He resented his presence in the house, resented Evan also. Having never truly experienced love, he had never experienced jealousy, but he did have a stubborn sense of property and that sense was offended by the warm relationship his wife enjoyed with the Taggs, father and son.

The first time they met, when he was on home leave from India just a few months after Margaret had engaged Arthur and had made arrangements for him and his son to live at Wiswell Towers, he said to his wife, 'This arrangement won't do at all, old girl. I can't imagine what possessed you. These people are strangers to us yet they are being treated like family members. They live in our house, they dine with us, and they seem to have the run of the place. It's damned unsettling to me and I won't have it. I'll talk to Angus Bradshaw and he'll tell me where we can find a competent local tutor who will come in for a few hours every day.'

Margaret smiled and said, 'We are fortunate to have a man like Arthur Tagg, William. It's unusual to find a person of his calibre who is willing, at his age, to devote himself exclusively to the education of one child. If you've talked with Sophie she must have told you what a fine teacher he is. As for his son, he's an excellent boy, and I'm delighted to have him here as a companion for Sophie.'

'Well, I'm not.'

'Also,' Margaret went on, 'since you can't be here, it's good for Sophie to see a gentleman in residence, someone she likes and respects who is not simply a member of the household staff.'

'But he is a member of the staff . . .'

'Not exactly, William. Arthur Tagg is an educated man, much better schooled than either of us or any of our friends in the county. He had an unfortunate marriage that ended badly, and it changed the entire course of his life. Otherwise I'm sure he'd be headmaster of a fine school.'

'That's neither here nor there. There's no need for us to have an endless discussion about this. You made a foolish commitment. I can understand your discomfort about it . . .'

'I feel no discomfort whatsoever,' Margaret said.

'Well, perhaps you should. In any case I will relieve you of the embarrassment of talking with Tagg. I'll take that on myself.'

'No, you will not. I have indeed made a commitment to Arthur Tagg and I intend to honour it. I do not regret that he and his son are living with us. I'm delighted they're here. I caution you, William, it would be not only unkind but extremely unwise for you to inject yourself into this situation. Not only is Mr Tagg an invaluable teacher, he has been most helpful in managing the estate. He is needed here, I consider him a friend, and I will not have him disturbed or embarrassed by you or anyone else.'

'Surely you're not forbidding me to talk with him.'

She shook her head. 'I am cautioning you. If you say anything that makes him believe he's not wanted here, I will assure him that he is. If you try to discharge him I will rehire him as soon as you return to India. And I'll increase his salary.'

Cranston stood up, crossed the library, and refilled his glass from the port decanter. He turned back to Margaret. 'Am I to understand that I have no voice in the running of this estate, in the decisions that affect my own family?'

'You have a very strong voice. You always make your position clear.'

'But you continue to do whatever you want.'

'I continue to do what I think is best. I make decisions because decisions must be made. Many times each day. Surely you're not suggesting that I write to you each morning in Delhi and then wait for your answer before I act.'

'That's not what we're discussing, Margaret, and you know it.'

'I know what I'm discussing. Perhaps you should tell me if your agenda is different.'

'I have the feeling that this is a contest to see who's in control here.'

Margaret smiled. 'I don't see it that way at all. You cannot possibly administer and control Wiswell Towers because you don't live here. And there has never been an understanding between us that you would control me.'

He took a long drink and sat down again. 'I've never understood you, have I?'

'Of course you have. I'm a failed trooper. I'm always out of uniform. I never salute properly or stand to attention. I'm a civilian and you've never known how to deal with civilians.'

For the next few years, on the rare occasions when Major Cranston was in England, he suffered in silence the presence of Arthur and Evan Tagg. His discomfort did not decrease, however. It increased. Since he was posted to Surrey in 1916, he was able to be in Northumberland more often than before, and he had reason to believe he would be retired as soon as the war ended. So the prospect of seeing Arthur Tagg on a daily basis was a painful prospect.

When 1918 came, however, when he was retired as expected, the cards seemed to fall in his favour. Sophie, although still living at Wiswell Towers, was married and expecting her first child, and Evan was preparing to go off to university. Cranston, eager for command again, restless already in mufti and inactivity, concluded that the moment had come to take the high ground. After three whiskies one morning following breakfast he found Margaret reading her correspondence in the morning-room and stated his case, not diplomatically as he had planned but, fortified by the whisky, bluntly.

'It appears to me, from the size of her stomach, that Sophie has permanently abandoned her studies. And young Evan Tagg tells me he'll be off next week to take up his university work, so unless you and I decide to study Greek or Sanskrit, I believe we have no further use for a schoolmaster here at the Towers. Am I correct?'

'William, we're not going to have this discussion again, are we?'

'New circumstances demand fresh discussion. Or so it seems to me. I'm here in residence now, about to take on whatever duties are required of master of the house. Sophie is grown. So, as I say, if His Majesty's forces can now get on without Major Cranston, I believe that Wiswell Towers can move ahead without Arthur Tagg.'

Margaret slowly folded her reading glasses and put them down on her desk blotter. 'William,' she said, 'I don't want to get angry with you. I've had a pleasant breakfast and now I'm reading my mail and planning my day. So I do not intend to have an extended debate with you on this matter. I will simply say this. Arthur has lived here with us for almost eight years. Whether you accept him or not, he is a part of our family. So is Evan. Arthur is perfectly qualified to find a position elsewhere. He's still a young man. I believe he's just forty-two. But I don't believe he has made any plans to leave us. So until he does he will stay on here. I am most anxious that he should stay. I've told him that, as recently as last week, and now I'm telling you.'

'But what will he do?'

'If you've paid attention since you came home to stay you must have seen that he's in charge of the entire operation of this estate. Everything passes across his desk. The book-keeper, the solicitor, the gamekeepers, the tenant-farmers, all the staff heads report to him. Not even when my father was alive did everything function so smoothly. He has authority but he's not domineering, and everyone responds to that. He is much admired here. And I am one of his staunchest admirers.'

'I hope that's not meant the way it sounds.'

'To my ears it sounds exactly as it's meant. And you must be cautious not to interpret it in some other way. Be extremely careful, William, that you don't say something to me that you can't take back.'

'I don't understand,' he said. 'I don't understand any of it.'

'Perhaps that's because you're searching for something that isn't there. The situation with Arthur Tagg is precisely as I have described it to you. Nothing more, nothing less. If he left us, we would have to engage three men to replace him.'

It was six years later when Sophie decided to move to London with her daughter, Sarah, and her son, Trevor.

Several months passed before Cranston once again took the field against Tagg.

'Dear God, William,' Margaret said, 'am I never going to hear the end of this?'

'Don't you see the situation is humiliating to me? I feel like a foolish character in an odd novel about county life. How do you think it looks to our friends?'

'I don't know what you mean. In the first place you and I don't have friends. I have friends here that I've known since my childhood, and you have a few retired military men whom you drink with in country pubs, but we have no friends together. You don't really want friends. When we were in India you had two activities: drinking and playing soldier. You still have just two activities: drinking and playing billiards.'

'I thought when I was retired, when Sophie was grown and married, that you and I would have a pleasant life together, just the two of us. Travel a bit, London once a month or so, visit America perhaps. But mostly I saw us here at Wiswell Towers. Golf together, doing some gardening, taking an afternoon walk by the river.'

'Oh, for the love of God, William, what sort of self-deception pill have you swallowed? You have never, never in our married life acted as though you wanted to spend time alone with me. Don't misunderstand me. I'm not complaining, or criticizing you. Not at this late date. But please, let's not pretend. Let's not fashion some spun-sugar dream about what might have been, some fantasy about our sweet retirement. We've been married for almost thirty years. I almost said we'd been together for all that time but we haven't. I'm not sure what *together* means but I'm quite certain it doesn't describe the life we've had.'

'I have no idea what you're talking about.'

'I believe that. I don't think you do. That's what makes it so hopeless.'

'By God, I don't have to listen to this. You're trying to get me angry but it won't work.'

'Of course it won't work. You don't get angry. You just get wounded and confused. You're a military man and there's no place for anger on the parade ground. You just close ranks, give new orders, and set things right. Steady on, and all that rot.'

'I don't recognize you. I've never seen you like this.'

'That's because I promised myself you never would.'

'I've tried to give you a good life. It's damned upsetting . . .'

'A good life? When? We never had a life together. You had a life, and Sophie and I had a life. But they never connected.'

'What did you expect, when you left India and came back to England?'

'I'm not talking about that. I mean before. Always. Here and there. Then and now. No life together. You weren't available, William. You're not available now. You're all locked up inside. No trespassers allowed.'

He sat silent for a moment. Then he said, 'If I'm such a rotten bastard, why did you marry me?'

Margaret smiled. 'That's a legitimate question. And I have the answer. I loved you. I was young and inexperienced and hopeful and idealistic. I'd had a lovely life here with my family. I loved Northumberland but I'd never been anywhere else. When I met you, you were like a visitor from another planet. Older than me, handsome, sure of yourself. I'd never seen anyone in total command, the way you were. And no one looks better in a uniform than you do. I was hypnotized. And so was my family. You were strong and quiet, and everyone seemed to respect you. So when you talked with my father and asked

52

if you could marry me and take me back to India with you I thought the world had opened up for me. I continued to think that for as long as I was able to.'

'Are you saying you were unhappy from the start?'

'Unhappy is not the word,' Margaret said. 'Deserted is the word I would use.'

'We lived a damned fine life in India.'

'I know it was a fine life for you. And your fellow officers felt the same as you did. I'm sure of that. But it was not a fine life for me.'

'You had every luxury . . . a full staff of servants.'

'But I lived alone, or so it seemed to me, until Sophie was born. Then she and I lived alone. You were totally involved with the regiment, with cricket, with polo, with drinking, with horse-racing, with the British Club. Your life in India was the same after you were married as it was before you were married. Things hadn't changed a bit. You had simply acquired two new recruits, a wife and a daughter.'

'I've never heard such bloody nonsense in my life.'

'Of course it sounds like nonsense to you. That doesn't surprise me. Because you don't have the slightest understanding of what I'm talking about. If you're surprised that I've never said these things before, that's the reason. I knew there was nothing we could discuss. There's still nothing we can discuss. Because you can't or won't understand. Through all those hot and dusty years in India I simply saluted smartly, fell into line along with the rest of the wives, and prayed every night for some miracle of redeployment. When my mother died in 1911, I knew my chance had come. My chance and Sophie's. When we left India and came home to Wiswell Towers it was like dying and going to heaven. I felt as if I'd reclaimed my soul. I promised myself I'd never give it up again.'

'I never stole your precious soul or anything else.'

'That's correct. You didn't. I surrendered it voluntarily. I'm not putting the blame on you. I'm simply trying to explain the situation.'

'It sounds as though you've always hated me. Is that what this is all about?'

Margaret shook her head. 'Not at all. I've never hated you and I never shall. You are what you are and you can't be blamed for it. I've never understood why you married me. I don't know why you married at all. Your life with the regiment answered all your needs. Now your only joy is remembering your life in the regiment.'

He sat staring at her, his neck and jowls growing slowly pink. 'It seems damned strange to me that the only time you ever talk this way to me is when the subject is Arthur Tagg.'

'There's nothing strange about it. The only time we talk about anything remotely personal is when you bring up the subject of Arthur, when you decide yet again that we must sack him.'

'Not that simple, I expect. You seem to be saying that he possesses all the fine and tender qualities that are lacking in me.'

'I've never said you lack tenderness. But it's all directed towards yourself. And God knows, you're not insensitive. But there again your definition of sensitivity concerns only your hurt feelings, your wounds, the sins that others commit, or that you imagine they commit, against you. You're like a vacuum cleaner. Everything goes in and nothing comes out. Your only real security is when you're firmly buttoned up and belted into your officer's uniform. And you only have true self-esteem when it's your full-dress uniform.'

'You're mistaken about that, my dear. I know my value. I've tested myself all my life, beginning at Sandhurst. And I'm proud of the results. I'm damned proud of my achievements. I've served my King and my country, and if I had it to do over again I would do just what I've done. I know of no higher calling than the regimental life.'

Margaret smiled. 'I know that, William. God, how well I know that. That's what I meant when I said we have no area for discussion. All the doors are locked.'

'But you're right about my sensitivity,' he went on. 'Nothing is lost on me. And I'm not embarrassed to admit that it hurts me deeply to see my wife of many years measuring me against the flimsy standard of a person like Arthur Tagg. And finding me wanting. Not only does that hurt me but it causes me concern about the condition of your mind.'

She smiled again. 'Perhaps you're right. Maybe I'll go down to London for some clinical testing. Or perhaps I'll simply eat more fruit and fresh vegetables and have a weekly consultation with the Vicar. That should bring me round.'

2

'It's my shout,' Kincaid said. 'You're my luncheon guest. That's why I rang you up. Since you were a key witness to some of my misfortunes I felt it was only fair to show you what a fine creature I've become.'

'I'm impressed,' Evan said. 'You look and sound like a young aristocrat who has never set foot outside Belgravia. Is that what you've chosen to be now, or will it be a new accent and a different costume as the mood strikes you?'

They were sitting in an upholstered booth at Doolittle's, a small restaurant in Bruton Lane.

'God knows the answer to that question. Next week I

may be sleeping in a doorway somewhere but for today and the near future I am an English gentleman of means.'

'And you've a damned good tailor as well.'

'Burke and Lansdon. Just nearby on Cork Street. Leonard Woolf's tailor. He says Savile Row's *déclassé*. His word, not mine.'

'Have you been taken suddenly rich?'

Kincaid smiled. 'By my standards, yes. By anyone else's, no. When I was in jail people began to send donations to several London newspapers to help me out. Quite a bit of money accumulated. And two weeks ago they turned it over to me. So I'm temporarily in the black.'

'I see in the *Observer* that you impressed a lot of people at the poetry reading a week or so ago.'

'That's what they say. But to me the whole thing was a send-up. A lot easier than working on the pavement and hoping for a few shillings. I was the only bloke on the stage who wasn't nervous. Why would I be? There was nothing at stake. I had no reputation to lose. So I just stood up there in my dungarees and a white shirt that Mrs Barwick gave me, and blasted everyone with a few poems and a long speech from *Dr Faustus*. They even came up with an Australian poem for me to do, so I spit that one out like a fair dinkum ocker. Half of those elegant poms didn't understand what I was saying but it seemed to churn them up a bit. I picked up some money from that evening too. Mrs Barwick and her pals thought I did fine. A couple of weeks from now, I'll be back in that same theatre, by myself this time, and I'll get half of every bob they take in. I don't know why a bunch of strangers would shell out real money to watch what I do but the theatre manager says they've sold most of the stalls already. So till people get wise to me I might as well ride along with it.'

'No doubt about that.'

'The first half of the show I'll wear my seaman's clothes and cape, and do the same stuff I did when I was busking outside the theatres. And after the intermission I'll wear a dinner suit, white tie and the whole mess, and do Dante's *Inferno*.'

'Next stop Buckingham Palace. A command performance.'

'None of that. I'm not fooling myself about any of this. Mrs Barwick and her friends will get tired of me in no time and people will say, "What's the fuss about? He's a chancy-looking bloke who talks loud and knows how to remember a lot of words," and that will be the end of it. I'll find a merchant ship and sign on for South Africa or Buenos Aires and all this craziness will be behind me just like a six-month stretch in jail. After a while you forget which jail it was, why you were there, and how long you stayed. And I'll forget about everything that's happening to me right now.'

As they got up later to leave the restaurant they met Sophie coming in. She was with her Aunt Sybil and Uncle Howard. Evan introduced everyone and they chatted together briefly before the waiter showed Sophie and the others to their table and Evan and Kincaid stepped into the street.

'Are you related to those people?' Kincaid asked as he and Evan walked towards New Bond Street.

'It's a long story. We're not actually relatives but I've known the family for most of my life. Sophie and I grew up together.'

'What did you say her name is?'

'Cranston-Black. She was married to a man named Black.'

'I've read about people with two last names but I never met one before.'

57

'She just calls herself Sophie Black. Nothing fancy about Sophie.'

'She looks fancy to me. People like her you usually see in expensive magazines.'

'I'll tell her you said that. She'll probably blush.'

'Don't tell her then.'

Evan did tell her, however, when she rang him up that evening.

'I couldn't believe that was Kincaid,' she said.

'That's him all right. The new edition.'

'I never would have guessed. But Uncle Howard recognized him as soon as he spoke to us.'

'Not so ordinary-looking now, is he?'

'Shows what a good tailor can do,' she said.

'It's more than that, I think. I think some windows have opened up for him. He's seeing things he never noticed before.'

He told her then what Kincaid had said about her. Evan also told her what *he* had said.

'I never blush,' she said. 'You know that.'

'You're blushing a little just now, I expect.'

'No, I'm not. Most of the women I see in expensive magazines are horrid-looking.'

'I never thought of that,' Evan said. 'Maybe that's what he meant.'

'You're a proper bastard, aren't you? I'm sorry I rang you up.'

'No, you're not. You know I think you're the most stunning woman in London.'

'That's better,' she said. 'Now I like you again.'

A few weeks after Evan came to live in London, after finishing his university work, he met a young woman late one evening in the underground station at Leicester Square. She was slender, but not tall, broad cheekbones and soft brown hair braided and pulled back in a knot. She was trying to carry a heavy satchel and a bulky box tied shut with rope. When he offered to help her to her train he found out she didn't know where she was going. It was her first time in London. A friend was to have met her at the station when she arrived from Dover but had not showed up. 'No one came,' she said. 'I waited two hours.'

She was Polish. Her name was Olga. She had been studying sculpture in Paris at the Académie de la Grande Chaumière. Now she had received a modest grant from the Polish government so she could study for six months in London at the Courtauld Institute.

'That's not far from where I live,' Evan told her. 'If you have no place to stay tonight there's an extra bed in my flat. It's in a room with a strong lock on the door so you needn't be afraid that I'll cut your throat in the night.'

She did stay in the room that night with the door locked. When she went off to the Institute the next morning she asked if she might leave her luggage with him till that evening. 'I will have found my friend by then and I'll be able to move in with her.'

She did find her friend but she learned that the friend had met a young man from Wales who was studying at the Royal Academy of Dramatic Art. 'He has moved in with my silly friend and brought his dog with him,' Olga told Evan that night, 'so there's no place for me.'

Evan took her to a Sicilian restaurant on Euston Road and they agreed that she would stay with him in his flat till she could make different arrangements. That night she slept in his bed, very tiny in one of his shirts. The next morning, as they ate breakfast in his kitchen, she said, 'You're very clean, aren't you? I only know painters and sculptors. They're never clean. They don't care about things like that. It's very pleasant to be in such a clean soft bed with such a clean man.'

She was nineteen years old. 'But I'm very old all the same. The war made us old. Men die in the war but the women just get old. People in my country have bad teeth. And many children have legs that don't hang straight. I have strong legs but my teeth will soon be beyond saving. Bad food and no dentists. All over Europe it's the same. In Cracow, even the merchants and the landowners have unhappy teeth. But look at you. Long straight legs like a dancer and strong white teeth like mother-of-pearl. I touched your teeth with my tongue last night. Did you know that? What a fine feeling it was. Like eating a lovely piece of fruit. And your toes, too. Straight and strong without bumps on them from bad shoes. There were many American soldiers in Paris. Not as fine-looking as you are. But almost always with straight backs and straight legs and chalk-white teeth in their mouths when they smiled. What food you must have in America to produce such legs and strong teeth. And the white part of your eyes is so very white. Almost blue. Do you see that? Do you use tobacco a lot? I don't believe you do. My father used to say that his eyes were yellow because of snuff and tobacco. And slivovitz also, I suspect. Papa was a devoted drinker of slivovitz.'

Evan had carried letters of introduction when he arrived in London. From his father, from his professors, and from Margaret Cranston. But he knew almost no people his own age. And for the time that Olga was with him he made no effort to meet other people. She went off to her classes each morning and he went either to the library to do his research and writing, or to the *Daily Telegraph* for whatever assignment Winkler might have for him. But every evening they met at his apartment soon after five o'clock. Occasionally they went out to eat but more often she shopped in the market on the way home so she could cook Polish dishes he'd never tasted before. They drank Italian wine, listened to fine music on the wireless, danced barefoot on the smooth oak flooring of his sitting-room, and spent long naked hours in his bed.

'We do such wonderful things to each other and then we get into the bathtub and sometimes we do other wonderful things there. But when we go back to bed to sleep we end up doing more wonderful and exhausting and painful things, and to make the hurt go away we climb back into the tub again. We must surely be the cleanest people in London. How fine it is to love so much and so long that we stick together like two caramel buns. Then we soak and wash each other and dry off sweet and dust ourselves with talcum and slyly do it all over again. How fortunate it is we met that first night in the underground.'

Her sculpture was angular and stark and cruel, Christ figures and dwarfs and men struggling for survival. 'But the anatomy must be correct all the same,' she said. 'Do you know Zadkine's work? At first it hurts your eyes. Then at last you see beauty in that work and nowhere else. He makes sculpture like Bartok composes music. They abandon nature and at the same time they never forget it. Look at us.' She would pull him often to the bedroom to stand naked in front of the tall mirror while she stood naked beside him. 'You see what I talk about so much. Your body is like a textbook on anatomy, on classical structure. Your bones and muscles and tendons and all your parts are like plaster models of what a man should look like. Now look at me. You are more perfect but I am better sculpture. I'm all out of proportion and out of drawing. I'm too little. I have hips like a young boy and small shoulders. But see my big pointed breasts. They don't belong on my little body. But there they are as if they have a life of their own. And they do of course. On you everything fits and meshes together. On me nothing is as it should be. But see when I move it all makes sense. Like my hacked-out wood sculpture makes sense.' She often turned to him then and put her arms around his waist. 'And we make sense, don't we? The golden perfect man with straight legs and shining teeth and the small soft machine of an imperfect woman. We fit together into a most extraordinary piece of ill-matched, tight-welded sculpture. We're an *objet trouvé*. A triumphant assemblage. Do you agree? Of course you do.'

They had known from the moment she moved in with him exactly when she would leave. The day and the hour. She had her return tickets in the drawer of the kitchen cabinet. Six months exactly she would be in London. 'When I leave, you will take me to Leicester Square where we met. You will put me on the Northern line to Waterloo Station.'

'Then I'll travel with you to Dover.'

'No,' she said. 'You must leave me in Leicester Square. That's the only way I can survive it. If you come one more step with me I won't be able to leave. We have to be very careful now so we don't do something bad to each other. If you care about me you must do it this way. We'll drink a great deal of wine and go crazy in our bed the night before I go. But the next morning you must let me leave you in the underground station.'

He had known about Josef also from the beginning.

'We have gone through a lot. We grew up on the same street in Cracow, we suffered through the war together. I

62

have known him since I was seven years old and we have lived together like married people since he was fifteen and I was fourteen. He is a sculptor too, as I am. He's a fine craftsman in clay and stone, but he lacks courage. There's no sense of adventure in his work. He will do public monuments one day, military heroes on horseback, and he will be very happy with that work. His parents were strict Catholics, as mine were, so he feels guilty because we're not married. As soon as we are able to support ourselves in a good way we will be married by the priest. Josef wants that very much. I want it too, but not in the same way he does. He thinks I'm a savage. He sees it in my work and it frightens him, I think. But he also loves me because of that. He knows I'm not afraid of things and he needs someone like me. I don't need him in the same way and he knows that too, I think. But he also knows, just as I do, that he's a permanent part of my life, that we're permanent together.

'He'd kill me if he knew how it is with you and me, the way we are together. He'd cut my throat and never feel sorry about it. And he'd kill you too, if he could. Because he's never done a reckless thing in his life, never responded to an impulse, he'd have no way of knowing or seeing how we connect to each other like children playing. If he found out how we are, he'd go to his grave believing you had stolen something from him. If I told him that I had given you everything freely and wept in the night because I had no more to give, he would never believe me. Josef is like a gorge cut into the rock, deep and dark and narrow. There's no sunshine inside him. He's nothing like you. He's never met a man like you. You're like the wide fields and pastures we saw when you took me that weekend on the train to Devon. Maybe I'd get tired of all that fine clean openness and energy and laughter if we stayed together, maybe my Polish soul would start to cry out for rainy nights and cold rooms and sombre colours. Josef, you see, has no hope of a joyful life. Maybe I'll find that I don't either. Maybe I'll think of this time in London as a summer trip to a country fair and be glad that I went back to my own reality, or Josef's reality, of guilt and torment and whispered confessions to the priest. My father thought I was a good Catholic daughter when I was younger, but I'm not. I never feel guilty, I never do penance. When Josef insists that I make confession, I simply lie. And I feel good about it. Since I was ten I've known what was right for me. I don't need to be instructed, or admonished, or punished. I belong to myself. And I must. Otherwise I'll be of no value to anybody. I am as innocent as a child because I never hurt anyone. I have no need to do damage to another person, even if they want to damage me. I feel very strong, as though nothing could really hurt me, not now or any other time. Then I wake up in the night and see you sleeping beside me like a great long-legged child, and I wonder how I'll ever be able to put that picture and all the other pictures of these months out of my mind and my memory.'

'Why do you have to?'

'That's the answer, isn't it? I don't have to, do I? We don't have to. *Ça existe*. It can't be forgotten. We just tuck it away and keep it for ourselves. We don't tell the policeman, the priest, or our grandchildren. We keep it snug and warm in some secret place and refer to it when we need to. When we want to. Then we tuck it away again.'

They promised themselves and each other that they would not be enslaved by either the clock or the calendar. Especially as the time drew near when she would leave. They pretended they could move smoothly ahead, dealing each day with the details of their lives. Then suddenly one evening Evan would say, 'By the way, isn't it tomorrow that you're leaving?' Or she would say at breakfast, 'I know you've forgotten, I almost forgot myself, but this afternoon I have to make the channel crossing to France.'

It didn't turn out that way, of course. During their last week each of them caught the other staring. Through the window, at the floor, at nothing. Sometimes it seemed they'd taken a vow not to touch. At other times they lay in each other's arms for hours, the window open, the curtain scarcely moving in the heavy August heat. For three days running, they went to a cinema every evening. They saw *Battleship Potemkin*, *The Big Parade*, and *The Joyless Street*. One night, to stay cool, they put their mattress on the floor of the sitting-room, opened all the windows and the transom over the door, and slept there.

One morning, her last Sunday, she made coffee and brought it to the bedroom and they stayed very late in bed, sleeping, talking, sleeping again, enjoying the weather, which had gone suddenly cool and fresh.

'I don't think you'll ever get married,' she said.

'That's because you're possessive and jealous and can't stand the thought of sharing me with another woman.'

'That's not true. I just don't think you'll get married. Do you think you will?'

'Of course I will,' he said. 'Everybody gets married.'

'No, they don't. And you know they don't.'

'Some people don't, I suppose.'

'Many people don't,' she said. 'I think you're one of those who won't.'

'But if I'm as irresistible as you say, how can I avoid it?'

'I didn't say you were going to live in a monastery or take independent vows of chastity. It's just that I can't see you swearing fidelity in a fancy suit, settling down in a proper house with grass and trees all round, having

65

children, going to a bureau every day, walking the dog, giving dinner parties for your neighbours, engaging in local politics. There's so much regimentation in all that. Rules and restrictions. It doesn't seem to suit you.'

'You're planning to get married. You've told me so. Why not me?'

'Some people need it. I don't but Josef does. It's like an armature inside his life. When we grew up in Cracow, all the families had many children. Every home, every block of flats, every *quartier* was teeming with children. There was one's own family and then there was the neighbourhood family. Everyone's life was regimented. By the man's work, by the wife's work at home, by the church, by the schools, by the government. So the regimentation of marriage was almost a freedom in that whole scheme of things. Having babies was an achievement. It was also a requirement. It's still that way for many people in many countries. Poor people have no real freedom. So they express themselves and define themselves by creating a family. Even a poor artist thinks and reacts like an artist. But a poor workman is obsessed only by how poor he is. He is free and equal in just one way: he can make love to his wife and she can give him babies. So he does, and she does, and they tell themselves they have triumphed over poverty and mediocrity. In their own eyes, they've become important. In the only way they can possibly be important. By reproducing themselves.'

'But that's what you're going to do, isn't it?'

'No, I'm an artist. I'll always be an artist.'

'Josef's also an artist,' Evan said.

'No. Josef's a craftsman. And once we have children he will be a father and a husband and the head of his family. That's what he has to be because he can't be anything else.'

'And you'll be a mother?'

66

'Yes, but I'll still be an artist. I must be. I have no choice about that. In Cracow, ten people live in a flat the size of this one. Josef and I will be no exception. But I will find a place to do my work. And time to do it. I know I will.'

Early that afternoon, when they got up at last, they walked along Euston Road to Marylebone Road and crossed York Bridge into Regent's Park. They strolled around the inner circle and sat on a bench in Queen Mary's Garden.

'You didn't finish explaining to me why I'm doomed to be an unmarried man.'

She laughed. 'You're not doomed. You're one of those lucky people who always gets to decide what he's going to do. You get to choose. I think you will choose not to get married.'

'Why do you think that? That's what I'm trying to find out.'

'You're a smart fellow,' she said. 'You know why most men get married. So they'll have a nice warm woman in their beds every night. Some women get married for the same reason. But more of them do it because a woman without a man is an outcast. To one degree or another. If you can't get a husband and you can't have a baby, even people who like you see you as a failure. Also marriage is a livelihood to most women. In Cracow it's very hard for a woman by herself to earn a living. It's hard to find a job. And if you do find one it's hard to live on what you make. I know that England isn't Poland and London isn't Cracow, but the reasons people do what they do don't change as much as you might think. What I'm saying is that most people get married because they need to, for one reason or another. They tell themselves and each other that they want to, but the fact is that they need to. You don't need to. That's why you won't.'

'What about love?' he said. 'Love doesn't count?'

'Of course it does. But it doesn't have much to do with marriage. I love you so much I feel as if my heart's going to stop. And you love me. But we're not going to marry each other. From what you've told me your mother didn't love your father much; your friend, Sophie, wasn't so crazy about her husband; and her mother's certainly not in love with her father. Still all those people are married. Or they were. Does that mean they were never in love? Of course not. It just means they loved one person and married somebody else. If you think that doesn't happen very often just ask a few questions here and there. You'll find out you're mistaken. Very few people marry the person they really want. They take the best that's available and spend their lives telling themselves that they got what they wanted. You're too smart to do that. That's what I mean. You'll always have a nice woman in your bed, you'll never have to worry about money . . .'

'Wait a minute. You have some idea that I'm wealthy. But I'm not.'

'It doesn't matter,' she said. 'You live as if you are and that's just as good.'

As they walked home later she said, 'You've gone very quiet. Did I talk too much?'

'No. I've just been thinking about what you said.'

'I'm not so wise, you know. I probably don't know what I'm talking about.'

When they were at home, having tea in their kitchen, he said, 'What if I told you I didn't want you to leave. What if I said I want you to stay here with me?'

She turned away from the stove, walked to him, and sat on his lap with her arms around him. She kissed him on both cheeks. 'First I would tell you that my visa expires in eight days. Then I would say that I don't believe you when you say you want me to stay. Then I would say that even if I did believe you, even if it was what I wanted more than anything else, I couldn't do it.'

'Why not?'

'Don't make me cry,' she said.

'Why can't you stay?'

'Because I can't. You know I can't.'

4

Sophie and Evan, as they grew up, had not related to each other in a cautious way. Like a genuine brother and sister, they had been relentless in their criticisms of each other. There had been no sacred ground. Their clothes, their manners, their habits, their friends were all fair game for assessment and ridicule.

Because it was so outrageously open, however, because they were always a match for each other, there was no cruelty intended and no real pain suffered on either side. It was, in fact, thoroughly beneficial and productive. Each of them helped the other to mature, to have quick perceptions, and most important, perhaps, to maintain, almost always, a sense of proportion and a sense of humour.

When they were a bit older, however, but still living under the same roof, they began to sense, each of them, that the other had private gardens and locked rooms that it was kinder not to enter. As we have seen, although he was aware from the beginning of the Hugh Causey affair, Evan never mentioned it to her and she never discussed it with him, either when it was happening or after it was over. Not till their luncheon conversation some sixteen years later.

For her part, as soon as she realized how serious Evan was about his work, about his desire to write plays that would appeal to serious actors and be accepted by theatre managers and audiences, Sophie sensed that old attitudes and light-hearted criticisms were no longer appropriate, certainly not in that sensitive area. So she asked no questions and made no suggestions. When he brought her something to read she always found something in it to praise. And any remark or judgement she made was prefaced with the observation that although she was an avid play-goer she knew nothing whatsoever about the art and craft of writing a play.

For her to make a serious observation, then, about Evan's work or his approach to it, was something she had not done before. For her to say that perhaps the reason he'd had no success with his plays was because there was nothing of himself in them was not only perceptive, it was deeply unsettling to him; it was a feeling he shared. He had been unwilling to admit it to himself, however, because he didn't know how to correct the flaw. The closest he had come, in an entry in his journal, was this:

I am too civilized, too kind, too educated, perhaps, for my own good. I can see everybody's point of view. It seems impossible for me to present my own point of view in a dramatic way, so that it colours the scenes and permeates the entire play. When I try for a rich tapestry I come up with a black-and-white poster.

In the next few weeks after that electric conversation with Sophie, her words came back to him again and again. Then, in some disconnected collage that seemed altogether illogical, his long-past conversations with Olga began to insinuate themselves into the mix. He began to remember clearly the things she'd said about family life in Cracow, the crowded flats, the tangle of small children. As she had related all that to him, he realized that he had only been exposed to failed marriages, to broken families, to children without fathers, to single parents.

He got up from his desk, then, one day, and sat in a deep chair by the window looking out on Gordon Square. For the first time he allowed himself to face the truth of his own childhood, to admit to himself how little he knew about his mother and father. What had brought them together, what their lives had been like, and what the facts were about their parting. He only knew that the truth, at least one side of the truth, was locked inside his father and would never come out.

Evan sat there in his armchair for a few hours each day, letting his mind wander. He had no fixed objective. He simply wondered, speculated about what had happened. As his imagination floated and darted and dreamed, he made no effort to channel or direct it. Countless thin, translucent layers of possibility settled on the framework of facts that he knew or thought he knew. Colours changed, and textures. Certain notions and conclusions returned time and again. He allowed his father to hold views, take positions, and make statements that were totally alien to the man he knew. He saw him as weak, as cruel, as sinning, and sinned against. Drunken, profane, abrasive, tearful, vengeful, adulterous, sarcastic, and whimpering.

Since he had no memories of his mother and had never been shown her photograph he expected that there would be no boundaries, no restrictions whatsoever in his portrait of her. Surprisingly, those infinite possibilities did not free him, they restricted him. Scrambling to assemble a multifaceted creature with specific moral and sensual lineaments, he repeatedly saw in his imagination, not a full-blown antagonist for his father but a fragile and defenceless young woman who seemed to be neither wilful nor self-assertive, but sweetly bewildered. Seeing her in

71

this way jolted him, sickened him somehow, and made him feel painfully disloyal to his father. The indolent harmless mind-wandering by the window had taken a dangerous turn suddenly. Topsy-turvy. Solid matter dissolved. Objects upside down and houses floating in the middle distance.

Evan felt the kind of sharp pain that betrayal brings. He had never felt it before. It wasn't clear to him if he had been betrayed or was about to betray someone. But the pain persisted.

Gradually, then, he came to realize that for all these days since his talk with Sophie, as he'd sat in his flat by the window, his subconscious had been struggling not to know or discover, as he'd told himself, but to write. He went to his desk, took out a sheet of paper and wrote on it: the play I must write is about my father.

5

When Evan was still at university, when he was reading English literature of the nineteenth century, he made the following entry in his journal:

Millions of people are unable to read. A much larger group are able to but choose not to. Others read constantly but understand nothing. These people, when questioned, find fault not with themselves but with the books they read. They believe that those books are needlessly complex, that the writers have deliberately set out to confuse and baffle their readers.

Such people insist that life itself is always knowable, that it strictly observes calendar time, that in the pattern of our days and years we know precisely where we are and how we came to be there. Such notions are nonsense, of course, and those who harbour them are simply seeking a logic and an inevitability in literature that they are unable to find in their lives. They are unable to find it because it is not there. As attractive as a moment-to-moment existence appears to anyone who examines it, as seductive as it may seem simply to live each day from breakfast to bedtime, with no thought of tomorrow and no memory of yesterday, we are both unable and unwilling to do it. The truth is that most of us derive our principal nourishment from what we have already done, or from what we hope to do. The present, alas, becomes simply a fulcrum on which to balance while we define ourselves by what has been and what will be. If we are thoughtful, or secure, or both, we accept it as a truism that each of us is not a river flowing straight and swift and clean between high banks, nor are we a knotted cord stretched taut between the moment of birth and the moment of death. We are, more accurately, each of us, a quilt made by willing but unskilled hands, tiny scraps stitched together in what may be intended as a beautiful pattern but which is, more often, an ill-conceived *mélange* of random colours and textures, carelessly matched and sewn together, some of its sections more cleverly done, others worn and frayed and haphazard, pale colours and primitive patterns. On close inspection one sees that many hands have done the work, using different scraps of material and different thread, while sitting in different sewing-rooms in different years, sometimes in good light, other times in near-darkness.

When the quilt is hung smoothly on a white wall, however, and studied from a distance, it seems to be of a piece. The intricacies and imperfections disappear, the patches seem to blend as distance dims their shapes

73

and colours. Both its chronology and its design become pleasant and satisfying.

This is the reading experience that most of us want, not all of us but a great number of us. We simply need to be told what happened. A smaller group is willing to consider how it happened, and the smallest group of all is eager to know why. These fortunate few do not require that strict clock time or calendar time be observed. They know, or can be taught, that in the human heart yesterday and today and tomorrow are one. Since they are able to follow ill-marked emotional trails they do not need road-maps or timetables to transport them from one year or one continent to the next. They do not expect the complex lives of imperfect people to be offered up in the form of a children's tale for five-year-olds. The only access we have to either art or wisdom is through ourselves. And all of us know what a winding path that is.

6

How do we discover the truth about a man like Roy Kincaid? Do we accept his own assessment of himself, however contradictory it may seem? Or do we rely on the instincts and observations of the people who are close to him? Or do we do both, fashioning his quilt out of whatever scraps we can lay our hands on?

Rosamund Barwick said to him, 'I think you have the potential to be some sort of public person . . . you have courage . . . you have presence . . . there's a small bright light inside you.' Margaret Cranston, after she met him, said, 'Men like Roy either spend their lives fighting to be accepted or they pull back all the way and tell themselves they don't need or want anyone.' Major Cranston said,

'Not damned likely that I'd want to have that bloody Aussie for a son-in-law. I had chaps like him in the regiment. Hard heads, callouses on their hands, and a sullen look on their faces, always ready to punch up an officer in a dark corner.'

Kincaid's prison friend K.C. Lott said to him. 'A few people will hate you because you've got a mean fucking face. But don't worry about it. Just stick with that expression, don't give away anything, and you'll have people falling all over you. People don't really like good guys. They pretend to but they don't. They like people who scare them a little.' Evan Tagg thought but did not say, 'I know he thinks of me as an intimate and loyal friend. In an orderly world I should feel the same about him. But I don't. There's an elusive separateness about him that I've never been able to deal with.' About himself, when he first met Evan, using his Australian accent, Kincaid said, 'I've got a bloody obsession to have things me own way.' Questioned a few years later about the discrepancies in his stories about his early life, he told a *Variety* reporter in Los Angeles, 'There's no such thing as absolute truth. I always tell the truth. But it's my truth. When I talk about myself, I can't be contradicted.'

Some years after he first appeared in London, when the name Kincaid had become known everywhere, an unauthorized biography of him was published by a company in New York that specialized in books about actors and politicians. The first chapter heading was 'Kincaid Speaks', followed by several pages of what were presented as direct quotes.

* I'm an outlaw, for Christ's sake, a convict, an aborigine. That's how I see myself. For the first fourteen years of my life the world offered me nothing. I kissed everybody's bum and got nothing in return. So I

decided to take what I wanted. Then I got something in return. They threw my ass in jail. In Tasmania. Not far from Port Arthur, where I was born. By the time I was twenty I'd been in eight jails in six countries.

* Everybody's looking to get rich or get laid. Or both at the same time. It's a whore's world. Everybody's putting out for somebody.

* I see nothing wrong with robbing people as long as they're not your friends. Everybody's stealing something. I'd rob a bank or roll a drunk in a minute if I wasn't afraid of getting caught and locked up.

* You know what I like about the movie business? Everybody's dumb and everybody's crooked. Nobody's surprised if he gets cheated on a deal. He doesn't call a lawyer or the police. He just says to himself, 'Even if I get screwed I can still get rich.' That's the motto. 'Next time I'll be the one who does the screwing. Next time it's my turn.'

* Here's the first law of Hollywood: If you're on the outside you're shit. If you're on the inside you're king. If you need money you call up the head of the studio. If the studio needs money they call up the bank. If the bank needs money they call up the mob. If the mob's short of money we're all in trouble. That means the world's gone broke.

* People keep telling each other to be honest and sincere. In this business nobody's honest and nobody's sincere. It's all illusion, they say. We're selling dreams. That means it's all fake. It's give and take, they tell me. To me that means they give and I take. So as long as it lasts, I won't walk away from it.

* For years everybody owned me. Every boss I had, every prison guard, every soup-kitchen worker handing out meals. I was public property because I didn't own anything. Not even myself. That's all over now. Now I've got my life by the ears. Full control. No surprises. I never knew for sure what I wanted till I got it. Now I'll never give it up. From now on I answer to nobody.

* I'm not a philosopher. I don't live by theories. I'm a worker. If I wasn't an actor I'd be a stonemason or I'd shear sheep. I've worked at both of those trades and I'd do it again if I had to. But right now Julian Thorne pays me a lot of money to show up sober every morning. So I show up. Somebody hands me the words to memorize, the director tells me where to stand and when to speak, and that's what I do. That's all any actor does.

* When I played Ned Kelly – it was my first acting job – an old actor named Sam Chudno told me, 'Only three things to remember. One . . . don't look in the camera. Two . . . when another actor talks, you listen. And three . . . when it's your turn to speak, say it as if you mean it.' That's it folks. That's what it's all about.

After the book came out, a reporter asked Kincaid if the facts in it were correct. He said he didn't know because he hadn't read it. The reporter then read him several quotes from the book and said, 'It sounds as if you had a pretty tough life growing up in Australia. Being an orphan and all.'

'The fact is I've never been in Australia. I was born in Argentina. My father was a professional soldier. A colonel in the Argentine Army. He's retired now. He and my mother have a little ranch outside Santa Rosa.'

'I don't understand,' the reporter said, 'I heard you

being interviewed last week on Jimmy Fidler's radio show and I'd have sworn you said your parents were missionaries in the Cameroon.'

'That's right. They were missionaries in the summer. Then Dad would go to Buenos Aires and be a colonel in the winter.'

After a long moment, the reporter said, 'It looks as if nothing in this book is accurate.'

'As I told you,' Kincaid said, 'I haven't read it. But it sounds to me as if they made it up.'

'That could be grounds for a law suit.'

Kincaid grinned. 'Oh, I don't think so. Those people are just trying to make a living like everybody else. As long as I don't have to read it, I don't care what they write.'

When the young woman who wrote the biography was told that Kincaid had said it was all untrue she offered to show her notes and research sources to anyone who doubted her. No one accepted her offer, the book sold a great number of copies, and as time passed it came to be regarded as a reliable source of information about Roy Kincaid.

7

Rosamund Barwick did her work well. Two weeks before Kincaid's evening of dramatic readings, a stylish advertisement appeared in the *Observer*, the *Guardian*, and the London *Times* with a photograph that made him look more romantic and attractive than he did in real life. In the advertisement it noted discreetly that all the seats had been sold. One week later a second advertisement appeared. Due to unusual popular demand, a second evening had been scheduled, on the day after the first performance. This second show would be at the Royal Court theatre on Sloane Square. Evan was in Alan Winkler's office at the *Telegraph* when he saw this new announcement.

'What do you think of that?' Winkler asked.

'I can't believe it. These are hard times. The theatres in the West End are half-empty every night and this renegade . . .'

'Ah-ah . . . watch yourself. You discovered him. Let's not begrudge him his success.'

'I don't mean that. He's a decent guy. At least he seems to be. And I don't begrudge him whatever success he seems to be having. But it surprises me. Why are all these people scrambling to buy tickets to see somebody they've never heard of before?'

'Word of mouth, our theatre man says. Kincaid impressed some people at that last poetry evening. And there's still a lot of curiosity among people who read about his run-in with the London constabulary. But mostly, my instinct tells me, it's Rosamund Barwick. I've been watching her in action for years. When she blows her bugle the troops come out. Some people say she could sell out the Albert Hall with a dancing-bear act if she set her mind to it.'

That evening, when Evan was working at home, Kincaid rang up. 'Haven't seen you for a bit. How about a pint at the pub on your corner?'

'I'm afraid I'm in the middle of something. A desk full of work.'

'Then you need a half-hour break. The fresh air will wake you up.'

'I don't think so. I'm really buried here.'

After a pause Kincaid said, 'Actually, I've got two tickets for you. For the evening at the Royal Court. Gift from the madam. No admission charge. Come watch the monkey play his drum.'

'Well . . . that's very nice of Mrs Barwick.'

'If you can't come out now I'll just walk over and drop the tickets off. I won't stay. I'll just ring your bell and hand them to you.'

'No, you needn't do that. I'll meet you. Give me half an hour to sort things out here and I'll meet you for a pint.'

Kincaid was waiting when Evan got there, sitting in a corner half-hidden by the curve of the bar. 'Sorry to muck up your work schedule,' he said when Evan sat down.

'You were right. The fresh air's good for me. It helps to take a break once in a while.'

Kincaid took the tickets out of his pocket and put them on the table. 'I told Mrs Barwick I wanted you to have the best seats in the theatre. These are seventh row on the aisle.'

'All the seats are good at the Royal Court. I hear you're all sold out both nights.'

Kincaid nodded. 'I don't know what the hell's going on. The old lady's been building me up as if I'm something special. Five minutes after I open my mouth they may start throwing eggs and tomatoes at me.'

'Are you nervous?'

'Not me. I know exactly what I'm going to say and what I'm going to do. No reason for me to be nervous. It's the audience that should be nervous. They don't know what they're in for.'

'Don't underestimate yourself.'

'I don't. I didn't mean that. I've got great writers behind me. It's not hard to make them sound good.' Then, 'I thought about sending some tickets to your friend, Mrs Black, but I don't know where she lives. Then

I decided it might not be such a good idea. All the tickets are gone now, anyway. I just gave you the last two.'

Evan took the tickets out of the envelope. 'What night did you say it was?'

'Thursday.'

'Thursday. That's right. I see it here on the ticket. Eight o'clock.'

'You can make it then, can't you?'

'I think so. Unless they send me off to interview Mussolini, or Jean Gabin, or Emily the gorilla woman. Sometimes I get a last-minute assignment but I'm not expecting one this week.'

'Good. I hope you can be there. And maybe you'll bring Mrs Black if she's not busy.'

'Well, we'll have to see about that. I have several hundred women on the string. I need to check my book and see whose turn it is.'

'Don't get me wrong. I'm not trying to tell you who to bring.'

'I know you're not. I was just making a joke. I'm sure Sophie would like to come if she's not busy. I'll call her when I get home tonight.'

Sophie was out when he rang her home. But she called him back just before midnight.

'Hope I didn't wake you. Should I have waited till morning?'

'No, this is better. I'm a night-bird like you. Did you go to the theatre tonight?'

'Yes. Gertrude Lawrence at the Haymarket. A new play called *Can the Leopard*?'

'And . . .'

'I'm not sure. I hope you'll see it so we can compare notes. I'm not sure I understood it. Or maybe I understood it too well. But no matter. I love to watch Gertie

Lawrence strut about. And Ian Hunter's awfully smashing to look at.'

'Bit of a stick, it seems to me.'

'You don't have to appreciate him. He's for the ladies. They all hold their breath when he walks on stage.'

'Perhaps they're afraid he'll stumble and fall.'

'Don't be nasty. He's gorgeous.'

'Speaking of matinée idols, that's why I called. Our former busker, Mr Kincaid, gave me two tickets to his evening at the Royal Court on Thursday. He seemed to think it would be a good idea if I brought you. I think you made an impression on him.'

'I remember. Like a page torn out of a magazine. Isn't that what he said?'

'Not exactly. But you're close. You want to come?'

'I'm not sure,' she said. 'Are you definitely going?'

'I promised I would if I'm in town.'

'Let me think about it,' she said. Then, 'No, I can tell you now. I really don't want to go. I get very restless watching those one-person evenings. But I'd like to ask you a favour. Can I persuade you to take someone else?'

'That depends. Who is she?'

'It's not a she. It's Uncle Howard.'

'Sorry. No dates with your uncle. He's a nice man but I don't want to escort him to the Royal Court. He talks too much.'

'Don't be a crumb, Ev. I told you before how much he likes to hear Kincaid doing whatever it is he does. And I know he tried very hard to get tickets to the Thursday do. But they were all gone. It would mean a lot to him.'

'I'm sure it would. You'd be surprised how many old gents ask me to go to the theatre.'

'Stop it. I'm asking you a favour. You have the tickets so why not share them with someone who would really appreciate it.'

'You're tearing at my heart-strings.'

'That means you're saying no. What a frog you are.'

'Doesn't mean that at all. I'm saying yes. I'll send the tickets over to you tomorrow and you can take Uncle Howard.'

'But I don't want to go,' she said.

'Then sacrifice yourself. Do it for uncle.'

'I can't do that, Evan, and you know it. Kincaid wants you to come. That's why he gave you the tickets.'

'I'll lie to him. I already told him I might have to dash off on an assignment.'

'I'm sorry. I wouldn't feel right about it.'

'You mean I'll have to take one of my succulent long-legged lady friends?'

'I'm afraid so. I'll just have to suffer. Along with Uncle Howard.'

On Wednesday night Evan called her again. 'You probably don't believe this but I have to fly to Lisbon tomorrow morning. I've just sent the Kincaid tickets to your house. You can use them or not, whatever you like. It's all the same to me.'

'Are you really going to Lisbon or are you just outmanoeuvring me?'

'I'm really going. The *Telegraph*'s been after Salazar ever since he got elected. He finally agreed to an interview. First thing Friday morning. So I'm it.'

'Well, thanks for sending the tickets but don't be cross with me if I don't go.'

'You're in the clear,' Evan said. 'Next time I see you, I won't even ask you if you went.'

The trip to Lisbon, as Evan later told his father, was a non-productive and frustrating chain of events from the time he left London till his return. 'By the time I got home I had decided that journalism had served its purpose for me. It was time to give it up and devote myself full time to play-writing. There's enough chaos in my brain as it is. I have no need to knock about from one place to another looking for more.'

'There was trouble with the aircraft, you said.'

'Exactly,' Evan said. 'It coughed and sputtered all along the coast of France. Finally we made an unscheduled stop at Bordeaux. The passengers got off and sat about in the terminal for six hours drinking cognac and eating cold sandwiches. Salami and gruyère. At last we boarded the aircraft again and took off. Smooth as silk for a while. But then the engines started acting up again and we began lurching about in the sky. By now it was almost dark. So the pilot announced that we would have to veer off course and make an emergency landing in Madrid. A new aircraft, we were told, would take us on from there. They expected that we'd be on the ground in Madrid for no more than an hour. Estimated arrival time in Lisbon was midnight. It was all a bloody bore but at least I knew I'd be able to keep my appointment with Salazar. What a naïve assumption that was!

'I finally arrived in Lisbon at five o'clock the following afternoon. As soon as I got to my hotel, I called Salazar's people. I talked to some cold and brittle bastard who insisted on speaking to me in French. He said Salazar had gone off to his family home in Castelo Branco for a three-day meeting with his economic advisers but would very probably, but not definitely, be able to talk with me on Monday when he returned. When I rang up Winkler at the *Telegraph* he said, "The food's great in Lisbon. Have a few good meals, drink some Portuguese wine, and see Salazar Monday. We're anxious to know what's going on in his head. Be sure to sound him out about the situation in Germany."

'But the main thing we wanted to know,' Evan told Arthur, 'was what he planned to do with the Portuguese wine industry. A lot of British money is tied up there and the old boys want to know what they'll be up against with Salazar.'

'Did you see him on Monday?' Arthur asked.

Evan shook his head. 'Not Monday. Not ever. They stalled me for two weeks, more than two, almost three. Every day, about noon, a sweet lady who spoke excellent English would ring up my hotel to give me the bad news. She was always apologetic. "But you understand, it is a critical period for our Premier. He is extremely occupied." So I waited. I rang up the *Telegraph* in London every evening, talked with Winkler, and continued to wait. At last the cold fish I'd talked with when I first arrived in Lisbon called one night, very late, at my hotel. He said, "It's a pity you were not able to keep your original appointment with the Premier. He was eager to speak with you. But since then the climate has changed. Many new issues have crystallized. I am not saying that our Premier refuses to speak with you now but I am saying that I can make no concrete promise as to when he will be able or willing to do so."'

'So you came home?' Arthur said.

Evan nodded. 'Next morning I was on the train heading north. I didn't want to play the aeroplane game again and I needed some time to look out the train window and decide what I want to do with myself. It was a wise move. I'd left Lisbon feeling like a discarded bar-towel but I arrived in London with what the Dean at Christ's College used to call "sense of purpose".'

9

When Evan came home at last to his flat he found among his letters a note from Sophie.

I've been trying to reach you. Finally spoke to Alan Winkler. He told me you're delayed in Lisbon. Please ring me as soon as you're back.

S.

As soon as he read the message he went to the telephone and called her at home. When Oliver, her butler, answered, Evan said, 'This is Mr Tagg, Oliver. I need to speak to Sophie. Is she there?'

'I'm afraid not, sir.'

'When do you expect her?'

'I'm afraid she didn't tell us when she'll be back.'

'She's normally home by five, isn't she?'

'Yes, sir.'

'Good. Ask her to ring me between five and six.'

There was a pause. Then, 'If she comes in this afternoon I will give her your message.'

'You just said . . . look, Oliver. This is Evan Tagg, not the greengrocer. Is something wrong there? You don't sound like yourself.'

'I'm sorry, sir.'

'Has Mrs Black gone out of town?'

'I can't answer that, sir.'

'I see. All right, let me try something else. Please call Mrs O'Haver to the phone.'

'Yes, sir. Just a moment.'

Ruth O'Haver had been Sophie's personal maid at Wiswell Towers. She had come along as housekeeper when Sophie moved to the Wiswell house in London. When she came on the second-floor extension Evan said, 'It's Evan, Ruth. I just came back to London and I had a message from Sophie asking me to ring her. Oliver seemed very mysterious for some reason. Is she all right?'

'Yes, I'm sure she is.'

'He didn't seem to know where she is, or when she'd be home. Has she gone off somewhere?'

'I'm sorry. Mrs Black asked me not to give out any information about her.'

'She told you not to tell *me*?'

'She told me not to tell anyone.'

'Do you know where she is?'

'I'm afraid I can't say.'

'Well, when did you see her last? You can tell me that can't you?'

'No, I can't. I'm sorry.'

'I've known you since I was eleven years old, Ruth. Stop playing games with me. I can't understand what you're doing.'

'I'm following Mrs Black's orders.'

'Tell me this, does her mother know where she is?'

'I don't believe so.'

'Have you spoken with Margaret?'

'Yes. She's telephoned several times.'

'Did you tell her any more than you've told me?'

'No, I didn't.'

'All right, Ruth. Here's what I'm going to do. I'm going to ring up Howard Wiswell. Then I'm going to telephone Sophie's mother. Then I'm going to come to Sophie's house to talk with you and Oliver. If you are still unwilling to talk to me, I will go straight to Scotland Yard and report Sophie as a missing person. I will encourage them to send an inspector to question you straightaway.'

When he talked with Alan Winkler he said, 'I understand Sophie was looking for me.'

'Yes. She called and asked where you were. Said she'd expected you back sooner. I told her I had, too. Then I explained about the problems you'd run into with Salazar.'

'Nothing urgent about her call, then?'

'Not at all. If there had been I'd have told her how to reach you in Lisbon.'

'When did she call? Do you remember?'

'You hadn't been gone long. Two weeks ago perhaps.'

'Maybe she was going off somewhere. Did she say anything about leaving London?'

'No. Just said she'd talk to you when you got back.'

When Evan rang up Howard Wiswell, Sophie's uncle was just leaving for his club in Pall Mall. 'Come have a bit of lunch with me,' he said. 'I want to hear about Portugal. I've always been damned fond of the Algarve. Praia da Rocha. Spent some lovely winters there. Flowers blooming. Port for a few shillings the bottle. A good life down there. Bloody nice people.'

At lunch Howard said, 'First off I want to thank you for those tickets to the Royal Court. The Kincaid evening.'

'I wasn't sure you went. I left in a rush and Sophie's plans were vague at that point.'

'She dithered a bit. Wasn't sure she'd be able to go. But I brought her round. Perfect stalls we had, the theatre was packed to the doors and Kincaid gave a good account of himself.'

'You enjoyed it, then?'

'More than that. I'm sure Sophie will tell you about it. I always thought there was something first-rate about that fellow when he was just a busker on the pavement. But he reaches a whole different plateau when he's on stage with lights and all the rest of it. That gravelly voice of his bounces off the rear walls. It was a bright notion, too, to present him at first in his seaman's clothes as he used to work the street, and then bring him back after the interval with his hair slicked back and decked out in a tail-coat.'

'The audience liked him then?'

'Couldn't get enough. When he finished the second half, the Dante piece, people stood up and let out a roar. Electric, the man in the *Guardian* said the next day. And that's the word, no doubt about it.'

'So Sophie enjoyed it.'

'Damned right she did. She's spent half her grown-up life going to the theatre. She knows something good when she sees it. She didn't clap and stomp her feet like I did, of course. But when we met him after the show she was most complimentary.'

'You went backstage then?'

'No, we didn't. I never got into the habit of doing that even when I was a young bachelor blazing a trail through the city. The fact is we were invited back, not to the dressing-rooms but to a private reception-room behind the Royal box. We'd had a note from Rosamund Barwick at the interval asking us to come round for champagne and sandwiches after the performance. Sophie wasn't keen to go and neither was I, to tell the truth, but as soon as the curtain went down and people started nudging towards the exits, Mrs Barwick came to find us and ushered us straightaway to where the party was. Not many people there, not more than forty, I should think, but a lot of faces you see in the daily journals. And some actors, of course. Cedric Hardwicke, Raymond Massey, and Wolfit. Edna Best and Jessie Matthews. I saw a few MPs I know who are members here at the club, and all the Bloomsbury crowd was there. Solid people for the most part. People who've accomplished something.'

'How did Kincaid react to all that attention?'

'I'd asked myself that same question before he came in from his dressing-room. I was curious as to how he'd deal with it. But when he showed up I could tell in a minute I didn't have to fret about that chappie. Cool as mountain water. He took a position in a corner of the room and stood there as long as the reception lasted. An hour and a half, I'd guess. He sipped a tall whisky and talked to everybody as they came up to him, one or two at a time. Quiet, pleasant to people, but not falling all over himself. Staying inside himself, as the jockeys used to say about a good mount. He didn't act impressed by himself or anybody else there. But he certainly impressed me. How old is he, do you know?'

'Twenty-four,' Evan said.

'Go on. I placed him at thirty. Maybe more.'

'He hasn't been easy on himself. I guess it shows.'

When they'd finished lunch, Howard said, 'Have you talked to Sophie since you got back?'

Evan shook his head. 'I just came home this morning. I rang her house but she wasn't in. I got the impression she may have gone off for a little holiday somewhere.'

'Maybe she did. She loves the sea. You know that. Almost every time I see her she talks about it. How much she longs for the sea. She might have run off to France with some of her chums. To her cottage in Dinan, perhaps.'

'You haven't seen her then in the past few days?'

'Haven't seen anyone except Sybil. We've had a snooker tournament here at the club for the past week and I've been fully occupied. I'm keen on snooker, you know. I'm chairman of our little group here and I'm pretty sharp with the cue myself. Not like I was before I developed this paunch but I can still surprise some of the younger chaps when I have a good day with the stick.'

'Do you think you've seen her since that evening at the Royal Court.'

'Oh, yes. And we usually chat on the telephone two or three times a week. But, let me see, come to think of it, I've only seen her once since that evening. Two or three days later she invited Sybil and me to her house for tea. She'd invited Rosamund Barwick and Kincaid and she wanted us to be there, too. So that's it. That's the last time I talked with the old girl. Fine little tea-party she gave. Sophie knows how to present things nicely. Learned that from my sister, I expect. Margaret always had a graceful way about her. Still does. Does things right. Knows the perfect word to say, how to wrap a gift, how to serve a cake and pour a proper cup of tea. And Sophie takes after her in those respects. As we were leaving that day, Mrs Barwick commented to Sybil and me what a handsome house Sophie has and what a perfect hostess she is. Mrs Barwick's car came round then and she and Kincaid drove off. As Sybil and I walked over to St James's to hail a taxi she said, "So that's the young man you told me about?" and I said, yes, it is, and she said, "He hardly says a word. I can't imagine him standing on a stage by himself for almost two hours speaking to a crowd of people."'

'But he did it, didn't he?' Evan said.

'He certainly did. *Enthralled*, that's what the audience was. Bloody enthralled.'

Evan, when he got back to his flat, did not call Sophie's mother as he had said he would. But he did telephone Ruth O'Haver. 'Have you thought about what I said?' he asked her.

'Yes, I have. But I can't tell you what you want to

know. I promised Mrs Black. And if you bring an inspector here from Scotland Yard I won't tell him either.'

'It's all right, Ruth. I'm not going to Scotland Yard. I know where Sophie is. She's in Brittany. In a place called Dinan.' There was no answer from Mrs O'Haver. But through the receiver he thought he heard a soft change in her breathing.

That evening Evan worked at his desk. Neglected correspondence. Unpaid accounts. He assured himself that his curiosity about Sophie had been satisfied. In any case, he concluded, it was none of his affair. He would accept the fact, as her uncle had, that she had gone off to enjoy some days by the sea.

The centre, however, would not hold. It was almost ten o'clock that night when he left his building, walked to Russell Square, and rang the bell at the side-entrance to Rosamund Barwick's house. A very tall brown-skinned man, a Sikh, opened the door.

'Pardon me,' Evan said. 'I know it's late but I'm most anxious to locate my friend, Roy Kincaid. He gave me this address and told me he lives here.'

'That's true,' the man said. 'But he's not here just now.'

'When do you expect him back?'

'That's difficult to say. He's gone off on holiday. He's been away for two weeks or more. If you'd like to wait inside I'm sure Mrs Barwick is still in the library. I will ask her and perhaps she can give you more specific information.'

'No, thank you. There's no need to bother her. And thank you very much.'

'I'm happy to be of service, sir.'

On his way home Evan stopped at a public house for a glass of claret. He made a concentrated study of all the people standing round him at the bar. He told himself he was cataloguing their movements, their expressions, and characteristics, memorizing their voice patterns, so he could include such people in one of his future plays.

When he got home later, a cable had been slipped under the door of his flat by the concierge.

MOST URGENTLY NEED TO SEE YOU. CAN YOU COME ST-MALO? WILL RING YOU EARLY TOMORROW.   SOPHIE.

· CHAPTER 3 ·

1

She telephoned him at eight the next morning. As soon as he rang off he booked a ten o'clock flight across the channel to Brittany. By early afternoon they were sitting in a small restaurant in an old building on a hill overlooking St Malo harbour.

'What a loyal friend you are,' she said.

'Just like an old dog. You whistle and here I come.'

'There's nothing about you that's dog-like. There never has been. If you were a dog you'd have to be muzzled day and night.'

She wore no make-up and her hair was pulled back loosely. She wore boating trousers, sandals, and an over-size fisherman's sweater.

'It's a long time since I've seen you dressed like that,' Evan said.

'It's not the garb for a woman of a certain age, is it?'

'You look fine. All of twenty years old.'

She smiled. 'I can't even remember when I was twenty years old.'

'Of course you can. It was twelve years ago.'

She made a face. 'Heaven protect us from a literal man.' Then, 'Seriously, I do appreciate your coming over here on such short notice.'

'You gave me no choice. It sounded like an order from on high.'

'I guess it is. As soon as I knew you were back in London . . .'

'You must have a good intelligence network. I just got home yesterday.'

'I know. Ruth rang me last evening. She said you were about to call out Scotland Yard. Did you do that?'

'It wasn't necessary. After I talked with your uncle Howard I guessed you'd come to Brittany. When I said that to Mrs O'Haver, I knew for sure.'

'Dinan has always been my secret place. You're one of the few people who knows that.'

The waiter came then to take their order. When they were alone again she said, 'Have you also guessed why I'm here?'

'Fresh air. Sunshine. Life near the seashore.'

'Don't play with me. You know, don't you?'

'I think so. I went round to the Barwick house last night and asked for Kincaid. The butler said he'd gone off on holiday about two weeks ago.'

'Can you believe it?' she said. 'I can't.'

'I can believe anything once I know it's happened.'

'I don't think I'm happy with your attitude. Have you decided to be matter-of-fact about all this? Cool and philosophical? Have you distanced yourself from me?'

'Of course not. I'm not taking any position. All I actually know is that you asked me to come over here because you needed to see me. But so far all you've done is ask me questions.'

'I'm nervous, damn it. I don't know what to say. I don't know what to do.' Suddenly there were tears in her eyes. 'I'm happy and frightened and bewildered. All at once. Half of me is trying to make sense out of everything that's happened and the other half simply doesn't give a damn.

I feel reckless and crazy and irresponsible, and I love the feeling. For more than two weeks now . . . God, it seems like two years . . . I wanted it all to be a secret. Something to lock up and keep just for myself. Then all at once I knew I had to tell someone or I'd burst. And the person I wanted to talk to was you.'

'Where is he now?'

'At the cottage outside Dinan. He knows I came here to see you.' Then, 'I want to tell you everything but I don't know where to start.'

'Howard told me you two went to the Royal Court together.'

'That's right. And did he tell you there was a reception afterwards?'

Evan nodded. 'Very pleasant, he said.'

'Yes, it was. Usually I detest that sort of thing but this was different. Because of Mrs Barwick, I expect. She has remarkable gifts as a social catalyst. She's like an odd mix of dowager, courtesan, and field marshal. You feel that she's in quiet control of everything and everyone, that people are most eager to please her. There were a great number of gigantic egos crowded into that small reception hall but they all behaved as though Kincaid was the only person of consequence there.'

'And how did he behave?'

'Very solemn. Very gracious. One felt he must have been the centre of attention many other times before and had come to think nothing of it. He was much the same as he'd been the day you introduced me to him at that restaurant in Bruton Lane. The difference was that this time I'd just witnessed what he's able to do on stage. Having seen all that force and energy and sensitivity in action, it was quite remarkable to see him suddenly reduced to human size.'

'Did you talk with him?'

'Only for a moment. All those high-decibel people were crowding up to him, so I just babbled out a few silly words of praise and withdrew. But as Uncle Howard and I left, Kincaid waved goodbye to us from the far side of the room.'

'Howard told me it was a remarkable performance. What did you think?'

'It's hard to describe. Either the performance or my reaction to it. As I told you before, I think, I'm never really taken with virtuoso evenings, with one-person performances. So I came to the theatre with misgivings, expecting very little. Nothing, from boredom to catastrophe, would have surprised me. Or so I told myself. But from the moment he walked on the stage I was reminded of something that Edna Best said recently in an interview. She said, "It's easy to tell when a really fine actor has come on stage. The audience relaxes and settles comfortably into their seats. They know instinctively that when this particular person is in charge, they are in good hands."'

'Is that what you felt?'

'That's what the entire audience felt. It seemed that everyone breathed a deep sigh and settled back to enjoy themselves. Howard said later it was like watching a fine musician doing a solo performance. At the beginning he started slowly, speaking in a clear but almost conversational tone, then gradually, almost imperceptibly, increasing the tempo, the intensity, and the level of projection through the love poems, the great soliloquies, and ending with Henry the Fifth's speech to his men. He seemed to progress from solo instrument, as Howard had said, to full orchestra. The effect was shocking and startling, almost painful. There was something aggressive about what he was doing, something cruel, almost vengeful, as though he was there not to please or enlighten the

97

audience but to punish them. You were conscious of no technique. All the emotions seemed like real emotions, occurring for the first time. The anger was real anger. The effect was that of a prisoner battling to escape from whomever or whatever it was that held him captive. At the interval Howard and I concluded that the second half of the programme could not possibly match the first in intensity but we were mistaken. He started the Dante on a higher level than he had begun before, used his voice differently; he kept the material locked inside him, it seemed, so it had to be torn loose. It was frightening and agonizing, like eavesdropping on a personal sorrow, or sitting in a room with someone who has attempted suicide and will clearly attempt it again. When he finished at last, when he read the last two lines in a hoarse whisper, then dropped to his knees just before the curtain fell, the audience was stunned and dead-silent. But suddenly they exploded in a roar and came up on their feet. I never stand and applaud and make a spectacle of myself in the theatre. You know that. But in this case I simply found myself on my feet like everyone else. I wasn't sure what it was I'd witnessed but I was absolutely certain it was something I had never seen before and might never see again.'

Evan smiled. 'And you have me to thank. If I hadn't forced those tickets on you, you might have been at home in your lounging pyjamas reading Lytton Strachey.'

'Don't think I haven't thought of that. A thousand times, I expect, in the past two weeks.'

'The way you describe it, it makes me regret that I went off to Lisbon. I seem to have missed the theatrical event of the year.'

'I didn't say that,' she said. 'At least I didn't mean to say that. As I said, Kincaid has no visible technique. Not the sort we're accustomed to seeing on the stage. So although the result was certainly theatrical, I suspect it was not *theatre*. It was like witnessing a personal revelation. Seeing a tortured person turned inside out. I'm certain it's not a performance he would be able to repeat. It was all intuitive and internal and electric. It offered no answers about Kincaid but it stimulated dozens of questions. Provocative is the word. It made you wonder, "Who *is* this crazy man?"'

'So you invited him to tea?'

'Not exactly.'

'Howard said you had him to tea a few days later.'

'Actually, when we said goodnight to Mrs Barwick, I invited her to tea. She asked if she could bring someone and I said yes, of course. So she came with Kincaid. Howard and Sybil came also, and it was a pleasant visit. Sybil and Howard and Mrs Barwick had a fine chat, and I joined in, of course. But Kincaid ate his cucumber sandwiches, drank his tea, listened attentively to all of us, and said very little. At one point Howard asked him if he planned to do other evenings like the one at the Royal Court, and Kincaid said no, he didn't believe so. At this point Mrs Barwick, looking sly and triumphant, said, "We believe we see a sea voyage in Kincaid's future. America may turn out to be the place where he belongs."'

'What was that all about?' Evan said.

'I didn't know then and I don't know now.'

'When she said that, Kincaid said nothing?'

Sophie shook her head. 'As I say, he said very little. But just before everyone left, when Howard had taken Mrs Barwick into the library to see the Daumier and Sybil was in the powder-room, Kincaid said to me, "The next time you invite me here, don't ask anyone else. I just want to sit and look at you. I don't want you to say a word. I know you're intelligent and clever but I don't give a damn about that."'

'What did you say?'

'I don't remember if I was angry or simply taken aback. I said, "But what if I don't invite you again?" And he said, "I hope you will. If you don't I'll arrive at your door without an invitation."'

'Did you invite him again?'

'No. I thought it was arrogant and presumptuous of him to talk to me like that. I decided that whatever I had admired on stage had not travelled with him when he left the theatre.'

'When did you see him again?'

'Three days later. In the middle of the afternoon Oliver came to my upstairs sitting-room with a box of chocolates and a large bouquet of roses. "Mr Kincaid is downstairs. He asked me to bring these up to you and to inquire if he might speak to you." I told him to take the flowers and the chocolates back to Mr Kincaid and to tell him I was not available. I walked to the window then, just above the street entrance to my home. In a moment Kincaid came out carrying his gifts. He walked across the pavement and stood there in Fulsham Court looking at my house. At last he walked away, leaving the flowers and the box of chocolates on the footpath, leaning against the far wall. As I watched, two schoolboys came past, heading home from their classes. They picked up the flowers and chocolates, looked them over carefully, then carried them off. For the next three days a large box of red roses arrived each morning, an identical box each time. No message or card was enclosed. On the fourth day, early in the evening, Oliver announced that Kincaid had come to see me. I had expected him to come. It had never occurred to me, however, that I would receive him. But I did. And I knew precisely what I was doing. The next afternoon we drove to Portsmouth and took the overnight ferry to St Malo.'

On his way from Newcastle to London on the train, Major Cranston had carefully planned his strategy. He was unaccustomed to asking favours, and certainly not from underlings or inferiors. On this case, however, he recognized that his tactical position required a change. Having resisted for twenty years the notion that the Taggs, father and son, had any familial rights whatsoever at Wiswell Towers, he was now determined to enlist Evan's services on the grounds that, though he was not Sophie's brother, she thought of him as a brother and would therefore be willing to listen to whatever reasonable advice might come from him.

If Evan's task was to persuade Sophie, then Cranston's assignment was to persuade Evan to function for the family, to present their case and accurately describe their trepidations in the matter of Roy Kincaid. He told himself, 'If I seem to accept Evan into the family after all these years I think he will be so grateful that he'll do whatever I wish. If I make the proper approach I'm sure I can bring him round.'

Cranston, however, never had an opportunity to seduce Evan as planned. As soon as they sat down together in the bar of the Savile Club, Evan said, 'I'm not sure why you came down to London to talk with me, but if it concerns Sophie in any way, I won't be able to help.'

Cranston's diplomacy disappeared at once. 'Why not, for God's sake? We have a crisis here. You're not a member of the family, it's true, but Sophie's mother and I believe that you could very well have some influence over her.'

'But I don't want to have influence over her. She's an adult. And a damned intelligent one. She doesn't need advice from me or from anyone else. She's able to make her own decisions.'

'I'm afraid you're mistaken there. I've never known a woman of any age who didn't need a man's advice. And the wisest women are the ones who realize that. Sophie's a fine young woman but she is female. And that means intuition and emotion get in the way of her decision-making. She needs to see things as they are, not as she would like them to be. And it's our responsibility to help her do that.'

Evan shook his head, 'Not mine. Even if she were my own daughter I wouldn't try to influence her in a situation like this.'

'Then you'd be a damned poor father. Since you have no children I would advise you to pay some mind to someone who has. I am her father and I will not walk away from my duty to her.'

'I can understand that. I'm sure if you want to talk to her she'll listen to whatever you have to say.'

Realizing he'd been sandbagged, Cranston went on the offensive. 'Damn it, man, he's after her money, pure and simple. Why else would that Australian riff-raff be pushing her to marry him?'

'Are they planning to be married?'

'Of course they are. They must be. When she rang up her mother yesterday from France, she gave Margaret the impression that it was damned serious business indeed. If they didn't have marriage in mind, she'd never have let him carry her off like that.'

'Maybe she carried him off.'

'That's a rotten thing for you to say.'

'This isn't the nineteenth century, Major Cranston, and Sophie's not eighteen years old. Since they went away to her cottage in Brittany it certainly doesn't look as if she was taken by force.'

102

'Men like him have ways of getting what they want. You know that as well as I do.'

'I also know that no man could even kiss Sophie's hand if she didn't want him to.'

'What are you trying to say?'

'I'm saying she knows what she's doing.'

'Is that what she told you? We know you went over to Brittany to talk with her. She told Margaret that. What did she tell you about her plans?'

'She told me nothing. But in any case I'm sure you wouldn't expect me to discuss things she'd told me in confidence.'

'We're not concerned here with your honour or mine. We're looking for a way to deal with a rascal who has no honour, a fortune-hunter.'

'You must have some information about Kincaid that I don't have,' Evan said.

'The man's been in jail. In prison. I know that. I can read the newspapers. And he boasts about it. A few weeks ago he was begging in the streets. What more do I need to know? It's clear the bastard has no background, no education, no character. He wants money. Why wouldn't he? He's never had any.'

'Sophie's not a fool. If that's all he wants from her . . .'

'I'm not saying that's all he wants. Sophie's a damned attractive woman. I'm sure he's told her she's the most beautiful creature in the world, that he'd give up his life for her, but mark my word, young Mr Tagg, money is the lure. Do you know how much money we're talking about?'

Evan shook his head. 'I have no idea.'

'I'm surprised your father has never told you. Thanks to Margaret, he knows all the details of the Wiswell holdings, you can be sure of that.'

'Well, he and I haven't discussed it and I don't want to discuss it now.'

For the first time since they had sat down together, Cranston suspected that for all his persistence he was up against a stone wall. 'I don't like what I'm hearing,' he said. 'Margaret believes you're a bright and reasonable young chap. She'll be disappointed when I tell her you've refused to co-operate. After all she's done for you, she thought you'd be eager to do something in return.'

'Did she say that?'

'You can take my word for it. I know how she feels.'

'But did she say it?' Evan insisted.

'I told you. She was counting on your doing your bit.'

'But she didn't say what you said.'

'Whether she said it or not, I'm saying it. We've done a lot for you and your father.'

'Mrs Cranston has done a lot for me. No question about it. But my father has been a reliable, valuable teacher. He's worked for you and he's certainly earned what he's been paid.'

'But we've also treated you like family members . . .'

'Not you,' Evan said. 'Mrs Cranston and Sophie. But not you. Don't you think we know that you've tried to get rid of us many times, that you wanted us out of the house and gone?'

'I don't know where you get your information.'

'We don't need information. It was in the air. It still is. Do you think my father is stupid? He would have left long ago if he didn't feel such strong loyalty to Mrs Cranston.'

'But you feel no such loyalty . . . is that what you're saying?'

'No, it's not. I'd do anything for her. And I believe she knows that. She also knows about my loyalty to Sophie.'

'But there's no such loyalty to me?'

'Major Cranston, I don't even know you and I never

104

have. When I was a little boy, whenever you and I were in the same room I felt as though I was invisible. It seemed to me you were unable to see me. So I invented a game to help me feel better about myself. I pretended I couldn't see you. It took a little while but finally I made it work. And it still works.'

Two days later Margaret Cranston telephoned Evan at home. 'I've tried several times to reach you,' she said. 'I want to offer you my apologies. William came home earlier today. He told me about his talk with you and I was humiliated. I hope you realize that he was not speaking for me. I knew he'd gone to London but I had no idea that he planned to see you. And I'm embarrassed that he asked you to intercede for us with Sophie. I know how close you two have always been. I would never ask you to violate any sort of confidence. Of course I'm concerned about her and I look forward to talking to her about her plans and to meeting Roy Kincaid. She's had enough heartbreak in her life and if I could prevent her from having more I would certainly try to do it. But I would never try to force my will on her or stand in the way of any choice she might make, whether it made sense to me or not. It's important that you believe that.'

'I do believe it,' Evan said. 'That's why I reacted the way I did to Major Cranston.' Then, 'He said you spoke with her on the telephone. Do you know when she'll be back in London?'

'She didn't say. But I expect she'll be there in ten days or two weeks. There's an event of some sort for parents at Sarah's school in Kent. I know she plans to be there for that.'

Some time later, when Kincaid and Sophie were separated by his work, she at home in England and he in California, when their only contact was through the post, Sophie wrote to him two or three times each week. In one letter she wrote:

I know what people think of me. They see me as a cool, controlled woman, well organized and kind. A loving wife and a devoted mother. 'Able to cope with whatever turns up,' they say. If they only knew what a floating, anchorless creature I really am, unsure of myself and my judgement, depending on all sorts of people, and most of all depending on you.

I think of you all the time during these cold unhappy days. And always I find myself returning to the miracle of our discovering each other in the first place. What drew us together is still a mystery to me. Perhaps that word, mystery, is the answer. Someone said, a poet, I imagine, that mystery is the core of love. If he's correct, then perhaps that explains us. I certainly had never known anyone remotely like you and you've said that I was equally strange and unfamiliar to you.

I have such a clear memory of the first time we met, when Evan introduced us in a restaurant. You've told me many times that you loved me at once. I can't say that. My first impression was that you were beautifully dressed, and that you had begun to acquire the speech and the sheen of your Bloomsbury friends. But that rebellious roughness, which is so much at the centre of you, could not be concealed. The broken nose, the scar above your eyebrow, your close-shorn hair like a dark helmet. Even your much-praised voice seemed ready to lapse into Australian slang at any moment. But the key thing I remembered after that first meeting was that you frightened me somehow. Something quietly menacing about you. That was a new experience and it clung to me. But it didn't make me eager to see you again.

But I did see you. I saw you on stage at the Royal Court and at Mrs Barwick's reception later. And I saw you when she brought you to my home for tea. And before I knew it I was seeing you yet again. I hadn't invited you. You just arrived. And two days later we were locked inside my cottage in Brittany with a fire on the hearth and the shutters closed.

That afternoon when you came to me in London you certainly didn't force yourself on me. God knows I wanted you, suddenly, as much as you wanted me. But it was like no love-making I had ever known. I felt as though my house had been sacked and I'd been carried off by looters. You were as silent as a mute and so was I. For those long dark hours in my bedroom I felt no connection between what had gone before in my life and whatever might come later. But after you left me I wept like a child. Not from pain or sadness. Simply in bewilderment. I had ceased to recognize myself. I was afraid to see you again but I knew I had to. I told myself that since nothing could possibly be permanent between us, I couldn't be hurt. I took refuge in our separateness. I was eight years older than you. I had two children. Everyone who knew me assumed I would never marry again and I assumed it, too. So whatever we had together, no matter what name we might put to it, would be temporary. It could be nothing else. By the time you rang me the next day I felt safe and protected by those circumstances. When you said you would see me at five o'clock I urged you to come. The following night as we lay together in our stateroom on the St

Malo ferry I no longer felt that I was protected in any way whatsoever, no longer believed that I could escape whenever I wished. And I no longer cared.

My father still insists that I should not have married you. He branded our marriage a failure before it happened. Before you and I had even decided to be married. But he's a fool of course. If he were not, if he were able to understand anything, and if I cared enough about him, which I do not, to try to make him understand, I would tell him that half of you and half of me will be welded together till we die.

There's another half of you, of course, that's not available to me or anyone else, the half that's made up of anger, old pain, and loss, the part that's rooted in Australia, in your childhood, and in jails and work camps and cheap hotels, in the dark bowels of freighters and tankers.

It was difficult for me to get beyond that first silent menacing part of you. When I did at last, when you began, slowly and grudgingly, to reveal other areas of yourself, when I saw and felt who you really are and where you come from, when I knew about the deprivation of your childhood, of your entire life, I loved you in a different way, an additional way. I told myself that you needed me. From that assumption it was easy for me to conclude that I could fix things, make everything right for you. That was the beginning of a painful period for me. After a very long time I was forced to accept the fact that certain things can only be fixed by you yourself, that only you can put them right. Nothing in my life has been more difficult for me to accept. Perhaps I'll never accept it fully.

And what about the half of me that may not be available to you? Just as you are permanently locked, somehow, into your past life, I am lovingly connected to my home, to England, to my mother and my children, to my way of life in my familiar surroundings. I am an Englishwoman. That's a part of me that cannot be given up, no matter how hard I might try.

Does that mean, does all this mean, that I am contented here? Far from it, my darling. I'm longing for you more than I can say. It's hell being away from you. I will count the days till we can be together again.

4

Evan and his father spoke to each other by telephone at least twice a month, usually on Sunday. On the first Sunday after Evan returned from Lisbon, when Arthur rang up, he said, 'I understand Major Cranston paid you a visit.'

'Yes, he did. Did he tell you about it?'

'No. Mrs Cranston told me. She also told me that she spoke to you.'

'That's right. Suddenly I'm quite in demand. Everybody's ringing me up.'

'She was upset because the Major had bothered you.'

'I know. That's what she said. But I knew when I was talking with him that she'd had nothing to do with it.'

'Of course not. She's perfectly capable of speaking with Sophie herself. And if she had wanted you to intercede in any way she would not have relied on the Major to give you a message.'

'That's pretty much what I told him.'

'You must have stung him. He's been stomping about the library and the drawing-room in his riding-boots as if he's about to declare war.'

'On me, perhaps.'

'No, I think not. From what Mrs Cranston says he's given up on you. She thinks Kincaid will be his next target.'

'The Major will have his hands full with Kincaid.'

'You know this fellow then?'

'Not really. I don't know him well. But neither does anyone else in London. I suppose I know him better than most.'

'What sort of chap is he?'

'Hard to say. He's full of surprises. Not a common type. He'd fall into place better in Liverpool, I expect, than here. Rough edges. A bad temper, I would guess, although I've never seen him really angry. He's like a packing-box that has "Handle with care" painted on it.'

'Who does he resemble? Anyone we know?'

'I'll put it this way. If he worked at Wiswell Towers he'd probably be a groom or a gamekeeper. At least that's what he was like when I first met him. Last time I saw him he could have passed for the son of a viscount.'

'Margaret said he's been taken up by some important people in London.'

'The Pygmalion syndrome. Except they didn't have to teach him how to speak. He's damned good at that.'

'How would you rate him? Is he a good fellow?'

'Don't be angry, but I'd like to know if you're asking for yourself or for Mrs Cranston?'

'For myself, Evan. That was a question you needn't have asked.'

'I know. But I wanted to make sure.'

'I daresay I'm as fond of Sophie as her parents are. I am concerned about her future as they are. Or as you must be.'

'Of course I'm concerned but I don't think it's my job to try to influence her.'

'Nor do I. This is simply a conversation between father

110

and son. If you did try to influence her, however, what would you be likely to say? How would you advise her about Kincaid?'

'As I said, I would never do it. If I did do it, however, I suppose I would tell her to proceed with caution. I think I'd give her that advice no matter who the man was. Regarding Kincaid specifically, I'd probably remind her that they come from very different backgrounds, that he has no education, no family, and no profession. I'd ask her to consider where they would live and what sort of life they might have together. And I'd suggest that she give serious thought to how such a marriage would affect her children. Kincaid is only eleven years older than Sarah and twelve years older than Trevor. If he's to be their stepfather those are matters to consider.'

'Yes, I think so,' Arthur said. Then, 'I gather, from what you've said that you don't think Sophie has made a wise choice.'

'That's not what I meant at all, Dad. I think the best choice for her is whatever choice she decides to make. If people picked their mates objectively most married couples would never have got married. I'm sure you and my mother didn't study a checklist before you got married and there's no reason for Sophie to do so either, no matter what her parents might think. No matter what you and I may think.'

'I agree with you, of course,' Arthur said. 'But all the same I have great sympathy for Mrs Cranston. Her hands seem to be tied.' He paused. 'I just wish we could help her in some way. We owe her a lot.'

'That's what Major Cranston said to me.'

'For once he's right.'

'Mrs Cranston should come to London as soon as Sophie gets home. Then they can sit down and talk non-stop for two days if they want to.'

'I'm sure she will go to London. Sophie will undoubtedly want her to meet Kincaid. But that will be a pro forma occasion. Mrs Cranston will still know nothing whatsoever about Kincaid. She'll have only the information that Sophie is willing or able to give her.'

'It will all work out, Dad, or it won't. You and I can't make things happen.'

'All the same I can't stop hoping.'

After a moment Evan said, 'You're suggesting that I should speak to Sophie, aren't you?'

'No. I'm not saying that. You've made it clear how you feel. Your prime loyalty is to her. I understand that. But in my position, knowing how Mrs Cranston feels about all this, it would be impossible for me not to help her in any way I could.'

'I know what you said when I asked you before but I'll ask again anyway. I hope you're not saying that you feel bound to tell Mrs Cranston everything I've been saying to you.'

'Of course I'm not saying that. Whatever you've said is privileged information. And any decision you make about speaking or not speaking to Sophie is a matter for you to decide.'

5

The day before they were to leave Brittany to return to London, Sophie and Kincaid motored south, found a sheltered beach in a small cove, and spent the day there. The skies were clear but there was a cool onshore breeze and the autumn sea was too cold for bathing. They walked southward for almost two hours, ate the lunch they'd brought, then walked slowly back to where they'd left the car. They spent the rest of the afternoon there, wearing their sweaters, sitting in a rock-rimmed niche protected from the wind.

'So where are we now?' Sophie said, mid-afternoon, the sun pale and sinking.

'Longitude or latitude?' he said.

'You know what I mean.'

'I know what you mean but I don't know the answer. And even if I did I don't think I'd tell you.'

'Why not?'

'It might not be what you want to hear.'

'What difference would that make?'

'It might make a big difference. I want to tell you things that make you smile. Whistle songs that make you dance. Where do you think we are?'

'I know where we are,' she said. 'Exactly where we want to be.'

He put his arm around her and pulled her close to him. 'You see. I don't have clever answers as you do. You're much more clever than I am.'

'I'm not trying to be clever. It's the truth.'

'But you knew how to say it. I didn't.'

'Maybe we shouldn't go back to London. Maybe we should stay here.'

'Sounds good to me.'

'Everything sounds good to you. You're an agreeable man.'

When he smiled she said, 'Is that funny?' and he said, 'No. It's just that nobody ever called me *agreeable* before. I'm supposed to be a hard-nosed bastard.'

'You are a hard-nosed bastard. But you're also agreeable. With me you're extremely agreeable.'

'That's because I'm afraid of you. You're an older woman and you have a hyphenated name. I never met a woman with a hyphenated name before. When we get married your name will be Cranston-Black-Kincaid. Is that right?'

'When we get married my name will be Sophie Kincaid.'

'Is that fancy enough for you?'

'It's not fancy at all. That's why I like it.' They sat quiet for a while. Finally she said, 'Can you believe what's happened to us?'

'I believe it.'

'A month ago we didn't know each other.'

'I knew you,' he said, 'but you didn't know me.'

'We'd met each other. We'd smiled and said hello. But that's not what I meant.'

'It's all right. Now we know each other.'

'One minute I feel as though we've been together for a year. The next minute it seems like an hour. I don't know where I am.'

'Sure you do. Everything's solid and warm and nice. We figured it all out. We've got answers for all the questions.'

'What makes you so smart?' she said.

'I'm not smart. I just know when I'm lucky.'

'What makes you so sure of yourself?'

'You do. If you like me I must be worth a lot.'

'Don't give me that. You're the cockiest man I've ever met. Women have been falling all over you since you were twelve years old. Isn't that right?'

'I remember a girl kissed me on the cheek once when I was twenty-two. That's about it.'

'Of course it is,' she said. 'And you learned to make love by going to the movies.'

'Not at all. Whatever I know I've learned from you.'

'Oh, God, I'm in for trouble. I can see that. I'm about to marry a *beau parleur*.'

'I only speak the truth,' he said. 'It's my fatal flaw.'

114

That night, as they sat before the fire in her cottage, she said, 'I want to ask you a serious question.'

'You can ask it if you like but I don't promise to give you a serious answer.'

'Why not?'

'Why should I? We're on a cloud here. Floating along. I always thought two good days in a row was a miracle. But since you kidnapped me and brought me over here to France, it's been nothing but wine and sweet music. I'm certainly not going to wreck that by having a serious discussion about politics or world finance . . .'

'Nothing like that,' she said. 'I meant a serious question about us.'

'That's worse. Besides, wc've dealt with all those possibilities. We've solved every problem. When it begins to get cold we either put more wood on the fire or we get into bed. When the wine bottle's empty we open another bottle. When we're tired we sleep, when we're rested we make love till we're tired again. When we're hungry we eat. That covers everything, doesn't it?'

'It certainly does,' she said. 'As long as we stay locked in this cottage.'

He smiled. 'Not just here. Wherever we are. We've invented a way of life.'

'Don't try to get me off the track. I have a question to ask you and I'm determined to do it.' When he didn't answer she went on. 'Does it bother you that I'm older than you?'

'No. Does it bother you?'

'Of course not.'

'Then why should it bother me?'

'I don't know. People think nothing of a fifty-year-old man marrying a twenty-year-old woman but when the wife is a few years older it makes people uncomfortable.'

'Not me. Only one thing concerns me and I think we

115

should give it some thought. When you're a hundred years old I'll only be ninety-two. Then we may have something to worry about.'

The next morning when they were having breakfast he said, 'Look, kid, I know you have a thousand questions and ideas bouncing around in your head. That's normal, I guess. But don't think we have to solve everything at once. Let's just do one step at a time. You're the important thing. Just remember that. The thing that matters most is for you to have what you want, to have what's good for you. That doesn't mean we should think of ourselves and forget about everybody else. I know the big considerations for you are your kids and your mother. But they must want you to have a good life. At least that's what they should want. On the other hand, they've had you all to themselves for a long time. They may not like the idea of giving you up. They may see me as the enemy. But they'll get over it. Finally they'll understand that I'm not just a wild bastard who wants to steal you and lock you up somewhere. It's better for you if they like me. So I'll be as civilized as I can be. But if they still can't stand the sight of me, if they think you've wrecked your life by choosing me, then you and I will have to deal with that when the time comes. The best thing we can do now is to keep ourselves to ourselves for as long as we can. There's plenty of time to focus on trouble after it shows up. Let's not waste time thinking about it till we have to.'

6

Alan Winkler, the man who had hired Evan just out of university and who had guided his work at the *Daily Telegraph*, was himself a failed novelist. 'Every news-paper man has a half-finished novel or a play stuck away

116

somewhere in his closet and half a dozen others moulder-
ing in his head. But most of those projects never get
finished. A good reporter relies on one side of his brain.
A good creative writer plugs into another area altogether.'

Winkler had known from the beginning about Evan's
intention to be a playwright. He had encouraged him, had
read most of the plays he'd written, and had given
thoughtful advice when Evan asked for it. Because of
Winkler, Evan had been given only feature assignments.
'You'll be able to spend more time with the people you're
writing about, to dig a little deeper, to learn what makes
them percolate. That should help you with your theatre
work. Good writing is always about people. The further
inside them you can get, the better your plays will be.'

As Evan sat with Winkler after his return from Portugal, as he explained that he wanted to work out a schedule
that would give him more uninterrupted time to work on
the new play he had in mind, as they discussed a schedule
that would give him that time, Winkler said again, 'Never
mind the plot. Screw the story and the structure and the
curtain lines and all that rot. Spend your time with the
characters. Work on them. Find out how they feel about
themselves, and how they feel about each other. When
you know those people like you know your pocket, you'll
find you have enough material for half a dozen plays.'

Evan knew by now that the play he planned to write
about his father would take the form of a son's efforts to
imagine, to duplicate in dramatic scenes, what the
relationship must have been between his father and his
wife, a woman the son barely remembered. As his broad
reference, he would use the marriage he had been
exposed to as he grew up, that of William and Margaret
Cranston. Following Winkler's advice, to immerse himself
as deeply as possible in that experience, to crystallize his
feelings towards the Cranstons, towards Arthur Tagg, and

117

towards his ephemeral wife, Evan chose, as an exploratory device, letter-writing. He would compose a candid letter to each of those four people, expressing his unguarded observations about them and their marital relationships. He began with the person he knew best, his father.

Since you're my father, the only parent I know, I could never actually say these things to you. Or allow you to read them. But since I am putting these thoughts down only for myself, to be seen by no one else, I feel free to be open and honest. And cruel perhaps.

I know you've sacrificed a lot for me and I love you. But I don't admire you. And I'm not sure I respect you. You have an obsession with laws and rules that has immobilized you. Any sign-post, any spoken command can make you change directions. When something positive happens to you, you call it good fortune. When something bad happens you believe you are to blame. You feel you deserved it.

You're an intelligent man. Well educated. You're kind. And perceptive. But not about yourself. You're an inspired teacher. You could have had important jobs in important schools. But you've always settled for whatever was offered. You've always felt grateful for any job available to you. Yet all the while you've taught Sophie and me that there's almost nothing we can't do. And you believe that. But you can't imagine that it also applies to you. I know you've told yourself, through all these years, that you've stayed with the Cranstons because it was good for me. And it was. But how can you imagine that it was good for you? Especially since the Major came home to stay.

Then there's Margaret, Sophie's mother. I know there's nothing physical between you two. I'm certain you've never made love to her and you never would. Even if she begged you. 'We come from different classes. That fact can't be changed or forgotten.' Since you made that speech to me about Sophie I can certainly believe that you would also say it to yourself. But how ridiculous it is.

Don't you see that you two are a match in every way. You are the true master of Wiswell Towers and you have been for twenty years. She defers to you, consults you in all matters, and I'm sure she loves you. Otherwise, why are you still there? Major Cranston wonders why, and so do I.

The answer is that you're a vital part of Margaret's life, as she is of yours. There was no reason for you to stay on at Wiswell Towers after Sophie married and I went off to university. I know, of course, that Margaret was eager for you to stay, but what was your motivation? The Major, when he came home in retirement, didn't want to have you around. He never wanted you. You had become, quite visibly, the functioning head of the household. Only when Margaret had made it clear to him that you were staying on did he appear to accept you, saving face with his cronies at the public house by saying you were an inexpensive convenience, willing to assume all his managerial duties for a low wage, leaving him free to be totally indolent, to gallop his mare across the moors and drink himself into insensibility every afternoon. As he pretended to endure you, you endured him. I never understood why. I don't understand now.

And there's the matter of my mother and your attitude towards her. She deceived you, went off with another man, deserted both of us, but do you still tell yourself what a kind and gentle person she was? Would you continue to send her money even now if you knew how to reach her? Do you value yourself so little? Do you truly see yourself as the world's servant? It seems so.

How many times have you told me that a parent teaches by example and not by persuasion? If that's true the things I've learned from you are self-abnegation, subservience, and abject humility. Thank God, I've failed to absorb those lessons. On the contrary, I have tried to teach myself to be as strong and self-reliant as I can be. I want to take chances. No fear of risk. I refuse to be an attachment to someone else's life. I'm willing to make mistakes but I refuse to lose myself. I need to make my own way, to be something; to stand for something. That's what I'm after.

Next Evan turned to Margaret Cranston.

If goodness can be exemplified in a particular person then you are surely that person. I do not think of you as my mother, but even if I did, that would not begin to cover the ground. I've never seen such a mix of kindness and strength in anyone else. Intelligence and emotion. Indignation and tolerance. With balance as the key ingredient. But thank God, for all your sense of fairness, you haven't forgotten how to hate. Your vengeance is to banish your enemies to Coventry.

You've been an armature of my life since I was eight years old. And of my father's life as well. You taught me what to read, how to look at fine paintings, and how to listen to serious music, from Bartok and Milhaud to Jellyroll Morton and Django Reinhardt.

Seeing you with Sophie was the best lesson of all. What a lovely relationship. Easy and intimate. Sophie's graceful sense of security comes directly from you.

There are two questions I can never ask, however,

which are the things I need most to know about you. The first is, why have you squandered yourself on a man like Major Cranston? And the second, what are your feelings towards my father?

Sophie and I have fantasized for years about the two of you, hoping you would somehow end up together. Sophie believes you've loved each other for a long time. I'm not so sure. I'm afraid my father loved no one but my mother and that burned him out for ever.

When Major Cranston was his subject Evan wrote quickly, as though he had waited a long time for the words to come out.

When you retired and came home to stay, the time was coming near for me to go off to university. Thank God. Still, I did spend almost a year at the Towers when you were also there. And I had seen you from time to time through the preceding years. So I had ample opportunity to observe you, listen to you, and draw conclusions.

I had been taught that there are admirable qualities in every person. I had no reason to assume that you were an exception to that rule. But at last I had no other choice. I could find nothing but coldness and disdain in your manner. Toward Margaret and Sophie, towards my father and me, towards the staff, the tradesmen, and the tenant-farmers.

At first I believed that your egotism had convinced you that all of us, when measured against you, were intellectual and emotional dwarfs. Later I decided that self-hatred was your distinguishing feature. Now I've concluded it's a rotten combination of the two.

Sophie says you had a disappointing career as an

army officer. Perhaps you did. But what possible disappointment could explain or excuse your mean and proprietary attitude towards your wife and daughter? They have given up on you long since. You must realize that. They have ceased to expect anything at all from you. They've developed, instead, a benevolent disregard that allows them to survive under the same roof with you in an almost civilized way.

I salute their equanimity but I can't join in it. Wouldn't if I could. I make higher demands on people and you meet none of those demands. Since you are unlikely to improve at this stage of your life and since I, therefore, see no reason to change my views about you, I simply reject you. While Sophie and Margaret are two of the most important people in my life, you do not exist.

Addressing himself to his mother was another problem altogether. He pulled several sheets of paper out of his typewriter, crumpled them and dropped them on the floor by his chair before he was able to fill one page.

If you think about me at all you probably assume that I hate you. Perhaps I should but I don't. I haven't seen you since I was very small so I expect that if I did see you now I wouldn't recognize you. And you certainly wouldn't recognize me.

We have no photographs of you, you see. None at all. My father says they were lost somehow, but I believe he burned them.

Although you went away when I was barely three, my father and I stayed in that little fifth-floor apartment in Superior Street for almost six years. He always believed you'd come back. Knowing you'd gone off with a man you'd been married to since you were seventeen, two years before you met Dad, realizing that he'd never been legally married to you, he still had hope. So all those years went by before he finally quit his job at the store. The next week we took a steamship to England.

I often wonder what my dad would have done if he hadn't met you at that exposition in Paris. He was just starting his teaching career at a fine public school in Hertfordshire. But when you went back to America he followed you.

What I'm saying is that I know almost nothing about you. Dad doesn't mention you and I don't ask. So when I think about you it's all a vaccuum. Maybe some day we'll meet so I can fill in the blank spaces.

7

Sophie did not deceive herself that the euphoria of the past few weeks would inevitably follow her from the cottage in Britanny to her house in London. She foresaw, from her family, everything from smiling resistance to open antagonism. Although she had long since ceased to solicit her father's approval she was apprehensive, all the same, about his reaction. Even when one was steeled to his self-righteous objections, the sheer decibel-level of his voice as well as the bulging veins in his throat were disturbing, the anticipation nearly as ugly as the experience itself.

Because she had spoken with her mother on the telephone from Dinan she told herself that she had, to a large degree, got past that critical hurdle. Margaret had heard her speak Kincaid's name, had understood what Sophie was saying to her and had hopefully, through her intuition, understood a great deal more. She was a reasonable woman, Sophie told herself, accustomed to change, able to accept change, whether in her own life or in someone else's. And the communication lines were permanently open between herself and her daughter. Their relationship had always gone beyond mere understanding; they had a sensory connection, reliable and rewarding. 'Thank God for Margaret,' Sophie had often said to herself. And she said it again now. Yet something intangible gnawed at her. What, in fact, had Margaret said to her when they spoke on the telephone? Were there any clues there? Were there more substantial clues perhaps in what she had not said? Sophie punished her memory but could find no solid evidence to indicate what her mother's position might be. Still, she would be an ally. Sophie was sure of that. And even if she had reservations they would disappear once she and her daughter had spent a few hours together. And once she'd been introduced to Kincaid.

In Britanny, Sophie had not thought of her children as stumbling-blocks to her plans. But as the time came near when she would journey to St Alban's to see Trevor, and to Cobham, Kent, to visit Sarah, even they began to present themselves in her mind as problems. She saw them suddenly not as children but as young adults with adult powers of perception, judgement, and rejection. She realized that they – particularly Sarah – would ask questions, a great number of questions perhaps, some of which she might not be able to answer to their satisfaction. 'They won't rejoice at the thought of sharing you with a stranger,' Kincaid had said. 'They've had you to themselves for a long time.'

At one point, as she and Kincaid had floated through the days in Brittany, Sophie had persuaded herself that the best solution would be to have a family party at her home in London. Her parents would be there, her aunt and uncle, the children, and the Taggs, father and son.

'That's the answer,' she'd said to Kincaid. 'We'll have oceans of champagne, a string quartet playing in the music-room, and a feast later in the dining-hall. Everyone will meet you at the same time, we'll all have a chance to chat and enjoy ourselves, and when it's over you'll be a member of the family. Isn't that a fine idea?'

Kincaid had not been enthusiastic. And soon Sophie also had lost her enthusiasm. She decided that the task must be accomplished one piece at a time, through a series of minor engagements rather than one major one. Slowly and carefully the individual units would be locked into place. And the linchpin would be Evan. Thank God for him. She congratulated herself time and again for having had the foresight to invite him to come to St Malo. If she had seemed to conspire against her family, then Evan, in her mind, was a co-conspirator. She knew he would support her, as he always had, that he would be seen, would allow himself to be seen, as Kincaid's friend, companion of the bridegroom, all that rot. He would function as her brother. He would unquestionably be Kincaid's best man at the ceremony; he would be seen, by his very presence, as her ally. Behind him, because of him, the others would fall into line. The more she thought about it, the more she saw Evan as the solution to her problems, great and small.

It was in this frame of mind, then, that she returned to London, full of joy and self-confidence. As planned, she and Kincaid separated at the station. He went to his flat above Mrs Barwick's coach-house and Sophie took a taxi to her home.

In her upstairs sitting-room Sophie found a letter from her mother.

I'm not certain just when you'll be returning but I thought it would be nice for you to find a letter from me when you arrive.

What a sweet surprise it was to have your telephone call from France. I know how much you love being in Brittany, so I'm always pleased when you're able to go there. I could tell by your voice on the telephone that you were having a lovely holiday.

And you've found a man you're serious about. What delightful news. I'm anxious to meet him. I hope you'll bring him along to Wiswell Towers as soon as possible after you're back. We'll have a grand party if you like and invite our neighbours the way we used to do. I'm so sorry you were never able to know your grandparents. What a gay and splendid place this was when I was Sarah's age.

Since I'm certain I will see you here before too long I will wait till then for us to have a long talk together. But I feel there are some subjects I should touch on now as well. Did you say specifically, when we talked on the telephone, that you are planning to marry Mr Kincaid, or did I misunderstand? Whatever you have chosen to do, you know that I will support you in every way. Your happiness is as important to me now as it's always been. I have seen you living alone for a long time since Toby died, putting your children's needs ahead of your own, being an excellent, responsible mother. You have certainly not been in a rush to marry again. So if you have found someone now I know it's a decision you've considered carefully.

Forgive me, then, if I treat you like a daughter and try to influence you a bit. This is probably unnecessary advice but I offer it anyway. Since you have waited so long, please don't be reluctant to wait a bit longer. You owe it to yourself and you owe it to Trevor and Sarah.

Of course I will approve of your marriage and your husband. As I've said, it's your choice and I trust you to choose carefully. But please, for your own sake, don't rush into anything. Take some time to get to know this man. Give your children an opportunity to know him. Give him a chance to know you. It will be time well spent, I assure you. Arthur Tagg is a tragic example of what can happen when two people marry in haste.

I know you are always in close touch with Evan and I know how supportive you are with each other. So I was extremely surprised to learn that he is not at all enthusiastic about the man you propose to marry . . .

Sophie read on quickly, her face gone suddenly quite pale. She crumpled her mother's letter into a ball then and threw it on the carpet. 'I can't believe it,' she said. 'I won't believe it.' She crossed the room to the telephone and rang Evan at home. When he answered she said, 'I'm back in London and I need to see you. Can you come over now?'

'How about this evening? That might be better for me.'

'It's really quite urgent. Otherwise I wouldn't ask you.'

'You don't sound like yourself. Are you upset about something?'

'Yes. I'm very upset.'

When he arrived at her house she was waiting for him downstairs in the library. As soon as Oliver withdrew, closing the doors behind him, Evan said to Sophie, 'You look like hell. Did something go wrong over there?'

'No. Something's gone wrong here. I found this letter from Margaret waiting for me when I got home today. I want to read part of it to you.'

She had retrieved the crumpled letter and smoothed it out. She adjusted the light by her chair and began to read. 'I know you are always in close touch with Evan and I know how supportive you are with each other. So I

127

was extremely surprised to learn that he is not at all enthusiastic about the man you propose to marry . . .'

'I haven't talked to your mother about Kincaid. The last time I talked to her . . .'

'Let me finish,' Sophie said. She went on reading. 'Evan said that Kincaid is best-suited to be a groom or a gamekeeper. He thinks you should proceed with caution. He says the man has no education, no family, and no profession. He thinks you should consider how such a marriage would affect your children. He says Kincaid is only eleven years older than Sarah and twelve years older than Trevor.' She looked up at Evan. 'Did you say those things to Margaret?'

'No.'

'What did you say when you talked to her?'

'The Major came to see me, to find out what I could tell him. Your mother rang me later to apologize for his coming.'

'Did you say those things to him?'

'No. I told him you were old enough and smart enough to decide who you want to marry without any help from him, or me, or anyone else.'

'Then what is she talking about?' Sophie held up the letter. 'Did she make these things up?'

'She didn't hear them from me!'

Sophie sat very still and upright in her chair. 'Did someone else hear them from you and pass them along to her?'

'Sophie, this is a new experience for me and I don't like it. I'm not accustomed to being interrogated like a bloody burglary suspect.'

'It's also a new experience for me and I like it no more than you do. When I put my trust in someone I'm not accustomed to having that trust violated.'

'What does that mean? I didn't steal from you, or tell

128

lies about you, or report things you've told me in secret. What do you mean by trust? Are you saying that no one is allowed to disagree with you? You and I have disagreed a thousand times and you know it.'

'This is different.'

'No, it's not. Do you think that if I'm concerned about you, that means I've betrayed you in some way? That's nonsense, Sophie. After all these years are you saying that my opinions mean nothing to you, that I have no voice in your affairs?'

'No, I'm not saying that. To my face you can say anything you think and anything you feel. But you didn't do that. I was begging you to say what you thought when you came to St Malo but you said nothing. Instead you ran off to . . .'

'I ran off nowhere. I told you exactly how I felt when I saw you in St Malo. I said it was nobody's business to tell you who you should sleep with or who you should marry. But don't tell me I'm not allowed to have private reservations, because I am. And if you want the truth I was planning to tell you exactly what those reservations are. I expected to talk with you as soon as you got back to London.'

'Well, I'm back and we're talking.'

'No, we're not. You're challenging me. You're trying to make me feel guilty but I don't feel guilty. It does concern me that you've known Kincaid such a short time. It does concern me that he apparently has a background as different from yours as it could possibly be. Is there a streak of violence in him? I don't know for certain and neither do you. Will he be able to be the right sort of stepfather to Sarah and Trevor? There's no way to know these things until you know him better. I'd hate to see you marry too quickly and get some nasty surprises later.'

'Life is filled with nasty surprises, Evan. You know that

as well as I do. You and I have known each other for most of our lives and we still surprise each other. We're doing it right now. Do you think I haven't asked myself all the questions you're asking? Of course I have. Some of them I believe I have answers for, others I don't. But it's madness to expect or insist on guarantees. Do you think Kincaid knows me any better than I know him? He doesn't. We will have to take each other on faith, as everyone does. Of course I'm concerned about doing what's best for my children. But I mustn't allow their reactions to overcome my own judgement and my own convictions. At his age, Trevor is certain to be fiercely jealous of any man I might marry. At her age, it's very possible that Sarah will be a bit smitten with Kincaid herself. But those things will pass. I will take great pains to make sure that I am as available to them, as accessible, as I've always been, and I'm sure they'll have a good relationship with Kincaid. There's no reason why they shouldn't. He's certainly not jealous of them and he has no uneasiness about my life with Toby or anything else. And it isn't as though he'll be asked to bring up two small children. I've already done that. They're away at school now and they will be for the next few years. They'll be adults before we know it.'

'As I said from the beginning, it's your decision to make and you seem to have made it.'

'That's easy to say. Of course I'm able to decide what I think is best for me. But I'd like to think there's some feeling of acceptance among my family. And from you, particularly. I still can't believe you could say those things that Margaret put in her letter.'

'If you expect me to explain myself or apologize to you, I'm not going to do it. I've just told you how I feel about you and Kincaid. And I told you before I said nothing at all to your father or your mother.'

'Then how can you explain . . .'

'There is an explanation but I'm not going to give it to you. It involves someone else and I . . .'

'But how do you expect me to feel?'

'I'll tell you what I don't expect. I don't expect to be called over here and put on the witness-stand. I'm not required to defend myself. To you or anyone else.'

'You're really angry, aren't you?'

'Let me put it this way. You're obviously disappointed in me. And I am sure as hell disappointed in you. So let's just leave it there.'

An hour later her mother rang up. 'Oh, I'm glad I reached you. Oliver must have told you I've been telephoning every day.'

'I'm just back today,' Sophie said.

'Oh, good. I hope you haven't opened your mail yet. I sent you a letter that I regret sending. Please toss it in the fire without reading it.'

'I've already read it.'

'Oh, dear. I hope you're not cross with me.'

'I'm cross with everyone just now. Including myself.'

'I don't know what possessed me. I've been under such pressure from William. But that's no excuse. I am concerned about you, of course, and anxious to talk with you about your plans, but the tone of that letter . . . I don't even like to think about it. It wasn't me, Sophie. Please throw it away and try to forget I sent it.'

'Did Evan discuss Kincaid with you?'

'No, he didn't.'

'With William?'

'No. I hope I haven't caused a problem between you and Evan. I'm not certain exactly what Evan said. He had a conversation with Arthur and it was passed on to me. But I'm not sure how accurate Arthur was in his reporting. Or if I remembered him precisely when I wrote to you.'

As soon as she rang off Sophie telephoned Evan. There was no answer at his flat. When she tried him again the following morning there was still no answer. Later in the day when she called Alan Winkler, he told her Evan had gone to Aberdeen on an assignment and would probably be there for ten days or two weeks. 'He'll be calling in but I don't know how to reach him.'

8

When Sophie visited her daughter at Cobham, when she started to tell her about her plans, and about Kincaid, Sarah said, 'I think I already know what you're about to tell me. You're going to get married. Grandfather rang me last week and told me about it. He says you're going ahead with it no matter what any of us say.'

Trevor, when she visited him at St Alban's, had also talked with Major Cranston. Trevor said, 'I don't understand why everybody else knows about it and you haven't told me and Sarah.'

'I have told Sarah and now I've come here to tell you.'

'But Grandfather's known about it for a long time.'

'No, he hasn't. I've never discussed it with him.'

'Then why does he know so much about this man you're going to marry. He told me all kinds of stuff about him. He said he's an ordinary sailor on merchant ships. And he's been in jail a lot.'

When she returned to London she learned that Major Cranston had paid a call to Kincaid, had made a nasty scene and had been asked to leave. Her mother telephoned in tears and said it probably wouldn't be wise for Sophie and Kincaid to visit Wiswell Towers, as planned, until 'things have settled down a bit'.

When Sophie invited her Uncle Howard and Sybil to come to supper at her house, they were unable to come. Nor could they come when she asked them a second time. After their third refusal Howard came to call late one afternoon and tried to clarify matters for Sophie. 'Damned awkward, all this business about Kincaid. He seems like a decent chap to me. But Sybil thinks we should stand aside, I think that's the way she put it, till the clouds blow over, till the Major comes down off his high horse and the family gets back to normal.'

That evening Sophie and Kincaid sat in a small restaurant in Sloane Square till past midnight trying to cut their way through the thicket of her family. The following morning they crossed the channel to France and the next day they were married at the *mairie* in Dinan.

· CHAPTER 4 ·

1

The week before Kincaid and Sophie went to France to
get married, Major Cranston blustered and growled his
way past Mrs Barwick's butler and presented himself at
the door of Kincaid's flat above the carriage-house. It was
early in the morning. Kincaid was still in robe and
pyjamas. 'My name's Cranston, Major William Cranston,'
he said when Kincaid opened the door. 'I'm Sophie's
father.'

Kincaid invited him in. 'It's a bit early for me,' he said.
'Not very well put together yet. Shall I ring for some
breakfast?'

Cranston shook his head. 'I had breakfast at my club.'

'How about some coffee?'

'Nothing for me. I have a few things to say to you and
then I'll be on my way.'

As they sat down facing each other, Cranston said, 'I'm
a career military man. Perhaps my daughter mentioned
that.'

'No. I don't believe she did.'

'I see. Well . . . in any case . . .' He seemed to have
lost his train of thought. Then, 'Have you served in the
armed forces? I'm told you're from Australia.'

'That's right. Born in Tasmania. But I wasn't a soldier.
When the war ended I was ten years old.'

134

'Sophie was almost eighteen.'

'I'm aware of that,' Kincaid said.

'In my regiment in India, I insisted that my junior officers learn to express what they had to say in the fewest possible words. State the facts, salute, and withdraw. A damned good formula, in my view. A lot of bloody time is wasted by people pretending to be polite to each other. So if I seem to be blunt in what I say, I am blunt.'

'That's all right with me,' Kincaid said. 'If I seem to be polite it's because I am polite. But I would be in any case because you're Sophie's father.'

'That's right. I am. And that's why I'm here. So I'll get right to it. Although there's been no official announcement or notification, Sophie's mother and I understand that you plan to marry our daughter.'

Kincaid smiled. 'She plans to marry me. We expect to marry each other.'

'When I was a young man it was customary for a gentleman to announce his intentions to the young woman's father.'

Kincaid was still smiling. 'I'm not sure that custom is still being followed. I'm also not sure that I qualify as a gentleman. But since I didn't call on you, I'm glad you've called on me. Now you know my intentions.'

'I notice you're smiling. Do you find all this amusing?'

'No, I don't. The smile is part of my politeness.'

'I've been told you're a smooth talker,' Cranston said. 'Warned about it, in fact.'

'Who warned you? Not Sophie, I'm sure.'

'I have many friends in London.'

'I'm sure you do. By the way, did Sophie know you were coming here today?'

Cranston shook his head. 'I don't feel obliged to inform my wife and daughter of all my movements. This is a meeting between two men. That's the only way to get things done.'

'What is it we have to get done?'

'As Sophie's father, I have some questions to ask you. Do you object to that?'

'Not at all. I may have some questions myself.'

'What questions could you ask me?'

'That will depend,' Kincaid said, 'on the questions you ask.'

'First off, I'd like to know if you've discussed me with my daughter.'

'No.'

'She's said nothing at all about me?'

'She may have told me a couple of things but I've forgotten what they were. No family secrets.'

'I didn't mean that. There are no secrets in my family.'

'Good. I'm glad to hear that.'

Cranston repositioned himself in his chair. 'I understand you're a sailor, a merchant seaman. Is that your profession?'

'I wouldn't call it my profession. But that's how I've earned a living the last few years.'

'What is your profession then?'

'I don't have one.'

'Do you have an independent income?'

Kincaid smiled again. 'I'm afraid not.'

'No money from your family?'

Kincaid shook his head. 'No money. No family.'

'What are your prospects then?'

'No prospects that I know of.'

'By God, you're a cheeky devil. I wish I'd had you in my regiment. I assure you, you wouldn't have seen so much to smile about.'

'Then I'm glad I wasn't in your regiment.'

136

'Just tell me what it is you plan to bring to this marriage?'

'Only myself, I'm afraid.'

'Does Sophie realize you're a man without resources?'

'I'm not without resources. I just have no money. And yes, Sophie knows my financial status. We've discussed it.'

'And I'm certain you've also discussed her financial position.'

'Not as much as you may imagine.'

'But you know she's a wealthy young woman?'

'Yes. She told me that.'

'Then if this marriage takes place . . .'

'We've decided to get married, Major Cranston. There's no doubt about that.'

'. . . if this marriage takes place,' Cranston went on, 'you'll be supported by my daughter, is that correct? You'll be her dependant, as her son and daughter are.'

'No. I'll be her husband.'

'But you'll be living on her money.'

'I'll tell you the truth, Major Cranston, I don't like the sound of that any better than you do. And I'll admit I've never been faced with this situation before. All the people I've known, men and women, have been as poor as I am. They scraped together a living in any way they could. The married couples I've known, in Australia or any place else, never had time to wonder about whose money they were spending. Both the wife and the husband, and the kids if they had any, worked as hard as they could to earn as much as they could, so they could live, so they could rent a place to sleep and buy some food and clothes.'

'That kind of living is foreign to Sophie. She could never live like that.'

'Of course not,' Kincaid said, 'but I could and I have.'

'You're proving my point.'

137

'No, I'm not. The point is I've never sought out people with money. I wouldn't know where to start. And I didn't seek out Sophie. But we met. We were introduced by Evan Tagg. Maybe I should have said to myself, "That woman is not for me." Maybe Sophie should have said the same thing about me. But I didn't and she didn't. We just knew that we wanted to be together and stay together. It never occurred to me to say, "I can't marry you because you have money." And I'm sure it never occurred to her to say, "I have to give you up because you're poor." As a business transaction, we make no sense at all. As a marriage, we think we'll be fine. I'm sure that explanation won't satisfy you but it satisfies us. However, if you think that Sophie doesn't see the situation as I do, then you should talk to her about it.'

'I will, young man. I will. I will also discuss with her your criminal record. You don't deny that you've been in prison, do you?'

'Of course not,' Kincaid said. 'I'm not ashamed of it. I tell anybody who asks me.'

'Do you also tell them what your crimes were?'

'Not always. But I'll tell you. Theft mostly. I've stolen a lot of food in my life. But I've also been convicted for armed robbery, burglary, and aggravated assault. I've been in lots of fights. Won some. Lost some.'

'You're not ashamed of anything, are you?'

'We're talking about my life. Things happened. I didn't have a chance to sit down and plan it. I started with nothing and I don't have anything now. But in the meantime I had to do a lot of things to stay afloat.'

'Is that how you defend being a criminal?'

'I'm not defending myself. To you or anybody else. You said you like facts. That's what I'm giving you. I'm telling you the truth about myself, just as I've told Sophie. She doesn't hate me for what I am or what I've been.'

'I don't hate you either. I think you're an ambitious, contemptible rascal and I put you on notice today that I will do everything in my power to prevent Sophie from marrying you.'

'That doesn't surprise me. If I were you, I'd find a taxi and go straight away to Sophie's house. Tell her everything we've discussed and maybe she'll change her mind about me.'

'Don't underestimate me, Mr Kincaid. I know you're full of self-confidence. Chaps like you always are. But I've faced nasty adversaries before.'

'Are you declaring war? Is that it?'

'That's it, precisely.'

'Good. If we're at war I don't have to be polite any longer.' Kincaid stood up. 'I'm going to shave and get dressed now and go down to the main house for my breakfast.'

'You can't dismiss me.'

'I'm not dismissing you. You can sit here as long as you like. I'll even have coffee sent up if you like. But I'm going down to the breakfast-room as soon as I'm dressed.'

Major Cranston stood up then, took a step towards the door, then turned back. 'For a young man with no income you seem to be managing quite well. You're living in a fine neighbourhood in a magnificent house with what appears to be a full staff. How do you manage that?'

'I'm a house guest. A guest of Mrs Barwick.'

'Perhaps I misunderstood you. I thought you said you never seek out women with money.'

'I don't like the sound of that, Major Cranston.'

'Neither do I. Sounds damned indecent if you ask me. I notice you're wearing fine silk pyjamas and an expensive robe. Does that mean you've received a few personal gifts from your hostess along with your meals and lodging?'

'Major Cranston, you came here uninvited and I've

tried to be hospitable to you. But now I want you to leave. I'm going to get dressed now. If you're still here when I come downstairs I'll ring for the butler, a man who has much less patience than I do, and have you escorted from the premises.' Kincaid turned and left the room, closing the door behind him. When he came out fifteen minutes later, Major Cranston was gone.

2

'There's no cause to fret about the family,' Mrs Barwick said. 'The family will come round. They always do. Major Cranston was the big problem. But he fired off his big guns and it did him no good. Now it's knuckle under or give up his daughter for ever. And even if he were hard-headed enough to do that, Margaret Wiswell would never allow it. I met her when she was just a girl, I knew her mother, and I tell you the Wiswell women are able to do what must be done. I met her at the Bradshaws, another fine family – Angus Bradshaw was like a king in North-umberland – Margaret was a close friend of Clara Brad-shaw and I'm sure they're still close. But what I'm saying is this: those families don't just give up a daughter, especially a fine young woman like the one you've just married. They may waffle and crab-walk and try to defend their foolish positions but at last, as I say, they'll come round. Families like the Wiswells still own eighty per cent of England's land, you know, passing it down from one generation to the next, so they'll put up with a lot rather than break a link in that chain of ownership.'

She was sitting in her drawing-room with Kincaid. He had returned a few days before from his short wedding-trip with Sophie. On this particular afternoon he had packed up his belongings in the carriage-house apartment

140

and had them delivered to Sophie's house on Queen's Walk.

'So you've got a fine wife now, young Mr Kincaid. Your fortunes have changed dramatically since I first saw you, just a few months ago, speaking your piece on the pavement outside the Duke of York's.'

'It's you who's due the credit for any good fortune I've had.'

'Oh, no, not at all. Anyone who knows me will tell you that I'm not slow to accept whatever applause comes my way. And I admit that I did a bit of engineering when you were in trouble with the police. I also found a proper place for you to perform and I saw to it that some appreciative and influential people were in the audience. But this triumph of yours, this lovely marriage to Sophie Black, is something you managed all by yourself. Even when she invited the two of us to tea I had no idea as I was sitting there that love-birds were twittering all about our heads.'

'They weren't,' Kincaid said. 'Not then. All that happened later.'

'Spare me the story, my dear. Even at one remove, the details of romantic love are too much for my heart. Thank God, old age is slowly destroying my memory. If I could remember clearly the things I did and the things that were done to me when I was your age certain areas of my rickety body would simply explode. Pour me another brandy, please, and tell me how you plan to adapt to your new wealth and indolence.'

Kincaid got up and filled her glass from the decanter on the low table between them. 'I haven't thought much about it,' he said, 'and when I do think about it I'm not certain I'll find the answer. Every bloke I ever worked with – in a quarry, or on a sheep station, or paving the streets of Melbourne – every single one of those devils dreamed of the day when he wouldn't have to work. And me right along with them, I suppose. But as much as I hated some of those jobs I had, I never really thought it would be so great to do nothing. Some days I'd walk along the street that runs by Melbourne Grammar and see those poor brats in their short pants and knee-socks and the milk-sop teachers with them and I'd say to myself, "Those bastards own Australia. And their children will own it after they're dead. All honey and cream teas for that lot. No sweating in the fields or in sawmills. No sleeping in barns or storage rooms. No hard work for those buggers." But even as I thought it I didn't envy them. I never saw myself sitting in a deep chair, pulling a bell cord so some dressed-up monkey could bring me a cup of tea or a brandy and soda. And I don't see myself that way now. Major Cranston thinks I married Sophie for her money but I don't give a damn for that. I married her for herself and she married me for the same reason. I know I got the best of the bargain but money has nothing to do with it.'

'Good for you. You've got proper instincts. No man who's worth his salt simply wants to lie about and be catered to. Especially a man like you who's seen something of life and is accustomed to using himself in a productive way. So let's talk about that. Now that a bit of time has passed, how do you feel about the theatre evenings you did, first at the Cromwell just down the way and then at the Royal Court?'

'A lot of things have happened in the past few weeks. I haven't had time to think about it. But I felt damned good when I was doing it.'

'I should think so. Those audiences responded to you. And the drama critics said nice things about your work.'

'All that was a surprise to me. But I certainly liked it.'

142

'And Sophie was impressed also. She told me so that afternoon when we had tea.'

Kincaid smiled. 'That's true. I'm quite sure she likes me.'

'So you've discovered something you can do. Something you excel at. Something that excites an audience and gives them pleasure. Would you like to continue with that?'

He shook his head. 'Even if I wanted to it would be impossible. That sort of performance isn't something you can do over and over. I can't spend my life doing that.'

'That's true. I agree with you.' She lit a cigarette, inhaled deeply, and said, 'So let's consider some other possibilities. Do you think you could be an actor? Could you play a part in a scene with other actors on the stage of a theatre?'

'God, no. I wouldn't know where to begin. I don't think I've seen more than five or six plays in my life. But I've seen enough and read enough about it to know that it's damned difficult work. Takes training and experience. I have neither.'

'That's true. But still what I've seen you do on stage is acting of a sort. It demonstrates that you've understood the text and you know how to present it. You can make emotional contact with the audience and hold their attention.'

'That's because we're face to face. Me against them. It's like a fight. I understand that. I'm good at that.'

She nodded. 'Many good actors could never learn to do what you do naturally. But you're saying you couldn't do what they do. Perhaps you're right.'

'And even if I could,' he said, 'I understand that most actors in the theatre are as badly paid as merchant seamen.'

'That's true. It's an act of love. But . . . there are

143

avenues to follow that are more rewarding. I told you when we first met that you have something of value, something that's saleable. I don't have the details worked out yet but I promise you I will. I'm delighted that you've found a lovely wife but I'm not finished with you yet.'

3

After his meeting with Sophie, after he realized that his father had repeated to Margaret, almost word for word, the things he had been told in strict confidence, Evan agonized for days about what his reaction should be. His first impulse was to ring Arthur at once and tell him what he had learned. Then he decided that a letter was the best solution, a carefully composed letter where the evidence and his reactions to it would be absolutely clear. His next conclusion was that their confrontation should be, not by post or by telephone, but face to face. His father should have the opportunity to see Evan's indignation and to defend himself.

At last, however, during his second week in Aberdeen, he wrote a short letter to his father.

Perhaps you know that Margaret Cranston wrote a letter to Sophie after she knew that Sophie planned to marry Kincaid, after the Major had tried to get some information from me, and after you rang me and asked me to intercede on Mrs Cranston's behalf.

In the letter to Sophie, which Sophie angrily read to me, were almost word-for-word quotations of the remarks I had made to you about her proposed marriage, along with my observations about Kincaid. When you and I spoke on the telephone it was clear between us that my remarks were made in confidence, not to be passed along to Major Cranston, Margaret Cranston, or anyone else.

I am not asking or hoping that you will deny what you did. Denial is impossible. I'm sure I know what prompted you. I'm aware of your intense loyalty to Margaret. But you also have a loyalty to me, just as I do to you. I'm not saying that what you've done is unforgivable. But I will need some time to absorb it and try to put it behind me. So when you don't hear from me you will understand why. Also, since we both realize you knew what you were doing, I would much appreciate it if you would not send me a letter of apology or explanation.

Although he had asked his father not to respond he half-expected to find a letter from him when he returned to London. But there was no letter. A few days later, however, he received an engraved announcement of Sophie's marriage to Kincaid, mailed, not by the bride's parents but by Sophie herself. Along with the announcement, she had enclosed a note.

I've tried to reach you many times since that afternoon at my house. I can't tell you how sorry I am about what I said. My family had me in a panic just then. That's no excuse, I realize, but it's the only one I have.

Kincaid and I have settled in and we're living in splendid isolation. But we would both love to see you. As soon as you can make it.

That afternoon Evan sent them flowers and a note.

Congratulations and best wishes. I've just returned to London and I am buried with work. As soon as I am able to dig myself out I will be in touch with you.

A few months earlier Evan would have believed it impossible that he would be out of contact with Margaret Cranston, his father, and Sophie. Now, however, he not only accepted it, he welcomed it. His reaction surprised him. Until one day it came clear to him. This unusual isolation was not only acceptable to him, it was necessary. He could be alone now with his play. He was free to be analytical, objective, even cruel if need be. These principal people in his life could now be dissected and dealt with – not as relatives or loving friends – but as characters in a drama. If love and loyalty could be disregarded in life, as he believed it had been, then he had no compunction about disregarding it in the work that lay before him on his desk.

4

'I hold you responsible for the impossible situation we're in now. It never occurred to me that I could feel estranged from my own daughter, but I do. It makes me sad in a way that I can't describe. It sickens me.'

Major Cranston was standing by the glass doors of the morning-room overlooking the east garden. Margaret sat at her writing-desk. 'That's bloody nonsense,' he said. 'If you're saying I'm responsible for trying to protect Sophie, for trying to prevent her from marrying some colonial rogue who's not fit to polish her boots, then I'm proud to take credit for that. You were no more keen on her marriage than I was. You're the one who wrote directly to Sophie. I didn't.'

'I know I wrote to her and I regret it. I told her I regretted it. But by then it was too late.'

'The way I look at it, there's nothing to regret. Sophie's the one who'll live to be sorry for what she's done. We did the proper thing. We tried to prevent her from marrying that rascal.'

'That's where you're mistaken, William. I was not trying to stop her from marrying Kincaid. I was simply trying to persuade her to take her time. And she would have, I'm sure. She and I have always been able to discuss things together. But you had to treat it as an idiotic military manoeuvre.'

'I don't know what you're talking about.'

'Of course you do. You tried to enlist Evan to take sides against Kincaid, you bullied Howard and Sybil into believing that the man they had met and liked was in fact a fortune-hunter, and then you went straight to Kincaid, where I'm sure you made a total ass of yourself. Finally you forced me to delay having Sophie and Kincaid to visit us here at Wiswell Towers because you swore you'd make a scene if they showed up.'

'I meant what I said.'

'I know you did. Otherwise I wouldn't have asked Sophie to postpone their visit. But as soon as she received my note she went off to France and got married. With no one from her family present, no proper ceremony, no public announcement, no reception for her friends. I blame you for that, William. For all of it. You blustered and threatened and bullied everyone. So now we have an awkward and painful relationship with Sophie that I may never be able to set right.'

'It's not your job to set things right. Sophie brought this on herself. It's up to her to come to us. And first off, I expect an apology from both of them, Sophie and that rotten husband of hers.'

'Good God, William, have you really gone out of your mind? Don't you realize that if we don't handle this carefully we won't ever see Sophie? Or if we do see her it will be only for the sake of Sarah and Trevor, all formal and cold, with no love or good feeling between us?'

'I'm not concerned about that,' Cranston said, 'and you shouldn't be either. She'll come round. Sophie's no fool. She'll quickly understand that she's the one who made the mistake, not us.'

Margaret sat staring at him as he stood by the window tamping tobacco into his pipe. At last she said, 'You really believe that, don't you?'

'Of course I do. And you will, too. As soon as a bit of time has gone by and you've come to your senses.'

Very deliberately she put her pens and envelopes and writing-paper into their proper cubicles in her writing-desk. She closed the desk-top, stood up, slowly walked to the door, opened it, and left the room. Behind her, Cranston continued to fiddle with his pipe as though he hadn't noticed she was gone.

5

One afternoon when Kincaid and Sophie came home after seeing a matinée performance of *Never Come Back*, there was a telephone message for Kincaid.

'A Mr Thorne. Julian Thorne. He asked if you could ring him back when you came in,' the butler said.

'I don't know anyone by that name,' Kincaid said to Sophie. 'Do you?'

'I don't believe so.' Turning to the butler she said, 'Did he say why he was calling, Oliver?'

'He said Mrs Barwick had suggested that he call. Asked me to tell you that.'

Sophie smiled at Kincaid. 'Your fairy godmother.'

When they were having a drink in the library a bit later Kincaid telephoned Mrs Barwick.

'Who's Julian Thorne?' he asked her.

'Oh, good. He's called you then. What did he have to say?'

'I was out. We saw Colin Clive at the Phoenix this afternoon. I just got the message that Thorne had rung up. Thought you might be able to tell me what he wants.'

'Well, now . . . perhaps I do know what he wants but I'm not going to tell you. I'll just say that he's an old friend of mine. A bit of a poseur, but behind the facade there's something of value.'

'But you won't tell me why he's got in touch with me? Why not?'

'Because I don't want to spoil your fun. Or his. Do you remember the conversation you and I had not long ago? About you and your future? Well, I can't be certain but I think Thorne may have an interesting proposition for you.'

'What sort of proposition?'

'I'll let him tell you that. But whatever he proposes to you, and you must trust me on this, you must refuse. Tell him firmly but gently that you are simply not interested. If I know him he will then offer you something else. Refuse that too. No matter what he offers, turn him down.'

'I think it would be simpler if I didn't return his call.'

'Oh, no. You must call him back. It will be an unusual experience for you. You've never met anyone like Thorne before. And neither have I. He keeps a lovely apartment at the Savoy and his company owns a building in Sutton Row. He will want to meet you, I'm certain, at one of those places. But you must say no. You must be available for a meeting only if he comes to your home, to Sophie's house, on Queen's Walk. Ask him for tea only. Not for drinks. And be sure that he meets Sophie. But just for a moment. Then when you've talked with him for half an hour, be sure that you're called away on some urgent business in another part of the house. A business call from New York. That sort of thing. After he's been there, ring me here at home, and you and I will talk again.'

When Kincaid rang off and told Sophie what Mrs Barwick had said, she was amused and delighted by the whole prospect. 'What fun,' she said. 'What a fascinating creature she is. She always has some sort of scheme under her witch's bonnet. And this time, we're to play a part in it. I can't wait. Ring up Mr Thorne and invite him to tea on Thursday.'

6

Julian Thorne, in appearance, was the prototype of a London gentleman. He wore a bowler and carried a stick. His suit was flawlessly fitted and tailored, his shoes hand-made on his own last, his shirt and his cravat were from Jermyn Street. Unmistakably. His wrist-watch and his ring were of heavy gold and his hair was carefully trimmed and shaped but left full in the English manner. His speech, too, and his choice of words were as British as he was able to make them. He had tried hard to place his voice where he felt it should be. He had managed to lose, alter, or disguise as much of his New York City accent as he possibly could. In his old neighbourhood he could certainly have passed himself off as an Englishman. In London, to someone who observed him carefully, he was simply a well-groomed and well-spoken American in his fifties who, for reasons known only to him, had taken great pains to transform himself into someone who might be thought to be British.

He arrived promptly at tea-time on Thursday, compli-mented both Sophie and Kincaid on the loveliness of their home and its location. 'I once had a fine old house in Mount Street. Historic building. But I sold it and bought a larger place in Belgravia, in Wilton Crescent actually.'

'How nice,' Sophie said. 'And do you still live there?'

'I'm afraid not. As much as I'd like to be here full-time, I'm only able to live in London for a few weeks each year. And I've found my needs are better served by keeping an apartment at the Savoy. But if I could settle here, a house on Green Park would be my choice.'

During tea he held forth on the subjects of Georgian silver, the National Gallery, and the Royal Albert Hall. And they discussed the current plays they had seen. 'I try to see everything that's worth while when I'm here. I tend to choose actors rather than plays. Excellent performers can bring even an ordinary play to life whereas a master-piece can be a disaster if the actors are not first-rate. This time, for example, I can't say that I've seen one memor-able play but I've seen some truly excellent performances. Cedric Hardwicke, Richardson, Gertrude Lawrence, Raymond Massey, Colin Clive, Madeleine Carroll. All fine actors with great futures.'

After Sophie excused herself and withdrew, Thorne resettled himself in his chair, his voice seemed to drop an octave, and he said, 'Has Mrs Barwick talked to you about me?'

'No, she hasn't. But I know the two of you are friends.'

'Dear friends. And I'm also her admirer. She's truly a woman of quality. Enormous energy and imagination. And I'm happy to say that she's introduced me to a great number of her friends here in London.'

When Kincaid didn't reply, Thorne cleared his throat and went on. 'Since you know nothing about me I feel I should tell you that I am associated with the motion-picture industry in America. Have you heard of Thorn-wood Studios?'

151

'No, I don't believe I have.'

'That's my company. Thornwood produced forty films in the past twelve months. I personally produced five of them. We have thirty-two actors under contract and we've just finished construction on seven new sound stages. The latest in lighting and recording equipment. After Warner Brothers, we were the first studio to convert fully to talking pictures. My brother and I believe we are at the forefront of the most exciting and lucrative form of entertainment the world has ever seen. Great fortunes will be made. Our performers will become international celebrities. Did you see *The Golden Wish* with Valerie Lund?'

'I'm afraid not.'

'We also made *Three Crusaders*. Several of your compatriots were in that one: C. Aubrey Smith, Ralph Forbes, Montague Love.'

Kincaid smiled. 'I'm embarrassed to tell you how few times I've been inside a motion-picture theatre. When I was a kid, wandering around Australia, trying to make a living, I used to slip into a theatre without paying sometimes. But those were silent films. Since then the life I've led hasn't seemed to include movie theatres. As I recall, I've only seen one talking picture . . . an actor named Brown . . .'

'Joe E. Brown,' Thorne said. 'The picture was *Painted Faces*. A circus clown on trial for murder.'

'That's right. So you see, I'm an ignoramus about your business.'

Thorne put down his tea-cup, touched his lips with his napkin and smoothed his tie with his other hand. 'Let me tell you why I'm here. Since sound films took over, all the studios have been trying to redesign their operations, trying to plan ahead for the new opportunities we see before us. Great technical strides are being made. We

152

expect to have perfect sound-tracks in the very near future. But what about our performers? Since *The Jazz Singer* it's been clear that voices are extremely important now. Interesting voices, dramatic voices, expressive voices. I believe that soon an actor will be recognized by his voice as much as by his face. First, we all looked to the theatre for our people. Thalberg and Mayer, Lasky and Zukor and Jack Warner are all bidding for stage actors from New York and London. And Thornwood is doing the same thing. But I'm taking a slightly different approach. I want those experienced people too, actors who can deliver a performance on film the first time out. But I'm also looking to the future a bit more than my competitors.

'You see, I've been in this business since I was a boy, younger than you, since the early nickelodeons. I've worked at one time or another with Bill Fox, Goldwyn, Lasky, and every other man who now heads up a major studio operation. I became an expert in publicity and promotion, and after we moved from one- and two-reelers and began to make full-length features I saw that the stories we filmed and the actors themselves would be the core of the new business. So I soon had the reputation of being able to find and develop film actors who would appeal to the public and have long careers. I had a hand in persuading the Barrymores to move from the stage to the screen. George Arliss, Anthony Bushell, and Ronald Colman all came to California because of me. Lillian Gish and Richard Barthelmess acknowledge that I gave them important guidance along the way. I mention these things only to emphasize to you that I have deep experience in recognizing talent and developing it. I am not only willing but eager to take a chance on a fresh young man or woman, to present them properly to a world audience and give them the opportunity to achieve the recognition they deserve. Because I know from experience that the famous and gifted people of tomorrow are totally unknown today.'

Oliver came into the drawing-room then and presented a message card to Kincaid. He read it quickly and said, 'Please tell them I will ring back as soon as I can. Within half an hour, I should think.' As Oliver withdrew, Kincaid turned back to Thorne. 'I'm sorry we were interrupted, but I was expecting a telephone call from New York and it's just come through.'

'But you must . . .'

'No, no,' Kincaid said. 'They can wait. I'll ring them back later. Please go on with what you were saying. As I told you, I know nothing whatsoever about your business. But you make it sound very interesting.'

'Dynamic is the word. We are now America's fourth largest industry. We have a world market. Growing every year. My studio, for example, owns forty-three theatres. We manufacture the product, distribute it, and own the houses where it is shown to the public.'

Thorne glanced at the clock standing against the wall to his left. 'I know you're pressed for time,' he said, 'so let me tell you quickly why I contacted you in the first place.' He stood up, made a small walking circle, like a fox marking his territory, and came to rest at last standing behind the chair where he'd been sitting before. 'You've just met me today,' he said, 'but I've been aware of you for some time. I was present for both of your theatre evenings and my office here in London, knowing of my friendship with Mrs Barwick, sent me all the press-clippings about your adventure with Scotland Yard and the part she played in your eventual release. So I've had some time to think about you. And I came here today to offer you a business proposition.'

154

Kincaid smiled. 'You probably came to the wrong place. I'm not a businessman.'

'I understand that. But I am. And both my business sense and my aesthetic judgement tell me that there is a future for you in motion pictures. I am prepared to offer you that opportunity if you're interested. I think you're a born performer and, even more important, I believe you're a physical type that I can sell to the public. Not just once but over and over.'

'Well,' Kincaid said, 'I don't know what to say.'

'You don't have to say anything just now. I just want you to know that it's not a casual offer and that I can deliver what I promise. I'll be here in London till next Monday. Think over what I've said and ring me at the Savoy when you've made up your mind.'

As Thorne was speaking, Kincaid was remembering the advice Mrs Barwick had given. 'I'm flattered by your offer, Mr Thorne, but I don't have to take time to think it over. You see, whatever you may think of me, I'm not an actor. I have no training or experience beyond the sort of dramatic readings you saw me give, and to be quite honest with you, I have no desire to become an actor. So although I'm grateful to you the only honest answer I can give to your offer is that it's not for me. I am simply not interested.'

7

After Thorne left, when Kincaid told Sophie about their conversation she said, 'Of course he's right. I would certainly pay to see you on a huge screen in a cinema. And so would millions of other women. They could all sit there in the dark, munching chocolate, and try to figure out what it is about you that is so threatening and so lovable all at one time. Mr Thorne would undoubtedly make you obscenely rich and well known.'

'Does that appeal to you?'

'No. I think it's a hateful prospect. And besides one cannot live in southern California. Mrs Hardwicke told my mother that only lizards and alcoholics can be contented there.'

'Then I made the correct choice.'

'You have no choice, my darling. If you told me we were going off to California to live, I would call Dr Fitzroy and have you committed to a well-guarded institution in Surrey.'

When he visited Mrs Barwick the next day she was in extremely high spirits. 'My poor friend Julian Thorne is stunned. He rang me yesterday after he left you and he was really quite pitiful. Absolutely unable to understand your reaction.'

'I did what you suggested. I told him I wasn't interested.'

'I know. So he said.'

'But that would have been my reaction in any case,' Kincaid said. 'Even if you and I had not talked before.'

'Well, we'll see about that later on. In any case you gave the perfect response yesterday. On another day, however, his offer may be different. You may want to respond differently.'

'I don't think there'll be another offer.'

'Of course there will be. Julian's gift is persuasion. That's what he does. He persuades banks to lend him outrageous sums of money, he persuades people to work for him, he persuades audiences that what they're paying to see is an important film. And he constantly persuades himself that he's doing creative work in a truly significant business. If one day he finally realizes that everything in his "industry", as he calls it, is indescribably trivial, he will simply wither up and die and be reclaimed by the Los Angeles desert.'

'I thought you liked him.'

'More than that,' she said. 'I adore him. He is a truly kind and generous man. And there's something innocent about him that is quite endearing. How one remains innocent in the cannibal society he's chosen for himself is a mystery to me, but he has managed it. That entire obsession he has about turning himself into an English gentleman is not just affectation, as some people believe. To me, it's a continuing effort he's making to distance himself from what he is, what he does, and where he lives. I count him as a true friend because I know he wishes me well. Always. I can't tell you how few friends we have, any of us, who truly wish us well.'

'But when you talk about him, I get the feeling you're manipulating him.'

'Of course I am. I must. He expects it. Because he manipulates me. Or so he believes. As I told you, he is a genuine friend. But he is also gracious and attentive and generous to me because I give him entrée to certain levels of London society that would otherwise be unavailable to him. It all works very subtly. He has never asked to meet a particular friend of mine, or to serve as my escort to an exclusive affair. Nor have I ever asked him to take a penniless but gifted poet to California and employ him as a scenario writer at a thousand dollars a week. But still such favours and services have taken place through the years, and they have in no way damaged our friendship.'

'Where do I fit into that pattern?'

'You don't. This is a new wrinkle. That's what makes it so delicious. You see, Julian didn't become aware of you through me. Did he tell you that his London office had sent him press-clippings when you were arrested and put in jail?'

Kincaid nodded. 'He said they sent the clippings because of your involvement in my release.'

'That may be true. But in any case he knew about you through no contact between him and me. And even after you'd come to live above my coach-house I made no effort to introduce the two of you. Nor did he ask to meet you.'

'But he saw me at the Royal Court.'

She nodded. 'And at the Cromwell. That's when I first learned there was something afoot. He told the staff at the Cromwell that he was planning a surprise for me. He persuaded them to let him conceal a photographer in the Royal box so he could photograph you as you performed on stage. The staff told me of course but I said nothing to Julian about it. He used the same device at the Royal Court but this time a film cameraman was concealed somewhere in the theatre, perhaps in the wings. I was never told where. Again the theatre manager told me about it before he gave permission. By this time I guessed that he was indeed planning some sort of surprise for me. I expected every day to receive a sheaf of photos of you. By then Julian had gone back to California. But nothing arrived. So when he returned to London this time, said nothing about the pictures he'd had taken but began to drop hints that he'd like to meet you, I decided there was something more complex in the works. So I mentioned to you that he might call. And he did. I was never sure what he planned to propose to you till he called me yesterday and told me you'd turned him down.'

'Then why did you tell me to say no, no matter what he said?'

'Because I knew he'd offer you something. Whether it appealed to you or not, it was necessary to say no. That's the only way to deal with Julian. People who don't make demands or present a problem are uninteresting to him.

158

If he doesn't have a problem to solve he's uninteresting to himself. That's why he's so well placed in that business. Because none of their real problems have solutions. Julian defines himself by effort and energy rather than accomplishment. No one is busier than an incompetent man.'

'Are you saying he's incompetent?'

'Of course not. I exaggerate. In the field he's chosen he's more than competent. He has mastered the intricacies of nothingness.'

'I take it you don't like motion pictures.'

She shook her head. 'Let me put it this way. I never go inside a church if I can avoid it. That doesn't mean I'm an atheist. It means I feel no connection with the church as an entity, or the people who administer it. The process of making a great concept or a seminal idea accessible to the masses always distorts or destroys the original, until at last it's unrecognizable and without meaning. Anything that's created with the purpose of appealing to everyone is worthless by definition. That is the fatal flaw of the motion-picture business, as it is of democracy. Popularity is not a virtue. Nothing that's truly significant can be popular.'

'You're too smart for me,' Kincaid said. 'I can't keep up.'

She smiled. 'I'm not smart. I'm just old. At my age, strong opinions pass for intelligence. But let's get back to Julian. I wanted him to see you at home so he'd know you have a rare and beautiful wife, and so he'd see also that you don't need money. He's very rich now himself but he's still hypnotized by wealth, especially if it's English. He'll be twice as eager to convince you now. The more unavailable you seem, the more dedicated he is to winning the day.'

'But I've already told him I'm not interested. Why would I continue to play games with him?'

'Because if you don't, you'll break his heart. At this moment, I assure you he's trying to determine what his next move will be. You see, in addition to everything else we've been discussing he truly does believe that you could make your mark in his silly business. And so do I. You're unique. I told you that long ago. You're heterosexual and you're full of self-confidence. What more does an actor need?'

'Are you saying that if I continue to talk with him I might change my mind about the whole business?'

'Perhaps not. But on the other hand, as we were discussing the other day, you want to do something to earn some money. You might decide it's foolish to turn away from five thousand dollars a week.'

'He didn't say anything about that sort of money,' Kincaid said. 'He didn't mention money at all.'

'Of course not. He's accustomed to people your age who are desperate to appear in one of his films, whether he pays them or not.'

'Then why would he offer me a lot of money?'

'He won't. Unless you continue to turn him down. Then God knows what he may offer you. In his world, that's the only reason people say no. Because the offer isn't good enough.'

'So you're suggesting I go along with him?'

'You should do what makes sense to you. But my advice is this: next time he approaches you, listen carefully and then say no again. Keep saying no until it reaches a point where you can't say no. That's when you should give him the impression that you might be interested under certain circumstances. Then you start making demands.'

'What sort of demands?'

'You demand anything you can think of that he hasn't already offered you. You're in a rare position, Kincaid.

For whatever idiotic reasons of his own, Julian Thorne has decided that he needs you. And you've decided, at least for the present, that you don't need him. That's power, my darling. Unless I miss my guess, it's a situation you've never been in before and may never be in again. So why not enjoy the process? You can always call it off, on a moment's notice. And if you have some latent guilt feelings just remember this: you can't hurt Julian by accepting his money. Or anything else he has to offer. You can only hurt him by turning him down. And incidentally, if you do decide to see him again, don't do it till he comes back to London the next time. And when you see him, do it at his office or in a public place. By yourself. Don't accept any invitation from him that includes Sophie. And never invite him to come to your house.'

'Why not? He's already been there.'

'That's the point. Don't ask him again. It will give him something to think about. Something additional to strive for.'

Later in the day, when he and Sophie were dressing, preparing to go out to dinner, she said, 'I don't understand what it's all about. Sounds like a great charade.'

'I don't understand it myself. Not totally. But she says I have nothing to lose and I think she's right. Nobody gets hurt and I might end up with a great deal of money.'

'We already have a great deal of money.'

'I know. Maybe that's why the idea of making some myself looks good to me.'

'You mustn't be silly on that subject.'

'I haven't been. I'm not searching through the classified section of *The Times* looking for work. But if something splendid turned up . . .'

'Like Mr Micawber.'

He smiled. 'Exactly. I could take you to California and stretch you out in the sunshine . . .'

'Steady on.'

'. . . feed you grapes and oranges, and offer you a proper honeymoon. You wouldn't mind that, would you?'

'Not at all. All honeymoons are welcome.'

'That's what I thought you'd say. Anyway, Mrs Barwick asked me to have lunch with a friend of hers who's with Gaumont-British. He'll tell me some of the inside stuff about the business so at least I'll understand what Thorne's talking about.'

'If he calls again.'

'That's right. If I ever hear from him again.'

'Do you really expect to?' she said.

'No, I don't, to tell you the truth.'

The next day they received by messenger a beautifully wrapped package, sent from Asprey on New Bond Street. Inside they found a Victorian silver ink-stand and a card from Thorne.

> It was a pleasure to meet you and spend some time in your home. I look forward to seeing you both again.

8

Although Wingate Fields, the home of the Bradshaws and the Causeys was rather a long drive from Wiswell Towers, the two families had always thought of each other as neighbours as well as friends. But the prime connection between the two households was the friendship between Clara Causey and Margaret Cranston. They had gone to school together, their children were close in age, and after Margaret returned home from India they had discovered still another common bond. Each of them had married unwisely and each of them had decided to make the best of it.

They met at least once or twice a month, usually for lunch, at an inn half-way between their two homes. After many years of this rarely changing routine they had come to believe that these meetings were a blessed constant in their lives, a period of three hours wherein there were no barriers or trap-doors, no need for caution or secrecy. They withheld nothing from each other, were not afraid to air even their most petty grievances. Husbands, parents, children, and staff were all fair game. Occasionally one of them wept. More often they laughed, sometimes uncontrollably. The freedom they felt to make any comment, complaint, or observation about their experiences at home was like a tonic to them. For themselves, they had changed the name of the inn where they met from the Blue Stag, its actual name, to the Confessional, and each time they met they told each other as they parted that they had become, as they talked and laughed together, ten years younger.

Sophie had always been aware of these meetings, had known of their importance to her mother, and had rejoiced in them. Knowing nothing in detail of what the two women discussed, she had sensed, nonetheless, that the meetings were of vital importance to Margaret. After the death of her husband, when she was living, first at home with her parents and then in London, Sophie often wished that she herself had such a woman friend, such an open, supportive relationship to rely on.

She was not surprised then, early in December, to receive a letter from Clara Causey.

Thank you for your note. I'm delighted that you liked the little wedding gift I sent. You're not easy to buy

for, you know, so at last I sent you that Ming figurine.
It's a gift my father gave me when I married Ned. I
loved it then and I love it still, so it makes me feel very
good to know that you'll have it in your beautiful
bedroom in London.

My children have scattered, as you know. Nora's still
in Paris. There for life, I expect. And her daughter with
her, of course. And Jesse, my adopted brother, is
there, too. Although he does pop in here occasionally.
Hugh has vanished to his shooting estate in Scotland
and my precious niece, Helen, has returned long since
to America. So here I am, feeling not sorry for myself
but very much alone some days. Thank God for
Margaret.

Since you know the chaotic state of my own family I
feel ill-qualified to comment on the situation in yours.
But I'll do it anyway. Perhaps I can say something that
will make sense and not make you angry. I am always
wary of people who threaten to do something 'for my
own good'. I'm sure you are, too. Nonetheless, I can't
ignore the unhappiness of my dear Margaret. So I will
risk offending you. By the way, she does not know that
I'm writing to you. You may tell her or not as you wish,
but this letter, for better or worse, is my idea, not hers.

You and Sarah and Trevor always spend Christmas
at the Towers so I know Margaret must have asked you
to come this year. Whether she has or not, it's vitally
important that you do come. I understand that William
made a frightful mess of things and I'm sure that's not
easy for you or your husband to set aside. But believe
me, and I speak from painful experience, such ruptures
are much easier to heal when they're fresh.

There's a great deal that I don't know, of course. I
don't know how angry you are. I don't know what was
said or left unsaid. But I do know that we all must be

slow to cast aside meaningful connections with valuable people. In a family, when the emotional continuity is broken, it is impossible sometimes to patch it together again. And no one profits from that.

In your situation, thank God, you didn't let family resistance change your plans. You went ahead with your marriage. So now, unless you have some terrible bitterness inside you, it's simply a matter of gradual acceptance and adjustment for all concerned. I assure you, Margaret is desperate for that process to begin. The Major is another matter, of course. One can never guarantee what his reactions will be on any given day. But you and your mother have managed through the years to deal with him and his eccentricities, and I'm sure you'll be able to in this matter as well.

The beauty of family occasions such as Christmas, birthdays, christenings, and anniversaries, is that the tradition itself has weight. People have become accustomed, through the years, to putting aside quarrels, rivalries, and petty jealousies. They're accustomed to doing their bit to make the day, the evening, the feast, whatever it is, a pleasant occasion. Because it's expected of them. They expect it of themselves. No magic transformation takes place, of course. But sometimes even a pretence of acceptance and civility can smooth the way towards the real thing.

I'm sure that anything I might suggest to you has already entered your mind a thousand times. But on the slim chance that it hasn't, I'm risking your disapproval by sending this note. There are only two principal players in this situation: you and Margaret. There is no reason for you to be estranged, not even for a moment. So I hope you will both be wise enough to come together again before the next year commences.

In mid-December, at eleven o'clock on a Sunday morning, Kincaid knocked on the door of Evan Tagg's flat in Gordon Square. When Evan opened the door, looking rumpled, Kincaid said, 'I'm not going to apologize for coming unannounced. I want to talk to you, and since you're always too bloody busy to come for a meal or to meet me in the pub for a pint, I decided this was the only way, to show up at your door.' He brushed past Evan, left his coat in the vestibule and passed on through to the sitting-room.

'I can't talk now,' Evan said. 'I was up all night working and I have a couple hours more to do. Then I'm going to bed to sleep till tomorrow.'

'Maybe you can't talk but I can. I think you've been acting like a jackass. For weeks now. Ever since Sophie and I got married. Even before that. I thought the two of you were like brother and sister. Matter of fact, you told me that yourself. So what happened? Why are you so bloody unavailable all of a sudden? She doesn't understand and neither do I.'

'Work,' Evan said. 'Too much work. That's the problem. I'm in the middle of writing this play . . .'

'I know all about that. I know that's your excuse. But are you telling me that a writer never has a meal, or takes a drink, or takes a walk, or goes to bed with a woman, or talks on the telephone? I don't believe that.'

'I don't care what you believe. You asked why I've been busy and I told you.'

'Sophie had a note from her mother, saying you've stopped talking to your dad as well. Too busy for him too?'

'That's between my dad and me.'

'Maybe so. But this, now, what we're talking about

here, is between you and me. You're the only bloke I've met in London that I felt I could talk to. A straight-ahead chap, I told myself. Everything that's happened to me in the past few months, all the good stuff, started with you. You went out of your way to do me a service. Or so it seemed to me. So I thought, "I've got a friend here. Not some over-dressed pom who talks through his nose, but a solid bloke who wouldn't back off in a street fight." So what happened? Once Sophie and I got married, you disappeared like a gypsy at the race course. Dropped out of sight. Wanting nothing to do with Sophie or with me. Nor with your dad, it seems like. So what do you expect people to think? If I didn't know better I'd think you wanted Sophie for yourself. But that doesn't make sense. If it did you'd have made your move a long time ago. When her husband died. Or sometime since then. But you didn't. So that can't be what's bothering you.'

'Nothing's bothering me. I've given myself a firm deadline for finishing this fucking play and that's what I'm trying to do.'

'Are you telling me that once you polish off what you're doing, you're going to ring us up and say, "Meet me at Prunier's. I finished my work and I want to celebrate." And you'll invite your old man down to London and get him drunk, and nobody will have to sit around wondering what's wrong with you. Is that the way it's going to be?'

When Evan didn't answer, Kincaid went on. 'That's what I thought. There's something else buzzing in your head.'

'I told you I didn't want to have this conversation and that's what I meant,' Evan said. 'If all you have to do is lounge about and try to find out what's in my mind, then you're a lucky fellow. I don't have time for those games. I have work to do.'

'Ah, now we're getting somewhere. You have to work

and I don't. Is that it? I married a rich lady, and now all I have to do is smoke cigars and live off the fat of the land. Sophie's old man told me I was marrying her for her money. Are you saying the same thing?'

Evan shook his head. 'That's none of my business.'

'You're right. It's not. But that doesn't mean you don't think it. Is that what you think?'

'No, it's not. But even if it were I wouldn't tell you. As I said, it's none of my business.'

'Sure it is. You're like a member of the family. Brother of the bride and all that crap. Why wouldn't you be interested in what man she married? If she was my sister I'd be very interested.'

'Sophie's not my sister. I grew up with her, I've known her for most of my life, and she's my friend.'

'Then why don't you treat her like a friend?' Kincaid said.

'Why don't you let me decide how I choose to treat her?'

'That's easy to answer. Because I don't want her to be hurt. She can't understand why you've cut yourself off all of a sudden. And I can't either. That's why I came here.'

'So now are you satisfied?'

'Not at all. I know less than I did when I came in.'

'That's because you're looking for a big answer. A clap of thunder. You're trying to make a big thing out of something that's quite small.'

'Just leave it alone and it'll blow over. Is that what you're saying?'

'No. I'm saying just leave it alone.'

For a moment Kincaid didn't answer. Then, 'You mean I should leave you alone.'

'I didn't say that.'

'You didn't have to.' He walked to the vestibule, picked up his coat, opened the door, and left.

'I think he's crazy about you,' Kincaid said. 'That's the only thing that makes sense.'

'Of course he's crazy about me,' Sophie said, 'and I'm crazy about him. But not in the way you think.'

They were sitting on a great soft sofa before the fire in their second-floor reading-room. Kincaid put his arm around her and pulled her close to him. 'This is not an inquisition. Just because we're married doesn't mean that I've owned you all your life. I'm just trying to understand what's come over him. The fact that he hasn't talked to either of us since we got married seems like more than a coincidence.'

'Of course it does,' she said. 'I agree with you. But that doesn't mean I can explain it. I really don't think Evan could have been desperately in love with me for all these years and I wouldn't have known about it. You have to remember, I'm almost two years older than he is. When I was sixteen and beginning to attract some attention from the young men of the county, he was only fourteen. By the time he was sixteen I was married and pregnant. So the timing was all off.'

'But not after your husband died. No age problem then.'

'Exactly. That's my point. If Evan had a yen to marry me, that was a perfect opportunity. I was a widow with two children and no man whatsoever in my life. But as soon as Evan came down to London from Oxford he had a saucy young woman on every corner. I was lucky to see him at all after I moved here with the children. We had our ritual luncheon two or three times a month, or he'd drop in occasionally to see the children when they were on holiday from school, but no word of love ever fell from his lips. There's another element too, now that we're examining the situation. That's Arthur, Evan's father. He apparently had a notion similar to yours, that two young people growing up together were very likely, somewhere along the way, to fall in love, or fall in bed, or something like that. I know his father lectured him more than once, probably quite often, on the fact that Evan and I were from different social and economic classes, that he must never forget that. Evan told me, of course, what his father had said and the two of us used to joke about it. He'd say things like, "I promise to stay out of your social class if you promise to stay out of mine." I must have said, a hundred times, "I pity the poor woman who marries you", and he always answered, "At least she'll be a woman of my own class." That's the way things were with us. Everything out in the open. We talked a lot about what sort of persons we would be when we were grown up. We were absolutely certain that we would have none of the anxieties and frustrations that seemed to define the adults we knew. I expect that Sarah and Trevor, when they talk together, promise each other that they will have none of my lesser traits.'

Later that night, as they were lying in bed, Kincaid said, 'I've been thinking about what you told me about Evan's father, about the lectures he gave him on the class system.'

'What did you conclude?'

'Nothing spectacular. But if, for example, somewhere in the back of his mind, Evan had a vision of you and him together, married and all that, and if his father's words had turned that vision into an impossibility, it must have been an ironic twist for him to see you married to me.' When she didn't answer he said, 'It's a possibility, isn't it?'

'I don't think so.'

170

'In that case we'll have to find another explanation for his putting us on his black-list.'

'No, we don't,' she said. 'I've given up trying to understand people. I just want to be happy and sleep with you in our warm bed, and to hell with everything else.'

BOOK TWO

· CHAPTER 5 ·

1

'I've been driving myself crazy trying to decide what to do about Christmas,' Sophie said. 'I think I've considered every possibility and every potential catastrophe. I even sat down and made dumb lists for myself, writing down what seem to be the plus and minus factors. I've worn myself thin with it. Should we go to the Towers or should we not? Each time I ask myself, I get a different answer. Finally, last night, before I went to sleep I said to myself, "If it's so difficult to decide, if the mere prospect of going there makes you unquiet then you shouldn't go. Make some lame excuse and put the whole matter aside till next year." When I woke up this morning that reasoning still made sense to me. What do you think?'

'Do you know how many times you've asked me that?' Kincaid said.

'Many times. But you're no help. Not so far.'

'It's your family, kid. I don't even know them. I've never met anyone except your aunt and uncle, and your sweet father.'

'I wish you'd never met him. He's the one who makes it so impossible to decide. One knows at the outset that he'll create some sort of problem, make some idiotic scene.'

'Who cares what he does? He can't change things between you and me. He has no control over us.'

'But he can make everything so damned awkward and painful for Margaret.'

'From what you've said it's going to be difficult for her no matter what you decide.'

'That's true.'

'If you want my advice, I think you should make up your mind one way or the other and then deal with it. Either way, it's not the end of the world. It's a few days out of your life. It seems to me you have three choices. You can make an excuse of some kind and not go, you can take the children and go without me, or we can all troop up there together.'

'I'm certainly not going without you.'

'That takes care of one choice.'

'Do you think I'd leave you here in London to spend Christmas by yourself?'

'It would only be for a few days. It wouldn't kill me.'

Sophie shook her head. 'Out of the question, my dear.'

'All right, let's look at it this way,' he said. 'Let's give everybody a vote. Your mother wants you there and your children certainly want to go.'

'They've never spent Christmas anywhere else.'

'That leaves the Major as the only no vote. So he's outvoted. Three to one.'

'What about us?'

'We're neutral. At least I'm neutral. So unless you decide to vote with your father . . .'

'But I'm thinking of you. I don't want it to be a terrible time for you.'

'Don't worry about me. I can take care of myself. You said yourself it's a big house up there. If the Major decides to act like a jackass I'll find an empty room and close the door behind me.'

'It's not that simple.'

'Of course it's not simple but sooner or later you have to make a decision. And now's the time to do it. Remember the letter you got from that friend of your mother? She said it's a lot easier to set things right today than it will be a year from now.'

'I don't know.'

'All right. I'll take the decision out of your hands. I'm no longer neutral. I vote yes. That makes it four against one and one undecided.'

'It's not just a question of mathematics.'

'Why not? The greatest good for the greatest number and all that poppycock.'

'Can you really struggle through a week in the same house with my father?'

'Of course I can. And so can you. We're going to be married for a long time and he's going to live for a long time, so the sooner we all get used to each other, the better.'

'God, how I hate all this. I hate it.'

'I know you do. But look at it this way: your father's miserable and we're happy. A month from now, no matter what we decide to do, he'll still be miserable and we'll still be happy. So if we have to absorb a bit of unpleasantness we can endure it.'

'I expect you're right,' she said after a long moment. 'It will certainly be better if I don't have to make an elaborate explanation to Sarah and Trevor. But I'm still concerned about you.'

Kincaid cupped his hand and put it next to her cheek. 'I told you, kid. Don't fret about me. Someday I'll tell you about some genuine bastards I've had to deal with along the way. Then you'll understand that your father is no problem for me.'

Kincaid and Sophie and her children arrived at the Towers the day before Christmas and stayed for just over a week. When they were back home in London he said, 'It wasn't a triumph perhaps but it wasn't a disaster either.'

It had been a triumphant occasion, of course, in the sense that the emotional undercurrents were never allowed to surface. Everyone seemed determined to concentrate on details, on flavours and scents and textures, warm and cold, soft and firm. Music and decoration and appropriate gift-wraps. Sleigh-rides and dancing, carols sung round the tree, and skating on the pond in the deer park. Rather than a warm family gathering for Christmas celebration, the celebration itself was the centre-piece and the family members only additional items of décor. They related with total concentration to their surroundings and all the carefully scheduled activities, rather than to each other. The love and devotion which they might normally have given to other people were squandered instead on objects and events.

The Major, who had been everyone's primary concern, behaved in an unbelievable and quite astonishing way. He was available, co-operative, at times almost pleasant, and most surprising, he was silent. He was a solid presence in the dining-hall, he chuckled at the antics of his grandchildren. And he was extravagantly polite to his long-time adversary, Arthur Tagg, and to his most recent one, Kincaid.

Only the Major himself and Sophie knew the reason for his incredibly civilized behaviour. She noticed at once that her father was not in the great hall to greet them when they arrived. Consequently, as soon as it was discreetly possible to do so, she found him in his upstairs study, closed the door behind her, and said, 'Before I allow my maid to unpack the cases and hang my things up, you and I must have a firm understanding.'

'I don't like your tone, young lady. I'll tell you that straight away. I've resisted your mother's efforts to programme my behaviour and I'd appreciate it if you wouldn't attempt to take up her cause.'

'I'm taking up no one's cause except my own and I . . .'

'That's quite enough,' he said. 'I have no more to say on the matter.'

She stood looking at him for a long moment. Then she crossed the room to the bell sash and pulled it twice.

'Can I get you something?' her father asked.

'No, thank you. I'll take care of it.'

The butler came in then. Sophie turned to him and said, 'Please go to our rooms in the west wing, Trout, and tell Mr Kincaid that we'll be going back to London as soon as our bags and the children's can be put back in the cars. Please see that all the luggage is gathered and tell Mr Kincaid I'll join him in a few minutes.'

'You'll do no such thing, Trout. Our guests will be staying on as we planned,' Cranston said.

Sophie had not turned away from the butler. 'Please do as I've asked you. Or must I do it myself?'

'No, mum. Thank you, mum.' He turned and left the room.

'What's come over you? Are you telling me you've travelled all the way up from London only to turn round and go directly back again.'

'That's precisely what I'm doing.'

'What about Margaret and your children? Don't you realize you'll be ruining their Christmas holiday?'

'That's what I don't want to do. That's why we're leaving.'

'What nonsense.'

'It is not nonsense. I told you that you and I must have

179

an understanding, but you were having none of it. If that's still your position, then there's no reason for us to waste each other's time. I'll make sure that the luggage is being taken care of and we'll be on our way.'

'Let's not go off half-cocked here. If you have something to say, let's hear it.'

'I certainly do have something to say,' she said, 'and I don't wish to be interrupted while I'm saying it. It's important that you listen to me and it's important that you understand me.'

The Major poured himself a drink and eased down into his chair. 'As you know, I didn't agree to come here for the holiday till ten days ago,' she went on. 'Until that time I was quite sure I would not come.'

'You've never spent a Christmas any place but here. Your children the same.'

'That's true. But this year was to be the exception. Until I decided at last that I must not disappoint Margaret and the children if I could avoid it. That meant, in my mind, that there had to be an understanding between you and me, a social contract if you will, that would guarantee your civilized behaviour for the short time we're here.'

'Where do you get such ideas? What makes you think . . .'

'I don't think. I know. Do you imagine that I don't know what you were up to when you were trying to prevent my marriage to Kincaid? I know what you said to Howard and Sybil. I know the hateful things you told Sarah and Trevor. And I certainly know the kind of tactics you used on Kincaid himself when you were trying to scare him off, or buy him off, or whatever rotten scheme you had in mind.'

'If you expect me to apologize for having your best interests at heart . . .'

Sophie shook her head. 'Too late for that, I'm afraid.

180

The damage has been done. I'm trying now to prevent further damage. That I'm determined to do. What I want from you now, in this room, what I insist on having, is your solemn assurance that you will say or do nothing during our visit that will upset my mother, my children, or my husband. He is my husband, you must recognize it and accept it, and treat him with the same courtesy you would show a fellow-officer if he came to visit. In case you don't understand, that means total courtesy, total kindness and consideration. Kincaid is a permanent member of the family. We know what a fight you put up to prevent our being married but the battle's over now and you've lost. You lost the battle and you must accept that. If you don't accept it or if you can't accept it, you will lose the war as well.'

'What does that mean?'

'I'll tell you precisely what it means. If I leave here today and go back to London, if I'm forced to leave because I'm afraid of what you might say or do, if I can't trust you to treat my husband decently, then I won't be back. Not this year, not next year, not ever. If that sounds like a threat, so be it. I think of it as a solemn promise to myself.'

'Are you saying you would deprive your mother of seeing her grandchildren?'

'I would not deprive Margaret of anything. I would continue to see her as often as possible. I would want her to come to London whenever she could. And I would certainly not keep Sarah and Trevor away from Wiswell Towers. But if you cannot accept my life, my marriage, and my husband, then you are no longer acceptable to me. If I leave today, or if I agree to stay and am forced to leave later because of some carelessness or cruelty from you, then I swear to God that you'll never see me in this house again and you will never be seen in mine.'

Sarah Black was only a year older than her brother, Trevor. Both were born in January. Consequently she did not have the power or the influence over him that she would have liked to have. She had always believed that she was mature for her age and in many ways she was. She felt intellectually and emotionally superior to Trevor and in many ways she was. But at the same time he had an unsettling ability to arrive at correct and sometimes startling conclusions by the most unorthodox methods. Or by no method at all. Their mother and their tutor, Mr Tagg, were accustomed to hearing Sarah shout at her brother, 'You're just guessing. You don't know the answer. You just made a lucky guess.' She concluded early on that her brother had social gifts, intuition, and a flare for unhinged fantasy. None of these was available to her. Or so she believed. So she continued to memorize rules and formulas and theorems, to study the behaviour of adults she admired, and to emphasize structure in her study habits and her thinking. She truly believed, from an early age, that logic would see her through, that if she took proper care of her mind, her memory, and her powers of reason, they would in turn take care of her.

Trevor, on the other hand, seemed to regard whatever he confronted as a game of chance. Fantasy and reality were interchangeable. Animals and plants – weeds as much as flowers – and raw materials – cement, bricks, shingles, lath, and wire – captured his full attention. Whereas his sister kept lists of her belongings, and a bound book that told her, in alphabetical order, where each object and possession was stored, Trevor was usually unable to locate even his most treasured toy. He would return from a short walk or a drive with his mother without the sweater he had worn when they left the house, or with one shoe missing. The servants were hard-pressed to keep buttons on his shirts and jackets, and laces in his shoes. One day he would seem unable to recall the name of a neighbouring county. The following day he might hold forth for an hour to whomever would listen about the Olmec and Toltec nations in Mexico.

Despite their apparent differences, Sarah and Trevor were as locked together emotionally as identical twins. Still they agreed on almost nothing. If there was not instant disagreement on a particular subject, they felt restless. In a matter of hours, one of them, either through research or simple contrariness, would present a dissenting opinion. It was not surprising then, that they would hold sharply contrasting views of Kincaid at the end of their holiday visit to Northumberland.

'There's something common about him,' Sarah said. 'He's a colonial and there's no way to disguise it. Of course he speaks well but it's too perfect to be authentic. And he's found a decent tailor and a proper bootmaker. But that's not difficult to do, is it? He's unusually careful, it seems to me. Cautious about his remarks. Says very little, you notice. Dead silent very often when we're at table. It's almost rude to be so silent, isn't it? It either indicates some sort of intellectual arrogance or a lack of confidence in one's opinions. In his case it's the latter, I suspect. He's very nice to Mum, of course. I'll give him that. And she, it seems, is dotty about him. I just hope she won't be bored with him after a bit. There's so little variety there. Nothing exciting or stimulating. Not to my eyes at any rate. He's like a dog who neither barks nor bites. I think Mum has found herself a lapdog.'

Trevor had another impression altogether of his new stepfather. 'Do you remember that groom who used to work for us? Tunstall, his name was. Quiet as a stone. Hardly spoke at all. And not a big man either. Half the size of Grandfather. But one day Otto, the head groom, got angry with him and discharged him. Shouted at him and used bad language in front of the other grooms and stable-hands. And do you know what happened then? Tunstall picked Otto up, held him above his head, and threw him over the rails of the exercise ring. Didn't say a word. Packed his gear and left. I think that's the kind of man Kincaid is. Everything kept inside. I like him. I like it that he doesn't talk so much. But still I had some fine conversations with him. He explained American baseball to me and I told him some things he didn't know about cricket and falconry. And he listened. He listened to every word I said and I'll bet he remembered too. He listens to everybody. Did you notice that? That's why he doesn't talk so much, I expect. It's hard to learn anything if you're talking all the time.'

'I still don't like him,' Sarah said. 'I think he's common.'

'You don't like him because you don't know anybody else who's exactly like him. You don't even know what you like, Sarah. You just like what you know. What's the fun of getting to know somebody if they're exactly like everybody else you already know?'

'There are some people one doesn't want to know.'

'Not me,' Trevor said. 'I like to find out about everybody. I'll bet you've never had a good talk with Trout, have you? Or Mrs Whitson, the housekeeper.'

'Of course I've talked with them.'

'No, you haven't. You've just rung the bell and told them what you need when they answer. But I've talked with Mrs Whitson for hours at a time. And Trout as well. They may not have been to university but they know a lot. They know about people and why they do the things they do. They understood a man like Tunstall. They knew he was a good chap and Otto was a piece of meat. When

Mr Tagg discharged Otto, the staff had a little party to celebrate. Nobody liked Otto except Grandfather.'

'You seem to know a lot about the staff. Are you training yourself to go into service?'

Trevor shook his head. 'Nobody would hire me. And they most certainly wouldn't hire you. That's why some people are born rich. Because God knows they'd starve if they had to provide for themselves.'

4

Julian Thorne came to London again sooner than expected. Rosamund Barwick rang up Kincaid one morning and said, 'I saw Thorne at a dinner party last night. Bright-eyed and full of beans as usual. He asked if I'd seen you. I think you'll be hearing from him.'

'If I do I should not invite him to the house and I should not bring Sophie if I meet him somewhere. Wasn't that your recommendation?'

'Exactly. And I understand you've had a meeting with Lloyd Banks, my friend at Gaumont.'

'I've seen him twice actually. We had drinks one day and we met for lunch a week later. Smart fellow. Funny and irreverent.'

'He has no illusions about the business he's in.'

'None at all,' Kincaid said. "He says, "It's a whore's business. But some of us are paid better than others."'

'Did he give you an inside look at how film deals are made?'

'That's his speciality apparently. In a few hours he gave me enough information to fill a book. Basically he said what you said. "If you're not hungry and the other chap is, you can make almost any deal you want to."'

'That's it, my sweet. Just remember that when you're talking to Thorne.'

When Thorne called, Kincaid arranged to meet him at the Thornwood building on Sutton Row. His office, on the top floor, was panelled with dark oak, carpeted and decorated like the library in an eighteenth-century manor house. Outside the French doors, a walled garden had been fashioned on the flat roof: a well-kept lawn, a fountain, great urns of flowers, and trees and shrubs strategically placed. The lamps were dim in the office but a soft pink light was positioned to play on Thorne's chair behind his wide desk. And Kincaid could feel a light on himself as he sat facing Thorne.

After an exchange of pleasantries Thorne said, 'The last time we talked you told me you weren't interested in the general proposal I made to you. I assume that nothing has happened in the meantime to change your mind about that.'

Kincaid shook his head. 'I still feel the same.'

'I assumed you would. But since I have confidence in you and a great deal of confidence in my own judgement, I decided while I was in California to go one step further. I asked you to come here this morning because there's something I want you to see. A piece of film our cutters put together. It's just two reels. My secretary, Miss Longworth, will take you downstairs to the screening-room. I want you to be by yourself when you're watching. When it's finished, if you want to see it again, just press the lighted button on the back of the seat in front of you and the projectionist will run it a second time. Then you'll be brought up here again and we'll talk about what you've seen.'

The projection room was blue. Pale blue walls and ceiling, thick blue carpet, and blue velvet armchairs, soft and deep, three rows of four seats, each row elevated a foot higher than the one ahead. 'Sit wherever you like,' Miss Longworth said. 'Can I get you some tea or coffee? Or a drink if you'd prefer.'

'No, thank you.'

'I'll be in the projection booth. Just press the button when you're ready for us to begin.'

'I'm ready now.'

Almost as soon as he was settled in his chair, music from a full orchestra came from speakers concealed in the ceiling and an aerial picture of a sprawling motion-picture studio faded up on the wall-size screen at the end of the room. Thorne's voice was heard then and slowly his image dissolved through. He was standing in the centre of an enormous, empty sound-stage, speaking in his precise approximation of Mayfair English.

All of us who have devoted our lives and our resources to the art of the motion picture like to believe that in the complex process of movie-making our particular job is the most important. The men and women who write scenarios believe that. So do the producers and directors, the set designers, the wardrobe people and make-up artists. The cameramen certainly know that they are indispensable. And the lighting people, grips, and juicers, and property men. Indeed all the people behind the camera are important. Everyone plays a critical role. The sound crew is now one of our most important components, as well as the editors, the composers and conductors. And musicians. We all deserve credit for the final product the public sees on the screen. But . . . in our flush of self-congratulation we must never forget that the actor is in fact the core of what we are about. Until that man or that woman begins to move and speak, unless those who do the pre-production work can depend on those actors to appear and perform on schedule, the work the rest of us do is meaningless. We become a symphony that is never played and never heard.

This little film then is a small tribute to the performers to whom we owe so much.

As Thorne's image began to fade and the music came up, a montage of the faces of actors and actresses filled the screen, still portraits of Fairbanks and Chaplin and Pickford. Lillian Gish and Barrymore, Valentino and William S. Hart. Vilma Banky, Emil Jannings, Carmel Myers, and Jackie Coogan. Ronald Colman, John Gilbert, George Arliss, and Buster Keaton. Then there was a twenty-second clip of Jolson singing in *The Jazz Singer*, followed by short scenes, smoothly cut together, of actors speaking. People whose faces were unfamiliar to Kincaid, young people for the most part, in close-up, making threats, promises, stating their intentions to other actors, vowing their love, swearing revenge. Suddenly then he saw his own face and heard his voice saying, 'These external manners of lament are merely shadows to the unseen grief that swells with silence in the tortured soul . . .' His face was gone then, suddenly, as swiftly as it had appeared, and the faces of other performers followed each other, some lingering longer than others, some saying three words, others a full speech. Kincaid sat watching, his hands gone cold suddenly from the surprise of seeing and hearing himself. Then he was on the screen again, wearing his seaman's outfit, then off, then on again, each time, it seemed, for a longer segment. Until at last, head-and-shoulders, he filled the screen in his sleek tail-coat and delivered four electric minutes of Dante's *Inferno*.

The music came up again and full-face portraits of twenty or thirty actors appeared in turn on the screen.

Younger people, those who had appeared, along with Kincaid, in the sound segments. And their names flashed boldly, like a headline, just above their faces. Finally, he saw, full-screen, a still picture of himself, the name Kincaid prominent, as the music reached a crescendo and the shot of Thorne's studios dissolved through again. The screen went white then, the room was silent, and the lights came up. After a moment Miss Longforth's voice came through on the intercom. 'Shall we run it again, Mr Kincaid?' He didn't answer till she came back inside the screening-room and asked him again. This time he said, 'No. No, thank you.'

A few minutes later he was back in Thorne's office.

'How'd you like the film?' Thorne said. All smiles.

'I hated it.'

'I'm not surprised. I hate it, too. Because I'm in it. Because every time I see it, I have to look at myself. I can't stand the sight of my face on film. Can't stand the sound of my voice.'

'Then why do you do it?'

'Because it's my job. It's my business. I represent my studio. I have to give speeches, make personal appearances, and often I have to say things that need to be said in front of a camera. But that doesn't mean I like to look at the result. I'll tell you something else that may surprise you. I know a great many successful actors, people who work in front of a camera every day, but of all those people I can only think of two who like to sit in a screening-room as you did and watch themselves. Of those two who can never see enough of themselves, one is a really atrocious actor and the other one is a mindless egomaniac. People say he saves his nail clippings after he's had a manicure.'

When Kincaid didn't answer Thorne said, 'This may surprise you, but almost any movie is a failure to the people who made it. It's a group activity, a business of compromise. Everyone does the best he can do under the circumstances. But the circumstances almost always are impossible. So if you feel as though a truck has hit you because you saw yourself on screen for the first time and heard a recording of your voice, I assure you that's the way most of us feel.'

'What I can't understand is why you went to all this trouble and work. Last time we talked I told you I wasn't interested in being an actor. I meant it.'

'I know you did. But I believe you'll change your mind. Also, I didn't put this whole film together just for your benefit. It was a promotion we sent out to our theatres a year ago. All we had to do was cut your footage into the negative and do some work on the sound-track. We were lucky to get any track at all when we recorded you in the Royal Court.'

'What did you expect me to say after I watched it?'

'I'll be honest with you. I didn't know what to expect. This is a new experience for me. I spend a great deal of my time fighting off people who want to work for me. They know I can make them rich. I don't have to convince them.'

'Is that what we're talking about? Making money?'

'No question about it. Each time I see you I'm more convinced than ever that you've got something I can sell. The more stubborn you get, the more I'm convinced. That stiff-necked, hard-nosed thing about you is what I like. And it comes over on film. You recite Dante as if it was a call to battle. You're a killer, Kincaid. Jack Warner's got a kid named Cagney who has the same quality. Tough-guy heroes. That's the future. All over the world people are having a difficult time. No money. No jobs. Men are up against it. Nobody wants to go to the movies to look at pretty boys in white collars. People who are struggling want to see actors who look as if they know what it is to work with their hands, to be broke, to steal if they're hungry, to fight in the streets, to go to jail. Warner's putting half of his production budget behind that idea. He's making pictures about truck-drivers and farm-hands and factory-workers who can't find work. There are men in America who are riding all across the country on freight cars, bumming rides, begging for meals at kitchen doors, looking for work, any kind of work. Warner's making pictures about those people and I intend to do the same thing. But I need the right faces and the right voices. The thing I'm looking for can't be acted. It has to be there. When Cagney does a film about the streets of New York, you know he's lived in those streets. When he punches a man in a scene, you can see he knows how to use his fists. That's what you've got, Kincaid. You've got a face and an attitude that tell me you've been somewhere in your life. You've done things. That look comes through on film and it's worth more to me than five years in acting school or ten years on the stage. I know you've seen very few movies in your life, you told me that, so I doubt if you recognized those actors you saw in that little film. Had you seen any of them before?'

'I recognized Colin Clive. Sophie and I saw him not long ago in a play. The others I've never seen.'

'Well, a few of them, like Clive, are English. Bushell, Ralph Forbes, and Leslie Howard. Men with a theatre background. But almost all the others you saw are young men who not so long ago were driving trucks, pouring drinks, or delivering milk. In towns all across the United States. These are people who couldn't begin to do what you saw yourself doing. Handling the classics. But they can memorize lines, walk around a set in front of a camera, and pretend to be something they're not. And because of that they're making more money than they ever dreamed of. They live in fine homes, drive Italian automobiles, drink champagne for breakfast, and they're recognized and applauded every place they go. I'm telling you all this because the last time we talked you indicated to me that since you've never actually acted, never done a scene with other actors, you felt it was something you're not capable of. You're wrong about that. I can do it. My wife could do it. My nineteen-year-old daughter would love to do it if I'd let her. It's not a mystery. It can be learned. And you, my friend, already know everything you need to know. I'll prove it to you. But first let me ask you a question. Have you ever been to California?'

'Yes, I have.'

'How did you like it?'

'It's not a bad place. Dry and hot most of the time. Desert mostly, the parts I saw. A great place for snakes and buzzards. A little rough on people. Always a struggle to find water. Reminds me of home a bit. Australia's the driest bloody country in the world. But then you'll find a place in the hills or by the sea that's so beautiful it makes your eyes pop out. But I didn't see much of the pretty parts of California. I was locked up most of the time I was there. In Chino, breaking rocks and shovelling gravel. And before that in Imperial County, at the work-farm east of El Centro.'

Thorne sat silent, looking at Kincaid. Then he smiled and said. 'All right. Now I'll tell you something you don't know. What you just did when you answered my question was film-acting. I was the camera and you were making an honest response to a question put to you by another actor. That's it, Kincaid. Human behaviour. One human being responding to another. That's what it's all about. Acting is reacting. Just like life. And the closer it is to life the better it is. It can't be vaudeville, or burlesque, as much of silent films were. And it can't be three times

192

larger than life, the way most stage actors work. Now that we have the actors speaking on screen, those voices have to be recognizable and familiar. Real people with believable problems. Naturalism is the key now. What you just did, the way you spoke when you answered me, is all you would ever have to do as a film actor. Forget about the camera and respond as you would in a similar situation in real life. You're a young man but you have a great deal of experience to draw on. You know how to work, you know how to fight, you know what it's like to be punished, to be locked up. Am I right?'

Kincaid smiled. 'You're right about that.'

'That's your training. That's what you have to offer. And that's what I'm after. So forget the way you felt when you saw yourself on film downstairs. That reaction means nothing. You are the worst judge of how you look and what sort of impression you make. All of us are. You have to trust me. When I see those first still shots we took of you on the stage of the Cromwell, when I look at the film we shot, when I sit here talking to you, do you know what I see? I see money. Money for me and my company, and a great deal of money for you. Now I'm a man of the world and I keep my eyes open. I've met your lovely wife and I've seen how you live. It's obvious that you don't need money. But I've never met a man who didn't want to make money. Half of the actors and directors I work with have already made fortunes. A few of them had money to start with. But when I start talking contract with those people they're out to bleed me for every dollar they can get. Because they know that's the way the business works. The bigger my investment, the harder I'll work to guarantee a profit on that particular project. The more I charge an independent exhibitor to show a Thornwood film, the more he'll scramble to get people into his theatre. From the outside it looks like greed. On the inside we know that our business is growing because talented people keep making impossible demands and money has to be generated to meet those demands. When you and I get to the point of talking money, and I guarantee you we will, you'll be surprised at how generous I'm prepared to be. But that doesn't mean I'm a fool. I pay people as close to nothing as I can, till I can look at my books and see how much that person is earning for me and my studio. Then, and only then, do I pay them what the figures tell me they're worth. That's the way everybody does it if they want to stay in business.' He sat back in his chair and smiled. 'But then . . . every so often, I read a book, or a story-idea, or I talk to a new director, or I see an actor I've never seen before, and some instinct tells me this is something or someone to invest in. Then I forget, for the moment, about profit, and I spend money like a wild man. Because I can smell a substantial profit down the line. I've been burned a few times but not many. Things happen. An actress gets pregnant at the wrong time. A director turns out to be a drunk, or he has a yen for ten-year-old girls. I've lost money on a few people but I've never lost that belief in my intuition. I know how to pick a winner. That's why Jesse Lasky hired me. And Bill Fox. And Sam Goldwyn. And that's why Thornwood studios today is one of the top five money-makers in the film business.'

'Are you sure it's not just because you're a good salesman?'

Thorne shook his head. 'We're all good salesmen. But that means nothing if you can't figure out what people are going to buy.' He smiled. 'Besides, if I'm such a good salesman why haven't I been able to convince you?'

'Maybe you haven't figured out what I want.'

'Maybe not. But I will. I'm a persistent bastard.'

'And then what happened?' Sophie asked. Kincaid had just come home from his meeting with Thorne.

'I thought we'd covered everything and I was about ready to leave but he persuaded me to go back downstairs to the screening-room with him and look at the film again.'

'But you said you hated it. Didn't you say that?'

'I did. But I hated it less the second time. Thorne kept talking on the phone to the projectionist, stopping and starting the film, rolling it back, looking at some of the short scenes over and over.'

'Yours as well?'

'No. That was the best part. He skipped over the film they'd taken of me at the Royal Court.'

'Then what was the point?'

'He wanted me to study the other actors. He dissected every scene, pointing out what was good and not so good. And mostly he kept telling me what a simple process it was from the actor's standpoint. Nothing like the theatre, he said. They shoot very few long scenes. Little pieces they do. A few lines here and a few lines there. They shoot every bit over and over till they get it right. Then the editors pick the best takes and put it all together. And that's it.'

'Did he convince you that you could do it if you wanted to?'

'According to Thorne, anyone can do it.'

'What do you think?'

'I don't know. But I could see how the process worked when we saw the same scene over and over.'

Sophie smiled and patted his knee. 'You do think you could do it, don't you?'

'I wasn't thinking about that. I was just listening to him as he explained everything.'

'But think about it now. Were those actors doing something mysterious that you could never do? Is that the way you feel?'

'It's hard to explain. When you hear it all taken apart and put together, a piece at a time, it doesn't seem to have much to do with acting, the way we see it here in the theatre. When Thorne talks about it, it's like hearing a carpenter or an engineer describing a structure of some sort he's about to build. It's all very technical and precise, and the actors are like pieces of the final thing but not so important as one might imagine. A lot of specialists do their particular jobs, then the actors do what they do, and a lot of other technicians pick it up from there. And finally everything gets mixed and processed and stuck together, and the result is a motion picture. Thorne said it takes as much hard work to make a rotten film as it does to make a good one. He says even the people doing the work very seldom know if it's going to be a success or not.'

'What an odd activity.'

'Of course. I told him that. I said it sounded like the way prisons are run. Lots of people giving orders but no one really in charge.'

'All the same,' Sophie said, 'you're intrigued.'

'I'm not sure that's the word. But when you hear about the lives those people lead and the great amounts of money they make, one can't help being a bit curious.'

'You know what I think? I think it sounds awful. Superficial and greedy and awful.'

'Of course it does. But so does any other business I've ever seen. I've heard smart people say the same things you're saying about the Catholic Church. Or the sewer system in Sydney. Or the British Parliament.'

'Be honest, sweetheart. Doesn't all this foolishness that Thorne describes sound terribly childish?'

'No question. But that's a fact of life. People do childish things. Most people make their living in childish jobs. The first time you ever saw me what was I doing?'

'You were being unbelievably handsome and seductive and appealing, wrapped in your cape, leaning on your sceptre and reciting thrillingly from *Coriolanus*.'

'You are now editing the truth as thoroughly as Thorne does. The fact is I was freezing my feet on the wet pavement, babbling away like a child, and making a total ass of myself. And all for one purpose. To pay for a bed in the seamen's shelter and a bit of soup. It's all commerce, Sophie. A few people get rich and most people don't.'

'I'm in trouble. I married you thinking you were dumb but beautiful. Now I see . . .'

'I am neither dumb nor beautiful. Lucky is the word.'

'How can you say that? From what you've told me about your life, it's been nothing but rotten luck.'

Kincaid smiled. 'Up to now. But starting with you, the bluebirds began to sing and my luck turned. From now on, it's sunshine and champagne.'

'And how about Mr Thorne?'

'I may never see him again. On the other hand I might. It all depends on what he has up his sleeve.'

6

Margaret Cranston had expected, as had the entire family with the exceptions of Sophie and Kincaid, that Evan would be at the Towers for Christmas, as he had been each year for more than twenty years. His father had also expected to see him there, had looked forward to his coming because he believed that once they were together, father and son, they would be able either to put aside or to talk away the incident that had been so disturbing to Evan.

Evan, however, had not appeared, had not telephoned, and had not sent gifts. And neither Arthur nor Margaret had been able to reach him when they rang his flat in London. In deference to Arthur, Evan's absence was not discussed in general conversation but it was discussed thoroughly between Sophie and Kincaid, between Arthur and Margaret, and between Sarah and Trevor, both of whom were extremely fond of Evan, whom they thought of as a family member. Sketchily connected, perhaps, but permanent all the same.

Sophie was certain that Evan was absent because of the unfortunate discussion they'd had before her marriage to Kincaid. In Kincaid's mind, he was at fault because of the visit he'd paid to Evan's flat after the marriage. Margaret was convinced that her letter to her daughter in which she quoted Evan's remarks about Kincaid was responsible for starting the chain of misunderstandings, while Arthur believed that he was the root cause, that he had prodded his son to make comments about Kincaid, had promised that he wouldn't pass them along to Margaret, and had then done precisely that. Trevor secretly believed, and had so believed for a long time, that Evan was enormously devoted to Sophie and was saddened by her recent marriage. Sarah, in her thirteen-year-old wisdom had assumed since she was eleven that Evan was a bachelor only because he was waiting for her to reach eighteen. Assuming further that his longing for her was as relentless and painful as hers for him, she concluded that he was staying away because he didn't trust himself to be near her.

The fact was that Evan had chosen not to go to the

Towers for the Christmas holiday because of his own guilt. He himself had started the machinery rattling and smoking because of his remarks to Arthur about Kincaid. He had complicated matters by expanding on those remarks to Sophie after she had received Margaret's letter. He still felt resentment towards Arthur for having passed on his remarks to Margaret but he felt no pride whatsoever in the sharp note he had sent to his father defining too precisely the scope of his resentment and the punishment he felt Arthur deserved. He also felt rotten about the way he had dealt with Kincaid when he'd come to visit him in an effort to mend the bridges.

So Evan had slunk off, had buried himself in a small hotel in Devon for the holidays, had worked on his play, or had tried to work, and had felt awkward and guilty. Guilt had become his familiar companion and as his play progressed, as it took specific form, as the characters began to grow in size and speak fearlessly, that guilt became more constant and more aggravated. While a part of him raced to complete his work, some internal beast raged against the day when it would at last be finished, when he would be forced to read it through, package it, post it, and expose it. And expose himself. Exposing, also, his father.

The thought of doing damage to Arthur was painful, but the thought of destroying or concealing a piece of work that he had wrenched and torn out of himself was a kind of self-punishment Evan could not contemplate. So he worked on, lay in bed at night with his guilt, and persuaded himself that everyone would be better served if he simply motored to Devon and failed to show up for Christmas in Northumberland.

He was elated then, when he returned to London, to receive a note from Margaret.

Dear faithless one,
I will be in London for five days commencing January 13. I will be staying with Sophie, of course, but she does not know I am sending you this note.

You must meet me at Claridge's for tea at four o'clock on the fifteenth. I will not take no for an answer. We have both been naughty and now we must talk and rediscover each other. If you tell me you cannot come I will be there anyway, expecting you to recant and put in an appearance.

> Much love,
> Margaret

When they met at Claridge's, when they'd settled into a corner of the central lounge, she said, 'I'm not good at this sort of thing. Do we apologize to each other or do we just smile and kiss and blunder ahead as though nothing had happened?'

'Neither one, I should think.' He leaned forward and kissed her and took her hand in his. 'I just want you to know that I have missed you enormously and I am delighted to see you. We have a great deal to talk about and as far as I'm concerned there are no forbidden subjects. To begin, I want you to know that I sent a note off to Arthur before I came here today. I told him that whatever temporary difficulties we may have stumbled into, they are in the past as far as I'm concerned. As soon as I can get a break from my work I plan to go up to spend some days with him. Or he can come here if he prefers. In any case I take my share of the blame, or all of the blame if that's the way it falls. Sophie's married now, I assume you all had a pleasant holiday together, so any foolishness that preceded the marriage can be forgotten.'

'You just made my speech for me. But you did it better.'

'Furthermore, in a few days, I will invite Sophie and Kincaid to join me for an evening so we can iron out any wrinkles that are left in that old garment.'

'There aren't any. I'm sure of that.'

'So much the better. The three of us will simply drink a few magnums of wine then, smoke Turkish cigarettes, and eat venison at a fine restaurant I've discovered in Brooks Mews.'

'How lovely,' Margaret said.

'Just a moment. I haven't finished. As soon as my play has gone off in the post I plan to motor up to St Alban's to visit Trevor. And from there to Cobham, along country roads, to see Sarah.'

'You've thought of everything, haven't you?'

'I must. I'm too eccentric to make many friends. So I have to be careful to keep the ones I have.'

Margaret smiled. 'Next I suppose you'll announce that you've invited the Major for a week of grouse shooting in Scotland.'

Evan shook his head. 'I only make peace where it's welcome. If I held out an olive branch to the Major he would either eat it or whip me with it.'

7

At King's Cross station, before she boarded the train that would take her home to Northumberland, Margaret bought a block of letter-paper with matching envelopes. As soon as she was settled into her compartment, as the train rolled slowly northward through the sprawl of London, she took a pen out of her bag and began to write.

My dear Sophie,

You know me so well. You know how much I love arrivals and detest departures. Since I was a child I've always hated to say goodbye. But today, as you stood in the station with me, I had a warm and lovely feeling. Because I knew that you and I, just by spending time together (something that was difficult to manage when you came for the holidays), had done away with that ugly thing – call it misunderstanding, or disappointment, or whatever you will – that had made us uneasy with each other for the first time in our lives. As I sit here on the train I feel there's something between us now, a sort of relaxed openness, that we haven't had before, not to this degree. It makes me want to confide in you, in this instance to write to you, to tell you whatever comes into my mind, whether trivial or critical.

You have always been the principal witness to my life with your father. I have tried never to denigrate him in your eyes but I've also felt it was unfair to present my marriage to you as something it is not. Now, however, I feel compelled to go a step further. Why now? I'm not sure. Perhaps because as we had breakfast together yesterday it occurred to me quite suddenly that you are the same age I was when you and I left India and came home to England to stay.

Although you have never asked me the direct question, I've always suspected that you've been puzzled all these years as to why I've stayed married to William. I myself have often been puzzled. The best reason I can give is that I never allowed myself to consider alternatives. Also, it took me a very long time to recover from the shock I felt when I realized at last what an unwise choice I'd made. By then you had been born, we were permanently settled in India, and the sheer mechanics of separating from William (I have never called him Bill) were more than I could conceive of or bring about.

As you surely know, divorce was not the civilized alternative that it is today. Unhappy marriages (especially on military bases) were not uncommon. But divorce as a solution was very uncommon. People simply muddled through and stuck it out. Wives made the best of it. And that's what I did. Although I suspected that William was no more ecstatic about our arrangement than I was, I also knew he would fight any attempt I might make to leave him.

Then, quite suddenly, both my parents died, within three weeks of each other. Heart-broken as I was, I knew it was, in its sad way. a godsend. It allowed me to go home and it gave William an acceptable story to tell his friends at the officers' mess. 'Large estate to manage. Financial matters.'

William, as you know, was in love with India. He still is. He would have accepted any circumstance that allowed him to stay there. When the war started and he was posted back to England, when he had to leave his beloved India, he left a critical portion of himself behind. He was a ferocious believer in Empire, the military aspect of it, and his role in it. The irony is that he was inept and incapable as a military officer, just as he's been inept and incapable at anything else he's tried. He loves the picture of himself on a horse but he is a wretched horseman. He is cruel to horses and they detest him. Nor was he ever able to master cricket. And he was the only officer in India, I'm sure, who couldn't manage a decent round of golf. He was, however, and still is, a world-class drinker. 'Major Cranston can bloody well put us all under the table.' That was his reputation and he revelled in it. He still does. So I decided, long since, to leave him to his whisky decanters and his cue stick. He didn't seem to mind. I'm not sure he even noticed.

I have compensated by staying vigorously alive in other areas of my life. I am aware that a mother is not supposed to live vicariously through her daughter but I have done that, nonetheless, and I'm not sorry. When you were hopelessly in love with Hugh Causey, I wanted to help you in some way but I didn't know how. And I wasn't at all sure I should. I was delighted that you were so much in love, lost and floating and out of control. I sensed you were going through something I'd never been lucky enough to experience and I didn't want to cheat you out of it. Didn't want to smother you with the beating wings of a concerned mother. I knew that Hugh would hurt you but I told myself I'd be able to step in before that happened. Or to soften the blow later. I was mistaken. It happened sooner and more destructively than I had anticipated.

I waited for you to come to me but you didn't. Still something told me it was wiser just then to keep my distance. Was I wrong? In any case, I had to watch you suffer alone, trying to conceal the fact that the sky had fallen on you.

Then, suddenly, Toby came into the picture, all handsome and cocksure in his officer's togs, eager to go to France and be killed. Crazy as all the young men were that year. Drunk with German blood and the smell of gunpowder.

Ironically, having stood aside for Hugh, I did caution you about Toby, who by almost any standards was an exemplary young man. I said something to you about not moving ahead too fast. But you wouldn't, or couldn't, hear.

As it happened, you and Toby were married for almost two years before you were able to live together the way people are meant to. After he was discharged from the military. By then you had two children and Toby was dying. I tell myself that if he'd lived, the two of you would have had a large family and a good life. And I believe that. But God knows, there are no guarantees. No one can say if that would have happened.

As Sarah and Trevor grew older, as you confined your life to them, I began to believe that marriage was not a part of your future plans. I often wondered what might have happened if Hugh had stayed on in Northumberland. I'm sure I told you that he got very drunk the day you and Toby were married – his mother told me this – and that he stayed drunk for five days. I only mention him now because I thought . . . I'm not sure what I thought.

In any case, Kincaid came as a surprise to me. As he must have to you. When we first talked about him it seemed you were fifteen or sixteen. All over again. I knew at once that you didn't care if William, or I, or anyone else, approved. I was glad about that. I should have told you so. But then your father got things all twisted round, I said things I shouldn't have said, and everyone suddenly misunderstood and mistrusted everyone else.

Thank God, all that's behind us now. Except for William, who feeds on chaos, we're all at peace again.

And what do I think of Kincaid? How do I feel about him? As I've just said, I know it's of little interest to you but I like to sort these things out for myself nonetheless. Your grandmother used to say, 'All men are more like than unlike.' Perhaps she was right. But Kincaid, I must say, is like no other man I've met. Perhaps I expected a beautiful young stallion like Toby. Or someone dark and threatening like Hugh Causey.

But Kincaid is altogether different from either of them. At first meeting he seems to present nothing other than his compact physical self and his hard-edged voice. He seems to be saying, 'If you want to like me or accept me I have no objections. But I will do nothing to influence you.' He reminded me a bit of the signs people put in their yards: Don't Stroke the Dog.

Before I'd met him, before you came to stay with us for Christmas, Arthur showed me the clipping from the *Daily Telegraph*, the article Evan had written. You remember it? He wrote: "This is a busker who never smiles. He makes no effort to ingratiate himself to his kerbside audience and seems to take no notice of whether or not they drop money in the hat."

What I'm saying is that I can see very clearly what attracts you to him, even if I can't define it. I admit I had never envisioned such a man for you. Nor had you, I'm sure. When I say that I expect your life with him will be neither smooth nor predictable, that is not a prediction which should make you wary. My life with William has been totally predictable and I would not wish such an existence on anyone.

If you asked me for advice, I would have none to give. I will only say this, exactly what I would say to myself if I were in your position: treasure the moments. And don't expect that your problems, whatever they turn out to be, can be handled with reason and patience and common sense, because they can't.

You're going to have a lovely adventure, Sophie. I promise you that. I expect you'll be happier than you've ever been and I'm quite certain you'll have moments of sadness and bewilderment that are completely new to you. But whatever happens, it will be a delicious trip. And God, how I envy you.

Margaret read what she had written, told herself that she would add a final paragraph later, carefully folded the pages and slipped them inside an envelope. She sat very quietly then, for half an hour, her eyes closed, the fields and trees flashing past outside her window. She knew as she sat there that she had put into words certain thoughts and feelings that she had never allowed to crystallize before. She felt unbearably light in weight suddenly, gauzy and transparent. It was a new and delicious feeling for her, a different sort of being. She opened her eyes suddenly. Like a blind woman who has miraculously recovered her sight. She laughed then like a trickle of water over stones. Reaching into her bag, she took out the block of letter-paper and her pen, and started to write again.

Dear valuable Evan,
How great it was to see you, to have tea and talk, to treasure our lovely and permanent kinship. I almost wrote *friendship* but that word doesn't cover it.

I'm on the fast train heading north. I've just written a long letter to Sophie and I've discovered, or rediscovered, perhaps, the joy of unburdening oneself with the pen. No wonder you're a writer. I know it's tedious and demanding work but what a joy it must be to have the courage and the ability to put everything you believe and feel into words.

I can't do that of course. I have no writer's gift. But today, for some reason I have found the other thing: courage. So I'm writing to you as I wrote to Sophie. With candour and innocence and love.

I've always known without being told that you and Sophie, for many years, have wondered and questioned each other about your father and me. 'They're the same age. They look well together. They like the same things, the same music, the same books. Why shouldn't they be together? Arthur is free and Margaret certainly could be, couldn't she? Why don't they do something about it?'

Why don't we? If I told you the thought has never occurred to me, I'd be lying. It has, of course. I can't be certain that it has also occurred to your father but I expect it has. I hope it has. My ego would be severely bruised if, through all these years we've spent in the same house, he had never once been tempted to put me under his arm and carry me off somewhere.

It may be hard for you to believe, or perhaps it won't, that Arthur and I were less than thirty-five years old when we met. Many times since then I've had an impulse to take his hand, to touch his cheek, to put my arms around him. I have also, less frequently perhaps, seen something in his eyes that revealed, then quickly concealed, something he was unable or unwilling to express. Loaded moments. Sudden clouds and electrical flashes that brought no rain.

Arthur, of course, bless his dear heart, is not a physical man. He is not ruled, or much influenced, it seems, by his senses. He doesn't touch people. He doesn't hug children or scratch the dog's head. He doesn't drink to excess and he doesn't use snuff or tobacco at all. Whatever dark impulses or strong passions he has, he has learned to control them. But we mustn't think less of him for that. I suspect that true passion doesn't feel the need to display itself to whomever may be watching.

It might surprise you to learn that I think of myself as a hopelessly emotional creature. At least I thought so at one time. But since I have never declared myself to Arthur, have never made an attempt to move our relationship to another plane, to abruptly change the way we are together, why should I be surprised that Arthur, the world's most structured man, has also scrupulously obeyed the rules, whatever he believes those rules to be. His values were forged in another century, just as mine were. But women are more flexible because we have to be, whereas many men, even adventurous ones, remain loyal all their lives to the principles and practices they were taught before the age of twelve. All men are Tories at heart.

We must remember too, that our precious England, however enlightened she may imagine herself to have become, is now, as she has always been, a society of classes. With rigid boundaries. Restricted entry. Some movement has been made at the edge but the centre still holds. People take pride in "knowing their place". Upward mobility is a foreign concept to them. Their hopes and ambitions are bounded by hedgerows of history, legacy, and good form.

Your father is certainly such a man. If someone accused him of trying to move beyond his class he would be shocked, I expect, and angry. If I fell on my knees before him and begged him to carry me off to a cave, I'm sure he would fetch me a sedative or a glass of sherry. If I persisted he would certainly say, 'But you're the mistress of Wiswell Towers. I am employed by you. Nothing can change that.'

I imagine you're smiling. Perhaps you're saying to yourself, as anyone your age might say, "What woman could ever be taken with such a man? How could someone so manacled by old ideas and concepts ever appeal to any woman?" I can only assure you that many women would find your father as appealing as I do. All men must be pursued, you know. Guided and instructed. Their brains may work well, and their muscles, but they must be taught to use their subjective areas. British men, in particular, must be brought along slowly. They must be carefully trained, like any other sporting animal. And the failure rate is high even then.

This is not to say that Arthur cannot be trained. Some woman may do it. Someone may already have done. But I'm not the woman for the task, however much I might like to try. Arthur has defined me and labelled me and firmly established my place in relation to him. I'm afraid that nothing will ever change that.

She put the letter to Evan away, just as she had done with Sophie's, promising herself that she would finish it, put it into an envelope and post it as soon as she was home at the Towers. But when she arrived there she put both the letters in a folder in the centre drawer of her writing-desk. She took them out and read them occasionally as the days passed, and the reading made her feel solid and courageous, just as writing them had done. But she thought of them now as messages to herself. She no longer pretended they were ever meant for eyes other than her own.

8

As soon as Evan had a final copy of his play in hand, after he'd rethought it, changed it, cut it, added new scenes, and rewritten every line of dialogue half a dozen times, when he felt at last that he'd made it as good and strong as he was able, he gave it to Alan Winkler to read. A few days later they met for lunch at Addison's Fish House in Whitefriars Street. As soon as they found a table and ordered drinks, Winkler said, 'I hope this won't be a farewell lunch.'

'I don't like the sound of that,' Evan said. 'Does that mean you hated the play?'

Winkler shook his head. 'Not at all. It means I think I'm about to lose a good journalist. You've written a sensational play, you bastard. I'm surprised and proud and envious.'

'I can't believe what I'm hearing. I was expecting to get two pages of notes and corrections.'

'No notes. No corrections. And only one piece of advice. Don't lose your nerve. Don't be afraid of what you've written. Don't let anybody talk you into changing it. I know it took a lot of guts to write it. Now you have to have the guts to go public with it.'

'I just hope I can find a manager who wants to put it on.'

'Don't even think about it,' Winkler said. 'I'm not a theatre man but I'm not deaf, dumb, or blind either. If you send this play to half a dozen producers, I guarantee you that at least two of them will want to do it. If I'm wrong I'll get you drunk and buy you the most expensive dinner the Savoy Grill has to offer. You know how tight I am with a shilling, so that should tell you how sure I am of what I'm saying.'

Evan smiled. 'Well, I hope you're right.'

'I know I'm right. A lot of people will come out of the theatre talking to themselves, however. You've written a play about guilt. That's a subject we all know about. Guilt in the family. Loving too much. Not loving enough. People telling lies to each other. Believing the lies. Denying the truth. That's what family life is all about. But nobody admits it. And nobody, sure as hell, writes about it. But you have. And it's sad and funny and heartbreaking. It will also make a lot of people angry as hell. Don't deceive yourself about that. Half the audience will think you're writing about them and they'll say, "How dare that bastard expose me like that."'

'Is that what you meant when you said I'd have to have courage to see it put before the public?'

'That's part of it. But mostly I was thinking of the father character. I assume you weren't writing about your own dad but everybody else will assume you were. They'll think that twelve-year-old boy is you, they'll think the mother the boy imagines is your real mother, and I guarantee you they'll think the father is your father. And they'll hate him as much as you seem to. Or as much as the boy in the play does.'

After a moment Evan said, 'Is that the way you felt? Did you hate the character of the father?'

'Hate may not be the right word. But certainly no one's going to like him very much. He's a weak, bewildered man. To an audience, weakness is a kind of villainy. A strong villain will wipe out a weak hero every time. In your play the kid has all the strength and all the sympathy. The mother looks good if only because she had enough gumption to leave the boy's father.'

'You really think there's nothing likeable about the father?'

'Don't get me wrong,' Winkler said. 'That's not a criticism. It's what makes the play work. When a child gets short-changed, whether it's a story or real life, somebody has to take the rap. It's usually the father or the mother because that's the way life is. In this case it's the old man. I know you didn't expect him to come across as a hero.'

'Actually, I didn't break it down that way,' Evan said. 'I just tried to get the moments right and make the three characters ring true. I had an idea that when the curtain came down the audience would see the story from everybody's viewpoint: the son, the mother, and the father. No

212

heroes. No villains. Just an emotional tangle that can never be resolved.'

'You've done that. You did a smashing job of it. I understood all three people. The father's motives were as clear as rain. Nothing wrong with his head. He knows how to solve problems. But that doesn't do it. When you're really upset it doesn't help at all when somebody tells you to calm down. In your play, the boy and his mother are heart-broken and the father isn't. Or if he is it doesn't show. So the audience won't like him. I didn't like him. When everybody's weeping at the graveside, the man who can't cry or won't cry is a hateful bastard.'

'Well, I hope you're wrong,' Evan said. 'If the audience hates him I think it hurts the play.'

Winkler shook his head. 'Not at all. If the audience doesn't hate him there is no play. Everybody who leaves the theatre will be thinking, "Thank God he's not real" or "Things may be bad at home but it's a blessing I don't have a dad like that." You created a terrific character, my friend. I'm just glad he's not real. I wouldn't want to meet him.'

After Winkler left to go back to his office Evan stayed at the table and had a second brandy with his coffee. Then he went into the lounge bar adjoining the dining-room, found a comfortable chair by a window looking out on the street, and settled in for an afternoon of gin and tonic.

At four o'clock he stepped into the phone booth at the end of the bar and rang up Sophie. When Oliver answered Evan said, 'This is Evan Tagg, Oliver. I have an urgent need to speak to either Sophie or Mister Kincaid.'

As soon as Kincaid came on the phone Evan said, 'Won't take no for an answer. Put on your thinking-cap and remember these details. Ritz bar. Seven-thirty tonight. Black tie and patent-leather slippers. Wine and

213

high hilarity for you and the missus. Then on to Le Faisan d'Or in Brooks Mews where I've booked a table for nine o'clock. Claret will flow and we'll devour a few game hens, followed still further by Hennessey and coffee as black as ink. I'm off to my home now to spruce up and prepare myself. Suggest you do the same. As I've said, no excuse will be accepted. Cancel all previous plans. If you try to ring me at home you'll find my telephone is *toujours occupé*. So prepare yourself for the festive evening of your life. We will celebrate the finishing of my play. The Ritz bar at seven-thirty.'

Evan rang off then, had another quick gin at the bar, hailed a taxi as it turned out of Fleet Street, and directed him to Gordon Square. At half past seven, when Kincaid and Sophie came into the Ritz bar, Evan was waiting for them, resplendent in his dinner-jacket and crisp white linen, his eyes sparkling, a fresh high colour to his cheeks.

'How splendid he is,' Sophie said. '*Il est beau comme tout.*'

'It's true,' Evan said, steering them towards a peach-velvet upholstered booth. 'I'm at my best. History may well record that this evening was my pinnacle.'

'How fast can you drink?' Kincaid said to Sophie. 'It seems we have a lot of catching up to do.'

'I am famous,' she said, 'for my ability to rise to the occasion, to do what must be done.'

After they ordered drinks and instructed the waiter to bring refills as often as he felt was necessary, Evan said, 'I swore to Margaret that as soon as I had finished my dastardly, life-threatening play – two long acts of fire and thunder – that I would ring you and treat you to a bout of debauchery and gluttony. So here I am, as good as my word.'

'So you've finished your lovely play?'

'Finished it, yes. But lovely it isn't. Ugly and truthful it

214

is. But before we get into that, my ego requires that you tell me about the appointments you had to cancel so you could join me here.'

'We're going to get very drunk, aren't we?' Sophie said.

'Some will be drunker than others,' Evan said, 'but all present will be properly drunk, provided Kincaid is willing.'

'Kincaid is willing,' he said.

'Tell him how difficult it was for us to make ourselves available this evening. And on very short notice,' Sophie said.

'Short notice is the best, isn't it?' Evan said. 'One feels spontaneous when one has no time to prepare opening remarks or to plan clever toasts.'

'The fact is,' Kincaid said, 'we had no plans for this evening. Until you rang up.'

'We were lolling about,' Sophie said. 'We'd been out three nights running and someone said, I assume it was Kincaid, that it might be pleasant to loll about, as I said before, and do nothing, or next to nothing.'

Evan made a face. 'I'd rather be your best offer than your only offer but I will settle for that.'

'We'll try to be entertaining, won't we, Kincaid?'

Kincaid nodded. 'I was brought up that way. It's an Australian tradition. When it's someone else's shout, it's the duty of the guest to be entertaining.'

'If it's my shout, that means I foot the bills. Correct?'

'Correct. But under these circumstances, Sophie and I decided that you should be our guest because . . .'

'Out of the question, old dear. That would mean I would have to be entertaining. And I expect to be outrageous. So let's speak no more about whose money will be squandered. I made the plan, I wrote the play, I made the call, and I will pay. With my last pound of flesh, if necessary.'

215

They began the evening on a high level of energy. Each of them was aware that this was a reunion, a welcome one, an end to an uneasy period. Sophie and Kincaid were eager to fall into Evan's rhythm, to laugh and drink, talk nonsense and *non-sequiturs* and to cement with wine and hilarity the present situation. Their three-way relationship was not ready yet for serious talk about what had gone wrong, who was to blame, and all the inconsequential rest of it. They sensed that the first step was to share an evening, one with no consciousness of what had gone before, one that made no effort to decide who had sinned or who had been sinned against. All of this behaviour, of course, was instinctive, as simple and childlike as a game of tag or follow-the-leader. Evan, by the tone he had set, was the game-leader. By his example he had clearly said, 'This is a gathering of the light-hearted, the intoxicated, and the irresponsible. Logicians, diagnosticians and common scolds need not apply. Let no pattern be followed, no rules established, no prisoners taken.'

When they arrived at the restaurant, in high spirits and sparkling, they were instantly forgiven for their rowdiness because they were a beautiful trio, good cheer and laughter, welcome guests to the *patron*, who was eager always to attract youth as well as money.

They selected many courses, ate unwisely, and rejoiced in the process. Bottles of wine arrived and were carried away empty, as fresh bottles took their place. At one point near midnight Sophie said, 'Perhaps we'll all go away to California and become rich and recognizable. Kincaid will be sought after everywhere, and I will be his consort, or concubine, or whatever loving female persons are called in that far-off place. We'll paddle our feet in the ocean by day, and dance and yodel all the night, and no one will ever be able to describe how happy we are. You too, sweet Mr Tagg. You must be there, surrounded

216

by careless ladies of every size and colour. We'll put Queen's Walk and Gordon Square for ever behind us. Kincaid will become known as a cowman . . .'

'Cowboy,' Kincaid said.

'That's correct, cowboy. Or a gangster perhaps. A man wearing grey suede gloves who murders people and avoids the electric chair by doing a kindness to a nun. I see a golden future there for all of us. Tagg will write scenarios, Kincaid will expose his muscles, and I will be envied as the friend to one and wife to the other. God knows what pinnacles of notoriety we might scale. How full of promise we all are.'

Evan came home at last at three in the morning, drunker than he had expected but more sober than he would have wished. His sense of balance was imperfect, his vision was cloudy, but certain areas of his brain were unaffected. His recall of the hours he'd spent with Kincaid and Sophie was patchy indeed, but his luncheon conversation with Winkler was clear in his memory, as though he was hearing it for the first time.

He undressed as quickly as he could, eager to be in bed. But before he could lie down he was sick in the water-closet. He was sick for the next two days. He blamed it on the wine he had drunk.

· CHAPTER 6 ·

1

Three days after his evening with Kincaid and Sophie, Evan went to Northumberland to spend a day with his father. That evening as they sat in Arthur's rooms Evan said, 'I expect you know that I hadn't seen Sophie and Kincaid since they were married. No good reason, I suppose. Just a misunderstanding. In any case, the three of us went out to dinner a few nights ago and had a smashing time together. So those fences have been mended and I'm glad.'

'So am I.'

'Perhaps you know that I also saw Margaret not long ago,' Evan said.

'She only mentioned that you'd had tea together when she was in London.'

Evan nodded. 'Another peace mission. And now I've come to see you.'

'No peace mission necessary here. I did something I shouldn't have done and you were perfectly entitled to take exception. If there's peacemaking to be done it's I who should be taking the initiative.'

Evan shook his head. 'It doesn't matter who does what. The important thing is to put it behind us.'

Arthur smiled. '"The child is father to the man." One of the oldest themes in literature.'

'Not sure that applies to me. I'm not wise enough to give you advice.'

'I'll be the judge of that.' He got up and poured more brandy in their glasses. 'Now that we've said our *mea culpas*, let's hear about your new play. You say it's finished.'

'It's finished, all right.'

'What does that mean? Aren't you pleased with it?'

'I'm damned keen about it. It's the best thing I've written. It may be the only good thing I've written.'

'Has anyone else read it?'

Evan nodded. 'Alan Winkler. He thinks it's excellent.'

'Good. And you trust his judgement, don't you?'

'More than anyone else I know. But all the same I've decided to put the play aside.'

'What does that mean?'

'I'm not submitting it to theatre managers. I don't want it produced.'

Arthur sipped from his glass. 'Why do I have the feeling I should drop this subject?'

'I'm sorry,' Evan said. 'It's an awkward area for me as well.'

Arthur got up and walked to the window looking out over the south garden. When he turned back he said, 'Am I hearing you correctly? You're saying you've worked for months on this play, you think it's a good piece of work, Winkler thinks it's a good piece of work, and now you're going to abandon it?'

'I know it doesn't make sense . . .'

'No, it doesn't. Are you proposing we drop the matter there?'

'That's right. I have to.'

'Why is that?'

'I just do.'

Arthur walked slowly back to his chair and sat down.

'All right. Have it your way. But since I'm destined never to see this play performed, won't you at least tell me a bit about it? What's the title?'

'*The Father House.*'

'Very good. Sounds like Tolstoy. And there's nothing wrong with that.' He smiled. 'Is it a play about a house or a play about a father?' When Evan didn't answer he went on. 'Have you written a play about me? Is that it?'

Evan sat silent, seeming to consider his options. At last he said, 'No, it's not about you. At least, it wasn't intended to be. It's about a twelve-year-old boy who never knew his mother. So he creates a mother in his imagination. The characters on stage are the boy, his real father, and his imagined mother. The scenes between the father and son are real, the scenes between father and mother, and mother and son, are created in the boy's mind.'

'I see.'

'As I said, it was never meant to be a portrait of you. And I still don't think of it that way.'

'But Alan Winkler did. Is that it?'

Evan nodded. 'He said that anybody seeing the play would assume I was writing about my own father.'

'But you say you weren't?'

'That certainly wasn't my intention,' Evan said.

'How about the twelve-year-old boy? Does he bear a resemblance to you at that age?'

'I don't know. Winkler didn't know me when I was twelve.'

'What do you think?'

'To me, he's a character in a play. But I'm sure there's a resemblance.'

'I don't know what I should say. You're certainly not asking for my approval, are you?'

'No. I hadn't meant to tell you about it all. It's a decision I had to make and I've made it.'

'Then there's nothing more to be said on the subject.'

'I don't believe so.'

'Well, forgive me for saying this,' Arthur said, 'but I believe there is something more. A great deal more. In the first place, we're not talking about an invitation for the weekend, or what sort of motor car one of us might want to select. We're talking about your work, something that means a great deal to you. I'm not a creative person myself but in my teaching I feel as if I've spent my life among poets and painters, so I believe I qualify as something of an authority on artists in relation to their work. History is filled with examples of men who abandoned, or destroyed, or refused to exhibit works that were unsuccessful, or which for some reason they felt did not come up to the mark. But I know of no instance where a creative person decided to put his best work in a cupboard and leave it there.'

'That may be,' Evan said, 'but in this instance . . .'

'Let me finish. My second point is this. All serious writers use their own lives or their own experiences to one degree or another. If all the novels and poems that dissected or defamed the writer's wives, parents, children were suddenly made to disappear from libraries round the world, all of us who are serious readers would be poorer for it. And there would be a great number of empty library shelves.'

'I realize that. I know writers are supposed to be ruthless but I am cursed with a conscience. I can't turn myself into an emotional burglar.'

'Why not? That's the profession you've chosen. And a glorious profession it is. All of us who have minds are indebted to writers in a thousand ways. Dickens and Tolstoy and Balzac tell us far more about the flavour and the truth of their times and their people than any historians. You say you can't be a burglar. I don't believe that. But if you truly can't, then you must find another kind of work. All writers, all serious writers, are burglars and thieves. They steal people's lives and memories and experiences like a ragman picks up old pots and scraps of metal. They carry those snippets and cuttings around in their minds till they need them. Then they're plucked out and brought to life again on the stage or in the pages of a novel. When a character is well written, when he breathes and reacts and makes human sounds, thousands of readers will swear that they were the model for him. Do you think I could write anything about a young man your age that wouldn't have a great deal of you in it? Do you think Trevor could write a school essay about a mother-son relationship that would not be in some way a portrait of Sophie?'

'I suppose not.'

'Let me ask you another question. What if you had come to me a year ago and said you wanted to write the play you've just described, what if you had asked my permission to proceed and I had given it freely, would we be having this conversation that we're having now?'

'I can't answer that.'

'What I'm trying to say is that I am proud of you for having written something that has value. I don't give a tinker's damn if it's about a character who resembles me, or if it concerns a true situation that existed between me and your mother. If you'd asked me before I would have said go ahead. And now I'm saying that you must go ahead. Once you've sweated and suffered over something it becomes a part of your life. You can't simply cast it aside because it might make someone uncomfortable.'

'We're not talking about *someone*. At least I'm not. I'm talking about *you*.'

'So am I. But I have no fears or trepidations about anything you might write about me. I know you better, I expect, than any other person I've known . . .'

'Exactly,' Evan said, 'and you believe that I could never say or write anything critical or hurtful about you. I believed that too, but . . .'

'Go on.'

'I can't go on,' Evan said. 'The reason I'm withdrawing the play is the same reason you and I can't finish this conversation. If I don't want you to see the play or read about it in the newspapers, then I certainly don't want to describe it to you in detail.'

'I can understand that,' Arthur said. 'That solution may work marvellously well for you, but not for me, I'm afraid. I know you're trying to be decent about this, but if I told you that I had heard your closest friend say something monstrous about you, and if I went on then to say that I couldn't repeat it because I couldn't bear to hurt your feelings, that is certainly not a kind or decent way to behave. I'm afraid we've gone too far with this conversation to simply abort it. That would leave both of us in a dreadful frame of mind.'

After a long moment Evan said. 'I told you that Winkler had read the play and praised it highly. What I didn't want to tell you, the thing that made me decide to abandon the play, was what he said about the character of the father. He said the play should be a guaranteed success because the father was such a complete bastard. He said all the people who hate their fathers will flock to see the play and recommend it to their friends who also hate their fathers.'

'But I've never for a moment felt that you hate me, so why should that concern me?'

'You don't understand,' Evan said. 'I was writing about a bewildered boy of twelve who couldn't understand why he didn't have a mother, why he'd never even seen her picture. But he loved his father, worshipped his father. So I wrote as truthfully about you as I was able to. Things you've said and done, the way you've been with me, sacrifices you've made. It's not just that I'm trying now to protect your feelings, it frightens me that I could set out to do something so specific, so personal, and end up with the opposite of what I intended. The reason I wrote about you, about us, was because someone told me I should deal with people and situations I really know. I never set out to make the father seem responsible for his son's confusion. It never occurred to me that he would be seen as a villain.'

'I never thought of you as an unhappy child.'

'Neither did I,' Evan said. 'I wasn't unhappy. But when I tried to portray myself at that age that's how it turned out.'

They sat there with their drinks in the silent room, no sounds coming from the rest of the house. At last Arthur said, 'I don't have great faith in psychiatry or its principles. I wouldn't apply them to this instance in any case. But I think I see very clearly what's disturbing you. You're afraid that you've written a different sort of truth than you've believed all these years. You don't want to make a public presentation of something you don't believe or don't want to believe. Am I coming close?'

Evan nodded. 'Mostly I'm concerned about you, about your believing that I've been making secret assessments of you for all these years. Behaving one way and feeling another way altogether. No play is so important to me that I would risk hurting you. Even in a small way.'

Arthur smiled. 'I once heard a prominent actress described as someone who thought that "acting is life, and vice versa". I assure you, I will never make that mistake as far as you're concerned. My perception of you is based on millions of heartbeats, millions of words, and millions of brush-strokes. You're a writer. What you write belongs to you. And I think you're just discovering that you can also belong to what you write. That can be a disturbing thought, I'm sure, but it's one you'll grow accustomed to. Because I think you'll discover that your work takes on a life of its own only when you're working at your highest level. Second-rate work has only a super-ficial, pasted-on life, and third-rate work has no life at all.' He set his glass down carefully on the table by his chair. 'I have tried to let you direct your own life, so I hesitate to draw diagrams for you now. But let me suggest a possible solution to this problem we've been discussing. I think it's imperative that you give your play every opportunity to have the best production and the widest possible audience. I think it's also important that you have no thoughts whatsoever of what my reactions might be to what you've done. Here is my proposal. As proud as I am of you, I will not read this particular play or come to London to see it performed. No matter what you've written or what light it might seem to put me in, I'm certain I could watch the play and it would in no way affect my feelings for you. But let's not take that chance. I strongly recommend that we should proceed as I've suggested.' He smiled. 'And somewhere along the way, after you've put this play behind you, we'll sit down together as we've done tonight and I'll tell you everything I can about your mother.'

One winter afternoon Kincaid received a cablegram from Julian Thorne.

Have instructed London office to deliver to you two round-trip tickets on SS BREMEN, Southampton to New York, sailing 7 March, returning England 10 April. And plane tickets New York to Los Angeles return. Also booked cottage at Ambassador Hotel. Most eager for two of you to visit California as guests of Thornwood Studios.

The following afternoon a package was delivered containing the promised tickets along with a great deal of travel information about Southern California. Plus promotional literature about Thornwood Studios and all of its triumphs, past, present, and future.

'He can't be serious,' Sophie said.

'Of course he can,' Kincaid said. 'I'm sure he's very serious.'

'I've never heard of such a thing. It's almost insulting.'

'Not the way Thorne looks at it.'

'It's like a command performance. Will he send a platoon of armed guards to take us along to Southampton and tuck us up in our staterooms?'

Kincaid shook his head. 'You can't judge Thorne by any standards except his own. He thinks he's being generous and hospitable. Like your uncle offering to send his car round to pick us up on a rainy night.'

'But my God, it's so gauche. What makes him think we even want to go to America? Or that we'd agree to spend more than a month in a hotel in Los Angeles? And does he think that if we chose to take such an idiotic trip we couldn't make our own arrangements?'

'He knows very well you can afford it, if that's what you mean. He also knew that Rosamund Barwick didn't need an emerald necklace but he bought her one anyway. As well as diamond earrings and a matching brooch.'

'Did she accept them?'

'Of course she did. She said, "He doesn't need his money and I certainly don't need his jewellery, but why hurt his feelings." She says Thorne's trying very hard to become a proper gentleman, and he's convinced that a gentleman must be generous with his friends.'

'If he thinks that then he hasn't made a careful study of the upper classes. No great generosity there.'

'He's trying to impress you, Sophie. You have a house on Queen's Walk and a family home in Northumberland. He's impressed by that. He wants you to like him. He wants you to know he's rich and important.'

'What do I have to do with it? It's you he's after.'

'That's true. But it's all connected in his mind with Mrs Barwick and her friends. And now, since he was here for tea, it's connected with you.'

'Well, I would like to be disconnected, please. It makes me uncomfortable having plans made for me. Receiving cables that tell me what I'm to do and where I'm to go. It must be really horrid out there where he lives. Is everyone for sale in California?'

'You're missing the point. Thorne knows we're not for sale. That's why he's fascinated. He's never offered me money when we've talked about whether or not I should work for him. Mrs Barwick says he never will, that if I ever make a deal with him I'll have to tell him what I want.'

'I thought those meetings were just a send-up. You're not taking them seriously, are you?'

'Not yet. But I like Thorne. Underneath his well-tailored surface there's something primitive that appeals to me. It's like watching a seal play a trumpet. No one expects him to play brilliantly. The miracle is that he can play at all.'

Sophie smiled. 'Please don't bring the sweet innocent seals into this conversation. We already have animals to spare. It's not enough that I married a wild Australian beast that I haven't learned the name for yet. We now have an odd reptile from the rain forest named Thorne, who can change colour at will like a lizard, whose skin is normally green like American bank-notes, and whose eyes glow like gold coins. Then we have dear Madam Barwick, a wingèd creature of bright plumage, who flits from tree to bush, quick and delicate, making a chirping noise that sounds like laughter, and feeding on nothing but fantasy and clever remarks.' She crossed the room to Kincaid's chair and sat down on his lap. 'Am I to believe that you would pack my slim tender body into a trunk, carry me across the ocean, and deposit me in a chancy hotel in some strange frontier-city populated by foot-pads and cannibals? Would you do that?'

'Why not? You carried me across the English Channel, locked me inside a cottage by the sea, and stuffed me with caviar, croissants and charcuterie, washed down with Sancerre and Calvados. Do you think that was a pleasant experience for me?'

'I bloody well know it was. Oh, why can't we go back there tomorrow? I was born there, you know, the day you and I walked inside that cottage.'

'That means you're far less than a year old. And dangerously precocious.'

'There's a sentimental love-song with a line that goes, "I can't remember now my life before we met, you've made it, oh, so easy to forget."'

'Don't get tender with me. We've just had breakfast. Besides, I like you better when you're mean and evil.'

'That's another song. "I'm mean and evil. Even rain don't fall on me." Seriously, you're not going to drag me off to America, are you?'

'We were married in France. Remember? My understanding of the French wedding ceremony is that the husband is free to make a slave of his wife, to drag her off to any place he sees fit. So there are all sorts of places I plan to drag you to. California may turn out to be one of them. I've spent a great deal of time there, so why shouldn't you?'

'Can't we just ring for Oliver and have him send the tickets and the travel folders and all those promotional materials back to Mr Thorne's office?'

'We could do that but it wouldn't be polite.'

'So much the better. If we're rude to Mr Thorne maybe he'll be offended and leave us alone.'

'Then what?' Kincaid said. 'What about my career? What about my future as an international celebrity? Aren't you a supportive and docile wife?'

'No. I'm a loving and adoring wife.'

'Same thing. That means you wouldn't stand in the way of my success. Quite the contrary. It means you would do anything to help me along the way.'

'Anything except journey to America and live in a California cottage in the garden of some bizarre actor's hotel.'

'You know something,' he said then. 'You are absolutely right. Why should you be burdened with all sorts of unpleasant duties that I should be able to handle alone. I'll ring for Oliver and instruct him to send back one set of tickets. I will go to America and have my business discussions with Mr Thorne and you can stay here in London where you belong. Where your heart is.'

'Just a moment, old dear . . .'

'I know you'll be concerned about my travelling alone

but you mustn't be. I'll miss you but that won't be nearly as bad as watching you suffer if you came along with me. After all, why should you come? It's not a holiday. It's business. I'll simply toddle off like a commercial traveller to do what must be done. And you can stay here in comfort. Then when I come back we'll go down to Brighton and spend a half-week by the sea.'

'For a moment I thought you were serious,' she said.

'I am.'

'No, you're not. You're a dreadful tease and you're teasing me now.'

'Does that mean you wouldn't let me go off to America alone?'

'That's precisely what it means. If I couldn't talk you out of going, I would most certainly go with you. But I still think we should send back the tickets. And the sooner, the better.'

'Perhaps we will,' he said. 'But there's no great rush.'

'What if you discover tomorrow that I've sent them back?'

'I won't discover that because you wouldn't do it.'

'But what if I did?'

'Then you'd have to be punished. I'd probably take the belt off my trousers and give you a severe beating.'

'Oh, my – that sounds exciting. I'm tempted to send back the tickets just to see if you'd keep your promise.'

Kincaid pulled her face close to his and said, 'I hate to disappoint you but I've never wanted to hurt anybody unless they were trying to hurt me. And even if I lived on human blood I wouldn't be able to take any from you.'

'Ah-ha! I've won,' she said. 'That means we're not going to California.'

He kissed her and said, 'No, it doesn't. It means we haven't made up our minds yet.'

'I've made up my mind.'

He kissed her again and said, 'It means we haven't made up our minds yet.'

3

When *Death in the Afternoon* was published, Major Cranston, assuming it was a book about armies and wars, sent off for it immediately. He had never read anything by Ernest Hemingway but he was aware that he had written a book about the fighting in Italy called *A Farewell to Arms*. He had bought that book the year it came out, but after glancing at the notes on the dust-jacket, he had put it away somewhere in his library of military volumes and hadn't seen it since.

When *Death in the Afternoon* came to him in the post, he sat down in his study at once with a cigar and a whisky, and opened the book. Within minutes he realized he'd made a bad purchase. He closed the book and rang at once for John Trout. When the butler appeared, Cranston handed him the book and said, 'This bloody book's about bullfighting. Send it back to the wretched bookshop and tell them I won't have it in the house. And tell them not to bill me for it because if they do I won't pay.'

Even the slightest disappointment or change in plans was always interpreted by Major Cranston as evidence of a conspiracy against him by persons either known or unknown. In the case of the returned book on bullfighting he was angry at both Hemingway and the bookseller, a timid bewigged gentleman named Roland Starkey. For several days he muttered their names to himself as he stomped about the library or the great hall in his riding-boots. Only because he was thus sensitized to the name Ernest Hemingway did he notice the article about him in the London *Times*.

He read the article with renewed anger, hoping to find further grounds for indictment of the author he had so recently come to detest. He sneered at every fact and opinion in the article. But one small segment caught his eye and stayed with him.

Commenting on Hemingway's work habits, the author of the article revealed that Ernest often read the Old Testament and wrote long letters to friends in the morning. 'To warm up' before he turned his attention to whatever story or novel he was working on just then.

Among his other self-deceptions, Major Cranston had always thought of himself as a writer. He had spoken of it so often to his fellow officers through the years that some of them had come to believe him and had chatted among themselves about it. 'Old Cranston will give us all a start one day, I expect. Some new revelations about regimental life, I shouldn't wonder. Or a steamy bit about the young lieutenant and the commander's wife.' The fact was that, aside from sloppy entries in his day-book and infrequent business-like letters to Margaret and Sophie, Cranston had never written, or even attempted to write, anything of an original nature.

Since his retirement, however, this literary impotence had been nagging at him. Because he had begun to take solace in a fantasy that the definitive act of his military career would be a book of memoirs, beginning on the day he arrived in India and ending on the day he was sent back, during the war with the Germans, to England, to his hateful duties at a military hospital.

The prospect of such a book, of the opportunity to express his love for the regiment and to vent his anger against certain superior officers and ill-informed aristocrats in Whitehall, was a tonic to him. It buzzed in his head constantly, drunk or sober, and gave additional fuel to his arrogance. But aside from illegible notes scrawled on match-books, paper napkins, and when in full creative fire on shirt cuffs, there was no written evidence of his passion to produce a book.

Consequently, the comments about Hemingway's work habits gave him fresh stimulation. He would eliminate his writer's block by writing to his friends, to his enemies, to family members, to himself, if necessary. He would warm up as Hemingway did, by expressing himself in raw and direct language, venting his passions and convictions, slaying his enemies, and clearing the battlefield for the definitive and final struggle that would produce at last his significant book.

The morning after reaching this conclusion, just after breakfast, he went straightaway to his study. Taking a glass of brandy with him, he sat down at his desk. He had decided that his first targets would be his own family, starting with Margaret.

I'm very conscious of the fact that we live in your ancestral home, rich in history and all that rot, that the income from this estate is your money, that, in short, you are a wealthy landowner and I am not. Even in India, I was aware that certain ambitious people sought us out because of your name and your family – the magnificent Wiswells.

The Major's wife is a fine lady. So they say. And no one ever questions that. No one comments on the fact, however, that you have tried to subjugate me from the start. Tried to confiscate my identity and force me to question my own worth. No one acknowledges that.

It's plain to see, for example, that our daughter is, in fact, your daughter. No doubt of that. Everything is yours, is it not? I'm surprised you've stayed with me. Perhaps it's because you count me too as one of your possessions, to be stored among the Wiswell heirlooms and family portraits.

Reading over what he had written, Cranston felt a flush of pride and accomplishment. 'Not so staccato,' he told himself. 'Be more detailed and expansive.' Taking out fresh paper he chose his second objective. This time it was Sophie.

I come from a family of men. I had three brothers. No sisters. My mother regretted that she never had a daughter. I regretted it also. I would have liked to have a sister.

When you were born I was proud and delighted. Looked forward to having a close relationship with you. Father, daughter. Advice and guidance. Respect and affection. But it didn't work out as planned. You were your mother's creature from the start. She taught you to hate India as much as she hated it.

After your grandparents died, when you and Margaret went back to England, I knew I'd never see you or your mother in Delhi or Calcutta again. And I didn't. Then, at last, I came home to stay. But it hasn't been a home for me. I've been made to feel like a liability, an encumbrance. Damaged merchandise.

This is not to say that I'm not treated in a civilized way. I am. But only that. You and Margaret are unbearably polite, very respectful to me when we're taking our meals, going out of your way, it seems, putting on a bit of a show, I expect, for the staff. Once we've left the breakfast-room or the dining-hall, however, you disappear, everyone disappears like a puff of smoke. Your children the same. Very polite. But nothing extra. No time to spend with the old gentleman.

As you know, I have no affection for Arthur Tagg.

No damned respect for the man. He's a bloody opportunist. Takes too damned much pride in his university degrees. But he at least gives me some of his time. Not on a regular basis, mind you, but occasionally, rarely, when he has stooped to include me in a discussion of estate matters, he will also linger long enough to take a cup of tea with me – never takes a drink, that chap, damned odd – and then we have a short chat about politics or world affairs. But then he's off too. Quick as a quail. Through the double doors and gone.

Tagg's son, Evan, when he used to be about, would occasionally, not often, play a bit of snooker with me. Then he'd be off too. No great investment of time. Snooker and a cigar. Then off and running down the corridor and up the stairs.

That's it then. That's about the size of it. Thank God for my mates at the Hawk and Swan. Without them to chew the rag with on the odd afternoon, I'd go dead mute in a fortnight.

Having touched on the Taggs, Cranston decided on a frontal assault, first on Arthur.

You're an odd bird, Tagg. Not a familiar type at all. You're not a lady's man, God knows. But not a man's man either. Don't know what to make of a chap who never takes a drink or smokes a decent cigar. Damned strange habits.

You know your place, however. I'll give you that. Solid upbringing someplace in your background. In spite of the fact that Mrs Cranston has always given you the run of the house, you still treat me like the master. It astounds me that I see you so seldom, but when I do, there's no doubt in my mind that you have proper respect for my authority.

On the other hand, your manner with my wife and daughter is a bit free and easy. Not improper, mind you. I would never accuse you of improper behaviour. I'm a good judge of men and I can tell you're not that sort. But all the same, old fellow, you are staff, aren't you? A bit more distance is required, it seems to me. There's altogether more familiarity, more laughing and use of first names than I would have permitted if I'd been on the grounds when you and your boy first arrived here. Sets a bad example, that sort of thing.

Since you have daily consultations with Mrs Cranston I'm sure you won't be surprised to learn that I thought you were redundant once your tutoring talents were no longer needed. But my wife wouldn't hear of it. She's a fiercely loyal woman. Got quite nasty with me, as a matter of fact. Said some nasty things. But I insisted. And since I am the master here, she had no recourse but to agree with me. At last, however, I relented. I told her I would keep you on if you could be trained to take over some of my duties as estate manager. She agreed to that and so far I have been satisfied with your work. I can't deny that you have tried to be helpful. That gives me more time to myself. Anxious to make a strong start on the old memoirs, set the record straight on a few matters.

Intoxicated by his rate of production, not preoccupied with accuracy of facts or the quality of his prose, Cranston didn't pause to read over what he'd written about Arthur Tagg. He plunged ahead with Evan.

It's a damned pity you were too young for the war. You might have made a decent soldier. And in any case, the experience would have put some fibre into you. I daresay you'd have come away with an ambition to do

236

something a bit more challenging than making up little stories and turning them into playlets.

But you missed it and there's nothing to be done. I had some chaps your age under me in India. Bright fellows, for the most part. Educated. Good families. Career officers. Eager to please. Quick to follow orders. Responsible. Respectful. And bloody good companions in the mess. Sing round the piano. Drink for drink with their fellow officers. Hands off the dark-skinned women. All-round decent chaps. Far from home. Doing their bit. Educating the natives. God and the King. Clean water and good drains. Schools and hospitals. And now the bastards want to throw us out. Not bloody likely is what I say. But there's a new breed in Whitehall. No feel for the Empire. No sense of the Commonwealth. They don't understand what we've done in India and round the world.

As for the radicals in Delhi and Calcutta, too much profit to the Crown, they say. Meaningless point of view. Of course we've profited. But at the same time we've lifted ignorant people out of the Middle Ages. Introduced them to the Church of England. Put britches on the men and taught the women to cover up their breasts. Decency and cleanliness. No more using the streets as a lavatory.

It's a rotten shame the military can't play a bigger role in government. Too much theory now, too much of an accent on values and extenuating circumstance. All of us in the regiment knew that a decisive officer, even when he's wrong, even when he makes a mistake, is more valuable to the regiment than a thinker. We built the Empire by telling people what was good for them, not by discussing it with them. Civilization depends on the willingness of people to obey orders.

Cranston put away his writing materials, locked the pages he'd written in the drawer of his desk, poured himself a whisky and soda, marched to the windows and looked out across the terrace to the formal garden. 'By God,' he said to himself, 'I'm on to something.'

4

'I've been remiss,' Sophie said. 'I can't believe that I haven't seen you since the afternoon when you and Kincaid came to tea. But as you know, that turned out to be a great occasion in my life. Since then it seems that everything has been topsy-turvy. In the most marvellous way.'

'It's I who have been remiss,' Mrs Barwick said. 'I've been trying to schedule a lovely party for you and Kincaid ever since your wedding but my home is a zoo each year from early December to late January and my life is a shambles. I am just now beginning to sort out matters that should have been dealt with six weeks ago. I am told by physicians and foolish friends that a woman my age must look after her health and conserve her strength, keep a lighter schedule. But I'm having none of it. I cancel more appointments in a week than most people make in a month. And for every one I'm forced to cancel, two others fall into place. Hundreds of people insist that I am absolutely necessary to them. I know they're lying to me but I behave as though I believed them, as though my presence in their homes at a given moment was indeed a critical necessity.'

They were having lunch together in the dining-room of the Stafford. As soon as they were shown to their seats, the waiter brought a wine-goblet of gin and put it down in front of Mrs Barwick. 'They know me here,' she said.

'Gin is my life's blood, you see. I don't over-indulge. Just three or four glasses each day, strategically scheduled. *Boodle's* gin and frequent naps. That's my secret. I can drop off to sleep for three minutes, or five minutes, and be totally restored. And I can do it anywhere. Standing, sitting, or leaning against a tree. Leonard Woolf says I could go to sleep standing up in a dinghy.'

For lunch Sophie ordered cold salmon and fresh asparagus. Mrs Barwick had a bowl of lobster bisque, cassoulet of snails, a pan-fried trout, and a cut of rare beef with roast potatoes. 'I eat to stay thin and fashionable,' she said. 'Or so my doctor believes. At one time he insisted that I must eat more to put on a bit of weight. Then I asked him to dinner one night and he saw how much I put away. Since then he's made no mention of my eating habits. One thing I don't do, however, is poison my system with salads and green vegetables.' She called the waiter over then and asked for a double portion of trifle with clotted cream.

Sophie realized at once that there were no breaks in the conversation when one was *tête-à-tête* with Rosamund Barwick. As she daintily chewed her food and sipped from her wine-glasses, which the waiter kept properly filled, Mrs Barwick skipped, like a humming-bird tasting blossoms, from one subject to another. 'I fail to see why people attack Willie Maugham with such gusto. Of course, he's a silly vindictive man sometimes and he often writes before he thinks. But he has skill. And time will sort out, as it always does, his best from his worst. He sees the world for what it is and of course that makes him cynical. But it also gives a weight to his books and plays that they wouldn't have otherwise. I say why not vilify Galsworthy, who's just been awarded the Nobel prize for literature? A ghastly and careless choice. Confusing to gifted young writers who aspire to excellence and who still trust their elders to have wisdom and good judgement.'

As she spooned up her lobster bisque she turned to *Brave New World*. 'Just published,' she said. 'Huxley showed me the manuscript a year ago. I told him it would be popular and successful for all the wrong reasons. I also told him he's done better work in the past and he'll do better in future. He didn't like to hear that but he knows I'm right.' Then, 'Keynes just sent me a copy of Henri Bergson's new book. I read it through like a good child but was bored beyond description. It's about morality and religion. Neither of those topics interests me. I told Keynes that, and he gave a great sigh as he always does when he thinks someone he admires has said something stupid.'

When Sophie brought up the subject of the presidential election in America, Mrs Barwick said, 'He's an intellectual, he's an aristocrat, and he's rich. He should make a perfect President. All leaders should be from the upper classes. Working people don't want one of their own kind to rule the country. Certainly the Americans don't. They've had a nostalgia for a king ever since the Revolutionary War. They won their freedom but they lost their way.'

As she deftly incised the trout with her fish-knife she said, 'T. S. Eliot is mesmerized by the Chinese. He says the next century will see the resurgence of the yellow race and the decline of us poor pale Anglo-Saxons. I told him to concentrate his vision on Germany. Let's deal with that situation, I said, rather than bemoan a time we'll never live to see. That odd little chap they call Hitler may do us all in. Eleven million votes he received in the election last year. His party won 230 seats in the Reichstag. He's anti-Semitic, maniacal, and shrewd. A deadly combination. Poor Edward Bernstein must be restless in his grave.'

During her meat course she spoke only of death. 'When one is my age one never hears mention of the word. Even the death of a canary or a pug-dog is a forbidden subject. What no one realizes is that all old people turn first to the obituary page to see how many people they've outlasted. Don't smile. It's true. One's friends begin to disappear. First, one at a time, then two or three each month, and at last like the victims of an epidemic. So one must find a way to soften the blows, or one would be weeping constantly. Each year, by the end of March, I lose count of how many I've lost since the first of January. I've always had hundreds of friends. In every country. I rejoiced in that fact. Now I've come to see that, because of all those friends, I now have an endless number of people to mourn. I don't have to check my diary. The names rattle off my tongue like a catechism: Arnold Bennett, Hall Caine, Frank Harris, all old and treasured friends, many of them younger than I. Gustave LeBon, Arthur Schnitzler, Vachel Lindsay, Dwight Morrow, Nellie Melba, Sir Thomas Lipton, and Anna Pavlova. All of them, and many more, in 1931. And last year, to name just a few: Lytton Strachey, René Bazin, Edgar Wallace, and Lady Gregory. And Hart Crane, a fine American poet who was just over thirty years old when he died.'

She studied Sophie carefully for a moment. 'I see you have a properly serious expression on your face. We all learn to exhibit sadness and concern when death is the subject. But now, having recited a long list of the recently dead, I must point out to you that every single person I mentioned, including Hart Crane, all those people, truly lived and used themselves in ways that conquer death. Their lives make death irrelevant. My father once told me, "There is one critical piece of advice to give to a young person: *use yourself*." Those who don't understand that wisdom are beyond help. Those who do understand it are as close to immortality as man can be.'

After she finished her trifle, when they had ordered coffee and liqueur, only then did Sophie ask the question she'd been waiting to ask. 'Tell me about Julian Thorne. What's he like?'

Mrs Barwick smiled broadly. 'Ah ha! At last. I've wondered for weeks when you would ask me about him.'

Sophie told her about the steamship tickets and the cabled invitation to be his guest in California. 'Of course,' Mrs Barwick said. 'That's Julian's style. He's famously generous. Such gestures mean that he likes you, or he's anxious for you to like him. Or both. It could also mean that he's determined to do business with your husband. Julian's far more generous than most of us. But he has a strong sense of self-interest as well. Through the years he has given me a great deal more than he's received in return. But the things he did receive were very precious to him. It's an intricate equation, you see, when one deals with men like him. Having said that, I must confess that I don't know another man like Thorne. That's why I've continued to see him through the years. He always interests me. And I'm not sure why. Perhaps it's because of his vitality. He's continually in motion. He seems always to be growing. The fact that he often discovers things and ideas and artists long after the rest of us have discovered them is beside the point. He truly believes that he discovered Monet and Utrillo. On the other hand, he was the first person I knew who owned a Münch. Sometimes he's hopelessly silly. Obstinate and trivial. But he's not cruel. At least, I've seen no evidence of it. And as I've discussed with Kincaid, Julian is helplessly vulnerable when he's in England. This country represents something to him that even he, I'm certain, could not articulate. Clive Bell, who's met him several times in my home and likes him, says, "When the rest of us die we'll go to heaven, when Julian Thorne dies he'll go to Maidstone, Kent."'

'Is that the secret ingredient? Is that the explanation for his pursuit of Kincaid?'

'Perhaps. But it's not quite so neat as all that. You see, Kincaid is not a prototype of the English gentlefolk that Thorne prefers to cultivate. Thorne first became aware of him, I believe, when he was trying to collect a few shillings by reciting Shakespeare on Shaftesbury Avenue. Kincaid was not married to you then, had no friends in London, and owned nothing but the clothes on his back. Also, I did not introduce Thorne to Kincaid. I found out about Thorne's interest in him only when the staff at the Cromwell told me he had asked permission for a photographer to take pictures of Kincaid while he was on stage. I realized at that point that Thorne had some interest that was connected to his business. Since then, of course, since he's been talking to your husband, Julian has kept me informed about their meetings, just as Kincaid has. I assure you, he is very serious about his intentions. He believes that Kincaid has a bright future as a film actor if he wants it. The point I'm making is that I have not been the architect of this scheme. Thorne hasn't been courting Kincaid because he thinks it might please me. As I've told Kincaid, I have in the past persuaded Julian to employ some of my out-of-pocket writer friends, and in one instance a composer, but this time no such conversations took place.'

'So you believe,' Sophie said, 'that all this generosity is strictly a matter of business.'

'Not strictly perhaps, but primarily. He also sees a chance, I think, to do a bit of sleight-of-hand. To present a new face, a new young man, that his competitors don't know about. By promoting Kincaid, he promotes himself and his studio, and scores a triumph over his rivals. Apart from the money and the occasional awards and statuettes those film people regularly present to each other, there are few opportunities for self-congratulation. So even a trivial matter, like which actor's name will be printed in larger type, can seem to be of world-shaking importance.'

'It all sounds hopelessly silly to me.'

'Of course. But when fame and money are cooked up together the result is always silly. Success and achievement are not synonymous and wealthy men are often not valuable men. But most people will instantly trade achievement for success and sacrifice value for wealth. So Julian's business, silly as it seems, is only symptomatic of a far more general circumstance. Does that make sense?'

'Of course it does. That's why I would hate to see Kincaid involved in that shadow world.'

'Very good,' Mrs Barwick said. 'That's what it is. Shadows on a screen in a dark room. But because millions of people are eager to pay money to sit in those dark rooms and watch those shadows, men like Thorne collect Renoirs and Louis Quinze settees, and live like rajahs among their groves of palm trees. I suspect that you and I would be surprised if we learned the details of how our ancestors managed to accumulate the great land-holdings that have made us so relaxed and secure.'

Sophie smiled. 'I wouldn't be surprised at all. I know a great deal about the early Wiswells. They were cunning rascals.'

'So there you are. The more we change, the more we stay the same. Commerce is the common language, as it's always been.'

'Tell me the truth. Quite apart from Julian Thorne for the moment, don't you think it's madness for Kincaid to take any of this seriously?'

'I can't answer that. It's something he'll have to decide

for himself. I don't see it as a crisis, whatever he chooses to do. He can say yes or no. Or he can say yes and then say no later. We're not talking about a choice that can't be changed.'

'I think he feels it would please you if he said yes to Thorne,' Sophie said.

Mrs Barwick lit a cigarette. 'As I told you, I have no stake in this. When I first heard about it, I was delighted. I saw it as an opportunity for a penniless young man to earn some money and perhaps even make a career for himself. So I encouraged him to explore the possibilities. That's all. I take it he's still interested in pursuing the matter or you wouldn't be asking me these questions.'

'You're right. I think I was hoping secretly that you would tell me some nasty secret about Thorne, about his dishonesty, or unreliability, or something, that would put the whole matter to rest once and for all.'

'But why would you want to do that?'

'For Kincaid's sake, I suppose,' Sophie said.

'Do you think he'd be pleased to hear that Thorne is a disreputable man, someone who's not to be trusted?'

Sophie shook her head. 'I doubt it. I think he likes him. But at least it might help him to make up his mind.'

'You mean it would give him a reason to put the whole thing out of his mind?'

'Yes.'

'Let me ask you this. What if Thorne made him an absolutely incredible offer? Wouldn't that also help him to make up his mind?'

'What sort of offer do you mean?'

'I mean a handsome offer. A great deal of money.'

'We haven't even discussed that part of it. I don't think any amount of money was mentioned.'

'Perhaps not. But it will be mentioned. And I'm sure

you'll both be stunned if the time comes when Julian discusses terms.'

Sophie smiled. 'I don't think anything like that would stun Kincaid. He doesn't seem to be much concerned with money.'

'Of course he is. All men are. That's one of the ways they measure themselves. With many men it's the *only* way they measure themselves. Their wives also measure them that way. And later on their children do the same thing.'

'Don't misunderstand me,' Sophie said. 'I know I was blessed at birth. I've never had to think about money and I never shall. I'm extremely grateful for that. And I don't feel guilty about it in any way. When I think about it at all, it gives me a warm feeling that my parents, my children, and Kincaid and I can live as we choose, doing harm to nobody else, enjoying our lives, being a part of the world, and having the good fortune to have no financial anxiety.'

'I felt exactly as you do when I was your age. But gradually I discovered that the most painful anxieties have little or nothing to do with money. Look at your parents and your children. Can you honestly say that their economic security has lessened any other problems they may have? The fact is that money only solves money problems. Everything else has to be dealt with on its own terms.'

'I'm not sure I understand.'

'I'm saying that people who were raised as you and I were raised have no conception of the internal workings of a person whose life has centred on one activity and one goal: survival. A wealthy person who loses his money still thinks and feels like a rich man. Someone who grows up poor never gets over being poor. No matter how much money they accumulate, they still scramble to survive.'

'You're talking about Kincaid now, aren't you?'

'Of course. He's a tricky subject, of course, because he's unique. Unusual protective colouration. Changes plumage as he moves from room to room. Looks at home in street rags or a morning-coat. Able to speak like a cockney drayman, an Oxford don, or John Gielgud. Perfectly at ease, it seems, in all settings. But we mustn't be deceived by that. That ability to conceal himself may be the definitive clue to Roy Kincaid. One thing is certain. Behind all those shifting screens is the Australian street-urchin, begging and stealing and sleeping in doorways. Since I've been inside your lovely house I don't have to be told how splendidly you live. I'm sure Kincaid is aware of every tiny detail in your home. But the life he lived for twenty-four years before he met you hasn't disappeared. Nor has the man who lived that life.'

'I feel as if you're warning me about something.'

'Not at all. Just because I'm old doesn't mean I'm wise. Age is guaranteed to bring dry skin and poor eyesight but not wisdom. Some of the stupidest people I know are eighty years old. Also, I don't presume to know a lot about Kincaid. I've known him a bit longer than you have but you undoubtedly know him a great deal better. Nor do I think I'm an expert about men as a group. I've been involved with a great number of chaps but my last serious love-affair, when I was sixty-seven, turned out as badly as the first one, when I was fifteen. I had two husbands along the way. One of them married me for my money. His name was Tom. The other one, Darby, left me *because* of my money. The irony is that Tom had more money than I did. But he wanted still more. Darby, on the other hand, was as poor as a man could be. When he met me I was pretending to be penniless in a garret in Montparnasse. We got married and were poor together there for almost three years. When I brought him to London at last and we came to my house in Russell Square, when he realized who I was and what sort of people I came from, there was a look of betrayal on his face that has been fresh in my memory ever since. I was afraid he would leave me that very day but he didn't. He stayed with me for almost a month. Then one morning he went out to buy me some flowers. Or so he said. But he didn't come back.

'When Tom left me it was for quite a different reason. He met a corrupt widow who had more wealth than Tom and me combined. She was most anxious to corrupt him, it seemed, and he was eager to be corrupted. So they married and as far as I know lived a corrupt and happy life together.'

Sophie smiled. 'None of this, of course, was as matter-of-fact as you make it seem.'

'Not matter-of-fact at all. I was heart-broken on both occasions. If this were a novel by one of the Brontes, I would be more destroyed by the loss of my poor Darby, a gifted and gentle man who seemed destined for destruction. But the fact is that my separation and divorce from Tom was the low point of my life. After him it never occurred to me to marry again. When he died, twenty years after we'd separated, I wept for days. And unless my memory is failing me, I haven't wept since. What a bastard Tom was. But he was a precious bastard to me.'

'I know what you're saying to me,' Sophie said, 'or at least I know what I'm getting from it. Because Kincaid is a man, because he is a certain sort of man, I should be wary. I should not be surprised if he's unable or unwilling simply to slip into my rhythm of living and take root there. He may have a need to define himself in his own way. Is that it?'

'You put it very well. But as I said, you mustn't think that I'm advising you. I'm not. I do know, however, how I would try to behave if I were in your position. Shall I tell you that, or should I keep it to myself?'

'I'd like it very much if you would tell me.'

'I would tell myself that what I do is not nearly so important as what I don't do. A great number of things have happened to Kincaid in the past six months, many of them the result of chance rather than planning. I would be careful to insure, as much as possible, that the next few decisions he faces be decided by him and no one else. Suddenly he's found himself in a different world, different from anything he's known before. So it's important that he be allowed to function, forced to function, if necessary. He's independent by nature. But he's suddenly involved with high-powered people. You, Thorne, and Evan Tagg. And me to a certain degree. He needs to prove to himself that he can hold his own in the game. He has to be allowed to take some chances, to make some mistakes. If he were my man, I'd encourage him to do that. What he might do is not nearly so important as how he feels about himself while he's doing it.'

5

Alan Winkler had gone to school with Hale Gossett. 'Why don't I send your play over to Gossett?' he said to Evan. 'He's a crude and tactless bastard and he's not to be trusted, but he's produced twelve plays in the West End in the past eight years, so he must have learned something.'

Two weeks later, Evan had a telephone call from Gossett's secretary. 'We're ringing you about your play, *The Father House*. If you're free tomorrow afternoon at three, Mr Gossett would like to have a chat with you about it.'

Gossett was a tall and rumpled fellow, brindle hair worn long and allowed to flop over his forehead. Tweed

249

lounge suit, dark-blue shirt, wool tie, and brown brogans in need of polish. Cigarette saucers on his desk, well-filled, ash on his jacket and tie, and a haze of smoke hanging inert in his office, catching the bars of afternoon sunlight through the window-glass.

'You're a young fellow,' he said to Evan. 'Under thirty, I'd guess.'

'Thirty-two.'

'Go on. I'd put you at twenty-six. Thirty-two, eh? Well no matter. Winkler, the rotten sod, tells me this is your first play. Maiden effort, they call it.'

'Actually, I wrote five plays before this one.'

'Trust Winkler to get it wrong.'

'Those plays were never produced.'

'A learning process, is that it?'

'Something like that,' Evan said.

'Did your university work at Oxford, did you?'

'That's right.'

'Not much help to a theatre man, going to Oxford. Nothing theatrical there, would you say?'

'I was reading English literature.'

'That's what I say. Nothing there to prepare someone for the business of noises off, curtain lines, and the leading man pissed on opening night. Another world, right?'

'I suppose so.'

'Ever gone to bed with an actress?'

'Don't believe I have.'

'Never slipped down to Brighton with a nice little sticky bun who's making her way from Bristol Rep to the Haymarket? Good experience for a writer, I should think. Good fun as well. Awfully keen to please, those little doxies, anxious to display their emotional range. Drop their knickers and display their bit of talent. Especially keen on playwrights, I'm told. Kindred spirits and all that. They tend to fuck actors for fun and writers for the intellectual experience. They'll roll over for a producer-chap like me as well but there's no camaraderie to it. More of a down payment towards future employment, I expect. Not a lingering experience. Not for them. No dallying or experimentation. No exchange of sexual anec-dotes. More often than not they like to get you on your back, do the straddle bit, and pump you like an engine till they've taken whatever you've got. Then they're on their feet in a twinkle, knickers in hand, and off to audition for a Hungarian play to be produced in a church annexe in Hampstead. A great number of people take it up, you know, the theatre life, for just those little rewards. Slap and tickle in the wings, ride the pink horse in the loo, a quick stand-up-and-cheer in the phone-box backstage. Theatre's my whole life, the man says. But that's what he means.'

Gossett stubbed out his cigarette and lighted a fresh one. 'Now, let's talk about your play. Damned good effort. Powerful. Family play. Always an audience for that. Needs some work. May need a good bit of work. On the other hand, we may say to each other, in a friendly manner, "Let's not touch the little bugger. Let's leave it as it is." Raw material. Loose ends. Dangling preposi-tions. Ragged and primitive. That sort of thing goes down well these days. Mustn't tie things up too neatly. *The Father House*. Not sure what it means but it has a good sound. Opening curtain: nothing going right. Final cur-tain: things worse than they were to start. I like that. It's modern. A bit of Ellerbie by way of Chekhov. But none of the sweetness Ellerbie sticks in there just to tickle the matinée ladies. No treacle or horse-dung in your play. No jokes. No musical turns or clog-dancing. No audience either, we may discover. But let's give it a go. I'll have my solicitor draw up an agreement. Standard terms. You won't get rich in any case from a play like this unless some esoteric bugger decides to turn it into a film. But I'll give it a first-rate production and keep it running as long as we can keep the rabble trickling in. How does that sound to you?'

'It sounds fine to me. I didn't expect things to go forward so quickly.'

'Well, there's no point to cocking around, is there? After all, I've had the play for two weeks. I read it the first night. Sent copies off to Geoff Bingham, and Hardwicke, and Roger Livesey the next day, and told Charles Streeter at the Criterion that I expect to have a good serious drama for him in a few weeks. Hardwicke, it turned out, is committed to a film in America and when he gets back he's set to do *The Late Christopher Bean* at the St James. Livesey's off to do *Dr Faustus* in Edinburgh and won't be back till June. So he's out too. But we had a bit of luck with Geoff, who was my first choice in any case. He's just come off *Too True To Be Good* and *For Services Rendered* and was scheduled for a Shaw comedy at the Haymarket. But Ann Todd pulled out for undisclosed female reasons and announced the next day that she would be appearing in *Where Ladies Meet* at the Lyric. So I caught Bingham at the proper moment. He goes into *Wild Decembers* later in the year but for now we can have him. He's damned keen on your play and he had a good thought for the mother. Mary Cecil. Ethereal quality. Pale innocence. Did a play with her three years ago. Did my best to take her to bed but she was having none of it. Loyal to that rotten husband of hers, I expect. But God knows why. Anyway she's as keen as Bingham is and they work well together, so we're all set. Except for the boy. And I know I can get Donald Rugger for that. He's almost eighteen but he can still play twelve and all the pansies love him. Bruce Applegate says he'll stage it for us, so we should be ready to go ahead just about any time we say. A few weeks from now you may be seeing your face in the daily papers, young Mr Tagg. On the other hand . . . you know what I mean. Chancy business we're in. No business at all, some people believe. But as Baudelaire said, "One man's meat is another man's *poisson*." Maybe we'll find a place for a few jokes like that to liven up your second act.' A hearty laugh then from Gossett. 'I saw you wince, you coward. Thought you were in for trouble, didn't you? Bloody producer going to wreck my play. Add a few songs and a dancing bear. Not a chance. I won't change a thing. If the play fails I'll see that everyone knows it was your play. It it's a big success, I'll let them assume that I'm the one who made it work. Welcome to the real world. If you don't shoot yourself I think you've got a future.'

6

Millions of people who came to know Kincaid by watching him in darkened cinemas believed they knew him well. Regular exposure to his imperfect face, magnified to full-screen size, and his penetrating voice, also magnified, by hidden speakers, had persuaded them that the total man had been revealed. Regular readers of *Silver Screen* and *Photoplay* magazines, as well as the film technicians, the grips, the juicers, and the prop man felt the same way. He was what he seemed to be: a self-contained, self-reliant, hard-edged man.

The people who knew him best, however, Sophie and Evan, Sarah and Trevor and Rosamund Barwick, realized how much they didn't know. When pressed for details about his life before he came to London at the age of twenty-four, he sometimes said, 'Why go into it? I don't feel sorry for myself and I sure as hell don't want

253

somebody else to feel sorry for me. Things are good for me now. I have a fine life. So why should I dig up a lot of things that weren't so good?'

As we have seen, he was extremely generous about himself in press interviews. Information, anecdotes, and revelations flowed freely. But after the first few months of these stories, no one believed anything he said, nor did they resent it. They accepted it as a form of entertainment. One columnist, Arnold Danish, concluded, 'He's not a born liar, as some have said. It's a device he uses to guarantee his privacy. Kincaid is a male Garbo. He not only wants to be alone, he insists on it.'

If he had chosen to tell the simple facts about himself, to Sophie or to anyone else, if he had decided to give a chronological account of his early years, this would have been the result:

'I was born near Nubeena, a village on the Tasmanian Peninsula, just off Wedge Bay and eleven kilometres from Port Arthur. My mother's name was Kania. She died in childbirth when I was born. I don't know who my father was. I've never known. I don't know if Kincaid is my real name or if it was simply made up and given to me by the Constables. August and Stella Constable were an elderly couple who had a small farm just south of Nubeena. They kept goats and sheep and chickens and two cows. They had an orchard and a large vegetable plot. Subsistence farming. They never tried to pretend they were my parents or grandparents. They were hard-working, silent people. They spoke very little to each other or to me. They got up with the sun and went to bed again as soon as it was dark. They fed me and gave me a place to sleep and clothes to wear. And as soon as I was old enough I had daily chores to do. We had no close neighbours. I never saw another child till I was four years old. The Constables rarely spoke about my mother, but when I remembered later certain things they'd said, I concluded that she had worked for them as a servant. Sometimes they mentioned Murduma when they spoke of her. Later I learned that many years before, there had been an aborigine settlement at Murduma and some of their descendants still worked in the forests and sawmills.

'Still later, when I was a seaman, I shipped out with an aborigine from the Bass Islands named Sam Langenna. He told me that Kania is the aborigine word for swan. When I was sixteen, working in a butcher's shop in Sydney, I spent all my free time in the public library. One day I found a list of all the prisoners and guards who had come to the Port Arthur prison from England. In 1870, only seven years before the prison was shut down, a man named Kincaid had arrived. Part of a contingent of marine guards. I decided that he might have been my grandfather. But the trail ended where it started.

'When I was six years old there was a hard winter in Tasmania, especially on the peninsula where we lived. Mr Constable got sick and died, and three weeks later his wife died in the hospital at Hobart. Some people from the Methodist church in New Norfolk found out about me and arranged to have me brought to a small orphanage they'd started there, in the old toll-house on the Derwent River. I spent two good years there. They worked us hard and they were strict as hell but we slept in beds and had enough to eat and they taught us to read and write and do arithmetic. They had a small library, mostly history and religion, and I read every book I could get my hands on. The place wasn't run like a prison. Some of us would be sent into town on errands. And once a week usually, they'd give the boys a few hours' free time. I always crossed the bridge, walked north-east on the river-bank, followed the trail beside the Derwent till it met the river Lachlan, then back into town, down Pioneer Avenue to

Burnett, across to Montagu and over the bridge again to the toll-house.

'I still remember those walks I took, looking at the solid hills on all sides of me and thinking it was the best place I could ever hope to see. I didn't want to leave there. But one day they called me in and told me I was going to live with a man named Doc Bozeman and his wife, Edna. They were there in the office waiting to take me along, two husky people with thin lips. He was a butcher and I rode to Hobart with them in the lorry he used to carry sides of beef from the slaughter-house to his shop on Salamanca Place. As I walked behind them to the lorry, Edna Bozeman said to her husband, "Don't growl about it. His skin's fair enough and he looks Irish. So nobody will know the difference. He'll get by."

'I wasn't adopted. Nothing official like that. Someone was paid off, I expect. I was taken on as an unpaid labourer. I washed, swept, mopped, polished, cleaned up blood and guts, and slept in the tool-room behind the butcher shop. I stayed there for almost two years. Then one day when Doc took me along to deliver meat to Glenarchy I hopped off the truck, ran into the wood beside the road and headed for New Norfolk. When I got to the orphanage at last, they called the local constable's office. Bozeman told them I'd stolen three butcher knives from him, as well as eight guineas from the money-box. I didn't mind much when they sent me to a juvenile work-farm just west of Swansea. I thought anything would be better than living with the Bozemans. And I was right.

'I never was afraid of going to jail after that. I knew I could eat there and have a place to sleep. And all my mates would be in the same fix as I was. Also I got to go to school again. Three hours every night. From six to nine. All day, from sunrise till late afternoon, we went out in work crews. Road work, sea-walls, masonry, sheep-shearing – any jobs within twenty miles of Swansea that wanted doing. I liked the outdoor work and the life with my mates, a few of them my age, most of them two or three years older. Picking pockets, pinching money, stealing food and whisky were the subjects they discussed most often.

'When I was thirteen they released me. Gave me a few shillings and a coach ticket to Queenstown. Told me I'd be likely to find work there in the copper mines. But I didn't. Work was slow at the smelters and any available jobs were given to the lads coming home from the war. Also they kept asking me how old I was. I told them sixteen but since I had no papers to prove it they didn't believe me. I was husky for my age and had work-calloused hands but no beard or moustache. So they saw me as the boy I was. After going hungry for a week, I stole a ride on a timber lorry going north to Zeehan. The same story from the smelters there. So I found work as kitchen-boy in the Hotel Lockman. They gave me a room and my meals and three pounds a month. Ten hours a day, seven days a week. But there was a library in Zeehan at the Methodist church-house and I was allowed to take books home, so I could read in my room at night.

'The reading was my undoing. The parson took an interest in me, questioned me to find out my age. Said I was a bright lad and he intended to see to it that I would be sent back to Hobart and then to a proper school. After my experience with the Bozemans, I wanted no part of Hobart. So I stole a ride on another lorry. For Queenstown again, then on to Strahan. There, on the docks, after five days' looking, I met a first mate who took me on as a galley-lad on an ore boat bound for Melbourne. The cook turned out to be a drunken bloody pervert but I kept him off me till we got to Melbourne. As soon as we

257

tied up I was down the gangway and hiking up Bay Street towards the city centre. I walked through those streets – Collins Street, Bourke Street, Elizabeth, and Lonsdale – and everything around me smelled of money. I was fourteen years old, full of energy and optimism. I knew there had to be opportunities for me in a city like Melbourne.

'A week later I was in jail for stealing food. Two weeks in jail, the magistrate said. When I was released he suggested I move north. Wangarotta. That area. Short of help there, he said, on the sheep and cattle stations because of all the young chaps who'd been killed in the war, or who'd taken grants of land from the government, trying to make a go of it on their own. The magistrate was right. South-east of Glenrowan I found work on a cattle station. A decent man named McBride. Worked my tail off but he treated me like a human being and he taught me what he knew about raising cattle. It was the best I'd had it since the work-farm at Swansea. The blokes working for him were a good lot. Chewing plug-tobacco, drinking themselves blind two nights a month when they got paid. And having fist-fights just for fun. To pass the time after supper and to burn up energy. I had at least one fight a week when I was there. I lost the first twenty or so. Then I began to win every other one. By the time I left McBride's station nobody wanted to fight me. They said, "That little bugger will do anything he can think of to hurt you."

'Why did I leave? The trip from Strahan had done something to me. It opened me up. And when I saw Melbourne something else slammed open. Maybe the world was filled with cities like that. That's what I thought. And since ships went everywhere in the world, why was I choking on dust and sleeping on a straw mattress at a cattle station in Victoria? No good reason, I told myself. So I drew my wages and bought a cheap ticket on the train to Sydney. But I couldn't find a ship there and it began to look like Melbourne all over again. So I settled for a meat-market job on Pott's Point. Another beefy rum-pot bastard of a butcher. Named Kilty. Slaughtered pigs and rabbits in his basement. Also skinned a dozen house-cats a week and sold them as rabbits. Every night, as soon as he closed the shop and I'd finished cleaning up, I prowled the streets looking for another job. Finally I found one on Atherden Street at a pub called Dugan's Schooner. Hard work again but I was close to the docks and most of the customers were seamen. I talked to as many of them as I could. Told them I was looking for a ship. Finally, after five or six months, it paid off. Not a galley-helper this time. An apprentice seaman. On a ship carrying timber to Belgium. The morning we weighed anchor and headed north-east towards the Panama Canal I felt just born but old as the world. I was seventeen.

For the next seven years, except for the times when we were in port or I was in jail, I was always on the sea. I shipped out on a dozen different ships and we tied up at every major port in the world. I was drunk and disorderly in Capetown, Lisbon, Bombay, New York, Marseilles, San Francisco, Rio, Buenos Aires, Oslo, Shanghai, Singapore, Jakarta, Havana, Honolulu, and many more. At the end of my first voyage I lay on my bunk in the harbour at Antwerp and told myself I had found a good way of living, a profession I could follow for the rest of my life. I expect I would have stuck to that idea if I could have stayed out of jail. As I learned the language of the sea everything about it appealed to me. It's a solitary life. All seamen are loners when they're sober. They volunteer nothing about themselves and they don't ask questions. The work-schedule is rigid and the food is good. But best of all for me was the feeling that everything started fresh with each new trip. The world became as small and manageable as the size of the crew. No one cared where I came from, or what I'd done before I walked up a particular gangway. For two months, six months, or a year, for as long as I stayed on that ship I could present myself in any way I chose. If I decided to stay totally inside my own skin I would be defined solely by my work. I was, for the first time in my life, an equal among equals.

'But as I say, jails and prisons changed all that. It started in California. California was a bad-luck place for me. All my mates fell into trouble when they were in California ports. Anything seemed possible there, in those days. All the bootleg liquor you could drink and women waiting on every corner. Plenty of orange juice to sober up with. And a jail on every square, it seemed, to accommodate you when you tried for something that wasn't available.

'My first time in San Diego, a six-day lay-over there, I wandered south to El Centro and had a long uncomfortable stay there in the Imperial County jail. A year later, California again, I was sent to the Chino institution for juvenile offenders. One to three years. After eighteen months I was released. I got on a tired old coast-wise ship that sailed to Seattle, Vancouver, Sitka, Anchorage, and back again. For eleven months I stayed peaceful and quiet. But then I picked up a ship in Vancouver that was going through the Panama Canal to Boston. And in Boston I got into trouble again. A big Italian kid decided to work me over outside a snooker parlour in South Boston and I put him in hospital. They arrested me for aggravated assault, the judge found out about Chino and El Centro, and he put me away for two years in the state penitentiary at Worcester. I did the full two years. Till October of 1931. A week after they released me I was lucky enough to get on a ship bound for Bombay, with further stops in Zanzibar and Mozadishu. Then on through the Suez Canal to Gibraltar, up the coast from there to Le Havre and London. I jumped ship then with Joe Dock, the dwarf, and a week or so later we were out in the street doing our act together, trying to earn a few shillings as buskers.'

· CHAPTER 7 ·

1

Five days after Kincaid and Sophie sailed for New York on the *Bremen*, Evan's play went into rehearsal. As he sat with the actors, the director, and the producer round a table on an empty stage, as he listened to the rich familiar voices of Geoff Bingham and Mary Cecil speaking the words he had written, he was thrilled. But only for a moment. Gradually, in his ears, those words began to sound familiar, then banal, as though he had heard them in other plays many times before. When he stole quick glances at the faces around the table he thought he saw boredom there. Gossett, who looked as though he hadn't slept the night before, seemed ready to nod off. And Applegate, the director, had a vacant expression in his eyes, as though his mind had wandered away to some more inviting place. Once or twice he made odd suggestions or comments which indicated to Evan that he was not really familiar with the text. The actors mumbled, coughed, smoked incessantly, and had grim expressions on their faces. Only an occasional bark of laughter from Bingham broke the rhythm.

During a break in the reading, Bingham refilled his pipe, took Evan by the elbow and steered him to the protected alleyway just outside the stage door. As they strolled back and forth in the damp rectangle of space,

Bingham said, 'By God, Tagg, I think we're on to something. A good sniff in the wind. Bluebirds flying. As soon as I read the play I rang up Gossett and said, "The lad's got an instrument, no doubt about that." Always some place to go in these scenes. Choices, you know. Woop and warf. Pull and tug. Conflict. That's all it is. That's what we're about, all of us jesters who stick on the crêpe hair and putty noses, and strut about on the boards. Conflict and resolution. Let old pussy out of the bag, then try to stitch her up again. Boy without a mother. Fine premise. Sensitive lad in search of a ghost. Making her up. Walking her about. Bringing her to life. Measuring the bastard father against her. He is a bit of a bastard, isn't he, the father? Don't mean to restructure your work for you, don't think that. No patience with actors who don't respect the playwright's intention, squirming about trying to put a stamp on the role that has no place there. Never been accused of that myself. Never will be. Content to play what's written. Bring it to life. Put a bit of spice in the stew perhaps where spice is required, but no bloody attempt to grab the writer's hat and cock it on my own head. No patience with that, by God. So when I say the father in your piece is a chap the audience might like to put a whip to I think I'm in harmony with the text. We won't plaster it up, I promise you. No painting the lily. That's not my way. No reason to glower and swear and stamp about to show the balcony birds that one's a rotter. Better to play against it. That's my notion always. Treat a whore like a lady and a lady like a whore. Nothing more hateful than a bastard who's trying to prove otherwise. So that's the tack I'll take, I expect. Let the words do the work. Don't tell the audience the same thing twice. That's my rule. Tell them as little as possible. When they jump in and decide a few matters for themselves, once they've done that, you own them for the evening. So we're off to a smashing start unless I miss my guess. Good troops. Proper personnel. Gossett's a bit of a twat on occasion. Unpredictable fellow. Not a theatre man at all, one thinks at times. But then he'll make a clever move, lift out one bit and drop in another and skin your eyeballs. He's the new breed, I expect, so we'd best get accustomed to them. Able to make up his mind, no doubt about that. I know actors who'd slit his gizzard with a smile but even they admit that he keeps the ball in the air. Relentless once he's taken on a job of work. And the best thing about Gossett, save the best to the last, he lets people do what they're hired for. He won't piss around with your play and turn into something it's not meant to be. Won't let the actors do it either. Won't ride Applegate like a steeplechase jockey. He'll let us do our jobs.'

A few days later, when they had tea together near the theatre, Bingham said, 'Exhausting time for a writer, these early days. All stumbling about, it must seem to you. Fish on dry land. Lines coming out wrong. No contact between the actors. Questions, discussions, nothing quite specific, dropped cues, wrong moves, endless repetitions of one page of dialogue. Time to pack up and go home. Give it over. Everybody gets that itch at this stage. The boy Rugger is out to sea. Doing another play. Hearing a different drummer. Poor sweet Mary is trying everything she can think of. Changing her voice. Doing a wounded sort of walk. Still looking for the character. Close to tears she was last night when I dropped her at home. But give her a week, give us all a week, and all at once the lights will flash, the kettledrum will send out a roll, and you'll see your play come to life in a way you never imagined. After that, day by day, tiny scraps of colour and texture and movement, of calculated hesitation and electric anger will stick it all together like a fine watch. That aimless silly Rugger, a chap you wouldn't

264

send out to buy crumpets if he weren't an actor, will turn his head to the light or do something with his thin little voice, and you'll have a lump in your throat. And Mary Cecil will break your heart, of course, because that's her gift. Don't ask me what I will do. That remains a mystery. I will learn my lines, stagger about from one place to the other, and if I'm fortunate, as I often am, when the curtain goes up and we have our audience, they will believe that I'm more proficient than I am, that I have indeed become the person you intended me to be.'

After one week of rehearsals, Mary Cecil, who had kept very much to herself since their introduction to each other, came to Evan one afternoon at the end of rehearsal and said, 'Could you spare me a few minutes? I'm having some problems and perhaps you'll be able to help me.'

They sat in the lounge of the Guildford and had a whisky. 'I suppose I shouldn't ask you this question,' she said, 'but I'm groping in every direction I know, so I'll take the chance. How much of this play is autobiographical?'

Evan had anticipated this question and had carefully prepared his responses. For his father's sake, he had chosen to tell any falsehood that was necessary to make sure that no audience, no critic, no newspaper might conclude that *The Father House* was about Evan Tagg's father. 'It's all contrived and made up,' he said. 'Nothing autobiographical about it. There's been no such trauma in my life.'

She smiled. 'Score one for me. When I first spoke to Gossett after I'd read the play, he said he was positive you'd written about your own life. But I said you seemed altogether too secure to have gone through such a childhood.'

'I'm not certain that I'm all that secure but I assure you I didn't write about myself.'

'Can we talk about the character I'm playing then? Is she modelled in any way after a living person?'

Evan shook his head. 'Not consciously. I made no effort to do a portrait of someone I know.'

She smiled. 'Not consciously, he said.'

'That's correct. No one can guarantee what goes on in the subconscious.'

'Of course not,' she said. 'That's a dark and swampy place.'

'I can only say that when I reread the play or hear you speaking the lines, I don't connect what I hear with anyone I know. I don't know how these things normally work in the theatre but since I've been watching you in rehearsal I've had the feeling that you are the character.'

'Oh, God, how wonderful. Now, if only I could feel that. I think maybe I'm thrown off by the fact that she's not real, that she exists only in the boy's mind. I keep thinking I should play that, make that clear to the audience.'

Evan smiled. 'If the play doesn't make that clear, then we're all in trouble.'

'I know that of course. In the abstract. But how much does my character know? Does she think she's a real woman and a mother, or does she know she's simply a product of the boy's imagination?'

'All right, let me ask you this,' Evan said. 'Let's assume the play had a different intention and a different text. What if the mother had died two years before the action starts. The boy had lived with her for ten years of his life. So he doesn't imagine her. He remembers her. Would that be a different problem for you?'

'Yes, I think so.'

'To the audience she's still unreal in a way.'

'That's true. But they know she was real in the past. So I'd play her that way. As I would any other part. It's impossible, in any case, for an actor to become a ghost. We can't be diaphanous. We have to take the position, since no one I know has ever seen a ghost, that ghosts look like people. If it's not true, it's still a theatre truth.'

'Exactly,' Evan said. 'And I think that's the only position you can take in this case.'

'You think this imaginary woman can simply be played as a documentary human being.'

'No. Fantasy has its own rules. We can't show her having a foot-bath or eating cucumber sandwiches . . .'

'But the boy knows she's imaginary.'

'Not exactly. He's made her as real as he's able to. He's satisfied with the result and we must be too.'

'And the audience will accept that?'

'Of course they will. They want her to be real for the boy's sake.'

'And what about the father? What does he see? What does he believe?'

'The father is a dual role in a sense. His scenes with the boy are real life, father and son. But when we see the father and mother together, then both of them are imaginary. They speak together as the boy fantasizes them. The process may be fantasy but the result is totally real and recognizable.'

'I'm still floating a bit,' she said.

'Remember what I said a moment ago? I said as I watch you on stage you have become the character I wrote. The character was imaginary until you made it real.'

She smiled. 'Clever, aren't you? I think I'm starting to see the light. Are you saying I can simply play this part as myself?'

'Exactly. A young married woman with a child and a husband. Fantasy is worthless if it doesn't seem real. Do you have children?'

She held up one finger. 'A daughter. Twenty years old.

Blissfully married to a veterinary surgeon and living in Cardiff.' She smiled. 'You're supposed to say, "I can't imagine that you could have a twenty-year-old daughter."'

'You're a mind-reader.'

'The Cecil women marry young. I was barely eighteen when Angela was born.'

When they left the Guildford she said, 'My car's just down the way. Can I drop you somewhere?'

'What if I told you I live on Chelsea Embankment?'

'Then I'd whistle you up a taxi. I go the other way, I'm afraid.'

'Actually, I live in Gordon Square.'

'Then you have a lift. We're practically neighbours. I'm just to the north of you. In Charlton Street.'

As they drove along Bloomsbury Street, past the British Museum, she said, 'Do you have children?'

'No wife, no children. I'm a celibate playwright.'

'How nice for you. I've never met one of those before.'

'Nor have you now,' he said.

'I suspected that.'

2

Two days before the play was scheduled to open, as the cast was walking through a lighting rehearsal, Gossett came up to Evan where he was standing at the back of the Criterion. 'You're supposed to be drinking yourself blind in the nearest public house. Or nibbling on your fingernails. Opening-night jitters, old chap. Are you immune to all that? A few days from now we will have revealed ourselves in public, naked to the bone, you the most naked of all, and you're standing here, limp as a rag, like a pensioner watching a cricket match. How do you explain that? It's high-stakes roulette, you know. All or nothing. I'd like to see at the very least a trace of perspiration on your upper lip.'

'I'm taking my cue from you,' Evan said. 'You don't seem a bit nervous so why should I?'

'Ah, but mine is a different case. I have nothing to lose but money. I have no reputation, so that's not at stake. You, on the other hand, are about to see your child dissected by a cruel and dispassionate mob whom we generously describe as an audience, led on by a coterie of native trackers who call themselves critics. This lot, an ill-mixed pudding of procurers, rum-pots, pederasts, and unfrocked academics will pool their combined ignorance and reach a decision about you, about your gifts, your potential, and your commercial value. The extremes are these. There's a remote chance they will call you a genius, the equal of Shaw, as biting as Maugham, as accessible as Novello. There's a much greater chance that they will savage your play, both its conception and its execution, sympathize with the poor ill-advised actors, and suggest that you and I and Applegate open a sweet-shop in Camden Town. How does that strike you? A little more apprehension now, I expect. Intimations of mortality perhaps.'

'Not at all,' Evan said. 'After I watched the first dress-rehearsal last night I felt as though I could never ask for a better presentation of the play I wrote. I hope people will like it. If they don't there's nothing to be done.'

'God save us from a reasonable writer.'

'Tell me what you think,' Evan said.

'You want the truth, I assume.'

'If you can manage it.'

'I see you've come to know me well,' Gossett said. 'All right, as difficult as it is for me to give a serious answer to a straightforward question, I'll make an effort. This has

269

been the most worry-free, seamless production I've ever been involved in. I had come to believe that tears and profanity, character defamation, and threats of castration were vital components of the theatrical process. I'm not accustomed to actors who like each other or directors who like actors. When the sets are properly built and installed on time, when the costumes fit and the props work, when the programme printer makes no mistakes, I start to worry. But when I sit in the theatre, as I did last night, and find no flaws in what I'm watching, when the actors are brilliant and fired with energy, when the light cues are perfect, and, most frightening of all, when I have tears on my cheeks at the final curtain, I can't help feeling that something's gone terribly wrong. You ask what I think? Since I've never had such an experience before I have to conclude that we've got a disaster on our hands.'

3

The morning after Evan's conversation with Gossett, a cold rain fell in London. Road surfaces in the city were treacherous. Donald Rugger, heading for the theatre on his motorbike, skidded into the side of a lorry and fractured his lower left arm. When he arrived at the theatre that afternoon he seemed strangely exhilarated by the experience. 'I'll use it,' he explained to the director and his fellow actors. 'My arm's in a cast. It's a good symbol. I'm playing a wounded young chap.' He patted the cast. 'Fits the character.'

'It's not that sort of wound,' Applegate said. 'It's his bloody heart that's broken, not his bones.'

The following morning, the day before opening, Geoff Bingham's manager rang him up to say that a motion picture Bingham had agreed to do in July had been moved forward. 'They expect you to start filming at Pinewood next week.'

'But I'm up to my hobs in this play. It wants my full concentration. I can't be skipping back and forth to Pinewood just now.'

'I got them to promise there'd be no night shooting. And they'll work around you on matinée days. That's the best we can do. We're committed, Geoff. And they're committed to Rank. It's a bloody nuisance, I know, but I'm afraid there's nothing to be done.'

On opening day the cast did a final run-through in the morning. Then they went home to rest and to concentrate their thoughts on the evening performance. Mary Cecil, however, whose habit was to be in her dressing-room at least two hours early, returned to the theatre only forty minutes before curtain rise. Her eyes were swollen from crying and there was a dark welted bruise on her cheek-bone.

Under the circumstances, Evan felt the performance went well. The house was filled, the audience was attentive. The applause at the final curtain was not thunderous but it was warm and appreciative. The actors took three calls. But the atmosphere backstage was tentative and subdued. Gossett, in a short speech, congratulated the cast and the support people, everyone praised everyone else, then all went off to drink or to sleep. Evan slipped out of the theatre alone, hailed a taxi, went home and went to bed.

The critiques in the newspapers were neither enthusiastic nor brutal. They were kind to the actors, particularly Mary Cecil – 'A rare, heart-breaking portrait of a wounded woman' – and they praised the production details. About the play itself, and about the playwright, opinions varied. From each review, one or two observations, usually negative, stayed in Evan's mind.

The Times
Evan Tagg has a gift for dialogue and a sense of character. But structure is not his forte. And in this work he has tried to solve a problem of time and space that would baffle a master.

The Daily Telegraph
It would seem that Mr Tagg has a future in the theatre. But he must learn to be more objective about his material. This play, for all its potential impact, is weakened by its obvious use of the playwright's personal experience.

The Daily Mail
The ring of truth, the shock of recognition in this play, may be its downfall. All of us are aware of family cruelties. Few of us enjoy seeing them replayed in detail on the stage.

The Observer
Fantasy in the theatre presents problems. When it must survive inside the structure of a family play, the obstacles may be insurmountable. When Evan Tagg learns to attempt less he will achieve more.

The Guardian
There is a villainous quality about the father that almost overwhelms the play. It makes for strong theatre but an uneasy audience. One senses a personal involvement on the part of the writer that is unseemly. Surely Tagg can't be writing about his own parent. If he is, we pity both him and the father.

There were also complimentary passages, of course, but the negative views were the ones that Evan could not forget, particularly the one from the *Guardian*. He prayed that Arthur would never see it.

The Father House ran for two weeks. Sixteen performances. The slim young men who attended all the plays in which Donald Rugger appeared were in the audience for this one too, many of them for more than one performance. At the curtain calls, they stood, applauded tirelessly and shouted 'Bravo', or 'Brava', depending on their perception of Rugger. Two of his particularly intimate acquaintances, when they returned to the Criterion a second time, had their left arms enclosed in casts, as his was.

Many of the ladies who were loyal fans of Mary Cecil also attended. But a great number of Geoff Bingham's admirers stayed away, discouraged, one assumed, by the critics' description of his role. By the time the closing notice was posted backstage the audiences had begun to thin out. Gossett's speech to the company after the final performance was brief and unsentimental.

'No regrets,' he said. 'Not from me. And none from you, I trust. I loved the play. I love it still. And I love all my actors. We did our best but we didn't find the audience we had hoped for. Not enough tickets sold to keep us running. We've all seen it happen before. And we'll see it again. So God bless you. I thank you and I hope we'll all work together again soon.'

Evan waited till he thought Mary Cecil would be changed. But when he went to her dressing-room she had already gone. 'Put on her coat and left straight away. Didn't even take off her make-up,' the dresser said. 'But she left this note for you, Mr Tagg.'

Evan walked back to the empty stage, tore open the envelope, and read the message.

You dear wonderful man. We failed you. It's a lovely, important play and we didn't do it justice. I simply

273

couldn't face you. I'm going to Cardiff to weep and stay drunk for a week.

As he walked slowly towards the exit Bingham caught up with him. 'There you are, Cocky. We're the last two into the lifeboat. Gossett and Applegate vanished like bloody ghosts. Afraid they'd have to pony up for a whisky, I expect. So bugger the bastards. You and I will take over the nearest grog house and make a reputation for ourselves.'

'I'm afraid I can't do it. I . . .'

'No excuses, old dear. The ship went down, no fault of ours, and we two survivors must cling for a moment to the wreckage. Absolute requirement. Success can be handled carelessly. But failure's another matter. It wants caution and close attention. Warm hands and fresh nappies.'

They walked to the Bluebell. Bingham strode through and found a sheltered table in the snug. 'No visitors welcome tonight. Geoff Bingham's not receiving. No carpet stretched door-to-kerb for strangers. No pretty little tarts laying hands for luck on the old actor's hump. A bottle of Irish, two glasses, and two new-found friends conducting a post-mortem on a child that went awry. Ugly word, post-mortem. Don't like it much. Not keen for the process either. When I was a young actor, younger than you, I had no time for such rot. Did my work and went to my bed with whoever was the lady of the moment. But I learned my lesson. Found out there was a value to post-mortems after all. When a play collapses, for whatever reason, it's good to ease the old girl down. Don't just drop her in the nearest dust-bin and toddle off. Bad medicine. Gives you nasty symptoms after a bit. An ugly fit of bad conscience. Bobby Newton said to me once, "A play is not a strumpet, not a little doxy you roll in the hay for a quick half-hour. You live with a play, eat and sleep with her for weeks; you laugh and suffer together. Hope for the best, try for the finest. So when she's sick you try to make her better. And if she dies, you pay some mind. You give her some attention, the way you would any other lady who has nourished you and tried to keep you warm in the winter. You talk with your companions and try to remember all the good things. If you don't do that, if you walk away as though nothing's happened, you'll feel like a rotten bastard. And you deserve to." Now Bobby was not a sentimental chap and he was pissed to the gills when he said those words, one ugly night in Brighton, but by God he had his head screwed on right all the same. He said something worth remembering.'

Bingham picked up the whisky bottle the barmaid had left on the table and refilled their glasses. 'Don't believe in luck in the theatre. For the most part I think we all end up with what we deserve.' He tapped his fingertips on the table. 'But by God, sir, I think this time we were royally buggered. Bad luck came down on us like a fog. You remember I thought little Rugger was a good choice for the boy. Well, I was mistaken. He's gone thirty per cent deeper into fairyland since I worked with him last. Got his head up his bum now. He's like a cream scone left too long in the sun. Once the curtain's up he's all pirouettes and sly movements. The play gets turned on its arse and Billy Blue Eyes does a little dance for his friends. And to make it worse, he had to cock around and break his arm. I knew then we were sliding off-course. The greatest actor living can't play Hamlet with a bandage round his neck. Put an ear trumpet on King Lear and the play's over. And to make matters worse, Rugger the Bugger handled that cast on his arm as if it was a Byzantine dildo. He did us in. We could have covered for poor Mary but there was

275

no saving the day with our juvenile out of control, waving his bloody arm like a broad-sword.'

'What happened to Mary? Do you know?'

'Everybody knows what happens to Mary. That wretched arse-hole husband of hers gave her his usual encouragement. Whenever she's in a play he bounces her around a bit, not enough to keep her at home, he likes to see her bring in the money, but just enough to mark her lovely face and humiliate her and destroy her concentration. He's an odd bastard. Hates himself and takes it out on whoever's available. Mostly he takes it out on Mary.'

'Do you know him?'

'Of course I know him. Alec Maple. Used to be an actor. Not a bad actor either. I hate to say it but it's true. Had a flair for classical roles. Thin as a heron and a sullen look about him. Played Richard the Third in Liverpool when he was just twenty-five years old and I've never seen it done better. But gin was his downfall, even then. Nasty drinker. And unreliable. Late for rehearsals. Practical jokes during performance. Give you the wrong cue. Never where he was meant to be on stage. Didn't last long in the trade. Nobody wanted to work with him. Never worked again after he was thirty. But he didn't care. Had a few thousand a year from his family and that saw him through. When it didn't he lived off women, borrowed wherever he could, and continued to soak himself in gin. Then he took hold of Mary. A fine young actress, barely seventeen, studying with Basil Digby at his little academy. I don't know where she met a fox like Alec but it happened. He was a hand with women, of course. That lot always are. So she was married and expecting a baby before she had time to retreat or ask questions. My wife, Dorothy, has known her all these years. She says Mary's always been miserable with Alec but she's stayed with him in spite of it. God knows why. She's had a nice career, though nothing to what it might have been, so perhaps that's what saved her. But still he continues to beat on her like a jungle tom-tom. So it's hard to know why she hasn't stuck a knife in his throat or set him on fire in his bed. There's plenty who would cheer her if she did.'

They sat drinking together for more than two hours. For the most part, Bingham talked and Evan listened. When they were close to the bottom of the bottle, Bingham said, 'People wring their hands and moan and wail about the poor producer whenever a play goes belly-up. They believe that he has the most at stake. All wrong. The producer and the director have the smallest invest-ment. If a play goes sour they simply dip into the file-box and come up with the next project. But all the same, the writer and the actors get no sympathy. Most people aren't quite sure what the writer does. Damned few people in the audience have ever read a play straight through. There are still theatre customers who secretly believe the actors make up the lines. It's a cocked-up world we're stuck with, laddie. Vinegar in the honey-pot, kippers in the porridge. So what do the actors do when a play fails? They trot off with their mates, have a few pints, play a bit of slap and tickle, and next day they're in a new play. Or so the public believes. The sad bloody fact is the failure is always ours to swallow. If we'd made different choices, if we'd been stronger or funnier, if we'd been better, the audience would have responded differently and every-one would still be working. That's the way actors think. And that's what I'm saying to you, my young friend. We should have done better by your play. You did your work and did it well. We didn't do ours well enough.' He picked up his hat, cocked it over one eye, and smiled like Beelzebub. 'Of course, the bloody final truth is that I didn't have the proper support. If the other actors had pulled their weight . . . You see what I'm saying? If they'd put the steam in their roles that I put into mine . . .' he winked, 'then we'd have had the triumph of the season.'

4

As soon as *The Father House* was announced in the theatre section of the *Times*, Margaret Cranston booked two stalls for the third week, as well as return rail-tickets to London for herself and Arthur. She planned to announce the trip to him only a day or two before the date so he would have no time to manufacture an excuse for not going.

She was deeply disappointed, then, when she learned that the play had closed. As a compensatory gift, she asked the village librarian in Hexham to go through her file of London journals and put together a folder of press-cuttings about Evan's play. When they were delivered to her, a week or more after the play had closed, she gave them to Arthur as they sat one day in the morning-room. He thanked her, glanced at them quickly, then set them aside so he could proceed with the estate affairs they were there to discuss. But Margaret said, 'No, no, Arthur. It's bad enough that we didn't manage to see Evan's play. The least you can do is read what was said about it.'

'I plan to,' he said. 'I'll take them to my rooms and read every word while I'm having my tea this afternoon.'

'That won't do. Then I'll be deprived of the pleasure of watching you.' She picked up the folder, opened it, and put it on his lap. 'If you won't read those articles, like the devoted father you are, I'll ring for Trout and have him hold you in your chair while I read them aloud.'

That afternoon, as he had tea in his sitting-room, Arthur put the folder away in his armoire. He had tried, that morning with Margaret, to skim over the printed pages, to give the impression of reading without actually doing it. But certain passages leapt out at him and stuck in his memory. And Margaret, true to her threat, had plucked out certain pages and read them to him.

Just as Evan had remembered most clearly the negative comments about the play, Arthur too fastened on the one that disturbed him most, the one he wished most fervently he had not read.

There is a villainous quality about the father that almost overwhelms the play . . . Surely Tagg can't be writing about his own parent. If he is we pity both him and the father.

Arthur had had no contact with Evan since their last meeting. He was torn between an impulse to telephone him to express regret that the play had not been a success and an impulse to wait until Evan showed he was ready to talk about it. He promised himself that he would not reveal to his son that he had read any of the reviews; to that end he asked Margaret to keep secret the fact that she had passed them on to him. 'I'd rather have him believe that I looked them up myself in the library.'

Having handled the mechanics of the problem, Arthur now tried to deal with the substance. But the talent he was most proud of, his ability to concentrate, to conquer the most complex issue by isolating its separate problems and solving them one at a time, seemed to have deserted him. His normal straight-line thinking had become a pattern of concentric circles. Conclusions and solutions refused to stay in place. They tumbled, floated, and ricocheted. Every answered question bred a dozen unanswered ones. Most worrisome of all was the fact that he could not define the principal issue. What was at stake? What was in jeopardy? Was it Evan's respect for him or his for Evan? Did he suspect that he'd lost the love of his son or had his own love always been inadequate?

Arthur was not a man of action. He had never tried to be. He believed that all serious choices are best made in contemplation. But now, suddenly, when his tested methods seemed to be failing him, he had a strong impulse to act, to go to London, to lock himself in a room with Evan, and rip down any wall that had sprung up, or seemed to have sprung up, between them. As he worried this idea, herded it back and forth in his mind, as he struggled with the pros and cons of such a decision, he remembered the details of the last conversation he'd had with Evan. 'I promise, after you have the play behind you, that I will sit down and tell you as much as I possibly can about your mother.'

Arthur began to make specific plans for a trip to London. But something held him back. Perhaps it was London itself, he told himself. Unfamiliar ground for him. Strange terrain. A place that had to be conquered and held at bay. An aggressive city. Not the best spot for the kind of quiet discussion he hoped to have with Evan. As he thought about it, he concluded that their conversation should continue where it had begun. He looked around at his familiar objects and furnishings that Evan had grown up with, and he thought, 'This is our centre. This is where we should talk about matters that concern us both.'

That brought him back to the original question. Who should make the first contact? Should he forge ahead or should he wait to hear from Evan? Or should he simply bridge the gap by writing a letter? That notion appealed to him. At the moment it was the wiser choice, he decided. No abrupt trip to London, no face-to-face contact. And no mention of the play at all. That could wait. Or perhaps it could be quietly put aside, postponed, or never discussed at all. That would be the better way to proceed, he told himself. A letter. With information he had promised last time they talked, a letter about Amy, Evan's mother.

As he moved to his desk, took out several sheets of stationery and began to write, he seemed to forget what his intention had been; when he'd promised to tell Evan something about his mother, his plan had been to fill in the blanks for his son, to correct whatever sins of omission the father might have committed against the child, to paint a gentle portrait of his former wife, to be kind, to lie a bit if necessary, to plant pleasant thoughts and memories in Evan's mind, a healing poultice, a hand-tinted misty picture of a woman the boy did not remember and would certainly never meet.

However benevolent his intentions had been, Arthur's hand betrayed him almost as soon as he began to write.

I promised last time we talked together to tell you about your mother in some detail. Some sentimental weakness told me that I should present her to you in the kindest possible way so that you would feel a fondness for her and believe perhaps that you were the product, as children are meant to be, of a loving and tender relationship between a father and mother.

I would love to be able to present such a picture to you. I would if I could but I cannot. I think the muscles and tendons in my fingers would cramp in rebellion if I asked them to write such lies. I also believe that such distortions of the truth would be damaging, in some way, to you. They would certainly be damaging to me.

The truth is this: I've never forgiven myself for being

such a fool, for marrying a woman who deceived me from the start. I feel dreadful that you grew up without a mother and I feel worse that the mother who gave birth to you was Amy. For years I looked for traits or characteristics that you might have inherited from her, but apart from some pleasant physical features you share (God knows she was pretty) I've seen no evidence of her shortcomings. You have intelligence and a sense of fairness. Those are not her characteristics. If you asked me why I was drawn to your mother in the first place, I would say it was my blindness and stupidity rather than her attributes that brought us together. If reading such things about your mother is distasteful for you, I'm sorry. But I think it's important for you to face the truth about her, just as I have had to do. When you marry I hope you'll remember my mistake and choose a young woman whose background is similar to your own. Then, when you have children, you'll be able to give them a more complete life than I was able to give you.

5

'I've had my spy-glass turned full-round,' Sophie said, 'looking at things in reverse.'

'How do you mean?' Kincaid said. They were sitting at breakfast the day after Sophie's luncheon with Rosamund Barwick.

'It came to me this morning as you were shaving and I was still lolling about in bed. If you were to say to me, "Let's take a reckless trip together. Cross the ocean. Take a look at New York. Then sip champagne in a luxurious train as we cross that wide and primitive country. Palm trees and California at the end of the line. Sunshine and bathing in the sea. Visit the tame Indians and the wild movie-stars. Stay up late, sleep till noon, and have a lovely extravagant time . . ."'

'A honeymoon,' he said.

'Exactly. A proper honeymoon. If you were to offer me such a trip I would clap my hands like a child and race to Southampton to board the first available steamer.'

'So why are we hesitating to accept Thorne's offer?'

'That's what I asked myself. Since it's all make-believe anyway, why shouldn't we have a magical, make-believe honeymoon?'

'I'll be Brian Aherne and you can be Madeleine Carroll.'

'I think not,' Sophie said. 'I mean, I will try very hard to be Miss Carroll if that's what you require but I would prefer to be with you rather than Brian Aherne.'

From that moment on, they rethought the trip to America. In their minds it no longer had a connection with Julian Thorne. No time was spent considering his motives or their responsibility to him. 'We'll be reckless rascals,' Sophie said, 'thinking of no one but ourselves. Sybarites and hedonists.'

'And the devil take the hindmost.'

'Correct. Scott and Zelda will take lessons from us. Noel Coward will beg for permission to dramatize our life together.'

When she wrote to her mother later from New York that original gay lunacy was still dancing through her letter.

My first transatlantic crossing, you know. But God knows it won't be my last. What heaven! What corrupt luxury. If other liners are half as lovely as the *Bremen*, then Kincaid and I may very well spend our declining years (starting tomorrow) crossing and recrossing the

283

world's seas. We have a divine suite on the sun-deck and we're being treated most royally. Champagne always on ice, great bowls of fresh flowers appearing each morning after breakfast.

We are encouraged to live a sinful and indolent life. Kincaid complains that he wears only two costumes: pyjamas and dinner-dress. Not true, of course. We also swim and play shuffle-board. And we are often seen in the sumptuous bar on the promenade deck.

As you can see, we're totally naughty and self-indulgent. Our steward, it seems, serves only us. So we ring for him constantly. He's a West Indian chap, well spoken and unbearably handsome. He caters charmingly to all our needs, both real and imagined. His name is Elgin, and we are tempted to steal him and bring him home to London.

We have cocktails with the captain each evening and we dine at his table. I feel as though I've gained a full stone but Kincaid swears I'm unchanged. If that's true it's because of the dancing. We dance at teatime, during the cocktail hour, and after dinner. At midnight a champagne supper is served, and cold chicken and caviar and pâté can be had in one's stateroom at any hour of the night. I recommend this life to you, my dear mother, and suggest you take it up as quickly as possible.

This shipboard note was enclosed with the letter she wrote from New York.

The pace continues. What an overpowering city this is. All pushed tight together on an island between two rivers, the buildings squeezed up thin and tall, it seems, because there's no room for them to spread out. Crowded, of course, people and motors and trams, like

London, but more workable somehow, because the streets are not higgledy-piggledy like ours but laid out like a grid. Avenues running north and south, streets east and west, from the Hudson River to the East River. And every vehicle and every person in a wild and noisy rush. But sadness everywhere as well. Unoccupied stores, poorly dressed children and great numbers of unemployed men in the streets, just as in London. Almost fourteen million people out of work here in America. Or so the papers say. And yet the fine hotels flourish, the theatres have big audiences, and expensive restaurants are fully booked at lunch and dinner. The world is not fair, is it?

We're here for just five days, leaving tomorrow. At the theatre we've seen *Roberta*, *Men in White*, and, unfortunately, *Tobacco Road*, most of which I couldn't understand and none of which I liked. Tonight we'll see, *Ah, Wilderness* with George M. Cohan. I never dreamed I could ever in my life be so happy.

6

'What the bloody hell's come over you?' Winkler said.

'What's that supposed to mean?' Evan said.

'Pretty obvious, isn't it. I haven't been able to get you on the telephone. I wrote to you twice and had no answer. Now I come here to your flat, it's four o'clock in the afternoon and you look as if you just crawled out of bed. Or maybe you haven't been to bed yet. Which is it?'

'Don't mother me, Alan.'

'Mother you? I don't mother anybody. And even if I did, that's not what you need. From the looks of this place you need a housekeeper. Or a four-man clean-up squad. And from the looks of you, you need a shave and a good wash. What's going on?'

'I've been working on something . . .'

'You have, eh? Looks to me as if you've been working on a bottle of Bombay gin. Smells that way, too. What is it you've been working on? A new play?'

Evan nodded.

'That's good news. What's it about?' Winkler said.

'What?'

'This play you're working on. What's it about?'

'I don't want to talk about it. Don't want to talk it away.'

'I see.' Winkler looked around the room. 'I don't see any pages on your writing-table there. And that looks like your typewriter-case over in the corner.'

'What do you want, Alan?'

'What do you think I want? I'm not selling cookies. I came over here to see if you were dead.'

'Well, I'm not. You can see that.'

'What are you doing, telling me to screw off and leave you alone?'

'I didn't say that.'

'You didn't have to.' He picked up his hat and walked to the door.

'I didn't ask you to leave. I didn't mean that.'

Winkler turned back at the door. 'Don't worry about it. I have to get back to the office. Drop me a postcard some time when you're not too busy writing.'

'You're really pissed-off at me, aren't you?'

'No. I'm surprised at you. I thought you had some balls. I know your play didn't turn out the way you wanted it to. It's a kick in the ass. But it's no reason to sit in the corner and suck your thumb.'

'Is that what you think I'm doing?'

'I don't know what you're doing. You tell me.'

'It's no big headline. I just hit a bad patch. Little things. But all at once. You know how it is.'

'Damned right I do. But how does that connect with your locking yourself in here like a bloody hermit?'

'I didn't decide to hole up here. I just haven't thought of a reason to go out.'

'Then go out just to go out. Go out for no reason. The best way to cure the black-ass is to walk out into the street. Any street. You're not writing, laddie. Don't fool yourself. You're sitting here feeling sorry for yourself, and if you don't watch your step that can become a profession. It doesn't pay much but it can sure as hell keep you busy if you allow it to. If you want an assignment, get a good night's sleep and ring me tomorrow. If you don't want an assignment, then I'll have to find a way to explain to Mr Head why you're still on the payroll.'

'I know you came here as a friend,' Evan said, 'but you don't sound very friendly to me.'

'I'm not trying to be friendly. I'm trying to wake you up. Keep in touch.' He opened the door and let himself out.

Evan moved to the window and watched Winkler walk off down the street towards the Russell Square Underground station. He stayed there by the window trying to restructure the scene they'd just played. He left all of Winkler's questions and statements as he'd spoken them but he tried to create better lines for himself, better than the ones he'd come up with before. But it was difficult. He didn't want to dissect the situation concerning the play, he didn't want to discuss the letter he'd received from Arthur, and he knew no way at all to explain to Winkler about the lovely and vulnerable actress who was afraid of her husband but who seemed unwilling to leave him. Evan told himself that the subject fascinated him because he saw it as the theme for a play. But he wasn't deceived.

7

When Jane Endicott, the headmistress of Sarah's school, rang up Margaret Cranston she said, 'I'm calling you because I've been unable to reach Sarah's mother in London.'

'My daughter's gone off to America for a short holiday.'

'Yes, so I was told by her staff.'

'Can I help you? Sarah's all right, isn't she?'

'I can't say for certain how she is. She didn't report for breakfast this morning, and if her classmates know where she's gone to they're not willing to say. Before I notify the local authorities I wanted to speak with her mother.'

'You're quite certain she's left the premises?'

'Yes, we are. And it appears she may have taken the early train to London. We sent someone to the station to inquire first thing and he was told that a girl who answers Sarah's description bought a ticket to London today.'

'I'm sure she's gone home for some reason. I'll ring my daughter's house and see if she's arrived. Then I'll ring you back as soon as I know something. I'd appreciate it if you wouldn't notify the police just yet.'

'I'm afraid that's a decision I'll have to make, Mrs Cranston. We're very disappointed in Sarah. Our girls don't behave this way. We have a strict code.'

'Of course, you do. And we appreciate that. But I'm sure that we'll be able to have Sarah back with you straight away.'

'You don't understand me, Mrs Cranston. I can't promise you we'll be able to take her back. Our disciplinary group will have to meet and come to a decision. It's not fair to the other girls, you see . . .'

Margaret broke in. 'Forgive me, Miss Endicott, but I have to ring off now and try to locate Sarah. And when I ring you back I trust you will use another tone with me. Is that clear?'

'I don't believe . . .'

'When I send Sarah back to you I expect you to receive her with patience and consideration. She is my grand-daughter. She is not to be dismissed. Do we understand each other?'

'I have my responsibilities . . .'

'That's exactly what I'm referring to,' Margaret said, 'and I'm sure you will handle them properly.'

As soon as Margaret rang off, Ruth O'Haver, Sophie's housekeeper telephoned her, sounding apprehensive. She said that Sarah had rung up from the railway station. 'She told Oliver she was taking the train to Northumberland to see you. I'm very concerned. She should be at her school. Trains are no place for a young girl by herself. Shouldn't we try to reach her mother?'

'No, Ruth. I'll take care of things. You mustn't fret. We'll meet the train at Newcastle and everything will be fine.'

She rang for Trout then. When he came into the room she said, 'Sarah's on the train from London that left King's Cross half an hour ago. Please call Wilson Cuff at York station. Explain to him that Sarah is on that train and ask him to make sure that the conductor is looking after her.'

When Sarah arrived that evening, Margaret said, 'Maureen will draw you a nice bath and we'll have some supper sent up to you. You've had a busy day. So have a good sleep and we'll have a chat in the morning if you like.' She kissed her on both cheeks. 'I'm delighted that you're here. It's lovely to see you.'

Late the next morning they sat together in Margaret's

private sitting-room just off her bedroom. 'I suppose Miss Endicott rang you up,' Sarah said.

Margaret nodded. 'She was concerned about you. That's her job after all, to look after her girls.'

'Well, I don't want to be one of her girls. She needn't look after me because I'm not going back.'

'When did you decide that?'

'I've been thinking about it a lot lately.'

'Did you talk to Sophie about it before she left?'

'No point to that, is there? She'd just tell me I had to stay on and that would be the end of it.'

Margaret smiled. 'That doesn't sound like Sophie to me. I thought you two talked about everything.'

'Not so much. We used to do but not so much now.'

'Since she's married, you mean?'

'I expect so,' Sarah said.

'I don't talk with her so often either. But I expected that. A married woman has all sorts of things to do that take up her time.'

'Good for her. I hope she's happy.'

'Oh, she is,' Margaret said. 'I've just had a letter from her and she's very happy. It made me feel good just to read those words in her letter.'

'Let's not talk about her. What's the use?'

'Why shouldn't we talk about her?'

'I just don't want to.'

'But I do, Sarah. Does your leaving school have something to do with your mother?'

'It will when she hears about it, I expect.'

'Are you going to write and tell her about it?'

'No. But somebody will,' Sarah said.

'I don't think so. I'm the only one who knows how to reach her and I don't plan to tell her.'

'Why not?'

'I don't want to spoil her holiday. And besides there's

nothing she can do in any case. You've made up your mind not to go back so that settles the matter.'

'Won't Mrs O'Haver tell her when Mum calls?'

'No. I've specifically asked her not to. Sophie will be home in a few weeks. You'll have plenty of time to talk things over with her then.'

'A lot of good that will do me,' Sarah said. 'She'll just bundle me up and send me back to Miss Endicott.'

'I don't think so. Not if you're unhappy there. We'll find you another school.'

'I'm sick of school. That's why I left. I don't want to go to any silly school.'

'I'm afraid you don't have a choice about that, dear. You're thirteen years old . . .'

'Fourteen.'

'You're just fourteen years old and you must be in school. The law requires it and your mother requires it. I'll make some calls this morning and we'll find a school for you here in the county until Sophie comes home and we can make a permanent choice.'

'I can't go to some tiresome school here in Northumberland.'

'Of course you can. Mary Magdalene is a perfectly good day-school. Or you could be a boarder at Trumbull's. I'm sure that could be arranged.'

'Can't I just stay here with you till Mum gets back? I could do some reading on my own . . .'

'No, Sarah. That's out of the question.'

'Couldn't Mr Tagg tutor me?'

Margaret shook her head. 'No, dear. Mr Tagg has other duties now.'

'Can't I just ask him?'

'I wouldn't permit it in any case. No matter what he said. You belong in a proper school. You've broken a major rule at Miss Endicott's. I'm sure you know that. I believe she can be persuaded to take you back but I can't guarantee it. If she won't accept you or if you refuse to go, then you'll be required to go to school here in the county. It's not a subject for discussion, Sarah. Do we understand each other?'

'I understand you but I don't think you understand me.'

'If that's true, then you'll have to help me understand.'

'It's hard to explain things to grown-ups.'

'I said those same words to my mother. And your mother said them to me.'

'I just felt different,' Sarah said, 'when I went back to school after Christmas. Things are different. Evan didn't come for the holidays, Trevor has turned into a rotten know-it-all since he's been at St Alban's, and other things have changed too. You know it as well as I do.'

'You're talking about Sophie.'

'Not exactly.'

'Yes, you are. You resent it that she's married, don't you?'

'I wouldn't use that word.'

'What word would you use? Did you expect that your mother would never marry again?'

'I never thought about it. It's a long time since my father died. Did you think she'd marry someone else?'

'I hoped she would.'

'Did you think she'd marry somebody like him?'

'Don't we say his name?' Margaret asked.

'You know who I mean.'

'Are you saying that you're upset because your mother got married? Or are you unhappy with the choice she made?'

'Do you like him?'

'It so happens that I do like him. But even if I didn't I would have to keep those feelings to myself. I love your mother with all my heart but that gives me no right to

292

select someone for her to love. If she's happy with her marriage, then I'm happy for her.'

'Don't you think someone should tell her if they see she's making a mistake?'

'I don't think she's made a mistake. And I know she doesn't think that.'

'Of course not. But she's deceiving herself. I think he's common.'

'I've heard you use that word before. I'm sure it has a very specific meaning for you.'

'My mother's special and important, and he's not. That's what I mean. He's not good enough for her.'

'When I got married,' Margaret said, 'my father didn't think Major Cranston was good enough for me. When Sophie married your father, Major Cranston didn't think he was good enough for her. I daresay when you pick a young man you want to marry, none of us will think he's good enough for you.'

'I've already picked someone. But I know I won't be able to have him. He's older than I am.'

'That doesn't surprise me. It's better when at least one person is a grown-up.'

'Why do you say that?' Sarah said. 'I'm a young woman now, am I not?'

Margaret smiled. 'I admit I haven't thought of you that way until now. But I suppose you are. At least in your own mind.'

'In certain primitive societies, girls are married when they're twelve. I know my physiology, Grandmother. I could have a baby any time I chose to. A town girl in Cobham had twin daughters last year and she was only fifteen.'

'I'm sure there's some wise comment I should make but I can't seem to think of one.'

'Don't think I'm planning to trot off somewhere and

have a baby,' Sarah said, 'because I'm not. The fact is I've given it a great deal of thought and I've decided I may never have a family. There are a great many things I want to do and I'd hate to be tied down with children, as my mother has been. It's a pity she didn't marry again when Trevor and I were small. I expect her judgement would have been better then.'

Sarah and her grandmother spent the entire day together. By late afternoon Sarah had decided that perhaps it would be wise for her to go back to her school in Kent after all. 'I'm sure I'll choose a different school next year,' she said, 'but for now I might as well finish the year with poky Miss Endicott.'

As they were being driven to Newcastle to catch the London train early the following morning Sarah said, 'I want to tell you something but it's only for you. I don't even want my mother to know. I know you don't like to keep secrets from her, so if you'd rather I didn't tell you, I'll understand.'

'Well, perhaps I can make an exception. As long as you haven't committed murder or burned down a building, I think I can give you a pledge of secrecy.'

'You remember, I mentioned to you yesterday that I was in love with an older man.'

'As I remember, you said you'd chosen someone.'

Sarah nodded. 'What would you say if I told you the man is Evan Tagg?'

'Are you telling me you're in love with Evan?'

'Yes. For a long time now.'

Margaret smiled. 'What would you say if I told you that I am also in love with him? That Sophie is as well.'

'I don't mean that kind of love. We were talking yesterday about having babies. That's the kind of love I mean. Lying awake at night, whispering to yourself. Crying yourself to sleep. Have you looked at your photo albums lately? All the pictures of Evan are missing. I have them. I can't stop thinking about him. I have scary dreams about him. So real, I hurt when I wake up. When I read in *The Times* that his play was a failure I cried for two days. I hated myself because I hadn't gone up to London to see it. I knew he must be very unhappy and I couldn't stand the thought of his being by himself.'

Margaret sat silent, her eyes on the green fields as the car rolled ahead. At last she said, 'Does Evan know how you feel about him? Have you told him?'

'I want to. I'm dying to. But it's too soon. He's known me since I was a baby. I see how he looks at me. He thinks I'm still a child. So I have to wait. When he finally looks at me and realizes I'm grown up, then I'll tell him. I know he has a lot of other women and it drives me crazy. But I tell myself it's not important what he does with them, as long as he doesn't get married. I pray every night that he won't do that for the next year or two. Till I have a chance to . . . till I can tell him how I feel about him. I know he loves me. I just have to change things so he'll love me in a different way.'

'What if he can't do that?'

'Why wouldn't he? He will. I know he will.'

8

Because he now identified himself, to himself, as a writer, Cranston was secretly determined that no other writer in the family should eclipse him. This ambition, rather than a specific enmity towards Evan, caused his spirits to lift when *The Father House* played for only two weeks in London. It also stirred him to a new burst of energy on his own behalf. He reread the notes he had previously made and sat down to add new pages.

Our India was all handed over to the bloody Hindus and Muslims. All of it pissed away by those cowardly bastards at Whitehall. Queen Victoria, Empress of India. That was the ticket. England leading the way. Heading the parade. Making a productive nation out of that rag-tag collection of indolent beggars. Giving their children the chance to learn a bit about civilization. Giving them trains to ride and cleaning up their foul water.

British engineers. British soldiers. Sandhurst men. Putting the rag-heads in uniform, the best ones, teaching them to drill and stand watch and fire a weapon.

Nine decades of Crown rule. That's what made a country out of India. Not bloody Gandhi in his white nappies. Not Gokhale, or Tilak either. Screeching about independence and autonomy. Riling up a crowd of fools who didn't understand what they were listening to. Bombs and guns in the hands of animals who'd never had a proper bath. Chopeka and his rotten brother and that lot. Two British officials bleeding dead in the street because of those wild-eyed orang-utans.

Too many meetings. That was the root of it all. Wretched liberal slogans. Fuzzy theorizing. Trying to set things right for every half-naked soul. The job of Britain has always been to make things smooth and right for the British. Dalhousie didn't go out there to spoon-feed every half-wit rabble-rouser with a towel wrapped round his head. We do business. It's what we've always done. Why else would we call it the Commonwealth? And a business wants someone in charge. So the Crown took charge of India. With a top-grade military force on hand to back them up.

By God, we invented India. And when we finally pack up and slip away with our tails between our legs, the buggers will have to reinvent themselves. But that's a job of work they can't handle. No fibre for it. It's not in them. I speak from experience. Firsthand. They know nothing about order. Don't know and don't give a damn. That's why they needed it forced on them.

Canning was a man with the right idea. 'No bloody nonsense,' he said. After the mutiny in 1857 he straightened them out. Put a few rascals to the wall. Taught everybody the rules and the consequences. But by the time I went out, in 1890, we'd lost the reins and the handbrake.

Kindness and patience. Those were the new watchwords. Slogans for cowards. All the cantonments were the same. Kiss brown bottoms. Be sweet and kind to the natives. 'They're just like us except for the hue of their skin.' I never bought that. I was never seduced or persuaded by any of that. Not for a minute. 'They're bloody not like me,' I said. And that's the way I handled myself and the men in my units. 'Demonstrate your power or you'll have no power.' Those were my orders.

Stuck to my beliefs and sacrificed my career. Made the choice and stuck with it. By the time I reached captain it was plain to me that I'd never go higher than major. And I never did. They tried to humiliate me with assignments that were below my abilities. Tried to sway me. But I kept my eye on the straight-ahead.

'You'll be our public affairs officer, Major Cranston.' Or R and R supervisor at Simla. In charge of the British Club in Delhi. Tucked away always. Into a corner. Outside the chain of command.

When the war came it was no different. Barely fifty years old, in my prime, but no combat for Cranston. Second officer at the military hospital in Surrey. Procurement. Supervising non-commissioned personnel.

That sort of rot. And ten days after the armistice, they retired me. Major Cranston. Handy chap to have around as a staff man but chancy as a command officer. Bugger the lot. Bugger them all.

· CHAPTER 8 ·

1

A few days after their arrival in California, Sophie wrote a note to Margaret.

I write in haste. Since we're on holiday why am I in a hurry? I have no satisfactory answer for that. I can only report that, since arriving here, we have been constantly in motion.

Our host, Mr Thorne, has removed all possible problems and anxieties from our lives. We are shamefully catered to. The cottage we had been told about turns out to be a spacious country house with a walled garden and its own swimming-pool sequestered in a corner of the grounds of the Ambassador Hotel. Full hotel services, of course, plus a couple in our staff quarters and a brisk young woman who answers our many telephones, takes messages, and makes appointments for us. A car, with driver, takes us wherever we want to go, and there is also a sleek red roadster if we want to drive to the beach by ourselves.

For Kincaid and me, it's like a splendid circus, a land made for children. Bright birds swooping about, little red trains to ride, towering palm trees, buildings that look as though they were copied from a child's colouring-book, clubs and restaurants that stay open all night, elderly ladies with peroxide hair shopping in silk lounging pyjamas, great sandy beaches with seals and dolphins playing just off shore. And the sun shines every day, it seems.

Also, everywhere we turn we see an English actor we recognize. In these first few days we've met Anthony Bushell, Leslie Howard, Clive Brook, C. Aubrey Smith, Constance Collier, and Ralph Forbes. They all seem to have taken root here. They've formed a British colony, play bridge and cricket and polo, and seem to shun the Americans. Everyone talks about the Depression but these film folk seem very prosperous indeed. It's an unreal life, Margaret, with an almost dangerous quality to it, but for us, because we know our precise departure date, it's a lark. We've gone reckless and impulsive, as if there were no other way to live.

The day after they arrived, they had an elaborate luncheon with Julian Thorne in his private dining-room at Thornwood studios. 'I toyed with the idea of inviting some of your compatriots to luncheon but I decided that since you've just arrived you might prefer something quiet. You'll have unlimited opportunity for social activity if that appeals to you. I have not publicized your arrival, but I expect the local papers will quickly discover you, all the same. There are no secrets in this community. If one is famous anything one does is news. If you're not famous they will try to make you seem so. If you go to parties you'll be in the columns. If you keep to yourself they will write about you as mysterious recluses from England. No malice intended. It's simply the way of our world out here. Gossip is truth. And everyone wants to see their names in print.'

'We don't,' Kincaid said.

'I know that. That's why I'm giving you this indoctrination lecture. The little gremlins who feed information to the papers already know that you've arrived, that you're staying at the Ambassador, and that you're having lunch with me today. The serious gossip columnists, like Parsons and Hopper, will cable their flunkies in London to see what they can find out about you. The others will simply make up things to write. I learned to ignore all that nonsense a long time ago and so did my family. I hope you'll be able to do the same. But whatever you read, please don't associate it with me. As I said, I have made no announcements about your visit and I don't plan to. My publicity people here at the studio have been instructed to volunteer nothing about you and to answer no questions.

'Another warning. You will be flooded with invitations from people you've never heard of. Also from some quite famous people you've never met. Miss Glass, the young woman who's handling your telephone calls, will report to you daily about those invitations. She'll advise you as to which ones might be interesting for you and which ones should be ignored. You can then decide for yourself what to accept. If you accept one invitation you'll get twenty more the next morning. If you turn down all invitations your telephone will never stop ringing. In this city, the unattainable is the most desirable.

'However you decide to spend your time I'm certain you'll enjoy yourself. Southern California is a playground. Some people believe that's all it is. But you'll have a chance to see for yourselves. I've made no secret of the fact that I want you to work with me, Kincaid. We can discuss that at a later date if you like. Or we needn't discuss it at all. I invited you here so you could see my studio and get some idea of the life we Californians live. I just hope you'll go back to England with a nice sun-tan and pleasant memories. If it turns out that we're able to do business together, I'll be delighted. If not, I will continue to count you among my English friends and look forward to seeing you when I'm in London.'

In the next few days the following items appeared in the two major Los Angeles papers as well as the motion-picture trade papers.

The newly-wed Roy Kincaids are in town, living in luxury at the Ambassador. Mrs Kincaid before her marriage was Sophie Cranston-Black. She's the widow of Toby Black, a British war-hero, and heiress to a great English fortune.

Who are the Kincaids and how are they connected to Julian Thorne? Rumour says that Thornwood may soon open studios in England and that Roy Kincaid will head up that operation. Kincaid is a wealthy film distributor from Australia.

Only the select few share private luncheons with Thorne in his offices. Garbo has been there. And Lubitsch. And Mayer. But why English millionaire Roy Kincaid and his wife? Does Thorne envision a movie career for the beautiful Lady Kincaid? In any case, the British colony here will certainly be bubbling with parties for these new visitors.

Thorne's predictions were correct. Invitations began to come in the day after their arrival. Along with those invitations and the telephone messages from Miss Glass came the newspaper cuttings.

'I don't believe this,' Sophie said after she'd read the items. 'Can you believe this?'

Kincaid laughed. 'We can't say Thorne didn't warn us.'

302

'But they've got everything wrong.'

'Not everything. We are in Los Angeles, we did come here from England, we are staying at the Ambassador, and we did have lunch with Julian Thorne.'

'How do they know all that?'

'Lots of spies in town. That's what he said.'

'And this awful photograph of us. Did you know they took our picture when we arrived?'

Kincaid shook his head. 'I saw a photographer or two. Maybe they take pictures of everybody who comes here.'

'Lady Kincaid, the heiress and actress. What poppycock. And you're suddenly an English millionaire. Or would you rather be an Australian film distributor?'

'I'll settle for whatever they want to give me.'

'I know you think it's funny and it is, of course, but aren't there any controls on these journalists? Can they write whatever they choose without consequences of any sort?'

'I'm sure we could hire a solicitor and spend our holiday here sitting in his office, but we want to do that, do we?'

'Of course not. But will this go on all the time we're here?'

'It could do. But I don't think I'll fret about it. I'll tell Miss Glass not to send along the press-cuttings. It's all silliness, but since there's not much we can do about it, it's best to ignore it.'

'Do you believe Thorne? Do you think he had nothing to do with all this?'

'I believe him. But if someone told me he'd taken the opportunity to get a bit of publicity for himself and his studio I wouldn't be offended. And I wouldn't be much surprised.'

'I wouldn't be surprised either,' Sophie said, 'but I would be offended. I'm glad you decided not to get involved with him.'

'Did I decide that?'

'That's what I understood. Before we left London. We said we would treat all this as a great send-up, an escape from reality, a chance to have a lovely honeymoon in never-never land. Isn't that what we said?'

'Something like that. But if I said I've completely given up on Thorne I don't remember that.'

'That means you're still considering his offer?'

'He hasn't made an offer. Not yet. But I'm still considering the notion of talking to him till he makes an offer.'

'I can't imagine any sort of offer that would justify living in this bird-land.'

'I can't either. I don't plan to live here. All I'm planning is to do what we said we'd do. We'll eat some lovely meals, drink some lovely wine, romp in the sea, bathe in our pool here, dance at the Coconut Grove, pour sun-tan oil on each other, and stay in bed for days at a time.'

'Heavenly.'

'When we're rested up, we'll take that snappy little red roadster and drive north along the coast, following any canyon roads that appeal to us.' He picked up the sheaf of invitations. 'And if we want to visit these hospitable actors and hear them gossip about each other, we'll do that. We'll be rude and careless so they'll respect us. We'll arrive late and leave early. And we'll barely touch our food so they'll realize we're accustomed to something finer. Everything's available to you, Sophie. All you have to do is smile, wiggle your pretty hips, and follow me.'

Sophie did, indeed, follow his lead. Their schedule, for the weeks they stayed in Los Angeles, was random, self-indulgent, and immensely pleasurable. They drove as far south as Tijuana, as far east as Palm Springs, as far north as Santa Barbara. They swam every day. The sun bleached their hair and tanned their bodies. In a country where alcohol had only recently been declared legal again, they drank too much every night. 'But how much is too much?' Sophie asked.

'The question is,' Kincaid said, 'how much is too little.'

They saw their first baseball game, their first jai-alai match, their first flagpole-sitter, their first bullfight, and their first marathon dance contest, they met Al Jolson and heard him sing for forty minutes in his own parlour. They danced to the music of Ray Noble and Hal Kemp and Enric Madriguera. They took the great steamer to Catalina and stood on the balcony of the casino looking across the channel to the mainland. They had a Mexican lunch on Olvera Street and dinner in Chinatown. And they listened to Paul Whiteman in the Hollywood Bowl. 'We're devouring everything in sight,' Sophie said. 'We're discovering everything there is out here. Eating it with a spoon.'

And when the impulse hit them they did indeed respond to a few of the invitations that continued to be passed along by Miss Glass. A formal dinner one Saturday night at the Rathbones. An afternoon of croquet and gin-slings at Laughton's. Another sporting afternoon at the Hollywood Cricket Club as guests of its founder, C. Aubrey Smith, and his co-founders, Ronald Colman, P.G. Wodehouse, and Boris Karloff. And there was a polo Sunday at Will Rogers' ranch just off Sunset Boulevard. Douglas Fairbanks, Jr. hosted a cocktail party at the Garden of Allah, and his father and Mary Pickford entertained them at Pickfair. Carmel Myers invited them to a lovely lawn-party celebrating Scott Fitzgerald's birthday. They were also invited, but declined, to spend a weekend at San Simeon, and Tracy, Cagney, Pat O'Brien, and Robert Montgomery had them picked up in a western stagecoach and delivered to a St Patrick's Day party at a saloon they'd commandeered in Culver City, just opposite MGM studios.

As they drove up and down the coast, they made a game of stopping to inspect every house that was for sale. In each case they asked serious questions of the owners or the estate agents, and listened attentively to the answers. 'If we see a house we're madly in love with,' Sophie said, 'we will sell the London house, sell Wiswell Towers, sell my children, and start a new life here betwixt desert and sea.'

Each time they stopped, when they returned to the car, Kincaid asked her, 'Were we madly in love with that sweet little one-bedroom, clapboard shanty?'

'Yes,' she would say. 'Madly but not insanely. I suggest we keep looking, and if nothing better turns up we can always come back here, make the proper arrangements, and settle in.'

One day, as they drove north on the coast highway between Malibu and Trancas, Kincaid suddenly signalled for a left turn, crossed the highway to the ocean side, and turned on to a narrow road.

'Bad move, darling,' Sophie said. 'There's no house here. I saw the sign clearly. Land, it said. Forty acres. We don't inspect land, you see. We only inspect houses.'

'That's true. But since we're rejecting so many houses we might as well reject a piece of land as well.'

The road, more a lane actually, was hard-packed dirt, with eucalyptus trees, like great sentinels, on either side. It wound like a lazy serpent through grasslands on a high bluff above the sea. At the end of the road, in a heavy grove of trees, was the burned-out foundation of a large house, the black chimney, solid still but charred, rising out of the rubble of stones and blackened timbers.

Kincaid and Sophie got out of the car, walked slowly round the ruins of the house and on towards the edge of the bluff, forty metres past the home site. A four-foot stone wall had been constructed along the rim of the land.

It stretched away in either direction as far as one could see.

'Cornwall,' Kincaid said.

'It does remind one of Cornwall. It's so unlike the rest of the coast along here. It's a true headland, isn't it? All rugged and angry and a straight drop to the sea.'

'There's coastal land like this in Tasmania,' he said. 'Almost no one living there. Mining and timber-cutting. Very wild country. Nothing like it anywhere else in Australia.'

They strolled south along the grey wall, vines and wild flowers tangled among the stones, four feet thick, hugging the edge of the bluff, solid earth and shale supporting it: no visible erosion, no rocks fallen away. A clean hard edge, like the western rim of the world, and nothing below that sharp-lined, wall-topped edge but a three-hundred-foot straight fall to the jagged rocks at the edge of the ocean.

A short walk south of the ruined house there was a break in the wall, an opening the breadth of a narrow road. The wall had not crumbled or fallen away. Stones had not been taken off for some other purpose. The wall-end on either side of the opening was finished and well buttressed. 'How odd,' Sophie said, when they stopped to look at it. 'Why would they leave a break in the wall like that? It looks as if someone planned to put a road through that opening.'

'The road to nowhere,' Kincaid said. 'The aborigines do things like that. They leave holes in fences sometimes, openings in walls, even holes in roofs. Not through carelessness. They're all neatly controlled and finished like this one. The younger people don't know why they do it, but they continue it nonetheless. Anthropologists try to say it's some sort of religious symbol, some formal tradition.'

307

'What do you think?'

Kincaid shook his head. 'It's a mystery to me. But I met a very old man when I spent a summer one year in the Bass Islands and he had a good explanation. He said, "That's an escape-hole for the human spirit. A man's soul doesn't always follow his feet. It needs a path of its own."'

'I hate those creepy symbols. They make me nervous. This place makes me nervous.'

'I think it's beautiful. I'll buy it for you, we'll keep a caravan here, and once a year we'll come over from England and give our souls a chance to escape through that wall.'

'Not I, my darling. If I bought this land, which I never would, the first thing I would do is fill in the space in that wall.'

'You're right,' he said. 'I'd do the same thing.'

2

A week before Kincaid and Sophie were scheduled to fly back to New York to board the *Bremen* for their return trip to England, the following item appeared in Justin Gold's column.

This columnist has solved the mystery of Roy Kincaid and his connection with Julian Thorne. Kincaid is not an Englishman as was reported elsewhere. Nor is he a film distributor. He's an Australian performer. Thorne saw him on the London stage and has been pursuing him ever since, trying to convince him to join his stable of stars at Thornwood Studios. Thorne sees him as a new kind of hard-boiled hero. So far, our spies tell us, he hasn't been able to get Kincaid's signature on a contract. His latest enticement: a film about Ned Kelly, the Australian Jesse James, to star Kincaid, of course. Will Kincaid go for it, or will some other studio grab him? We'll keep you posted.

After the first press-cuttings they'd received on their second day in California, they'd asked Miss Glass not to send along any others that might turn up. But this one she included, along with their morning mail and a short note.

Thought you might like to see this clip. Also, you've had calls in the last few hours from L.B. Mayer's office, from Selznick, and from Henry French at Paramount. All of them are anxious to see you. I told them you have a full schedule. Was that the correct answer? Also, Mr Thorne asked if you could call him when it's convenient for you. He'd like to see you at five this afternoon, if possible.

'I can't believe it,' Sophie said. 'I'd better get you away from here or someone will steal you. We haven't finished our breakfast yet and already these strange people are clamouring for an audience. I know you're wonderful and rare and valuable, the answer to a maiden's prayer, but how do they know it? Are those people really reacting to that little item in a trade paper?'

'The sharks smell blood,' Kincaid said.

'Whose? Yours or mine?'

'Thorne's, I expect. It's a game. Mrs Barwick and Lloyd Banks, the Gaumont man, told me all about it. If one studio wants you, they all want you. If one studio drops you, then nobody else will hire you at any price.'

'But these people have never even seen you. You could be Joe Dock the dwarf for all they know.'

'Doesn't matter. If they think Thorne smells money, then they smell it too.'

309

'You're starting to enjoy this aren't you?'

'Of course I am. Who wouldn't? It's a great charade. Like going to the circus.'

'But they want you to ride the elephant. Or maybe the tiger.'

'It doesn't matter what they want. It's all a question of what I want.'

'And what is that, may I ask?'

'I haven't decided yet.'

The maid came into the room then. 'Miss Glass is here. Shall I tell her you're not dressed?'

'It's all right,' Sophie said. 'Have her come in. She's seen us in our robes before.'

Miss Glass was delicate and business-like. Short-cropped auburn hair and glasses on a ribbon. 'There's a great basket of roses at the hall porter's desk. They're addressed to you, Mrs Kincaid. Shall I have them sent in?'

'Who are they from?'

'I didn't open the card but the hall porter said they were delivered in an RKO car. I assume they're from Mr Selznick.'

'I don't know Mr Selznick. Who is he?'

'He's the head of RKO studios. Very important man.'

Sophie turned to Kincaid. 'Do we want Mr Selznick's roses, darling?'

'Why not? They might be very important roses. We will accept the roses, Miss Glass. And please send Mr Selznick a thank-you note.'

'Will you see him if his office calls again?'

'No, I think not. Polite refusal,' Kincaid said.

'With regret,' Sophie said.

'That's right,' Kincaid said. 'Sincere regret.'

'The same for Mr Mayer and Mr French?' Miss Glass said.

Kincaid nodded. 'Exactly. Polite refusal.'

'There's also a gentleman named Fred Benjamin who seems to be killing time in the Ambassador lobby. He's L.B. Mayer's man-of-all-work. The diplomat of the company. He solves problems. I avoided him in the lobby but my instinct tells me he has some notion of waylaying you when you leave the hotel. I assume you don't want to see him either.'

'That's right.' Kincaid said. 'Ask the driver to bring the car round to the garden entrance at half past twelve. We'll meet him there.'

As she rose to leave, Miss Glass said, 'Would you like to call Mr Thorne, or shall I give him a message?'

'Please tell him I'll be at his office at five.'

They had lunch at Perinos. When the captain took them to their booth a bottle of champagne was cooling there. 'I don't believe we ordered champagne,' Kincaid said.

The captain smiled. 'Compliments of Mr Mayer.' When they were seated, he signalled to a waiter, who came over quickly, handed two small gift-wrapped boxes to the captain, and withdrew. The captain placed the boxes just beside their place settings and said, 'Compliments of Henry French.'

As the wine waiter opened the champagne, Kincaid and Sophie opened their gifts: two identical silver cigarette cases, hers monogrammed SCK, his monogrammed RK.

'How did they know we were coming here? What time did you ask Miss Glass to book the table?'

'Just after eleven.'

'Is she telling everyone in town where we are at every moment?'

'I don't think so. She works for Thorne. She's there to keep people away from us.'

'Then how do they know? Is this whole place an elaborate peek-a-boo network? Will we find out sometime

311

in the future that there were cameras and microphones concealed in our bedroom?'

'Ahhh, what a fine idea. A permanent record of Sophie Kincaid doing what she does best.'

'How dare you.'

'What a priceless bit of history. Worth preserving. Worthy of a special place in the gallery of Wiswell armour and antiques.'

'You're really odd, my darling. I've married a very strange man. One of those unusual mammals from Australia.'

Kincaid laughed. 'In answer to your question, a straight and honest answer to your serious question, I'm sure there's no photographic record of what you do best.'

'Can you imagine what it must be like,' she said, 'being actually involved in all this madness? Seeing yourself distorted and deformed by these furtive creatures masquerading as journalists.'

'Have you forgotten the London tabloids?'

'I never read the London tabloids,' she said.

'Of course you don't. But they exist all the same. And they're widely read.'

'Don't play devil's advocate with me, Kincaid. You certainly haven't enjoyed reading this drivel about yourself, have you?'

'Of course not. My point is that it needn't be read.'

'What the eye doesn't see . . . et cetera. Is that it?'

'Exactly.'

'Your tolerance is greater than mine, my darling. My best moments here have been when we were out of town. On the road. Me and the mister, driving along.'

'If you spent a year here you'd probably never want to leave. How do you explain that little British colony we've met? Most of them have taken root. They haven't become Americans. Far from it. You noticed they invite very few locals to their parties. They've simply decided they're a colony, as I said. They see Santa Monica as Brighton in the summer. They've made no effort to adjust to American life. They've made a tiny replica of England, walled it off, and they're smug and contented living inside it.'

'Perhaps they are. But I could never be so adept at fooling myself. Every day I spent here I would be looking at the calendar. Counting the days till it was time to go home. That's what I'm doing now.'

'I seem to remember your telling me yesterday that you were having a smashing time.'

'I always do when I'm alone with you. But all this chaos this morning has intruded on our privacy. If it were left to me, I would pack up and leave for New York tonight.'

'We can do that if you like.'

'Don't be so agreeable. You only become agreeable like that when I've made a totally idiotic suggestion.'

Kincaid smiled and said nothing. She reached across the table and put her hand on his arm. 'Do you think I'd tear you away from all this ahead of schedule? Do you think I'd spoil your fun? All this is fun for you, isn't it?'

'Of course it is. I'm having a jolly time. The business with Thorne and these other motion-picture people is like a trip to Galapagos. Strange new species to be seen. Animals roaring in the night. Bright birds screeching and whirling about. And if I told you it doesn't amuse me to have strangers making a fuss over us . . .'

'Over you, my sweet.'

'Over me, then. If I told you that some adolescent part of me doesn't respond to that kind of attention, I'd be lying to you. Everything that's happened these last few months has been new territory for me. Most of the time I feel as though I'm standing to one side watching somebody else. And now, here we are, in this amusement-park world. And for reasons that escape me, some of these people think I deserve to be treated in a special way. I don't think that. I feel like saying, "Mistaken identity, folks. I'm not who you think I am." I have said that to Thorne. But he pays no attention. And now these people with names I never heard before, Mayer and French and Selznick, people who, as far as I know, have never laid eyes on me, are sending us gifts, trying to see us, acting as if I'm somebody important. If nothing else, it makes me curious. Curious about them and curious about myself. A year ago I had only two things to feel good about. Two accomplishments. I knew I could make a living any place in the world if I had to. And I knew I'd learned how to survive in prison. That was it. Those were my achievements. Now people are telling me they see something in me I've never seen in myself. I don't believe them but they've got my attention. I feel as if I have to find out what's round the corner, what's behind the next door. Does that make sense to you or doesn't it?' When she didn't answer, he said. 'Yes or no?'

Sophie smiled. 'Of course it makes sense to me.'

3

'This is not a pressure meeting,' Thorne said. 'Nothing like that. The fact is I've pretty much accepted the fact that this could be our last discussion of the business at hand. I'm supposed to be a persuasive fellow, but I've had my failures, just as everybody else has. So if you can't be persuaded, then I'll simply have to add your name to my failure column and try to do better somewhere else.' He held up a copy of *Film Daily* that had been lying on his desk. 'Also, since I read Justin Gold's column I've had the feeling that I might be competing against some other persuaders now. Am I right?'

'You're not competing against anybody, Mr Thorne. I'm not playing games.'

'Well, that's good to hear. But you're not telling me there hasn't been any response to Justin's column, are you?'

Kincaid smiled. 'No, I'm not.' He told him then about the efforts that had been made to contact him. The gifts, the flowers, the whole story.

'Cigarette-cases,' Thorne said. 'That's quite generous for Henry. He usually has somebody take you to dinner first to see if you're worth the trouble. But Justin must have got him energized. He's the power columnist in the trade. We all read what he has to say before we shave in the morning. He's the one we trust. He usually gets his facts straight.'

'Where'd he get his facts about me?'

'I don't know but he wasn't far off. I thought maybe he'd talked to you.'

Kincaid shook his head. 'I decided he must have talked to you.'

Thorne shook his head. 'I wasn't about to put you on the platter so Selznick, or French, or MGM could take a crack at you. No, Justin has his own sources. Information is power in this town. Everybody talks and everybody listens. We all have secretaries and office-boys and people who run the ditto machine. And all those people have friends in the business. So nothing stays secret for very long. I've got people in every studio in town who report to me. And people who work for me do the same thing elsewhere.'

Thorne stood up behind his desk, walked around it, and sat in an upholstered chair facing Kincaid. 'Tell me what you're thinking. About my proposition, I mean. Last time we talked I was trying to convince you that you're capable of a lot more than you think you are. Have you given that some thought?'

'Yes, I have. And I decided you know more about your business than I do. If you say I can do it, then you must be convinced that I can.'

'That's right. I am convinced. And I'm not the only one. I tried a couple of experiments since I saw you last. I decided to get some other opinions about you. We have forty or fifty young people working for us. In their teens or early twenties. They don't have big jobs. Typists, messengers, mail-girls, gardeners. Young people making a start. What we do when we want a fresh opinion about a picture, or an actor, or an actress, is invite these kids to take an hour off from their jobs and come to our main screening-room. We don't give them questionnaires. After we screen something we talk to them. A director or a publicity person sits down with them and they all talk about what they've seen. In this case I was the one who met with them afterwards. We screened the piece of film I showed you in London. Then I asked them to talk about it. I didn't steer them. These are bright kids. They work around film-making every day and they spend their own money to go to movies two or three times a week. I asked them to make comments about the young actors they'd seen on the film and they all had something to say. But almost all of the comments were about only five or six of the actors. You were one of those they talked about most often. Then at the end I asked them to write down which one of all those actors they thought would have the most promising future. I took the notes to my secretary and had her tabulate them. And three people got almost all the votes. Joel McCrea, Doug Fairbanks, Jr., and you. You got almost as many votes as McCrea and four more than Fairbanks. Does that tell you something?'

'I guess it does.'

'All right. Now listen to this. My next step was to call in four directors: Jack Conway, Dudley Murphy, Frank Tuttle, and Jim Cruze. Before I screened our little film for them I said, "Let's pretend we have to pick an actor we've never worked with to star in a film. Tell me which one of the actors you're about to see you'd want to hire." Murphy picked Edward Nugent, Conway picked Paul Kelly, and Tuttle and Cruze both picked you. You saw for yourself how many young actors appeared in that short film. And those four directors know what to look for when they're casting a picture. So there you are. In case you're still in doubt about your potential I've just given you some encouragement from two totally different areas. Young people who go to the picture theatres and some fine directors who make the films. It's up to you now. I've done all I can do. You have to tell me if you're going back to London in a few days or if you want to sit down with me and hammer out a deal.'

'I am going back to London in a few days . . .'

'Is that your answer?'

'Not completely. I'm also willing to talk with you about a deal. Before I leave.'

'I'm delighted,' Thorne said. He stood up, crossed to Kincaid's chair, and shook his hand. 'You won't be sorry. I can promise you that.'

Kincaid smiled. 'I just said I was willing to talk. What if we can't reach an agreement?'

'That's impossible. If we talk, we'll agree. Unless you ask me to turn over the studio to you, we'll be able to work out a contract you'll be happy with.'

'Before we go any further I have to tell you a seven-year contract is out of the question.'

'Why is that?'

'Because it doesn't make sense to me. I could turn out

to be a dud. Six months from now you might wish you'd never made a deal with me.'

'That's no problem. The seven years is an outside number. There are shorter option periods inside that time. If we don't pick up your option . . .'

'I understand that. You can cancel the contract at the end of any option period. Correct?'

Thorne nodded. 'That's the normal contract agreement.'

'Does that mean that if I want out of the contract, I also have an option to break it?'

Thorne carefully fitted a cigarette into an ivory holder and lit it. 'I see you've done your homework. As I recall, you told me you'd had some meetings with Lloyd Banks.'

'Yes, I did.'

'We hear complaints about that one-way option constantly. From many of our contract people. But most of them are more interested in extending the contract than they are in breaking it. The problem is we can't do business without contracts. The insurance people wouldn't permit it, even if the studios were willing. Also, we invest a lot of money in our actors, in addition to their salaries. We publicize them, train them, sell them to the public. It's a continuing process. That kind of effort makes no sense if we're not certain we can depend on that actor for a period of years. Many of our actors make five or six pictures before the chemistry is just right. Only then do they begin to attract attention and become valuable to us. If those people were free to toddle off to Universal or Paramount just when they're becoming known, we would have squandered our investment. On a few occasions, however, we've made five-year deals. Does that sound better to you?'

Kincaid shook his head. 'I'm not interested in a term contract for any period of time.'

318

'Let me be sure I understand. You said you are interested in coming to an agreement with me but you're not willing to make a contractual agreement? Is that what you're saying?'

'No. I realize there has to be a contract. I said I'm not willing to sign a term contract.'

'Are you suggesting another type of contract?'

'I'm not smart enough to do that,' Kincaid said. 'You know everything about your business. I know almost nothing. But I'm sure there must be other sorts of contractual agreements with actors. What happens, for example, when you borrow an actor from another studio for one specific picture?'

'That's a loan-out deal. The actor has no part in those negotiations. He's simply paid his regular salary by the studio that holds his contract.'

'But you negotiate with the studio for the actor's services. I assume you pay the studio more than they pay the actor.'

Thorne smiled. 'Usually a great deal more. Since you've talked with Banks, I'm sure he told you that.'

'Yes, he did. But I'm not interested in the amount of money that's paid. I just wanted to see if there was a pattern of negotiation for a particular actor to appear in one particular film.'

'There is. On a loan-out. But apart from extras and bit players, almost every good actor in town is under contract to somebody. The only actor of major stature who isn't bound to a studio is Basil Rathbone. Even Chaplin and Fairbanks and Pickford, when they formed United Artists, found that they were contractually bound to themselves.'

'If you're saying that you are only able to deal with me in terms of a long-term contract and I say I'm not willing to sign a long-term contract, then perhaps there's nothing more for us to talk about.'

'I don't intend to give up that easily,' Thorne said.

'But you certainly don't need me to do business and I don't need you to keep me out of debtor's prison. So it may be hard for us to find a way to compromise.'

'It may be impossible. But I don't accept that. Not yet. After weeks of waiting we've just begun to talk. So I'm not prepared to back off so quickly. Let's look at the positive side. My enthusiasm for you and your future has not slackened off in any way. And you have become interested enough to begin to talk terms with me. So let's leave it there for the moment. I think I see where you're heading and I'd like to give the situation some more thought. Then in a day or so we'll sit down again.'

'That's fine with me,' Kincaid said. 'But there's one other thing I wanted to ask you. That item in the paper said something about Ned Kelly. What's that all about?'

'I don't know where Justin got hold of that. I talked with some of my production people about it a few weeks ago after you and I had our meeting in London. Since you're Australian and the Ned Kelly project is an Australian story, I thought there might be some possibility there. But no one here seemed to have much interest. We've kicked that story around for years. At one time we had it scheduled as a silent film. But we were never able to get a screenplay we liked. Do you know anything about Ned Kelly?'

'He's an Australian hero. Everybody down there knows about him. I worked on a cattle station near Glenrowan. That was his stomping-ground. People in that area still talk about him in the present tense. As if he was still alive.'

'Doesn't sound like the same man. As I remember the scripts he was just another outlaw. Preyed on the people.

The whole community rose up finally and killed him. Burned him up in a shack.'

Kincaid shook his head. 'The people loved him. He was like an Australian Robin Hood. Fighting against bad government and rotten police. And he didn't die in a fire. The police hung him.'

'I'll have to have those scripts sent up and read them again. Or maybe I'll let you read them. Have you ever read a screenplay?'

'No.'

'You haven't missed much. Pretty boring stuff. Most of our screen-writers see themselves as directors, so they spend more time figuring out the shots and the camera angles than they do on dialogue and story. But if you stick with it, you can usually figure out what's going on.' He picked up the telephone by his chair. 'I need some material urgently. Send Simpson down to the script department. Tell him to bring you the carton marked *Ned Kelly*. There must be a dozen treatments and screenplays in the box. Pick out the last five or six – the most recent ones – and send them by messenger to Mr Kincaid at the Ambassador. Be sure they get there this evening.' When he hung up the receiver he said to Kincaid, 'You read a little, I'll read a little, and next time we talk we'll compare notes. Don't have high expectations. The last script I saw on Kelly was hopeless.'

4

When Kincaid and Sophie had spent their croquet afternoon as guests of C. Aubrey Smith, they'd met a jovial young man whose family lived in Lincolnshire. Burt Windrow. Later they'd met him again at a dinner party given by Anthony Bushell and his wife. 'He's charming,'

321

Sophie said after they'd met him the second time. 'But just that.'

'What does that mean?' Kincaid said.

'It means he has everything a man could possibly require except the most important thing.'

'And what is that?'

'What is what?' she said.

'The most important thing.'

'I'm not sure I can put a name to it. It's something that often isn't noticed when it's there but which is very much missed when it's absent. It's like the human spine. No one ever sees it but it's an accepted necessity.'

'Whatever his flaws,' Kincaid said, 'they don't seem important to those young beauties who flock round him, chirping to be noticed.'

'Of course not. I'm not questioning his virility, you understand. He's gorgeous and humorous and tall and slender and gracious. But when all's said and done, there's no one home. If I were asked to describe him in one word I would say *unfinished*.'

'I see. Cruel judgement. How would you describe yourself in one word?'

'Well, now, let me see, I expect I would say *willing*.'

'Odd choice.'

'Think about it. I'm open, receptive, vulnerable, and accessible. Eager to please. Scratch my ears. Throw me a bone. If I were an animal I'd be a Dalmatian.'

'Dalmatians are beautiful but stupid.'

'So be it,' she said. 'You know the word for Evan?'

'No.'

'*Haunted*.'

'Haunted? Like a house?'

'No. Like a person.'

'And his father, Arthur Tagg?'

'*Immobile*,' she said.

322

'How about your mother?'

'My dear perfect mother, Margaret, is *noble*.'

'And the Major?'

'Oh, God, what word would describe my father? I hate to say it, but there's only one word, I think: *ossified*.'

'How about me?' Kincaid said.

'Not fair. Too many words for you. Strong. Tender. Stubborn. Relentless. Shy. Passionate. All kinds of good words.'

'Anyone can reel off a list of words. You have presented yourself as the genius of one-word descriptions. But you can't do it in my case. Is that correct?'

'Incorrect. There is one word for you: *unknowable*.'

'No good,' he said. 'That's a complete miss.'

'It's not for you to say, Coco. I am the high priestess of one-worders and I have labelled you *unknowable*. Don't fight it. Like Cleopatra, you have infinite variety. One is never quite certain what you are about to do or what you may have done in another life. You are inscrutable and unknowable.'

'I think of myself as an Airedale,' he said.

'Of course you do but no one agrees with you.'

When Kincaid saw Windrow walking towards him in the parking lot of Thornwood Studios, dressed in cream-coloured trousers and a white tennis-sweater, he remembered Sophie's one-word description of him and he felt a twinge of sympathy for this flawless, beige-and-white young man, high colour in his cheeks and yellow hair growing long on his neck.

'By God, I thought it was you. I have eyes like a falcon, you know. Saw a distant figure coming out of the studio entrance and I said to myself, "*Voilà!* There, as sure as Sunday, is Kincaid." Then I said to myself, "Gin and bitters in the bar-room at Lucey's." So come, I'll stand you a drink. Or half-a-dozen drinks if you like. I just picked up a small cheque and I'm brimming with generosity.'

'Just time for a quick one, I'm afraid,' Kincaid said.

'I'll be sorry to lose your company but that only means there will be more gin and bitters for me. I'm superstitious, you see, about cheques coming through. My habit is to find a comfortable seat in a nearby saloon, give the cheque to the barman, and proceed to drink till the money's spent. I am able to go home then with empty pockets and a light heart.'

When they'd settled into a booth at Lucey's with drinks before them, Windrow said, 'Now, what's all this I read about you in *Film Daily*? Suave English gentleman, we all assumed when we met you. Well spoken. Beautiful wife. Taking the waters and seeing the sights in the colonies. Now it turns out you're a ruddy actor like the rest of us. Am I right?'

'Afraid not.'

'Not a film actor, you mean. All your creative energies devoted to the stage. Marlowe, Ibsen, Shaw. That lot.'

Kincaid shook his head. 'I've never appeared in a play in my life.'

Windrow signalled for fresh drinks. 'Keep an eye on me, old fellow,' he said to the waiter. 'Bring fresh drinks at regular intervals whether I signal or not. If I say stop or if you find me sleeping in the booth, that will be your signal to cut off service. Otherwise, keep the old Bombay flowing.'

'No more for me,' Kincaid said as the waiter moved off.

'Don't discourage the staff. Whatever arrives will be consumed. If not by you, then by me. If not by me, by the undertaker when he comes to claim my tortured body, destroyed by impossible dreams and marathon sexual combat.' He took a long drink. 'Now, you're saying that

Justin Gold, the nearest thing this community has to a Messiah, has published filthy lies about you in his obscene column in *Film Daily*?'

'Not exactly. You asked me if I'm a stage actor and I said no. I did some poetry readings for a group in London, one at the Cromwell, the other at the Royal Court.'

'Were you a triumph?'

'I wouldn't say so.'

'No matter. In any case, you've now come west with the wagon trains to make your fortune as a *skuespiller*. Do you recognize that word? Norwegian for film actor. Taught to me during a steamy weekend in Lillehammer by an enormous Norwegian strumpet who whipped me into submission with wet towels, then painted Nordic designs on my buttocks while I slept. Where was I?'

'You assumed that I'm here to become a film actor. Actually Sophie and I will be going home to London in a week or so.'

'Does Justin Gold know that? If not, I'd like to tell him. Love to catch the old bugger in a lie. He's never deigned to mention me in his rotten column but he told Clive Brook, who told me, that he thought of me as an *arriviste*. Clive said he speaks miserable French. So, I wrote Mr Gold a note and said that if he ever slandered or libelled me again I would see him in court, and that failing, I would do serious damage to his person in the alleyway behind his miserable little cottage on Wilcox and Yucca. As a footnote, I informed him that if all the *arrivistes* in what is laughingly referred to as "our industry" were suddenly identified and whisked out of town there wouldn't be enough people left to fill a telephone-box or the poopy cabinet in a public latrine. Have you met Mr Gold?'

'No, I haven't.'

'Never slipped a few dollars in his shirt pocket, never

polished his car, bought him a sandwich, or kissed his bum? If the answer to all those is no, then it's surprising that he wrote about you in such detail. On his tomb will be carved *Quid pro quo*. He does nothing for nothing. One can assume that if you didn't titillate him in one way or another your friend the Reverend Mr Thorne must have done the job. Ah, well, so it goes. You still haven't told me what Julian Thorne is up to. Is he truly planning to foist you off on the public as an actor, a man whose only experience is dreary recitation? There are many of us you know, qualified chaps, who are full-time residents here, trying to work at our trade, struggling for a major opportunity, and it doesn't go down well at all when a bloke floats into town with his rich and tender wife on his arm, smelling of money and French perfume . . .'

Kincaid's arm came up suddenly. His hand fastened on Windrow's throat. When he spoke his voice was a husky whisper. 'Listen to me, you son of a bitch. One more word out of you about my wife and they'll find you dead in this fucking booth.' Windrow's face was red, his eyes bulging. He tried to talk but only a dry wheeze came out of his mouth. 'Now,' Kincaid said. 'I'm going to take my hand off your throat. But if you say one rotten word, if you make one sound, I'll drop you. Do you understand what I'm saying? If you do, blink your eyes.' Windrow blinked his eyes like a child's doll and Kincaid slowly relaxed the grip on his throat. Windrow sat staring at him, his hands limp in his lap, his face blotchy now, white and red. 'Not a sound out of you,' Kincaid whispered. 'Do you understand that?' Windrow nodded again. His eyes never left Kincaid. 'I don't know who you think I am and I don't care,' Kincaid said. 'I only care about your filthy mouth. If you ever say one word to me about my wife, if I ever hear that you've mentioned our names, I promise I will make you wish you'd been born a mute. Remember how my hand felt on your neck. Then pray to God I never have a reason to put it there again.'

Kincaid eased himself out of the booth and walked slowly up the dim-lit aisle to the doorway. He crossed the street, found his car in the parking lot, and drove home to the Ambassador. He gripped the steering-wheel hard to stop his hands from shaking.

5

Two days later Thorne and Kincaid met again. This time for lunch. In a private dining-room of the Union Club on Hill Street. 'I believe there's more privacy here than in my office,' Thorne said. 'At the very least you'll be guaranteed a fine meal. The chef here used to be at *Les Pigeons* in Dijon.'

As they ate their meal Thorne reminisced and philosophized. 'In my business we studio heads are known as greedy people in a cruel industry. And there's some truth in that. When I was a boy I used to hear similar stories about vaudeville and burlesque and travelling circuses. Perhaps it's inevitable when there's a great deal of money at stake, when people are eager to be entertained and other people are just as eager to offer entertainment. There's competition at every level. Hard competition between performers, between managers and impresarios, between theatre-owners and exhibitors. That sort of struggle creates friction and damage. And hatred sometimes. But still, lifelong friendships are formed, fortunes are made, and the cameras keep turning. Those of us who were there at the beginning, showing one-reel films for a penny in vacant stores in New York, never cease to be amazed at how far we've come. In 1931, one thousand feature-length films were made world-wide. This year, more than five hundred talking pictures will be made in this country alone. Sixty of those will be Thornwood films. At least one new production finished each week. And all this while the experts have predicted our imminent downfall. First they told us the public wanted only one- and two-reelers. Then they said that only comedy would sell. When we went to sound, the wise men theorized that film had to be a silent medium, that it could not compete with plays on stage. And in 1929 and 1930 the money men said that poor people, out-of-work people, could not afford to go to movie theatres. It turns out that movies are the only entertainment they can afford. We've had cutbacks of course, we've been forced to spend our money more wisely, but two years after the stock-market crash, Jack Warner paid Constance Bennett thirty thousand dollars a week to work in a routine film. And think of the fine actors we've attracted: Muni, the Lunts, the Barrymores, Helen Hayes. An awkward young woman named Hepburn makes one picture and becomes an important actress. People like Emil Jannings, Garbo, Dietrich, and Laughton come to us from overseas. We've built a mecca here. We've invented a form of entertainment and enlightenment that will never die. Something to be proud of. Look at some of the releases in last year alone: *Grand Hotel*, *Dr Jekyll and Mr Hyde*, *Scarface*, *Strange Interlude*, *The Sign of the Cross*, *A Farewell to Arms*, *Mata Hari*. Thornwood released *The Disciples*, *Golden Harvest*, and *Rebecca's Children*. Of course I compete with the other studios and they compete with me. But one thing we never forget: a really good picture is good for all of us, no matter who makes it. When the movie habit is strong, when people go to their neighbourhood theatres once or twice a week, we all benefit.'

At last, when their coffee was served, Thorne said, 'I

looked over some of the Ned Kelly scripts and I assume you did too.'

'Yes, I did.'

'Do you want to tell me what you thought or should I give you my opinion?'

'Go ahead.'

Thorne shook his head. 'Nothing there, I'm afraid. It's routine outlaw violence. Nobody here gives a damn about Australia and the fact that it's set in Australia is the only fresh thing about it. Our people did some research on the terrain down there and they said we can duplicate it in Thousand Oaks and Malibu Canyon. Brush country and sand and eucalyptus trees aren't hard to find around here. I don't see it as a production problem or a budget problem. There's just no story. A man steals horses and cattle and robs banks till the police catch him and kill him. And that's it. Am I right?'

'As I told you the other day I'd never read a screenplay before. But I know the story of Ned Kelly. And none of that story was there in what I read. I think if any of your writers had told the real story you'd have made the picture a long time ago.'

'I don't know. I read three or four drafts of the script, all by different writers, and the story didn't seem to change much.'

'That's right. It didn't,' Kincaid said. 'All of them had it wrong.'

'That's what happens out here. Once you get a sour draft of a story it goes from bad to worse. When that happens, the best thing to do is abandon it.'

'Maybe you're right. But if it were up to me I'd say, throw out all those scripts and start over. Once a writer puts down the real Kelly story I'll bet there's not a studio in this town that wouldn't make the picture.'

Thorne smiled. 'When a producer or a writer says that

to me it usually means he's about ready to place a call to Schulberg or Columbia and leave me holding the bag.'

'I'm not a producer or a writer, and even if I were I wouldn't cock around with you. I told you that the other day. This just happens to be a story I know something about. If you really want me to make a picture for you, this is the one I'd like to do.'

'Well, that's good to hear. Maybe you and I are about to make some progress. I'm just not sure this Kelly property is the answer. What are we talking about now? If I put you together with a writer and you told him the story you think we'd have a decent piece of material?'

'Yes, I do.'

'Well, let's talk about that. Let's see what sort of writer we might need. Tell me a bit about Kelly. What do you know about him that's missing in the screenplays you read.'

'Everything's missing. The whole situation is missing. The Kelly family were small farmers in the state of Victoria, living on a piece of land that was given them by the government. The father was dead. Just the mother and her sons. Those people with small farms were called selectors. And the big landowners hated them. Tried to get hold of their property using any means they could – bribing officials, supporting crooked police. Finally they managed to send Mrs Kelly to jail. Also one of her sons. That started it all. What they call the Kelly Outbreak: Ned Kelly and the four or five men who followed him bucking the big landowners and the law, trying to survive. He was intelligent and clever. A born leader. And he had great public support. But finally the police hunted him down and hanged him. Some people in Australia say he's the only national hero the country has.'

'That's not the story I paid for.'

'But it's the real story. Even Australians don't usually

get it right. Only the people around Glenrowan know all the dirt.'

'All right, let's see where we are. From what you said the other day, the deal you want to make with me is what we call a picture deal. The picture you want to do is the story of Kelly and you're willing to work with a writer till we get it right. Am I on the mark so far?'

Kincaid nodded.

'Let's break this down one piece at a time. I told you day before yesterday that we only make term deals with actors. Five years or seven years. Very occasionally, with an established star we'll do a picture deal. Three pictures or five pictures, usually one a year. I've thought about our conversation and discussed it with Sam, my brother. He's tougher than I am in these matters but I finally persuaded him. We'll give you a five-picture deal. Exclusive. You only work for us except on loan-outs.'

Kincaid shook his head. 'I only want to sign for one picture.'

'Can't be done, I'm afraid. I can't believe that Lloyd Banks advised you to ask for that. He knows better.'

'That's right. He agrees with you. He says nobody would give me terms like that.'

'I think I've made it clear,' Thorne said, 'that I'm willing to go as far as I can to sign you with our company. But I can't go that far.'

Kincaid smiled. 'I didn't finish telling you my terms. When I sign with you for the first picture I will give you an option for a second one. A project I approve of. Terms to be negotiated. I will also sign an agreement of exclusivity for one year. Automatically renewable until a year goes by when I don't do a film for you. When that happens the exclusivity agreement is void. That's my assurance to you that I have no intention of doing films for anybody but Thornwood, assuming you still want me. Since I'm not under contract I will not do loan-outs.'

'You're proposing one picture a year, terms to be negotiated, and an agreement of perpetual exclusivity as long as you continue to do one film a year. How can I guarantee you a film every year when you have power of refusal? If you turn down everything we offer for one year, then we've lost our exclusivity.'

'It's not flawless, I admit. But short of putting myself in bondage for life, I don't know another answer. Let me put it this way. If I become important to your company I have faith that you will make every effort to keep me working. I ask you to have faith that I mean it when I say that I have no intention of working for anyone else. There's another advantage from your standpoint. If the first picture's a failure, or the second one, I'm automatically off your payroll. You don't even have to say goodbye. I'm gone.'

'I've made a thousand deals. But this is a new one on me. I'm not sure what you're after.'

'That's easy. I want control over my own time. I want freedom of movement. And I don't want to embarrass myself, or my wife, or you.'

'All right. Let's assume for the moment we could get together on a cockamamie deal like that, let's talk about another problem. Are you in a position to move ahead at once with the Kelly project? Can you stay here in California and work with a writer?'

Kincaid shook his head. 'We're flying to New York in three days. Then back to London.'

'So where does that leave us? You're carrying the story around in your head.'

'Here's the way I see it. I think you should find a different kind of writer for this story. Those screenplays I read seemed to be written for the cameraman. You mentioned that yourself. Ned Kelly's story is about people, people who are being trampled on. They don't have much and what they do have is being taken away from them. Australia's full of people like that. So is America. But somebody has to bring those people to life for us. And it seems to me the writer has to do that before the actors can do it. So why don't we forget about men who've written twenty slick screenplays and find a writer who can write scenes about people who are being pushed over the edge?'

'We're always looking for people who can do that. Rosamund Barwick will tell you, I've hired writer friends of hers who'd never laid eyes on a screenplay. Didn't know a boom from a dolly.'

'The man I'm thinking of knows a boom from a dolly. I guarantee it. He's also a playwright. And a damned good one. Just had a play in the West End with Geoff Bingham and Mary Cecil.'

'*The Father House*. I read some good things about it.'

'Maybe you've read some bad things too. But don't let that turn you away from Evan Tagg. He knows how to bring characters to life. He's a man first and a playwright second. And Ned Kelly's story has to be written by a man, not some freak in a lavender shirt. When I tell him the facts the way I began telling them to you, I guarantee you he'll put them together like a brick wall.'

'You're quite a salesman. After we finish your first picture, I'll have to send you round the country to meet the exhibitors.'

'I'm not a salesman. I'm just stubborn and I have a big mouth.'

'What if we decide to go with Tagg?' Thorne said then. 'How do we proceed? Should I have my people in London contact him?'

'Not yet. Let me talk to him first. I'll have to see what

his work schedule is. Then, if he's willing to do it, you people can talk to him about money. But meanwhile I'll have to give him some rough idea of what the job is worth.'

'It's hard to say. At Thornwood we get the best we can for as little as possible. There's no set rules. Some of the worst hacks in town make a fortune year after year and some really talented people get two or three hundred a week.'

'Do you remember how much you paid for that last Kelly screenplay?'

'Lou Hibler did that. We probably paid him twelve hundred a week. He's an old hand.'

'How many weeks?'

'Eight weeks probably. Lou's a slow worker.'

'Close to ten thousand. I guarantee you Tagg will do a better job.'

'Let's talk about six thousand dollars for eight weeks.'

'He may have to give up some regular work he does for the London *Telegraph*.'

'That's all right. We'll negotiate with him.'

'If I don't make it sound inviting, you won't have a chance to negotiate with him. He doesn't give a damn for the movie business. You won't be able to jerk him around.'

'What are you suggesting?'

'Why don't I tell him I think the job pays a flat ten thousand no matter how long it takes?'

'With a rewrite and a polish,' Thorne said.

'You can handle that stuff with him later on. First we have to get him to say yes.'

'All right. Tell him ten thousand and we'll crucify him later,' Thorne said. Then, 'Am I being too optimistic or are you and I edging slowly towards an agreement?'

'I wouldn't be surprised.'

'I'll dictate a deal memo as soon as I'm back in my office. Those were pretty complex terms you were talking about but I think I've got a handle on them. We'll send a copy of the memo to you tomorrow, you can check it over, and we'll talk again to make sure everything is understood. Then I'll have the contract drawn up and sent to you in London.'

'That's fine.'

'Since you seem to have turned yourself into a first-rate negotiator I'm sure you're aware that we've discussed everything except billing and money. About billing, the contract will read that you'll be billed above the title, first position, in every picture you make for me. Until you become important, we'll make you important. That's our job. Now, what about money? You seem to have thought about everything else. How much money did you and Banks decide to hold me up for?'

'No money,' Kincaid said. 'I don't want any advance payment. And no salary while we're shooting the picture.'

'Wait a minute. What are you talking about?'

'Let me finish. I'm an untried commodity. Neither one of us knows what I'll come up with in front of a camera. Nothing perhaps. What I'm saying is this: when the picture's finished, if you decide to junk it and not release it, you don't owe me a penny. If you do release it, you owe me a hundred thousand dollars. If the picture's a success and you want to negotiate with me for a second one, then you owe me another fifty thousand as final payment for the first picture. If it takes ten weeks to shoot the picture, then you will have paid me fifteen thousand a week. But only if the film's a success. If it's terrible and you throw it in the dust-bin, I get nothing. How does that sound to you?'

'It sounds insane.'

'Maybe it is. But you can't say it's not fair.'

The day before they were scheduled to fly to New York, Sophie and Kincaid, the top down on their red roadster, drove north to Santa Barbara for a Mexican lunch at La Golondrina. As they drove along the edge of the ocean he told her about his negotiations with Thorne.

'What in the world did you think you were doing? You mustn't sign your life away over lunch. That's why one hires solicitors.'

'I signed nothing. I simply told him what I thought was fair and he put it into a memo. Now the solicitors, his not mine, will put it into a contract. Then I will show it to your elegant solicitor, Sir Charles Tremont, and if everything's in order I'll sign it. I'll ask you to read it too, so you can make a final judgement about my sanity.'

'I made that judgement long since. You are certainly mad, and probably dangerous.'

As they had their lunch, in the cool, high-ceilinged splendour of La Golondrina, Sophie said, 'I'm leery of this entire business. Everything seems to be happening too fast. Why is Thorne so agreeable to everything?'

'Why shouldn't he be agreeable? He hasn't spent a shilling yet except for our steamship tickets and our lodging here. And I promise you, he won't spend a shilling till it's clear in his head that he'll be able to get ten shillings back.'

'But if you go ahead and make this Ned Kelly picture and it's no good he'll lose money, won't he?'

Kincaid shook his head. 'Not according to Lloyd Banks. He says Thorne budgets pictures so he can't lose money. He owns a hundred and thirty theatres. If the picture shows only in those theatres he can break even.'

'So it's almost certain he'll release it once it's made?'

'That's right.'

'And then he gives you a big bundle of money.'

'That's right.'

'Aren't you clever? I thought you were a poor orphan, uneducated and insecure. Now it turns out you're clever as well as smart. How do you explain this remarkable change?'

'As you've noticed, I am a serious reader and a good listener. Also, I'm married to a wealthy older lady so I can afford to gamble. Since Thorne knows I don't *need* anything I have a better chance of getting what I want.'

'Ah-ha. So you did marry me for my money?'

'Not at all. I married you because you're unattractive, timid, and ill-at-ease. I felt sorry for you.'

'Do you still feel sorry for me?'

'Of course not. Now I think you're the world's most fortunate woman.'

'Because I'm married to you.'

'That's right.' He patted her on the knee.

'You're truly an insufferable man, aren't you? Feeling your oats. King of the hill. Ready to mount your charger and take on the world.'

'Exactly. Stand aside or you'll be trampled.'

'And now you're about to shanghai poor Evan.'

'Poor Evan stands to make a nice sum of money. He might welcome it after the disappointment of his play.'

'But can he do it?'

'Of course he can do it. He's a good writer.'

'You've never read a line he's written.'

'But you have,' Kincaid said. 'And you say he's good. You say he's very good. So I know he is.'

'You're out of control, my darling. When I get to New York, I plan to write Julian Thorne a sweet thank-you note. I will also tell him that he has taken my perfectly nice husband and turned him into a monster.'

'How dare you.'

'You are disgustingly energized. As soon as I get you back to London I will put you on a diet of bland foods and sweet puddings. Mineral baths and a glass of warm milk at bed-time. That failing, I will bring you to Wiswell Towers and have the Major take charge of you.'

Kincaid smiled. 'As soon as we're back in London I promise I'll be obedient and cooperative.'

They drove towards Los Angeles late that afternoon along the coast highway. When they passed the narrow road where they'd turned in before to look at the headland with the remains of a burned house and the stone wall running along the edge of the bluff high above the sea, Sophie said, 'It's sold. Did you see the sign?'

'What sign?'

'That piece of land we looked at not long ago. The estate agents have plastered a sold banner across the sign at the end of the driveway.'

'It doesn't matter. You didn't like it anyway.'

'I know. But you did. I think you saw yourself walking those acres with a fine pair of dogs.'

'Good health and a bad memory,' Kincaid said. 'That's my secret. When I'm disappointed I simply forget it.'

'We'll find you a headland in Cornwall with a whitewashed cottage that looks out across the sea. And we'll buy you an excellent brace of dogs to follow you wherever you go. How does that sound?'

'Sounds good. I like Cornwall.'

7

The following day as they were being taken from the Ambassador to their plane, the chauffeur drove down Figueroa to Century, then west to the airfield. At the corner of Figueroa and Slauson, Sophie said, 'My God, look!' Just ahead of them, on the right, was a great wide sign-board on an elevation forty feet above the pavement. In huge block letters at the top was the name KINCAID printed in red. Below it, filling the centre of the space was a black-and-white portrait of Kincaid. At the bottom, white letters on a red panel, it said, THORNWOOD STUDIOS. By the time they reached the airfield they had seen five more signs exactly like the first one.

When they were in their seats, inside the plane, waiting to take off, Kincaid said, 'You're very quiet this morning. What's happening in your head?'

'I'm stunned. I don't like to see your picture plastered on signs above the street. It makes me feel extremely odd.'

'I feel the same way.'

'Why would he do such a thing? You're not committed to him or his studio. You haven't signed any sort of agreement. Or have you?'

'Of course not. There's just the deal memo that he sent me yesterday.'

'Then why would he go charging ahead like this? Will we see your picture high above Piccadilly Circus when we get to London?'

'I don't imagine so.'

'We should have rung his office as soon as we arrived here at the airfield and told him to take his bloody sign-boards down.'

'It's not that important, is it?'

'It's important to me. Would you like to open a picture magazine and see a photo of me in my night-dress sipping a cup of Café-hag? Would you like me to be public property? I don't think you would. Well, I don't like it either.'

Later, when the plane was in the air, flying east, high above the desert, Sophie said, 'I was just thinking what we said to each other when we decided at last that we would take this trip to America. We said we'd treat it as a lark. Did you mean that when you said it?'

'Of course I did.'

'I'm not so sure of that. I can't help feeling that you planned from the start to go along with Thorne.'

'There was no way I could know how things would turn out. We'd never discussed terms. We'd only talked in a general way.'

'But you really wanted it to work out, didn't you?'

'We talked about this in London,' Kincaid said. 'I told you I wanted to pursue it.'

Sophie smiled. 'You pursued it till it caught you.'

'I don't look at it that way and I didn't think you did. Yesterday, as I recall, you said I'd been awfully clever.'

'Yesterday I hadn't seen your face alongside advertisements for washing-powder and cigarettes. But I do think you were clever. You handled me very cleverly.'

'Are you sure you want to talk about this now?'

'Why not? It seems like a good time to me.'

'All right. I don't need to handle you, Sophie. I don't have to be clever with you. This business with Thorne came to me unsolicited. You know that. As things developed, I told you everything he said to me and everything I said to him. I never actually believed it would happen and it's obvious you felt the same way. It still may not work out. Thorne is free to walk away from it and so am I.'

'But you don't want to walk away from it, do you?'

'Are you saying you want me to?'

'You didn't answer my question.'

'And you didn't answer mine,' he said.

'It's not that simple. I know how you feel. At least I think I know. But I feel as if I'm standing at the bottom of a hill and great boulders are rolling down on me. I'd hate to see us make a silly decision that might change our whole lives. I'm not a public person. You know that. Neither are you. Or at least you never have been. I'm not angry with you. If it sounds that way I don't mean it. I'm not angry at Thorne either. I'm just scared. Apprehensive. Everything's been perfect for us. I'd just hate to see anything change. I love England. I need to be in England. The thought of being in California, of spending time there, of having a synthetic life with Thorne's studio as the centre-piece, fills me with panic. That's the only word for it. Maybe you'll never make this movie you're talking about. Or if you do, maybe you'll hate doing it or it will be a failure, and that will be the end of it. But on the other hand, Thorne may be right about you. You might be a raging success, and your face and your voice would be known everywhere, and you'd do one film after another. You might end up being a different person, someone very different from the man you are now. That would break my heart and it might break yours too. You know how much I love you. It never occurred to me that you could love someone and still want them to fail at something. But ever since I saw your face on those sign-boards, that's the way I've been feeling.'

'I can stop all this business with Thorne right now.'

'No, you can't. And I suppose I shouldn't want you to. I just have to find a way to feel good about it.'

BOOK THREE

· CHAPTER 9 ·

1

One afternoon when Margaret was away on a three-day visit with Clara Causey at Wingate Fields, Cranston went to the desk in her upstairs sitting-room, opened the drawers, and came upon the letters she had written but never mailed to Sophie and Evan. Till his dying day Cranston assured himself that he had gone to her desk to find a bit of sticky tape. He had no explanation for why he had studied the letters so carefully once he'd found them.

There was no misinterpreting his reaction, however, after he'd finished with the letters. As he closed the desk drawers and stood up, his face was flushed. He went downstairs to the library, poured himself a glass of whisky, and pulled the bell cord. When Trout appeared Cranston said, 'Go find Arthur Tagg and tell him I need to see him. As quickly as possible.'

When Tagg came into the library a few minutes later, Cranston had just poured his third whisky. 'Sit down, sir,' Cranston said. 'You and I have a bit of business to conduct.' He walked to a chair facing Tagg and positioned himself behind it. 'No reason to mince words,' he said. 'Straight from the shoulder. Man to man. That's the way I like to operate. No fancy pants. No dancing round the issue.' He took a long drink from his glass. 'No doubt in my mind about your feelings towards me. Twenty years now since you came here to the Towers. Give or take a few. And I've always known you have no time for me. No interest in my ideas. No concern for my opinions. I'm a cipher to you. A necessary evil. You nod when we pass in the corridors, spend a few minutes with me occasionally on estate affairs, but that's about the size of it. You think of me as an outsider in my own home. But by God, sir, I'm not the outsider, you are. And as of this moment you will be, quite literally, on the outside. This is an occasion I've looked forward to since the moment we were introduced. You're discharged, Mr Tagg. Your services are no longer needed here at The Towers.'

Tagg didn't answer. Cranston went to refill his glass, then returned to his station behind the chair. 'No reaction? Nothing to say? I'm not surprised. A bit of a shock, I expect. Thought you had a sinecure, eh? A solid situation, guaranteed for life. Is that it?'

'Not at all. I've always known you'd like to get rid of me if you could manage it.'

'If I could manage it? Oh, but I can, you see. I've just done it. And the quicker you respond, the better. It would simplify matters if you could be gone before Mrs Cranston comes home.'

'There's a great deal to be done before I can do that. It will take at least a week to tidy up affairs on my desk.'

'Don't be sly with me, Mr Tagg. I see through you. I've always seen through you. You're a chap who likes to hide behind a woman's skirts.'

'Don't speak to me like that. I don't like it.'

'Like it or not, it's the truth and you know it. You think once Mrs Cranston comes home things will get turned round. But you're sadly mistaken this time. I'm well aware of the fact that it was my wife who first engaged you and who pays your monthly wage. You've traded on those facts for a long time. But I am still the master here. The final decisions are mine. I've decided your employment here should be terminated and I've decided you should be gone by tomorrow afternoon. Someone else will handle whatever details remain on your desk.'

'Since we're speaking so bluntly, Major Cranston, let me make sure that I'm clearly understood. I am going to continue with my duties till Mrs Cranston comes home. After I talk with her, I will either leave or I will stay, depending on what her wishes are.'

'Not this time, bucko, this time you'll do as I say.'

'I assume you're not planning to have the grooms truss me up and carry me off the premises.'

'I'm sure that won't be necessary.'

'Yes, it will. If you insist on my being gone by tomorrow. And by the way, I wouldn't count on staff hustling me off to the main gate if I were you. I hired most of those people. They're my friends.'

'By God, you're ruddy sure of yourself, aren't you? In the regiments, when a man's dismissed he's bloody well dismissed. There's no discussion about it.'

'I don't believe this qualifies as a discussion. You stated your views and I stated mine. I don't expect we'll be able to compromise.'

'Not till Mrs Cranston is here to referee, is that it?'

'I wouldn't put it just that way. But I do expect she'll have her own views.'

'Damn it, Tagg, I thought we could settle this between us, like two gentlemen. Put it behind us. When there's sticky business to deal with, I hate to get the women involved.'

'But she is involved,' Tagg said. 'You can be the master if you like but Margaret's my employer. And I'm not sure I know what you mean by "sticky business".'

'You know, all right. Don't play the rosy-cheeked lad

347

with me. Don't paint yourself innocent. I've got a head on my shoulders, you see.'

Tagg stood up. 'I don't know what you're trying to say and I don't want to know. So I think we should stop this discussion before you say something you'll be sorry for.'

'Don't threaten me, by God. Are you threatening me?'

'No, I'm not. But I am saying this: whatever position you've decided I hold in this house, don't imagine that you can say whatever you like to me. I will not take abuse from you or from anyone else. I will also not listen to any comments you might make about Mrs Cranston.'

'Ahh, Mrs Cranston, is it? A moment ago, you called her Margaret. A slip of the tongue, wasn't it?'

'Not at all. I often call her Margaret and she always calls me Arthur.'

'I'm well aware of that. That's one of the things I'm putting a stop to. That's one of the reasons you've been dismissed.'

'When Margaret dismisses me I'll leave. Until then, I'll be here.' Tagg turned, walked to the door, and left the room.

2

When Margaret came home from her visit, as soon as she was in her rooms upstairs, her maid said, 'I'm to tell you that Major Cranston would like to see you in the library as soon as you're able.'

'Thank you, Rose.'

'It was Trout who gave me the instructions, mum. He thinks it's an urgent matter.'

When Margaret walked into the library, Cranston stood up and said, 'I'm glad you're back. Did you have a good time with the Bradshaws?'

348

'Yes, I did.'

'Will you have a drink?'

'No, thank you. I understand you have something to discuss with me.'

'Yes, I do. Have you seen Arthur Tagg yet?'

'No. I just arrived a few minutes ago.'

'Good. I wanted to speak to you before he did.'

'Why?'

'I wanted to tell you I've discharged him.'

'You what?'

'You and I have discussed this before. But now I believe the time has come. So I dismissed him. Told him his services are no longer required.'

'Where is he now?'

'At his desk, I suppose. The bugger refused to leave until you got back.'

'Don't you dare to refer to him like that.' She walked to the bell cord and pulled it. When Trout appeared at the door she said, 'Ask Mr Tagg to join us here in the library.'

'Why are you calling him in?' Cranston said. 'He and I finished our discussion. Covered all the ground.'

'Good for you. Now we'll cover all the ground again.'

'By God, I won't be caught in the crossfire between the two of you.'

'There won't be any crossfire between me and Mr Tagg.'

'This is no way to handle things. We don't need a committee to deal with staff problems.'

'There is no staff problem, William.'

'Let's be clear about one thing, Margaret. I've made up my mind and I'm not willing to change it.'

'It's not your mind that concerns me. It's your mouth. I have to find out what you've said and see what I must do to correct it.'

'There's nothing to correct, by God. I don't need anyone to clean up after me.'

'Oh, yes you do. That's exactly what you need.'

Trout opened the library door then and Tagg walked in. 'Major Cranston tells me he discharged you, Arthur. Is that true?'

'Yes, it is.'

'You don't want to leave us, do you?'

'No, I don't.'

'Then you shan't.'

'But I don't want to stay on if my presence will cause a problem. Major Cranston made it quite plain that he doesn't need my services, so perhaps it would be better for all concerned if I went elsewhere.'

'No, it wouldn't be better for all concerned. It wouldn't be better for the staff or the estate. And it wouldn't be better for me. We want you here and we need you here. Major Cranston may not require your services but I do.'

'By God, you're talking past me as if I were an umbrella-stand. I won't be disregarded,' Cranston said.

'You're not being disregarded,' Margaret said. 'All eyes are on you. You're the centre of attention. Do you have something to say?'

'I certainly do. I won't be humiliated in front of this employee. I dismissed him for sound reasons and I expect my wishes to be respected.'

'They are,' she said. 'And they are respectfully overruled.'

'The man is a schoolmaster. You hired him to tutor our daughter. Sophie is grown-up, twice married, and has two children of her own. Why must we still have a tutor on the premises?'

Margaret turned to Tagg. 'I'm sorry you have to listen to all this, but since it involves the three of us I think it's important that we all hear it first-hand.' She turned back to Cranston. 'You said you have good reasons. Is that one of them? Because we don't need a tutor?'

'There are other reasons.'

'What are they?'

'They're good reasons, by God. I assure you of that. But I refuse to discuss them with you when Tagg is sitting here watching me.'

'Why is that? He must have been watching you when you dismissed him.'

'Different circumstances. We didn't go into all my reasons at that time.'

'Why not?' Margaret said.

'Not necessary. When a man's dismissed he's dismissed. He's not entitled to an elaborate explanation.'

'Yes, he is. This isn't India, William. And even if you don't think he's entitled, I am entitled.'

'You and I can discuss this another time.'

'No, we can't. When I walk out of this room, this particular discussion will be permanently finished and tucked away. So whatever arguments you want to make, it's now or never.'

'You make me damned uncomfortable with your attitude. I feel as if I'm the one who's on trial here.'

'You may feel that way but you're not. No one's on trial. You said you have good reasons but you can't seem to remember what they are.'

'All right, by God, I'll tell you. I'm a gentleman. I don't like to bring up rotten things. Gutter-talk. It's not my style.'

'What on earth are you talking about?'

'For one thing this man doesn't know his place. He never has. From the first day I met him I could tell he had presumptions. Misconceptions about himself and his position. At first I blamed it on those years he spent in America, soaking up half-baked ideas about liberty and

351

equality. But little by little I saw it was a part of him. It was the way he saw himself. He became a resident of the Towers, he and Evan, legitimate full-time occupants of the Wiswell home, members of the family, first names all round . . .'

'That's enough, William. We've been through all this before. I won't subject Arthur to it.'

'Arthur . . . Arthur . . . you see what I mean. Arthur and Evan and Margaret and Sophie. Children in the sand-box. Party-favours and cream teas . . .'

'You're not making sense, William. You're going on like a wild man.' She stood up. 'I think we should end this meeting before you make yourself ill.' As she turned to leave, Cranston lumbered ahead of her and stood with his back against the door.

'You wanted to hear my reasons, now I'm going to tell you. We haven't been through it all before because I didn't know it all. A man has a right to protect his home. Any court in the world will defend that right . . .'

Arthur and Margaret looked at each other. 'What do the courts have to do with it? What are you talking about?'

'Don't act so innocent. I know about you two. I know a great deal more than you think I do. Twenty years you've lived in the same house together, two young people at the beginning. I should have guessed what was going on . . .'

'William, for the love of God, what's come over you?'

'Nothing's come over me. You asked why I want this man out of my house and I'm telling you. I read the things you wrote about him, Margaret . . .'

'What things?'

'In your desk. Letters that were never mailed . . .'

'You were going through my desk?'

'No. Not in the way you mean. I was looking for a bit

of gummed tape and those pages were there. They weren't in an envelope . . .'

'How dare you read things in my desk,' she said.

'How dare you write things like that about another man when you're married to me.'

Margaret turned to Tagg. 'I know what he's talking about and it isn't the way he makes it sound.'

'It's bloody well exactly the way I make it sound. And you know it,' Cranston bellowed.

Margaret turned slowly to face him. Finally she said, 'If you don't move away from that door, William, I'm going to ring for Trout and order him to open it. Even if he has to take it off the hinges.'

Cranston stood his ground like a cornered bull. At last, however, he shrugged his shoulders and crossed to the whisky decanter. 'Bloody women,' he said.

At the door Margaret turned and said, 'Tagg has not been dismissed. He'll be working here for as long as he wants. And one more thing: I'll be taking my meals in my rooms for the next few days. I suggest you do the same. I'm not sure how long it will take me to get over this performance you've just put on. I may never get over it. In any case, until I decide what I'm going to do about you, I would prefer not to see you or talk to you. Judging from the things you've said, I assume you feel the same about me.'

3

For the next ten days Margaret did, indeed, stay in her rooms; took all her meals there and talked to no one except her personal maid. Trying to heal herself after the shock of confrontation with Cranston, she sat for hours in her bath, read old treasured books in bed at night, sat on the *chaise-longue* by her wide window looking out across the afternoon gardens to the brook.

She was accustomed to solving problems, for others as well as for herself. She was proud of her ability to sort out situations, to untie difficult knots. She frequently advised people that almost any dilemma could be sorted out by breaking it down into its smallest elements and dealing with them one at a time. Specific action, she counselled, was the solution: when one doesn't know which direction to take, it's essential to take some direction. Arbitrary action is preferable to stasis. Inactivity festers, action heals. She had a credo, a method. It had always worked for her. But now it didn't. No matter where her mind turned she saw an obstacle. A hundred times she reread the two letters Cranston had discovered. They seemed soiled to her now. Exposed. Misread. Although she saw them as innocent, she realized how they might be seen by other eyes, how they had certainly been seen by Cranston.

Her principal concern was not what her husband thought, however, what he had concluded, or what action he might take. Tagg was her concern. She continued to see his face, his expression, as he'd listened to Cranston's babbling about the incriminating letters. Since they'd left the library together that day she hadn't seen Tagg. They hadn't spoken together. Knowing the chaotic state of her own mind, she could only imagine the roman candles that were exploding in his head. She had the critical evidence in hand. Tagg knew only what he'd heard from Cranston.

She longed to sit down in a quiet corner and talk with him but she had no notion of what she might say. Rare for her. At one moment she decided she must let him read the letters, that until she did that he would be floating in an impossible, uncharted middle distance, without information, with no solid ground under his feet.

But what if he did see the letters and read in them something she had not intended? Or what if he sensed exactly what she had intended? Was that not an equal danger perhaps? Like a plastic ball inside a sphere of airjets, she bounced, floated, and ricocheted to and fro, falling first on one side, then on another. She had no fear whatsoever of facing up to Cranston but she was numbed by the thought of seeing Tagg, of talking with him, of trying to explain.

Just as Cranston had plunged her into her roundabout of indecision, he sent her a note, more than a week after she had begun her self-imposed isolation, that jolted her straight up again.

I've suffered enough humiliation. I see now that there's no hope for us. As soon as I'm able to meet with my solicitors I will file an action for divorce naming Arthur Tagg as co-respondent.

That night Margaret dressed and went down to dinner in the dining-hall. Neither Cranston nor Tagg was there. The following morning she asked Trout to bring Arthur to her sitting-room. When he joined her she showed him Cranston's note. He read it, then handed it back to her. 'I think the quicker I leave here, the better it will be for everybody,' he said.

'That's what I expected you to say. But unless that's what you truly want to do, I don't think it's the answer. As you know from our discussion with William last week, I certainly don't want you to leave.'

Tagg nodded. 'I appreciate that. But Major Cranston seems determined to cause a fuss. And now . . .' he indicated Cranston's note on the table between them, 'if he goes ahead with this, there's certain to be a scandal. So I'd be forced to leave in any case.'

355

'My husband is a bully,' Margaret said, 'but like most bullies, he's also a coward. He's able to make threats and raise his voice and write notes. What he's not able to do is make hard choices and carry them through. Once he's announced what he intends to do, that announcement often serves him as a substitute for taking action.'

'Are you saying you don't think he plans to divorce you?'

'He may be planning it, but going on his past record, I don't think he'll do it. Whatever he does, however, or threatens to do, I refuse to allow it to affect my decisions or to change the course of my life. And as far as scandal is concerned, there is no scandal. You know that and so do I. So does everyone else who's connected in any way with Wiswell Towers. You and I have nothing to hide. Nothing to be ashamed of. William can sue me for divorce if he likes but no respectable solicitor would allow him to humiliate himself by charging me with adultery. William is simply trying to have his way by making threats. I refuse to be manipulated by such tactics and I don't think you should be either.'

'But how can I do my work when I know how he feels about my being here?'

'This is not a new development, Arthur. You've always known how he feels about your presence here and so have I. You're a great deal more intelligent than he is. He senses that and it makes him uncomfortable. He also knows that you and I together handle responsibilities and make decisions that would normally be his. Since he's intellectually lazy and indescribably indolent he's delighted to have someone do that work for him, but at the same time he needs to think of himself as lord of the manor. He wants power and respect without responsibility. So although some part of him tells him he needs you, another voice tells him he must be rid of you. In

356

William's case, his indolence usually triumphs over his paranoia and I assure you it will in this instance. He'll continue to storm about in his study, his billiard-room, and in the nearby public houses, but life in this house will proceed as it always has.'

After a long moment Tagg said, 'But what if you're mistaken?'

'How do you mean?'

'What if he does go ahead with the divorce action, as he threatens to do?'

Margaret smiled. 'I have an excellent solicitor. We would not contest the divorce. We would in fact, do whatever we could to accelerate the proceedings. So in a short period of time William would be living elsewhere.'

'And you have no fear of what he might say or of what people might believe?'

'None whatsoever. And neither should you.'

'But how could I stay on here if there were some hint of . . .'

Margaret smiled. 'What a kind man you are. You're concerned about my reputation, aren't you? Do you think I might be branded as a scarlet woman?'

'I wouldn't want you to be damaged in any way because of me.'

'Of course you wouldn't. Nor would I want you to be damaged. But it's a dangerous world, Arthur. Unless one lives in a cocoon, damage of some sort is always a possibility. If I had been concerned about other people's opinions and suspicions I should never have engaged you in the first place. I was a 36-year-old woman whose husband was thousands of miles away in India, and you were a young man without a wife, the same age as I. I'm sure certain people raised their eyebrows. That's what eyebrows are for, I suppose. But I put such ideas out of my mind. I knew you were a wonderful teacher and you became a dear friend, and that was all that mattered to me. It's all that matters now. So when William raves and makes threats I find myself totally undisturbed. But if he caused me to change the tempo and the direction of my life, if he manipulated you into leaving this place, then I would be extremely disturbed.'

When Tagg didn't answer she said, 'I think I know what's on your mind. William carried on at some length about certain letters he'd found in my desk. Letters about you, he said. There are such letters. If you would like to read them, you're welcome to do that. Or I will tell you about them, whichever you prefer.'

'It would never occur to me to read any letters of yours. Nor do you have to tell me about them.'

'Of course that's how you feel. I knew that without your saying it. But since you've only heard William's version of what's in those letters, I feel obliged to give you a more accurate picture. Not for your sake but for mine.'

Again Tagg did not answer. After a long moment Margaret went on. 'When I went to see Sophie in London just after Christmas it was a splendid visit for me. We were able to spend a great deal of time alone together. So when I left London to come home I felt that we'd solved any problems that had come up between us because of her marriage, healed the wounds and explained away the misunderstandings. I felt truly exhilarated as my train left London bringing me back here.

'I had also seen Evan, as you know, and we had spent a lovely two hours together. So I felt good about that too. As I rode north on the train I decided to write a short note to each of them, Evan and Sophie, telling them how much I'd enjoyed seeing them. But the notes turned into full-length letters. Although I'd had no such intention originally, in Sophie's letter I told her in detail about my

358

relationship with her father, how he had failed me and how I, perhaps, had failed him. It wasn't intended to be an excoriation of William. More accurately, it was like an intimate conversation between an older married woman and a younger woman who had recently married for the second time. It was the most candid letter I had ever written. I'm sure that's why I decided, once I was at home here, not to post it. I've learned, to my sorrow, that even when we choose a person to whom we're willing to bare our soul, we have no assurance that the person we've chosen is as willing to listen as we are to talk. For much the same reasons I also decided not to post the letter I wrote to Evan that day. In the letter to him I discussed my feelings for him and for you. I wrote quite a lot about you and I believe I made some comparisons between you and my husband. Those passages, I expect, were the ones that riled William the most.'

She got up from her chair and walked to the window that looked down on the garden. 'I told him how important it has been for me to have you here. How kind you've been to me and Sophie. How helpful and dependable. I told him what a pleasure it is for a woman to have a man friend with whom she can have a civilized conversation. No conflict or competition involved. No manoeuvring for position. I must have told him how rewarding it is to be in daily contact with someone who truly wishes you well, who accepts you as you are.' She turned away from the window. 'Am I embarrassing you?'

'No.'

Margaret walked back to her chair and sat down. 'There seems to be a social rule in England, perhaps in the rest of the world as well, that one must never put one's true feelings into words. Love and respect and admiration are all better left unsaid. Protestations of affection are insincere by definition. Do you believe that?'

Arthur smiled. 'I'm sure many people would say that I invented those rules you're describing.'

'Don't misunderstand me,' she said. 'I'm not saying there's anything wrong with such an attitude. But it seems wasteful, somehow. If I were truly fond of someone and I learned they were not aware of that fondness, I would feel like a failure. Do you know what I mean?'

'Yes, I do.'

'If someone told you that I thought of you simply as an intelligent, helpful person but not as someone I admired or whose company I enjoyed, that would surprise you, wouldn't it?'

'Yes, I suppose it would.'

'Of course it would. You and I have spent many years together, along with Evan and Sophie, and for the last years with William. That's a large share of our lifetimes. If I said to myself that you have never been anything but a staff member, someone to teach my daughter and help me manage the estate, if I said I had never really noticed you as a warm and thoughtful human being, as a personable man of my own age, I would be lying to you and to myself. If you said that in all these years you have never looked at me as a woman I simply would not believe you.' She paused. 'I've never talked to you like this and I suppose I wouldn't now if William hadn't made it necessary. Have I made you uncomfortable?'

'No.'

'Thank God,' she said. Then, 'What I've said to you just now is an approximation of what I wrote to Sophie and Evan and what William read. You've been a part of my life, Arthur, for all these years, and you always will be, whether you go or whether you choose to stay. There's no label for the sort of partnership we've had and if there were one I would avoid using it. Whatever it is, it doesn't have to be defined, or explained, or defended. Nor do I

360

believe it can be casually discarded or brought to an end. That's what I've been trying to say to you. I don't want you to go away. There's nothing William might say or do, no problem he might create, that could be solved by your leaving this place. However modest you may be about it, you're a vital part of Wiswell Towers and everyone who lives here. If you choose to leave us you'll leave a space that can't be filled.'

Arthur sat very straight in his chair, looking past her at the trees outside the window. At last she said, 'Have I said too much?'

'No.'

'Have I said enough?'

He sat looking at her in that soft, silent room, but he didn't answer.

4

The day after he returned to London from America, Kincaid had lunch with Evan. 'I'm not going to tell you about the wonders of New York and California. Sophie made me promise to leave that to her. I'm going to tell you about a business proposition that might interest you.'

After he'd described the Ned Kelly project, the failed screenplays he'd read, and Thorne's offer to Evan, he said, 'What do you think?'

'I don't think anything. It doesn't make sense,' Evan said.

'Of course it does. All you have to do is nod your head, I'll cable Thorne in California, his office here will draw up a contract, and the money will flow.'

Evan shook his head. 'I think you misunderstood somehow. As I said it makes no sense. I've never written a film scenario. I've never set foot inside a motion-picture studio. And I've never laid eyes on your friend Thorne. So why would he hire me?'

'Why would he hire me?'

'That's different. All you have to do is walk around and make an ass of yourself in front of a camera. A writer has to *write* something.'

'Exactly. And that's what you're good at.'

'I thought those studios had writers lined up like horses in stalls.'

'They do. That's where he got those rotten screenplays I told you about. Now he wants something different. He wants you.'

'Just because you told him I could write believable characters?'

Kincaid smiled and nodded. 'Told him you were better than Chekhov.'

'Did you also tell him you'd never read a play of mine?'

'No. I lied to him. Everybody lies out there. It's expected. If nobody lied there'd be no conversation at all.'

Evan shook his head and Kincaid went on. 'It wasn't just my suggestion. He knew about your play here in London. He heard good things about it.'

'Did he hear it only played for two weeks?'

'Doesn't matter. When you sign up to do this screenplay he'll have the world believing you're more successful than Noel Coward.'

'When I talked with Sophie on the telephone this morning I got the feeling she hated it in California. But it sounds as if you liked it.'

Kincaid grinned. 'Felt very much at home there. Just like being in prison. Nothing but con men and hustlers.'

'And that's what you're trying to drag me into?'

'I'm not dragging you into anything. All you have to say is no and this conversation's over. This is a job you can do, Evan, and I thought you might like the money. I think you could have some fun as well. But you're not committed to anything.'

'Take it or leave it. Is that what you're saying?'

'No. That's what you're saying. I'm saying I've agreed to do this picture if we can get a decent screenplay. I know the story. You know how to write. So the whole thing seems like a good idea to me.'

'Only the money seems like a good idea.'

'Of course it does. So why don't we do this? You said before you have to talk with your man at the *Telegraph*. What's his name?'

'Winkler.'

'That's right. Go ahead and talk with him. Meanwhile I'll send over the material I mentioned to you. Then we'll see where we go from there. It's not a trap, Evan. Three or four weeks at your typewriter and you're home free. You might end up with a whole new career.'

'I might end up with a big headache.'

When Evan talked with Winkler the next morning in his office, Winkler said, 'Are you really asking my advice?'

'I suppose I am. I think the whole business sounds daft. So I wanted to know what you think. When people start throwing money about I get suspicious.'

'That's because you work for the *Daily Telegraph* where nobody throws money around. But if you're going to be dealing with those movie creatures you have to readjust your rights. If you don't trust the deal because they're offering too much money, tell them you'll do the job but only if they double the amount. You might get a nice surprise.'

'So you say I should do it?'

'I didn't say that. I'm just saying you shouldn't turn it down too fast. You said Kincaid's sending you the story and a couple of screenplays to look at to see how they put them together?'

'That's what he said.'

'So don't outmanoeuvre yourself. Look at the material, and if you think you can make something of it, have a go. Nobody else will hand you that amount of money for a few weeks' work.'

When Winkler walked with him to the lift he said, 'Mary Cecil. Isn't she the actress who appeared in your play?'

'Yes, she is. What about her?'

'She's in hospital. Heard it on the wireless this morning.'

'What happened?' Evan said.

'Not sure I got it just right. Pneumonia, I think they said. Rehearsing a new play. Collapsed on stage three or four days ago. Middlesex Hospital, I believe.'

Downstairs in the street, Evan found a phone-box and rang the hospital. 'She's doing nicely,' the ward nurse said, 'but I'm afraid she's not allowed visitors just yet.'

5

Margaret had told no one about her difficulties with Cranston. Even Clara Causey, her lifelong confidante, had not been told. The situation that existed between Margaret and Arthur and Cranston, known only to them, hovered like a soft cloud in the corridors of Wiswell Towers, undiscussed and ignored but nonetheless disconcertingly present.

Margaret had told herself that after Sophie returned she would certainly discuss the situation with her. But when they talked on the telephone, when Sophie rang up from London, Margaret didn't mention it. Nor did it come up in subsequent telephone conversations. It could be dealt with more fully in a letter, Margaret concluded. But when she wrote to her daughter, a week or more after her return, she still kept the matter to herself.

How wonderful it is to have you home in England. I know it was just a few weeks but to me it seemed that you were gone for months. As I told you when we talked, we had our usual late-winter weather. Cold and wet and nasty. Coughs and colds and bouts of influenza among the staff and the families of our tenant-farmers. Hurlbut, one of our gamekeepers, had to be taken in an ambulance to the hospital in Newcastle. Fortunately, he recovered nicely and is back with us.

I've been in touch with Sarah and Trevor, of course, and their lives are as serene as it's possible for lives to be at their age. Actually, Sarah is going through an awkward adolescent patch. But since you've talked with her, perhaps you already know what's in her thoughts. As I write this, I'm aware that her mind may have changed direction countless times since I rang her at school a few days ago. In any case, you and I will chat about dear Sarah when we see each other face to face.

Speaking of face to face, I hope that will be soon. The only excitement I have to report is that *Country Life* has asked permission to do a photo essay about Wiswell Towers for a series to be called 'The Great Homes of Northumberland'. Your father, of course, opposed the idea and I too hesitated for several weeks, but at last I gave permission. They will also do articles on Wingate Fields, the Goodpastor home, and one or two others. So there will be some unusual activity here for five or six days while the magazine people and photographers point out splendours in our home which they imagine we have forgotten. Before giving my approval, I tried to imagine what my father would have said if such a proposal had been made to him. He valued his privacy, of course, but he was also extremely proud of Wiswell Towers and its tradition. I decided that he would have agreed to the article and the photographs. Then he would have arranged for a small army of uniformed guards to be present to see that no damage was done to the tapestries, the portraits, or the carpets. So I have done just that. There will be some guards from an agency in York keeping an eye on things. And your father, in full uniform, will undoubtedly keep close watch on the guards.

Is there any chance you might be here for the event? Apart from your children, you are our youngest and most attractive family member. I'm sure the photographers would welcome you, just as I would. When I agreed to their coming, I told *Country Life* that we would require several sets of the photographs, not just the ones used in the magazine, but full sets of all pictures taken. So you will have those in any case.

For her part, Sophie had decided that her negative feelings about California and Kincaid's possible involvement there should be kept to herself. As they'd sailed home on the *Bremen*, as she'd stopped expressing her misgivings to Kincaid, as they pretended to each other that their trip had been for pleasure and nothing more, she grew impatient to see Margaret, eager to sit down with her and tell her everything, plus and minus, that had occupied her thoughts these past weeks.

Once she was at home in London, however, in the cream-and-gold splendour of those familiar rooms and halls, Green Park beginning to be fresh and spring-like outside her windows, the threat of California seemed faint and not worth sharing. Not yet at any rate. Consequently, her letters to Margaret were like manifestos of her new attitude.

Of course I'm happy to be home in London. But not because our stays in New York and Los Angeles were anything short of sensational. I'm a city woman, as you know, or at least I've become one. The pavement feels warm and familiar under my feet, the traffic soothes me, the crowds of people reassure me. All this to say that perhaps, for those reasons, I preferred New York to California. I do not agree with Mark Twain, who said it might be a pretty nice place if they ever get it finished. For my tastes, it is finished. And splendid and grand. Great art, fine music and opera and theatre, marvellous stores filled with lovely clothes, and excellent restaurants wherever one turns. If London is a man's city, as people say, then New York, like Paris, is a woman's city. Or so it seemed to me.

Los Angeles, on the other hand, is nobody's city. Not yet. There's a kind of gangly adolescence about it as though it hadn't yet defined itself, as though no one is sure yet what final form it will take or if it will, in fact, remain formless, continuing to grow and expand, being crowded and cluttered, but lingering still in uneasy transition. Not quite a desert settlement, not quite a city. Just a random collection of people and ill-matched buildings waiting, it seems, for some master hand to give them order and definition.

As I write these things I realize I'm being unfair. My method is wrong. California and its cities, its customs and its residents cannot be judged by standards one has learned elsewhere. One realizes at last, and comes to accept the fact, that Californians are making it up as they go along. They are benevolent pragmatists structured by two simple questions. Number one: does it

367

work? Number two: is the sun shining? Ronald Colman, who in his circle is thought to be an intellectual, said to me one Sunday as we watched a tennis match in his garden, 'This is the place and the state of being that most humans long for.' When I hinted to him that I longed for other things he excused himself and went off to sit with Dame May Whitty on a bench built round a giant gum tree.

Am I being snide and rudely English? I don't mean to be. Having been too analytical of a place that defies analysis, and too critical perhaps of a society that does not embrace either the principles or the practice of criticism, I must now confess that Kincaid and I had a smashing holiday. Lying on wide white beaches, dancing barefoot in elegant clubs, drinking exotic foaming drinks concocted of gin and syrup and fresh fruits. We seldom looked at our wrist-watches, always exceeded the speed limit when we drove, and barely noticed the women who stroll the streets of Beverly Hills in costumes that closely resemble underclothing.

In short, in those brief weeks, we adjusted. We were fêted and accepted on all sides, treated as equals by our inferiors. Our houseman and his wife called us by our first names and the gentleman who parked our red roadster at the hotel called me 'Honey'. Rudeness is common but seldom deliberate, so people come to accept it. And so did we. When one is confused, or offended, or feels degraded, one simply smiles. If one is publicly insulted one laughs and orders drinks all round.

Having said all this, I add that I would not hesitate to return to California. And of course we may be forced to. If by some miracle we find that Kincaid will actually be working there, then he will certainly return for several months and I will either accompany him or join

368

him later. If I hear that you've been very naughty I may punish you by taking you along with me.

I will indeed come to see you when the magazine people are there. I don't promise to pose before the portrait of Sir Abner Wiswell but I will be as helpful as possible in all other areas.

6

When Evan went to Middlesex Hospital, early one afternoon, an elderly nurse told him Mary Cecil was not in her room. 'She's only been up and about these last two days and her doctor wants her in the sun-room as much as possible. That's just down the corridor and to the left. I'm sure you'll find her there.'

She looked up and saw him as he crossed the room to where she was sitting by the window. 'Oh, my God,' she said. 'I can't believe it.'

'I called this morning,' he said. 'I asked them to tell you I'd be coming to see you this afternoon.'

'They didn't tell me. The nurses are sweet but not awfully good about messages.' She put her hands up to her face suddenly. 'Don't look at me. I look dreadful.'

'No, you don't. You look lovely. Ethereal.'

'I know what ethereal means,' she said. 'Thin and pale.'

'How are you? How are you feeling?'

'How am I? I don't feel qualified to answer. They tell me I no longer have pneumonia, but I am enormously weary all the same. I feel like a tiny old lady with wispy hair and brittle bones.'

'You want a lot of rest, I expect.'

She smiled. 'I expect you're right.' Then, 'I wish they'd told me you were coming. I could have put on a bit of paint.'

'Why is it that beautiful women never seem to know they're beautiful?'

'It's not false modesty,' she said. 'I have a very good and presentable day every now and again. Extremely pleased with myself. Happy to see my face in the glass. But this is not one of those days.'

'You look marvellous to me. Seems like a long time since I saw you last.'

She nodded. 'I ran from the theatre that last evening like a street thief. Did you get my note?'

'Yes, I did.'

'I can't remember ever being so shattered by a play's closing. I was on a train to Cardiff first thing next morning. I felt bloody dreadful and guilty and sick. I don't believe in luck, you know. Never have. Especially in the theatre. It's all a matter of work. If the play is solid, if the actors are right for their roles, if the director's not a sadist or a fool, and if everyone does his job, then, more often than not, things will come right.'

'I agree with you. Luck doesn't count.'

'Ahhh, but in your play it did. Not good luck. Bad luck. One actor with his arm in a cast and another with a discoloured, swollen face. Such things aren't supposed to happen but they did.'

'But no one was to blame. And it's all over now.'

'Not for me. It will haunt me for ever.'

'I don't think so,' he said. 'Tell me about the play you were rehearsing when you got sick.'

'Nothing to mourn in that case. I'm not sure it would have opened. It was a tedious little piece called *Overleaf*. Roland Hartman wrote it and he was also trying to stage it. The play might have been set right by a truly skilled director but it was too much for Roland. There were some good crisp scenes but the story had no spine. I only did it because Tony Quayle asked me to. I like Tony and I

370

admire his work but after two weeks in rehearsal he knew as well as I did that we were slowly sinking to the bottom.'

'And then you got sick?'

She nodded. 'But not because of the play. I had a nasty bout with a chest cold when I was in Wales. And an infected throat. It was raw and rainy there but I was tramping the roads a lot because I needed to be outside. Wouldn't listen to my daughter or the doctor and I paid the price for it. This pneumonia that finally put me down had its beginnings in Cardiff. I always fly in the face of the gods. It's my instinct. Not laudable but unchangeable, I'm afraid.'

'So you're not ethereal after all?'

'Not a bit of it. Hard-headed and relentless. Unreasonable and intractable.'

'Why are those traits invisible to everyone but you?'

'Because I hide them. That's why I became an actress. So I could conceal my evil nature.' She looked at her wrist-watch. It was pinned to the sleeve of her robe.

'I'd better leave you now,' Evan said. 'I think I've stayed long enough.'

'No. Please don't leave. It's only twenty past four. I'm sorry I looked at my watch. Just a nervous habit. Don't go yet. I need to know what you're doing. Are you working on a new play?'

'No, I'm not.'

'I hope you haven't gone gun-shy. When a play closes it's important to get back to work as soon as possible.'

'As a matter of fact I may be writing the scenario for a motion picture. I haven't done that before and I think I'd like to try it.'

'When I work in films I'm always disappointed with the result. I hope that won't happen to you.'

'It's a few weeks out of my life, so there's not that much at stake. It's a strong story, different from anything I've ever tackled, and I think I can do some good things with it.'

'Good for you.' She looked at her watch again. Then, 'I lied to you a few minutes ago. I am nervous about the time. He usually visits me at five but he could come earlier. I never know for sure.'

'Are you talking about your husband?'

'Yes. I'm sorry. I should have said that.'

'Are you afraid of him?'

'No. Why do you say that? Why would I be afraid?'

'You just seemed nervous all at once.'

'It isn't that. It's just that I . . . oh, God . . . why can't things ever be simple?'

'Never mind. You don't have to explain anything.'

'Yes, I do. I want to. My husband's name is Alec Maple. Did you know that?'

'I think someone mentioned ·it. Geoff Bingham, I expect.'

'God knows what he told you. He hates Alec.'

'He didn't say that. He told me he was a good actor.'

'What else did he say?'

'Nothing. It doesn't matter.'

'Yes, it does. What did he say?'

Evan smiled. 'He said you fall down a lot. And run into doors. That sort of thing.'

'He told you about Alec, didn't he?'

'Yes, he did.'

There were tears in her eyes suddenly.

'Don't cry,' Evan said. 'I'm going.'

'I'll be out of here next week. I'll have to rest a lot, so I won't be able to work for a while. I'd like to come see you one day. Is that all right?'

'Not if it's going to cause trouble for you.'

'It won't cause trouble. I'd just like to talk to you. We've never had a chance to talk. I'd simply like to ring

372

you up one afternoon and say I'm coming to call. Could I do that?'

'I'd like it.'

'I'm sorry if I'm saying something stupid. You're probably living with someone. Are you?'

Evan smiled. 'Not just now. I threw the last two girls out yesterday.' He looked at his watch. 'It was just about this time of day, actually.'

'I am being stupid,' she said.

'No, you're not. But even if you were it wouldn't matter. I'd be very happy to see you standing at my door. I'll serve you tea and sugar toast.'

As Evan walked along the ground-floor corridor leading to the exit on Mortimer Street, a tall, very thin man, his hair curling long over his collar, came towards him, then stopped in front of him suddenly, blocking his way. It was a strong face, angular and bony, but the eyes were flat and pale. 'You're Evan Tagg, aren't you? Making a social call on my wife, I expect. A little chat about old times. Greasepaint, footlights, carefree life in the theatre. Sweet words whispered in the wings. High drama, low comedy, all that rot.' Before Evan could answer, the man stepped aside and walked away up the corridor, one hand in his trouser pocket, the other swinging free at his side.

7

When Evan rang the hospital again, a few days after his visit with Mary Cecil, he was told she'd been discharged and had gone home. He considered calling her there but decided at last that it was not a wise idea. He persuaded himself that patience was the answer. She had promised to be in touch with him and she surely would. Still, it was difficult to put her out of his mind. Before his visit to the

373

hospital his image of her had been strong and clear. A vibrant and lovely actress. In rehearsal. On stage. Keen and crisp and animated. Larger than life. Now, however, he saw her pale and uncertain in her hospital robe, her hair pulled back, her feet in blue slippers, nothing public or self-assured or theatrical about her. Her hands lying in her lap seemed incapable of gesture, her voice seemed too small to reach the far seats of a theatre. Her present self, there in the bare sun-room of the hospital, seemed little more than an armature on which her former self had been so fetchingly moulded.

But it was this new and fragile person that clung to Evan's memory. It was that frail and vulnerable creature he longed to see, to spend time with, doors closed and the world shut out, all thoughts of the sullen Alec Maple tucked away in some walled corner.

While he practised patience, while he waited, he had, thank God, his work to do, the strange and complex carpenter work of piecing together the scenario for a film. There was a resemblance to the craft he knew, structuring a play for the theatre, but there were great differences as well. The unsaid, he soon realized, was as important in this new medium as what was spoken. The face and the eyes could speak eloquently. A glance. A gesture. After he'd carefully read the previous scenarios and the story-line Kincaid had given him, after he had decided to accept Thorne's offer, he went to see ten motion-pictures in three days. As he watched each film on the screen, listened to the dialogue, and marked in his mind the revelations of movement and silent action, he tried to envision the printed scenario for that film, what the writer had put down that had elicited the final sounds and images he was watching. At home he wrote down some of those scenes from memory and described the actions in his own words. Then he took out a copy of his play, *The Father*

House, and rewrote the first act as he believed an accomplished screenwriter would have done it preparatory to filming. And most important, he discussed the process in great detail with Kincaid.

'We're a perfect choice for this job,' Evan said. 'Two people who have no idea what they're doing. Two fools who have ridden camels all their lives and have never seen a river or an ocean are now going to design a ship.'

'Don't worry about it,' Kincaid said. 'The good part is that we don't have to hide our ignorance. We can ask each other any question we like without embarrassment. We can reinvent the wheel. Since we know nothing about technique, all we have to do is tell the story so it makes sense to us. I told you what Thorne said. "Forget about the camera. Forget everything except what happens. Write down what people said and did in the order they said and did it."'

On the *Bremen* sailing from New York to Southampton, Kincaid had made notes about the Kelly story as he'd learned it from the people of Glenrowan, many of whom had been alive in 1880 during the Kelly Outbreak. He'd put the events in chronological order and had them typed by a stenographer on the ship. When he gave the pages to Evan he said, 'This is the story and the people who were involved. I can't tell you how to write it but I can guarantee you this is the truth about what happened.'

After he'd read all the material, when he and Kincaid sat down to discuss it, Evan said, 'Let me tell you how I see this story, the characters, the events, the whole situation, and then you tell me if I've got it straight. Let's forget about the early scenarios. They seem to have very little to do with the facts you've told me and the things you had typed up in this chronology. Am I right?'

'Exactly.'

'All right. It seems to me we're dealing with an extraordinary character. He robs banks but he's not an outlaw. He's a genius at survival but he knows he's doomed. If he can be called a bandit at all, he's a social bandit. He's a poor man trying to battle a system that can't be changed. He represents something to the people who are in the same fix he's in. When he takes money from banks he also burns all the mortgage papers. That's a social act. If he hadn't the support of poor families like his own he could never have survived as long as he did. But even so he was hanged when he was twenty-five years old. He fought the system the best way he could, the only way he could, and they killed him for it. I'm not about to go all the way and say he was crucified but there's no escaping the fact that we've got a big theme here. One that people understand. Especially just now. The world is suddenly crowded with hungry people who think somebody should help them. Am I right? Am I on the right track?'

Kincaid nodded. 'That's the way I see it. And the people in Australia see it that way. Kelly's not a national hero because he robbed a few banks. People think he stood for something.'

'So do I. Now let me tell you how I feel about strong themes. They're dangerous. Once you realize you have one by the tail you have to try very hard to lose it. You have to forget about how the story ends and concentrate on the details. Christ was a carpenter. St Joan was a farm girl. I mean we can't tell the audience what a fine chap Kelly is. We have to let them discover it for themselves. Or maybe they won't. The important thing is we mustn't tell the story of a martyr or a hero. We have to concentrate on a young man who's up against it and who lives by his wits. He steals horses and cattle, robs banks, shoots people, punishes traitors and at last he's captured, tried, convicted, and hanged. We tell that story. We also tell about the police inspectors, the constables, and the big landowners. We stick as close to the facts as we can. It's all there. Love, honour, betrayal, and death. But when Ned Kelly falls through the scaffold, the story's over. The choir won't sing. Nobody will say gentle words or weep by his headstone. We won't make judgements. We'll let the audience do that.'

'Sounds good to me.'

Evan smiled. 'And no long speeches from Kelly. Strong and silent. That way, if the actor who plays him is not so good it still won't destroy the picture.'

'That's the best idea you've had yet. I think I'll tell Thorne I want you to write all my movies.'

'Maybe there won't be any more. Maybe after they see this one they'll escort both of us out of town.'

Kincaid winked. 'I don't think so. I think we're on the rails.'

8

When Sophie went to Northumberland for the *Country Life* event her father was not on hand to greet her. But when she was in her rooms, her maid gave her a note from him.

Please come see me in my upstairs study as soon as you can. I am most anxious to talk to you.

When she was in Margaret's sitting-room a bit later she told her about the note. 'I hadn't meant to burden you with all this,' her mother said. 'Not just yet. But since you'll be talking with William, I'd better prepare you.'

Half an hour later Sophie joined her father. As soon as she came into the room he said, 'I'm glad you're here. I hope you haven't had time for a tête-à-tête with your mother.'

'I'm afraid I have. She told me what happened.'

'By God, it's always the same. Scheming and manoeuvring. Keeping a chap off balance.'

'I'm not scheming and manoeuvring. I've just arrived this afternoon.'

'Didn't mean you precisely. Just the general tone. The normal pattern of events. Nothing out in the open. I'm a stranger in my own house.'

'Mother says no one ever sees you. She said she hasn't seen you for days.'

'And you can tell her for me she won't see me for a while. She was the one who announced that she'd be taking her meals in her rooms. So what's sauce for the goose, as they say. I decided two could play at that game. Now I take my meals upstairs as well. The worm turned. Also had the small snooker-table brought up here to my sitting-room. Should have thought of that years ago. I'm snug as a bear here. Everything I need.' When Sophie didn't answer, he refilled his drink and said, 'I expect I'm in for a lecture from you. You usually line up on your mother's side of the parade-ground.'

Sophie shook her head. 'I don't even lecture my own children. I certainly wouldn't lecture you.'

'Well, that's good news.' He took a drink from his glass. 'What exactly did Margaret say to you?'

'She just told me what happened and what's going to happen. If it's all right with you I'd prefer not to review the details.'

'What did she mean by that? What's going to happen.'

'The divorce,' Sophie said. 'She said you want to divorce her.'

'That's right. That's what I told her. I said if she didn't come to her senses that's where we'd end up.'

'What does that mean?'

'If she didn't tell you I won't either. Let's just say I want to see some changes around here, and I think when she's had time to think about it those changes will be made.'

'Does that mean you may not want a divorce after all?'

Cranston smiled a tight smile. 'I have a feeling it may not be necessary.'

'If Mother makes certain concessions – is that it?'

'I think she understands the situation.'

'I don't believe she does,' Sophie said. 'She's already talked with her solicitor.'

'About what?'

'About the divorce. She's had several talks with Charles Tremont.'

'I can't believe it. Why would she do that?'

'I'm not an expert on divorce but I believe it's standard practice for both parties to be represented by legal counsel.'

'By God, I haven't spoken to a solicitor.'

'I see. That explains it then.'

'Explains what?'

'She said she'd expected to have some legal papers sent along by now. She's surprised you're still living in the house.'

'Why wouldn't I be? Where am I expected to live?'

'I don't know. But I believe people often live apart once they've decided to separate permanently.'

'I won't be driven out of my house if that's what she's aiming at.'

'I don't think she's aiming at anything. She seems anxious to co-operate so you can have your divorce as quickly as possible.'

'You're bloody cool about this, young lady. I guess you

don't give a damn whether your mother divorces me or not.'

'But she's not divorcing you, is she? Didn't you send her a note saying you . . .'

'Damn the note. Margaret knew what I was saying.'

'What were you saying?'

'She knows. She bloody well knows, all right.'

Sophie sat silent, looking first at her hands, then at the vase of roses beside her chair, and at last at her father. 'The note you sent me said it was urgent that we should talk. What was it you planned to say to me?'

'I wanted to make sure you heard my side of the story. Did Margaret tell you what brought all this on?'

'She told me but I'm not sure I understand.'

'What didn't you understand?'

'Perhaps *understand* is not the correct word,' she said. 'What I mean is I couldn't believe it. Surely you weren't saying that if Arthur stays on here, you would divorce my mother.'

'That's precisely what I said and I meant it.'

'And what did Margaret say?'

'She said Arthur Tagg would continue to live here for as long as he wants to. But I don't believe she meant it. Or even if she meant it, then I'm sure she's changed her attitude by now.'

'What makes you think that?'

'Because she's a sensible woman. When she's had time to think she usually makes the proper choice.'

Again Sophie was silent. 'I don't want to hurt your feelings or give you bad news but I have to tell you this: Mother's made a choice. She wants Arthur to stay on and he's agreed to.'

'Are you saying she's chosen that schoolmaster over me?'

'Of course I'm not saying that and neither is she. You're

380

her husband and Arthur is her friend. He's been a dear friend to all of us for many years.'

'Not to me, by God. Nor to your mother either. Those two are certainly not friends, not by my definition of the word.'

'What are you saying?'

'You're a grown-up woman, Sophie. You know something of life. You know exactly what I'm saying.'

'I'm sorry, Father. I don't believe I do.'

'Are you saying you don't know or you don't want to admit it?'

'Admit what?'

'Damn it, Sophie, I don't like to dwell on it any more than you do. But I can't pretend to be blind. I'm talking about what's been going on between your mother and Arthur Tagg for all these years.'

'Are you saying what I think you're saying?'

'Yes, I am.'

'Do you truly believe that?'

'I most certainly do.'

Sophie shook her head. 'Then why have you waited . . .'

'I didn't want to believe it. I had no proof till just a short time ago.'

'What proof do you have?'

'I have no photographs if that's what you mean. But I know how she feels about him. We can all imagine the rest.'

'My God, I can't believe what I'm hearing.'

'I thought your mother told you.'

'Not all the details,' she said. Then, 'If you really believe this, why haven't you done something? Why are you still here?'

'I'm willing to forgive her. But not if Tagg stays on.

You see it's not just a question of my feelings. There's the staff to consider as well.'

'The staff? What in the world does the staff have to do with it.'

'They're part of this household. Everyone must be considered.'

9

The Ned Kelly scenario was finished, bound, and delivered to Thorne's London office before Evan finally heard from Mary Cecil. Late one morning she rang up. 'I'm a new woman,' she said. 'Not a better woman, perhaps, but a new one. Colour in my cheeks, sparkling eyes, gleaming white teeth, and a daring new hair-style. I'm a flapper now. You won't recognize me.'

'I think I will. When will I have the chance?'

'Not till this afternoon,' she said. 'Is this a good day? May I come calling? Nothing sinister. No designs on your person. Just a pleasant visit over a pot of tea. I feel as though we're close friends who know nothing about each other. We must correct that. Is three o'clock all right?'

'Of course.'

'Excellent, I'll see you then.'

At a few minutes past three Evan's street-bell sounded, he pressed the buzzer, and a moment later there was a light rap on his door. When he opened it Alec Maple was standing in the corridor. Leather jacket and corduroys, and a silk scarf knotted loosely round his neck. He held out his hand and said, 'Alec Maple. Long-time housemate of Mary Cecil. Known, in fact, to some of my drinking mates as Mister Mary Cecil.' He edged past Evan and crossed the sitting-room. 'Mary was unable to come.

Dreadfully disappointed. Asked me to express her regrets.'

'Is she ill?'

'Not at all. Well recovered from her pneumonia, the saw-bones says. But indisposed today. Lovely word that: indisposed. A catch-all. Dust-bin of meaning. Covers all possibilities.'

He settled himself in a deep chair and said, 'I see you've put together a fulsome tea. Awfully good china, isn't it? Haviland, I expect.' He reached across and lifted the wine bottle out of its cooler. 'Ahhh, Montrachet. Mary will be put out when I tell her you'd uncorked her favourite wine. Not mine, however. Not a wine-guzzler myself. But we must defer to the ladies on occasion, mustn't we?'

'Can I get you a drink?'

'By God, yes, you can. A beaker of gin if there's one handy. I'm partial to Tanqueray but if you have something else I daresay I'll be partial to that. I don't think of myself as a heavy drinker. Don't stumble about or damage the knees of my trousers by collapsing on the footpath. But all the same one doesn't feel comfortable when one doesn't have a glass in hand.' He took the drink from Evan and sampled it by half-draining the glass. 'It is Tanqueray, isn't it?'

'Yes, it is.'

'Fortune smiles,' Maple said. 'Now, let's get right down to it. What's going on between you and Mary?'

'What do you mean by that?'

'What else could one possibly mean by such a question? It means are the two of you having a *do*, are you contemplating having a *do*, or was this to have been an afternoon of tea and sandwiches and a spirited gabbo about the state of the arts?'

'Let me tell you something, Mr Maple . . .'

'First off, only my solicitor and Mary's banker call me Mr Maple. One is called Alec by the rest of the world.'

'I don't give a damn what you're called. I don't like your attitude . . .'

'No one does. Don't care for it much myself.' He walked to the cupboard and brought the gin bottle back to the table by his chair. '*Le bon dieu* helps those who help themselves. Hope you don't mind. Can I pour you a bit of the Montrachet?'

'No, thanks.'

'No matter. I'm quite accustomed to drinking alone.' He sipped from his glass. Content to drink more slowly, it seemed, now that the bottle was sitting at his elbow. 'Now,' he went on, 'I sensed impatience in your voice. Anger. I'm accustomed to that reaction. I myself never lose my temper. One takes pride in being always in control. But that makes others uncomfortable. Altogether dotty sometimes. There's no violence in me, you see. No punch-ups or rolling about on the pavement outside bars. Never violent or physically abusive. Nonetheless, people who have those inclinations steer clear of me. Because I have a reputation, you see. For vengeance. I'm a vengeful chap. It's a well-known fact among those who know me. A pyromaniac. I would never abuse a man with my fists nor hit him with a stick, whatever the provocation might be, but I wouldn't hesitate to set him on fire. A splash of petrol and a match, and the job's done. It's never fatal. Very seldom a serious injury. But it gives a man good reason to reflect when his trousers are burning off his legs. Parked cars have been known to catch fire also. Almost anything that God or man creates can be burned.'

'Why are you telling me all this?'

'It wasn't planned. The subject just came up. One follows the flow of ideas and emotions. The conversation then turns in one direction or another. I felt you were getting angry, and I thought it only fair to tell you that if you hustled me out of your flat here, down the stairs and into the street, I would not fight back.'

'But in future you might douse me with petrol and set me on fire.'

'Most unlikely, I should think. But as Celine said – I think it was Celine – "The heart has its reasons that reason knows nothing of." To me that means that even reasonable people like myself can't be expected to be reasonable at all times.' With an almost beatific look on his angular face, Maple sipped from his glass of gin. Evan poured himself a cup of tea and said nothing.

'By the way,' Maple said then, 'I saw your play, *The Father House*. Saw it three times actually. Fine writing, I thought, but the director and the actors did you in. Too literal. Ibsen on the brain. They missed the poetry. That's not altogether true, either. Bingham came the closest. Of course, there's always a hint of poetry in his work because the man's a certifiable lunatic. Didn't you know that? I thought everyone knew it. One need never fear that Geoff will be trapped in realism because he doesn't know what it means. Bays at the moon, I'm told. Poor Dorothy, his wife, is like a keeper in the zoo. Geoff is as likely to be on the roof or in the lily-pond as in his bed. He's like a cat. The impulse and the action are one. No consideration. No reflection. That's why he's fascinating to watch on the stage. The audience senses that anything can happen and they're right. Have you had many conversations with him?'

'Two or three.'

'I'll wager he mentioned to you that he detests me.'

'I don't remember that he used that word.'

'Then another word like it,' Maple said. 'You see, he rejects me because he knows I see through him. When I was a young actor in Liverpool a journalist interviewed me. Asked me which actors I admired, who I'd learned most from. I told him I admired Bingham but that it was impossible to learn from him because in the first place he was a genius and in the second place he was insane. Geoff liked being called a genius but he never forgave me for thinking him insane.'

'I suppose anything he might say about you would be unreliable then?'

'Not necessarily. What did he say?'

'He said your Richard the Third was the best he's seen.'

Maple smiled. 'No insanity in that judgement.'

'He also said you have a history of striking your wife. The day my play opened she came to the theatre with a badly bruised face. Bingham said you caused that.'

'Contrary to what you may believe, Mary Cecil is a complicated woman. She's the sort of person things happen to. A psychiatrist might say she makes them happen. She and I have been together for more than twenty years. Almost everyone who knows us wonders why she's stayed with me. The two or three people who know us best are astonished that I've stayed with her.'

'And what do you think?'

'I don't think it matters a great deal, one way or the other. Whether we should be together doesn't really concern me. The fact is we are together and I expect we'll stay that way.'

'Is that what you came here to tell me? If it is, you've wasted your time. I have no designs on your wife. I have never seen her in anything but a public place. I know her as a playwright knows an actress who's performed in his play. We have no other relationship.'

'I believe that. But it wouldn't matter in any case. Mary and I have what is called an enlightened arrangement. Fidelity plays no part in it. She is faithful to nothing but her career and I am faithful to no one but myself. You say you have no designs on her. Perhaps she has no designs on you either. But I know her quite well. And both my instinct and my experience tell me that she is longing to talk to you, to tell you about herself, her bizarre family, her days in the convent school, her determination to remain innocent in a sinful world. It's a performance you shouldn't miss. As long as one remembers that it's just a performance.'

'Did you come here to warn me, to protect me, or threaten me?'

'None of the three,' Maple said, 'and a bit of each perhaps. Primarily, I suppose, it's a matter of order. I have devoted myself to disobeying laws and defying rules but through it all I have maintained a fanatical sense of order.'

Late that night, Evan lay sleepless in his bed still trying to solve the puzzle of Maple's visit. At last he went to sleep. Just before dawn his telephone rang. When he answered, Mary's voice, soft and blurred, said, 'I'm sorry, sweetheart. I'm so dreadfully sorry.' Then, 'Don't give up on me, Evan. *Please*. Please don't give up on me.' Before he could answer she replaced the receiver with a soft click and the wire went dead.

• CHAPTER 10 •

1

Two weeks after he received Evan's scenario, Julian Thorne flew by clipper to London. Kincaid and Evan met with him there in his office.

'This is the first time we've met, Mr Tagg,' Thorne said, 'and I want you to know it's a distinct pleasure. I had a great deal of time to think about this project as I flew over here, and they were all good thoughts. I can't decide if the three of us are extremely clever or extremely lucky. A bit of each I expect. One thing I'm sure of. If someone had told me a year ago that I'd be planning a major production about an Australian outlaw, written by a man who had never tackled a screenplay before, and starring a man who had never appeared before a camera, I'd have laughed in his face. But that's what I'm about to do. And when I say *major* production, that's what I mean. As soon as I finished your script, Mr Tagg, I started making plans. My first choice for director was Tim Garrigus. He's made a dozen quick westerns for me and now he's ready to take on an important film. I don't know if he's Irish but he drinks like an Irishman, so I knew he'd respond to those names in the script. Skillion, Byrne, Hart and Quinn. And Kelly, of course. I was right. Tim can't wait to start shooting. He's already on his way to Australia with Russ Tunstall, our cameraman, Bob Deal, our production guy, and Loren Iverson, our art director. They'll shoot a lot of film and still pictures between Glenrowan and the New South Wales border, do research on wardrobe and 1870 buildings down there. And as soon as they're back we'll start turning Thousand Oaks and Malibu Canyon into a little corner of Australia.'

'When do you expect to start on the picture?' Kincaid said.

'We're aiming for August 1st. And there should be no problem with that date. Bob says we'll need a ten-week schedule, ninety per cent of it on location, but all our key people will be optioned for four more weeks in case we need them.'

'When do I have to come over?' Kincaid said.

'The sooner, the better. We'll be doing a lot of advance publicity and we'd also like to involve you in some of the pre-production details. You know the story and you know the people and the territory. We want to get it right. I'd like you to fly back with me if you can. Day after tomorrow.'

'I can't do that. What's the latest I can be there?'

'June 15th preferred. Early July – if that's the best you can do.'

'I'll be there first week in July,' Kincaid said.

Thorne turned to Evan. 'How about you? Do you have schedule problems? When can we expect you?'

Evan looked at Kincaid, then back to Thorne. 'I read in an article somewhere that movie people don't like the writers hanging around when they're making a picture.'

'That's normally true. But not this time. Garrigus wants you on hand and so do I. And for you we can't wait till July. As we finalize production plans we may need to make some script adjustments and we want you there to do that work. We like what we've got. We don't want some hack to screw it up. Since you'll be sticking with the

389

production you'll have a separate contract for that. And you'll be happy with it, I promise you. So you check your schedule and let me know when we can expect you. June 1st the latest. My people here in the office will make the travel arrangements.'

He sat back in his chair. 'We're going to have an adventure, gentlemen. I expect that before we're done, the three of us will make quite a few pictures together. We could also make a great deal of money. And all of us want to do that, don't we? If we have a little already, we need a lot more. Nobody needs money the way a rich man does.'

2

When Kincaid told Sophie about his meeting with Thorne she listened attentively as he went through all the details. When he finished she said, 'It sounds as though it's coming together nicely.'

'Smooth as custard, Thorne says.'

'And what do you say?'

'Hard to believe it's happening.'

'But it is, sweetheart. And like Thorne told you, it will be a fine adventure. You'll feel you're back in Australia again, with all your mates. And Evan will be there as well. You'll have a grand time, I expect.'

'I don't think so,' he said. 'If you were coming along it would be a grand time. This way, it's just a job to be done.'

'But if you're a great success as Thorne predicts, you'll be off to California again.'

'I'm not thinking beyond this one project. You and I

agreed that I would have no future commitments. One step at a time. Isn't that what we said?'

'Yes, we did. But now the first step's been made. So I daresay the second one will come easier.'

'We'll have to see about that,' he said. Then, 'I hope you're not saying that if I'm offered another film after this first one, and if we decide I should do it, that you'd pack me off alone again.'

'I'm not packing you off alone.'

'You know what I mean. I thought you'd be coming with me but you're not.'

'That's true. But it wasn't an arbitrary decision on my part. We discussed it weeks ago, even before you knew the film was a definite thing. Sarah and Trevor have their school holiday and I had promised them a summer by the sea. Uncle Howard offered me their house in the Algarve, so I accepted it. At that time I thought you would be with us. But now that this movie is working out for you I'll take the children off by myself. Howard and Sybil will spend some time with us, I imagine, although she doesn't care for Praia da Rocha in the summer, and my mother will be with us down there some time in July. You'll be working hard, and I'll be loafing and listening to the chatter of my children, and time will go quickly.'

'I'm sure we could find a house by the ocean in California. Then the children could have their beach holiday and we wouldn't have to be separated.'

'Of course we would. You said yourself that you'll be shooting somewhere in the countryside most of the time. And it's a six-day working week, isn't it?'

'I believe it is.'

'You know it is, darling. So if I can't have you in my bed every night, if I'm to live like a nun, I prefer the convent life of Portugal to that of Thorne's California.'

'Don't you think Sarah and Trevor would like it out there?'

'I've thought about that,' she said. 'And I think they would adore it. But for me, that's a good reason not to go. California's a seductive place for people their age. I could see that even in the short time you and I were there. All the best things are visible and accessible. All there for the taking. Feel the sun, smell the flowers, splash in the sea. Dance in the moonlight, drive in an open car, kiss a pleasant stranger. Los Angeles is not simply a place where movies are made. It is a movie. And everyone who lives there is busy acting in it. If you want to eat sausage in a roll, you go into a building that's designed in the shape of a sausage. Fish restaurants are shaped like whales. Barristers wear cowboy-boots in the court-rooms. The whole place is a playground. Conceived for children. Inhabited by children. So of course my children would love it. They might very well prefer it to any other place in the world. That's why I'm not keen to take them there. They're too young to realize that Los Angeles can be swallowed in one gulp like a spoonful of trifle. It's a meatless meal. Life seems easy because there is no life. Comfortable clothes, easy choices, pastel colours, belladonna, and plastic surgery. And when eventually one dies from boredom it's possible to be buried beside your cat in the pet cemetery.'

Kincaid smiled. 'Amusing but exaggerated.'

'Of course I exaggerate,' she said, 'but not by much. Gertrude Stein was brought up in California. When someone inquired about her home town she said, "There's no *there* there." If I were asked to compare Los Angeles with London I could only say that there are no grounds for comparison. So I don't intend to put my children in a position to make such a comparison before they're mature enough to make it properly.'

'You still didn't answer my question. Are you saying that any time I have to go to California in future, you'll find a reason to stay behind in England?'

'Of course not,' Sophie said. 'I'm not punishing you by staying here. I'm punishing myself. I hate to be away from you for even one day. I'm not just bound to you by marriage vows. I need to be with you. I'm miserable without you. But I know you have things you must do. So for this time, for this one time, I'll be doing something I must do with my children. You know I could never abandon you. But you also know that shrubs like me are hard to transplant. English flowers need rain. They don't do well in the desert.'

3

After her conversation with Kincaid, Sophie wrote a letter to Margaret, telling her the details of his schedule and their respective departure dates, he for California, she, with Sarah and Trevor, for the Algarve. In the final paragraphs of that letter she allowed herself to go beyond the operational aspects of the arrangements to the subjective ones.

As you can see, I am my usual calm and self-contained self. How I wish that were true. You know from our previous talks how insanely happy I am with Kincaid. After all my years alone after Toby died, I had given up hoping for a good warm life with a man I could love and respect. Then Kincaid appeared. Like a fabulous gift from somewhere. It seemed to me that no two people had ever complemented each other as we do. We have an instinctive understanding between us that is remarkable.

As you may have guessed there are long silences with a man like Kincaid. But all the same, the connections are never broken. He never retreats. Never goes away. I'm always aware of his presence even when he's not in the room.

But now he is going away. A long distance. And for several months. And I'm going off, too. In another direction. We sit and discuss all this in a calm and reasonable manner but inside me something is saying, 'What are you doing? Why is this happening? Why are you allowing it to happen?' I tell myself that it's the sort of conflict that often happens inside families. Men have business to conduct. Trips to make. Land to buy or sell in other countries. Holdings to look after. I've heard Clara talk about how much of the time Angus Bradshaw used to be away from England.

But then I say to myself, 'You needn't be separated. You can go with him.' I'm using the children and their school holiday as an excuse but I know in my heart I could make other arrangements. They could spend part of their summer at Praia da Rocha with Howard and Sybil, and the rest of it with you at the Towers. They would miss me a bit perhaps but they're old enough to understand that it's important for me to be with Kincaid.

I could also take them with me to California. I've explained to Kincaid in great detail why I don't want to do that. He pretends to accept my reasoning – he knows I have grave reservations about the quality of life in southern California – but I don't think he agrees with me that those reservations are a valid reason for us to be separated until God knows when. As you can tell from the tone of this letter, I'm not sure of that myself. So why am I taking this position?

I hope I'm not saying to Kincaid, 'If you've chosen

this odd adventure, if you feel the need to toddle off to California rather than stay comfortably at home with me, then you'll have to do it by yourself. All domestic pleasures and rewards will be denied you till you come to your senses and return to London.' Women do that sort of thing, of course, the Lysistrata syndrome, but at this point in history it seems desperately primitive. And in any case it's nothing I would do. Or would I? Am I capable of saying to someone I love, 'It's my way or no way?' The answer, of course, is that I'm not. But still, the result seems to be the same.

Here's another subtle shading. I've admitted it to no one else and I reveal it to you in strict confidence. My oft-repeated criticisms of Los Angeles *et environs* are not simply what they seem. The place is all tangled in my head with this new activity that Kincaid seems to be rushing into. It's so foreign to me, so far outside my experience that it makes me wary. One knows that many great chefs keep dirty kitchens but we put that out of our minds when we're dining in an excellent restaurant. Just so with a motion picture or a stage play. A very pleasant way to spend two hours in the evening. But I don't want to go backstage. I don't want to find out if the actor playing Othello goes home at night with the actress who plays Desdemona. Nor would I like to visit the production sets of Gaumont-British to watch the actors at work.

Here's what I'm saying. I would be disturbed to learn that my darling husband had signed on as pastry chef at the Café Royale. I confess that I am also unquiet about his new involvement in the making of motion pictures. If he fails in this first effort, however, I will not rejoice in that failure. Anything that might hurt him is a frightening prospect to me. I suppose I would be most content with a qualified success, one with neither humiliation nor great acclaim. The third possibility, that he would become in a short period of time a public person who could go nowhere without being recognized, pursued, and petted, who would be adored by strangers, hounded by journalists and photographers – that prospect is so repellent to me that I cannot describe it.

So perhaps my refusal to go with him to California is not so simple a decision as it seems. By temporarily distancing myself from him, by admittedly distancing myself from the place where he'll be working, am I hoping to drive an opening wedge, to plant the thought in his head, before he has irrevocably defined himself as public chattel, that such a definition is unacceptable to me? If so, then I truly am saying, 'Choose me or choose that odd, fairyland occupation.'

How can I defend such behaviour? Knowing how I feel, knowing how desperately I love him, how can I do anything but follow him and have faith that no change of location, no new emphasis or activity can alter the way we are together? When I ask myself that question I always give the correct answer. But a moment later I've taken another turn and the power of reason takes control. 'This has nothing to do with love, with your feelings for him or his for you. You have a brain and you have intuition. If you're not guided by those faculties you are extremely foolhardy. When someone you love makes an unwise choice, for whatever reason, you have an obligation to be concerned. You have a duty to try to see where the pitfalls are and to plot a course around them if you're able to.'

I don't expect that all of this, that any of this perhaps, will make sense to you. Other people's problems often seem to have simple solutions. So don't think I'm asking for guidance. I'm not. I know this is something I must sort out on my own.

4

If Kincaid had read Sophie's letter to her mother he would not have been surprised. He had learned, almost at once, how her mind worked, that it did work in almost all situations. Sophie believed, as the people of her class always believe, that problems can be solved, that what one has learned at home, in class, in Sunday school, at university can be used, must be used, to eliminate barriers and obstructions along the way. Letters can be written, phone calls made, strong-boxes unlocked, threats or promises made, friendships renewed, various handclasps and pressures applied, and eventually, by close observation of the lessons of economics, social history, and fear, a solution can be found. What are the values of good lineage, property, contributions to the church, and education if they can't be used to get one's own way?

Without these tools, however, other tactics are necessary. Since triumph, or even compromise, is rare when one is both poor and lacking in courage or optimism, one quickly learns the techniques of acceptance. Acceptance with resentment, with anger, and occasionally with grace. People who have never heard the word *fatalism*, who would not understand it if they did hear it, are the ones who practise it most consistently in their daily lives.

These were the people Kincaid had known, people without great expectations or grand plans. Only in prison had he met people with such plans. A grand plan had put them inside the walls and another one, each man hoped, would get him out. But these were the exceptions. The men on the cattle runs and sheep stations, the men digging

397

ore or cleaning fish, the migrants and draymen, the blokes with brooms and shovels, the ocker whose swag was all he owned, these grubbers and workers and drunks and street-brawlers whom Kincaid had worked and drank and fought with along the way were the children of chance. They believed that chance was the only constant in their lives. By chance a bit of work turned up, by chance a lorry overturned and crushed its driver, or a mine flooded and all the miners were drowned or put out of work. Chance produced a lift on the road, a drink of whisky under a bridge, a woman who would spread her legs for a shilling. Chance brought misery, hunger, heart-break, and only occasionally a bit of joy. But it was an ally. Something to be relied on. The only thing, if one paid close attention, that was always in evidence.

Because he'd been very young when he'd buffeted about Australia and later round the world, because he was still young, more aware of good fortune than bad, Kincaid had made an ikon of chance, had given it more credit than it deserved for the few good turns he had taken, and had often assumed the blame himself when things had gone sour. Needing, through those meagre years, to cling to something, he had stuck with his belief that chance was his friend and would at last serve him in some quite remarkable way. Ironically, the more he read and learned and educated himself, the more he clung to his pagan faith in tomorrow.

When his fortunes began to turn, therefore, in London, when a slow and sputtering series of events started to bring him into sharp focus, when strangers befriended him, although those individual happenings came, each one, as a surprise, the general sensation of moving ahead was not surprising to him at all. When he was an eight-year-old boy in the New Norfolk orphanage, when he took long walks alone by the river, the thought that came to him most often was, 'Some day I'll have my turn.'

He became a busker in desperation. Since he had no specific goal he could make no plans towards achieving it. He saw no value, until Evan persuaded him, of being featured in the *Daily Telegraph*. He accepted the generosity of Rosamund Barwick because it was forced on him by the court. But all the while some unfamiliar warmness inside him began to promise a sea change. After a week in the flat over Mrs Barwick's coach-house he knew without question that he had caught a benevolent tide. By the time he performed at the Cromwell and the Royal Court, he had demonstrated to himself how chance and his own efforts could blend together.

Julian Thorne, therefore, was not the surprise he might otherwise have been. Nor was Sophie. The child from whom gifts had been withheld was suddenly being rewarded. Or so it seemed to Kincaid. Just as he had accepted his earlier misfortunes, he now accepted the good things. If chance had been responsible before, he reasoned, it was responsible now. The pagan inside Kincaid asked no questions and made no demands. That small creature simply smiled and followed what seemed by now to be a well-marked road.

5

One morning as he went through his mail, consisting primarily of business circulars, military bulletins that concerned retired officers, and catalogues for hunting and fishing gear, Major Cranston came upon a short letter from Margaret's solicitor, Sir Charles Tremont.

We have been advised by your wife, Mrs Margaret Cranston, that you intend to commence a divorce action against her. For several weeks we have awaited some word from you or your solicitors but no information has been forthcoming.

. We hereby inform you, therefore, that we have now been instructed by Mrs Cranston to bring an action against you. We intend to file the proper papers in ten days or two weeks. Please furnish the name of your solicitor to this office so we can supply him with copies of our filing. If we don't hear from you, notice will be sent to you from an officer of the court.

Cranston went directly to the morning-room where he found Margaret with her mail. He put Tremont's letter on her desk and said, 'Perhaps you will be good enough to explain why this was sent to me.'

Margaret smiled at him. 'Good morning, William.'

'Just read that and tell me what it means.'

'Good morning, William.'

'Don't try to put me off . . .'

'Good morning, Major.'

'Good morning, damn it.'

'That's better,' she said. She read through the letter and handed it back to Cranston. 'Sir Charles is well known for his ability to say what he means. This note seems clear to me.'

'I'm the one who's suing for divorce.'

'I'm aware of that. But we've had no notice of it. I thought perhaps you'd changed your mind.'

'That's what you'd like, isn't it? But don't count on that, old girl.'

'Oh, I wasn't counting on it. I was afraid that's what you had done. That's why I'm suing you.'

'I won't have it. I'm the one who's been taken advantage of and by God I'm the one who'll sue for divorce.'

'That's fine. The sooner, the better. But meanwhile I'm sure Sir Charles will proceed with my suit.'

'Don't be an ass, Margaret. You can't divorce me. You have no grounds.'

'It would be difficult, I expect, since you've been an exemplary husband. But I'll have a long meeting with Tremont and I'm sure he'll come up with something.'

'But you don't even want to divorce me. I was the one who brought up the subject.'

'That's true,' she said, 'but as you can imagine, I've thought about it a great deal since then, and I've decided you're right. So now I think we should proceed and put the whole nasty business behind us.'

'I don't like the sound of that. Are you planning to put me in a bad light?'

'Not at all. I think people will sympathize with you. There's always something sad about a husband whose wife has turned to another man for affection.'

'I never used the word *affection*,' he said.

'That's true. I believe you said *adultery*.'

'That's the legal term, isn't it?'

'I can't tell you. I've never gone through this before.'

'Nor have I. But whatever my feelings, you know that I'm a gentleman. I won't allow this to be a public scandal. I have no desire to make you look bad.'

'You don't? That's certainly not the impression you gave me before.'

'I was angry, damn it.'

'Yes, you were. But in any case, the die is cast now and we must proceed. I agree with you that it's the best course.'

Cranston referred to the letter in his hand. 'Don't think I'm unaware of this man's reputation. God knows what sort of lies he may tell about me.'

Margaret shook her head. 'No, William, you're mistaken about that. Tremont is the soul of honesty. He's been our family lawyer for years. He wouldn't lie about you or allow me to do so. In fact, I'm sure he will insist on my telling the total truth about our life together.'

'By God, I don't like the sound of that either. That means he's found a way to turn the truth about and make me look like a jackass.'

'Oh, I don't think so. But perhaps we'll have to wait and see. Let's file the papers and let the solicitors talk things over. Then we'll go on from there.'

'By God, I don't understand you. All at once you're damned keen to get rid of me.'

She shook her head. 'Not at all. After the things you've said to me, and to Arthur, and to Sophie when you talked with her, it's plain to see that you can't wait to pack up and get out of here. And I don't blame you. That's why I'm making every effort to make things easier for you. Once the papers are filed I'm sure your solicitor will advise you to leave here as quickly as possible. When we talked before, you mentioned that we also have to consider the staff. And I think you're right. It must be awkward and confusing for them, having the master and the mistress in separate wings. Living in separate quarters.'

'But we've always lived that way.'

After a long moment she said, 'That's true. So we have.'

Jack Brannigan came to photograph the Northumberland homes for *Country Life*. He did Wingate Fields first, then the Goodpastor home, and next he came to Wiswell Towers. When he was introduced to Margaret and Sophie by Cynthia Leek, the editor for the article, Brannigan turned at once to Sophie and said, 'You're a truly gorgeous young woman, Mrs Kincaid, a subject for a sonnet. Surely you need bodyguards no matter where you choose to walk. If I'd met you at any other moment in my life I'd have fallen to the floor and kissed the hem of your garment. But today, just now, at this moment, I can barely see you. I have eyes only for this woman who introduces herself as your mother.'

He turned to Margaret and said, 'By God, madam, you are a revelation. Ah, I see in your eyes that you're offended. Don't be. You mustn't be. I am Irish. I have an Irish eye and an Irish mouth. But if I thought I'd offended you, I'd cut my throat right here in your reception-hall. I was brought up Catholic, you see. Learned my lessons well. And I assure you the Lord never intended that man should be silent when he sees something beautiful. If I had to stand here mute and pretend that you are just another charming and gracious Englishwoman, I would feel like a traitor to my soul. Beauty doesn't exist until someone notices. Who said that? Perhaps I did. And please don't imagine, just because I'm a stocky chap in his fifties, hair-line receding a bit and a half-step slower than I once was, do not conclude, I beg you, that this ordinary lad from Donegal does not recognize beauty when it appears. I've devoted my life to it. The seasons, the fields, the skies, and the seas. And all the lovely, heart-stopping creatures, animal and human. My brain and my heart are store-houses of all the wonders I've seen. Because once my eyes have focused on something truly extraordinary I own it for ever. It's etched on my brain, or in my soul, or wherever the good stuff comes to rest. And it never fades or gets misplaced. So when I've finished my work here, dear Mrs Cranston, when I've climbed into my caravan and driven off, if you feel a bit weak or changed somehow, you'll know why. I will have stolen something from you and taken it away. Whenever you look in the glass, remember this: the reflection you'll see is a pale copy of the picture of you that I'll carry with me till they place me under the sod just outside my village of Letterkenny.'

Mrs Leek had tried to prepare Margaret, as well as Clara Causey, Patricia Goodpastor, and the other ladies involved, for the surprise of Jack Brannigan. 'You mustn't judge him too quickly. He's a brilliant chap, actually. Has lived all round the world and studied in Dublin, Auckland, Rome, and at the University of Chicago. He boasts that he has no career but the fact is he excels at everything he does. He was a prize-fighter as a young man, then a teacher, a poet, and a painter. He sings and plays the lyre and is fluent in half a dozen languages. He taught himself photography only five years ago and he calls himself an amateur. But we struggle to hire him whenever we can. However, he condescends to work for us only once or twice a year. When he does, he demands the highest fee we're able to pay. But he takes exquisite photographs for the Donegal tourist bureau and asks for no payment at all.'

'Sounds like an unusual man,' Margaret said.

Mrs Leek nodded. 'And he is. But he has a drawback that I must make you aware of: he has very little patience with what we call the social graces. He is absolutely dedicated to the practice of saying whatever comes to his mind.'

'Oh, my. That can be a problem.'

'Of course it can. When he first worked with us we thought it might be a serious problem. Stuffy people, you see. Not accustomed to such a flow of opinions and judgements. Particularly from an Irishman.'

'Of course,' Margaret said.

'But we've never had a problem actually. The things we were anxious about never came to pass. We decided that his basic sense of fairness always rescues him. He's a kind man. Never sets out to wound anyone. And his energy level is truly hypnotic. People are swept along. Also, he adores women and most women are quite taken with him. He's not an Englishman, you see. He's very different from what we're accustomed to. But you'll see that, of course, when you meet him.'

After her first two days with Brannigan in the house, Margaret rang up Clara Causey. The first question Clara asked was, 'And what about Jack Brannigan?'

'I'm not sure I know what to make of him.'

'Nor do I,' Clara said, 'but I think he's enchanting. He's like a gamekeeper with intelligence and sensibility.'

'Awfully brash, isn't he?'

'Of course he's brash. Why shouldn't he be? We could all do with a bit more brashness. Clears the air, doesn't it, when somebody speaks out a bit? Angus loved him and that's a good test. They drank together and stayed up every night till two in the morning. He scored a big success here. Only the staff was suspicious of him. Thought he was not a gentleman.'

'And he isn't, of course.'

'Of course not. And thank God for that. But he is a gentle man. And what a lovely sense of humour.'

'How old would you say he was?' Margaret said.

'Our age, I expect. Perhaps a bit younger. People like him are young when they're eighty.'

Margaret told her then about the speech Brannigan had made when they were introduced.

'Well, I must say, you got special attention,' Clara said. 'He treated me like a treasured sister. And Patricia Goodpastor the same.'

'The odd thing is that he's said almost nothing to me since that first meeting. When I see him in the morning he says, "Good morning, Miss Maggie. A soft morning, isn't it?" Then he's off somewhere taking pictures for the rest of the day. And in the evening he's at the public house in Hexham.'

'That is odd. Maybe he's smitten with you. Remember the boys when we were in dancing school? They never wanted to dance with the girl they liked best. I suggest you corner him one day for a nice chat. That's what I did. And I assure you he bears no resemblance whatsoever to your husband or mine. He knows how to talk to a woman. How many men have you met who could manage that?'

Margaret did not follow Clara's suggestion. She made no effort to corner Brannigan. But they did talk together. The last afternoon he was there, when Mrs Leek and her two assistants had already left to return to London. Brannigan asked her to walk through the gardens and the deer park with him. 'I'd like a fine portrait of you with flowers all round and the house in the background. We'll put it on the cover of the magazine. You'll be a famous beauty for the rest of your life. And I'll be known the world round as the man from Letterkenny who took the famous portrait of Maggie Wiswell. I know your name's Cranston, but since I've got no love for that military person you're married to, I prefer to think of you as Wiswell.'

'And I think of you as cheeky. No one in my life has ever called me Maggie.'

'That's because you've never met anyone who was good

406

enough for you. You happen to be a Maggie, not a Margaret. A woman with straw in her hair. Not a stiff-necked crow with starch in her corset and ice in her veins.'

'Do you always talk to women the way you talk to me?'

'Ah-ha. In case you haven't noticed, you and I haven't talked at all. Not since we met that first day.'

'Is there some reason for that?'

'Of course,' he said. 'I didn't want to talk blarney and I saw no opportunity for anything else.'

'My friend Clara Causey said she enjoyed talking with you.'

'That's kind of her. And I enjoyed talking with her. She's an interesting woman. But nothing like you.'

'I'm surprised to hear you say that. Most people think we're very much alike.'

He shook his head. 'Not alike at all. Except you both picked the wrong husband. Yours is a bully and hers is a bore.'

As they talked, they strolled through the gardens and the park, and he kept shooting pictures. Some of the house and the gardens, many of her.

'Did you tell Clara what you thought of her husband?'

'I didn't have to,' he said. 'She already knew it.'

'But you told her anyway.'

'That's right. I did.'

'Was she offended?'

'No. Are you?'

'A little bit,' Margaret said.

'No, you're not. And neither was Mrs Causey. As a matter of fact she laughed. She's got a great sense of humour. She got it from Angus.'

'You call her Mrs Causey and you call me Maggie. Why is that?'

'I told you. Because the two of you are different. She's cautious and you're not.'

Margaret smiled. 'You're wrong there. I've been cautious all my life.'

'Being cautious doesn't mean you are cautious.'

When he finished taking pictures they sat on a wrought-iron bench in the deer park overlooking a deep pond. 'How old are you?' he said.

'What difference does that make?'

'Makes no difference at all.'

'I'm fifty-three,' she said.

'I'm fifty-four. So we're twins. You're the youngest person in your house, you know. Major Cranston thinks he's ninety. How old is he?'

'Sixty-eight.'

'How about that other man? The one in the grey suit?'

'Arthur Tagg.'

'How old is he?' Brannigan asked.

'Fifty-seven.'

'He looks good but he's old inside. So's your daughter. Do you know that?'

'Sophie's young and gorgeous.'

'Gorgeous but not young. She's old inside as well.'

'You're mad,' she said.

'Of course I am.'

'How about you? Old inside? Or young?'

'Old as the moon. I'm Irish and I'm from Donegal. Every man from Donegal has a little wrinkled-up man living inside him.'

'Why are you so concerned about people's ages?'

'I'm not concerned at all. We're talking about sad creatures who think themselves old. You're living in an old house with two old men, an old housekeeper, and an old butler. It's not good for you. It's not even good for me. I've been here five days and I swear to God I'm developing symptoms.'

'Of what?'

'God knows. It doesn't matter. It's just a rhythm a person can fall into if he's not cautious.'

Margaret smiled. 'I don't see you falling into anything. You seem to do only the things you want to do. Am I right?'

'Of course you're right. What else should I do? Why would anybody spend his life doing things he didn't want to do? Does that make sense to you? Makes no sense at all to me.'

'I guess you're one of the lucky ones.'

'Maggie, my darling, my angel, my dear, luck has nothing whatsoever to do with it. Nobody's destined to be in a certain place at a certain time. Or to stay there once he gets there. I don't need a set routine to make me feel safe. I make a hundred free choices every day. Sometimes a thousand.'

'Don't you ever make a bad choice?'

'Never,' he said. 'I don't even know what a bad choice is. The choices I didn't make remain a mystery. The ones I did make can always be changed.'

'You sound like a confirmed bachelor. Have you ever been married?'

'Three times. Three children.'

'I thought you said you're a Catholic.'

'I did say that. I didn't say I'm a perfect Catholic. It so happens that I married a Baptist, a Presbyterian, and a Holy Roller from Tennessee. So in the eyes of the Pope I'm still single. Haven't been married for nine years now.'

'How about your children?'

'Two boys. One girl. The oldest one thirty-two, the youngest twenty-seven. All full-grown. All married. One living in Capetown, one in Florida, another one in Galway. They like me and I like them. We're always happy to see each other. They're lovely young animals, my children.'

Very early the next morning, the sun just edging up, Margaret went out to the courtyard in front of the coach-house where Brannigan's car was parked. As she crossed the paved area he opened the door to his caravan. 'Ah, there you are. What a fine way to start the day.' He held the door open and followed her inside. 'Throw those trousers off the bench there and take a seat. I've made an Irish coffee for you that will change your entire life. Heavy cream, dark brown sugar, and a jolt of the Irish splashed in.'

When he handed her the mug of coffee she said, 'It seems you were expecting me.'

'Not at all. But when I lay there in my bunk last night I said to myself, "Just in case she does drop in to say goodbye and godspeed, you'd best have a decent cup of coffee ready for her."'

'Actually,' she said. 'I came to take your picture.'

'Can't be done. I never pose. And you seem to have no camera.'

'I'll use yours,' she said. 'But I'm ignorant about such gadgets. So you must adjust it for me. All I'm able to do is point it and click the shutter.'

He reached to a shelf behind him and took out a small camera. 'This one's foolproof. Impossible to fail with this little monster.' He made some quick adjustments then handed it to her. 'Centre my well-used face in the viewfinder and press the black button. I will scowl so the picture will show me as I am.'

She took five quick pictures, then handed the camera back to him. 'When you've developed them,' she said, 'just send me one. The one you like best.'

'I've never seen a good photo of myself. Only my soul is photogenic.'

'Then send me the one you hate the least.'

'And what will you do with it?'

410

'I'll keep it in my linen cupboard to frighten the mice.'

When she was back inside her house she went to the second-floor room that overlooked the coach-house. She pulled the curtains aside and watched his caravan back up slowly, turn about, and head south on the tree-lined road leading to the main gate. As she stood there in the window, the warmth from the whisky still coloured her cheeks. She assured herself it was the warmth from the whisky.

7

'Well, you're on your way, aren't you?' Rosamund Barwick said.

'I'm not sure,' Kincaid said.

'Oh, you're on your way, bucko. No doubt of that. When the money starts to flow you can be sure that matters have progressed beyond promises and conversation. And I've talked with Julian Thorne. More accurately, he's talked and I've listened. In my case, I've seen the light in his eyes. That particular glint can mean only one thing. He smells money. He thinks he has hooked a very large fish and from what he's told me I'm inclined to agree with him. You see, in Thorne's business, no one is really interested in innovation. Any change is usually the result of desperation. Talking pictures came about because the Warner brothers were going broke. So they risked everything and started making pictures with sound. It worked and they changed the whole business. It wasn't a matter of foresight or creativity. Financial panic brought it on. Thorne and all his rivals are dedicated to the principle of doing what they've done before. If it worked once, it will work again. That's the credo. Don't change the contents. Change the label. Don't sell the house.

Paint it a different colour. Wrap the package in fresh paper but don't, for the love of God, change what's inside.'

'I understand what you're saying, but look at what he's doing. He's got a new writer, a new actor, and the story's about a piece of Australian history that no one in America has ever heard of.'

'I know that's what you're thinking. You're convinced that Thorne's taking a big chance with you. I say he's taking no chance at all. You're the fresh wrapping I was talking about. The film itself is a western. Whatever trappings and historical events are draped on it, that's what it is. As foolproof a commodity as American films have discovered. Horse-thieves, gunfights, trials and hangings. Bank robberies, suffering women, and a noble hero. And a bit of a social message thrown in to give it weight. If that's called taking a chance, I know a few industrialists who would be happy with that same amount of risk. And as far as you're concerned, do you think those shop-girls and lorry-drivers who buy tickets know a good actor from a bad one? Of course not. They go to the movies to fall in love. When the billboards and magazines tell them Jean Harlow is the world's sexiest woman and Ronnie Colman is the most appealing man, they believe it because they want to believe it. Producers like Thorne tell the world what they should like, and what they do like, and for what reasons. Long before your movie is shown in a theatre, millions of people will already be convinced that you're great.'

'But when will I be convinced?'

'That's not important. You don't have to be. I'm told that many successful actors can't bear to watch themselves on screen. Cedric Hardwicke for one. Ethel Barrymore for another. The important fact is that other people want to watch them. And that's how it will be with you. Or so

Thorne believes. And I believe it too. Your problem is that your memory is too good. You keep thinking of yourself as a deck-hand on a freighter or as a busker in St Martin's Lane. Those days are over, Kincaid. You're a brand-new creature with a new destiny. Relax and enjoy it, my friend.'

8

Geoff Bingham, glass in hand, was holding forth. 'By God, you're a secretive bastard, Evan Tagg. Not a word from you in months, then a furtive little weasel named Pecorini, who says he's with Thornwood Studios, tells me he wants to talk to me about a film role in California, out there among the cacti, as they say. And before I have time to tell him to get stuffed, he says the bloody picture he's talking about was written by you. *Bushranger*, he called it. He was keen to buy me a lunch at the Savoy as soon as possible.'

'What did you say?'

'I say no to everything when it's first offered. Donald Wolfit taught me that. "Not available, old dear." That was his rejoinder. It's a good tactic. Gives the jackals and the hyenas who prey upon us something to think about. So I told this chap Peccadillo that I'm solidly booked for some time to come, but that I would speak to you about this *Bushranger* business. What in hell is a bushranger?'

Evan laughed. 'Don't ask me. All I know about Australia is what I learned from Kincaid. Actually, a bush-ranger seems to be a homeless chap who borrows other people's horses, butchers a stray cow every now and again, steals a bit of money when it's needed, and generally lives by his wits.'

'Not going all the way to Australia to make this picture, are they?'

Evan shook his head. 'Shooting it in California.'

'Why can't anyone make a film in Scotland or County Mayo, where there's scenery worth looking at. How do you feel about the Aussies?'

'I only know one. He's a decent chap.'

'Worked with an Australian director once. Don't know how that came to pass. Big burly chap. Insisted on calling me Geoffie, the silly twat. They love to turn everything into a diminutive, those people. Damned annoying if you ask me.'

They were having a drink together at the Black Eagle in Great Windmill Street just three days before Evan was due to leave for America.

'So they've sucked you into the business of flickering shadows, have they? Another playwright gone to perdition. I'm told they keep writers in cubicles out there. Like hens on an egg farm. So beware. You're too young and too gifted to be seduced by those rug merchants. Actors from London have flocked there, you know. All of them love the bloody sunshine and the coconut trees. They seem to be making a great deal of money and a few of them have got richer than Croesus. Odd thing, however, most of the really rich ones are people who didn't fare so well here in London. Ordinary chaps most of them. But now, one of our really good people, Bart Marshall, has taken Edna and gone off. Rathbone's there now, and Raymond Massey. Always liked Raymond, a bright fellow, but I have no idea what compelled him to be an actor. Amusing and likeable man at a party, crackerjack story-teller, but deadly dull when he walks on stage. Too bloody tall. Maybe that's it. Swinging those long arms and rolling his eyes. But he'll go well out there. He takes himself seriously and that lot is impressed by a serious

414

chap. Look how they've taken to poor old Karloff. But mind your step, Tagg. Don't sign anything that hasn't been checked by seven solicitors, don't fall in love with a dancing girl, and don't forget you're a playwright.'

'I've only signed for one picture.'

'That's it. If it's no good, they'd fire you anyway, no matter how long you've signed for. And if it makes some money they'll have you rewriting the same story under different titles for as long as you live.'

'I take it you're not interested in making a picture in America.'

'*Au contraire*, as my housemaid says. I try to be an artist in the theatre but when Rank or Gaumont-British rings me up I turn into a buccaneer. "Money," I cry out. "Give me great sheaves of money." If they respond properly I then accept their project, no matter how tedious the script, no matter how tiresome the role. I learn my lines, walk, run, or stumble to the required spot that pleases the camera operator and the dunce who calls himself a director. Then, when all possible damage has been done, I gather my pound notes together, go home, get drunk, and begin to prepare for my next job in the theatre. In short, if Julian Thorne and his procurer Mr Piccadilly are willing to pay me what I'm worth I will be happy to make an ass of myself in California. What role would you imagine they're considering me for?'

'I haven't discussed it with them but I expect they would want you for either McBean or Nicholson. They're both proper bastards.'

'So much the better. It's hard to feign benevolence and good cheer on a film set. Much easier to scowl and make threats.'

'McBean is a big landowner, mean as a snake, and Nicholson is a police superintendent. There's also Superintendent Hare and Captain Standish, the chief commissioner.'

'All bastards, I trust.'

'Not a decent chap among them.'

'Good. That's encouraging news. Perhaps I'll be offered a paid vacation in California, and if the money flows properly I will undoubtedly accept.'

When they left the lounge bar and walked along Shaftesbury Avenue together, Bingham said, 'No word of our erstwhile producer, Gossett. I assume he's opened a house of ill fame in Torquay, sly bugger that he is. Always suspected that he's a bit on the lavender side. Talks so much about his female conquests it makes one suspicious. Thought I saw young Rugger giving him a few sidelong glances when we were rehearsing your fine play. But who knows? And who gives a damn? A man has a right to do what he wants with his tally-whacker. It's no concern of mine as long as he keeps his fat fingers off my property. Am I right?'

'Seems like a sensible attitude to me.'

'And our dear Mary. What about her?'

'You mean Mary Cecil?'

Bingham nodded. 'Dear Mary Cecil. Have you seen her?'

'Once, after the play closed, we had tea together. But that was some time ago.'

'Dorothy, my lady wife, sees her occasionally. Perhaps I told you that. She thinks Mary may have left her rotten husband at last. Do you think that's possible?'

'I would have no way of knowing.'

'Tossed the bugger out, Dorothy said. I hope it's true. He's a worthless drone. Have you met him?'

'I don't think so,' Evan said. 'May have met him backstage at the theatre but if I did I don't remember.'

'None of my affair, old chap, but I had the feeling you had a little fever for our Mary. Am I wrong?'

'I liked her a lot. She's a fine actress.'

'Ahh, yes. That wasn't what I had in mind. You see, Dorothy suspects that Mary has chosen another companion. Thrown out the husband and brought in a new chap.'

'Good for her.'

'So it's not you, eh?'

'It's not me at all,' Evan said.

'I'll be damned. I'm usually right on in these matters.'

Evan smiled. 'Not this time, I'm afraid.'

'I'll be damned.'

9

Clara Causey came to spend the day with Margaret the week after the *Country Life* people had come and gone. When they were having coffee and port together after dinner, Clara said, 'You haven't mentioned Jack Brannigan. Does that mean you have secrets to conceal?'

'No secrets,' Margaret said.

'Did you manage to have a conversation with him as I suggested?'

For reasons that were unclear to her Margaret had decided, from the moment she knew Clara was coming, that she would not discuss the time she had spent with Brannigan. 'No,' she said now. 'It didn't come about somehow and I didn't see any reason to force it.'

'Oh, but I gave you a reason. You would have had a thoroughly delightful time, I'm sure. He's another sort of person. Not at all what we're accustomed to. After talking with him for half an hour I felt as if I'd made a sorry job of my life. It wasn't a matter of having failed my children, or Ned, or even myself. It wasn't that I'd done things badly. I simply felt that I've had such a narrow vision, that I've accepted things I should have questioned and rejected. I felt as though I've had many choices that I've refused to make, that I've bypassed all sorts of lovely opportunities to see and hear and understand. I've lived as though Northumberland were the universe and Wingate Fields the world. Do you know what I'm saying?'

'Of course I do. But I think you're being too critical of yourself.'

'I don't mean to say that I feel like a failure. Nothing could have changed the responsibilities I've had or my duties to my family and myself. Some things had to be done in any case. Certainly I wasn't cut out to be a hedonist. Neither are you. And neither is Brannigan in my view. What I'm talking about, I suppose, is a sense of joy, an ability to see things in a fresh way. It doesn't require a fundamental change in one's life – leaving home, moving to the Côte d'Azur, putting your children in an orphanage, or becoming a papist. It's just a small adjustment you make in your brain that redefines things, changes labels, allows you to decide for yourself what's important and what isn't, and above all permits you to change your mind.'

Margaret felt strangely ill at ease suddenly. 'You've become positively evangelical, my dear. Maybe it's best that I didn't expose myself to Brannigan.'

Clara laughed and put her hand on Margaret's. 'God forbid that I, of all people, should become evangelical. If I seem to have done, then that's a contradiction of everything I feel. Words always betray us, don't they? Let me put it this way. Remember how we felt when Nora and Hugh and Sophie were tiny children just learning to run and play and fall and get up laughing? You and I have discussed this many times. There was such a freedom about everything they did. Squealing and tumbling and dashing about. And we felt that same freedom from just watching them. A kind of exhilaration, unlike anything we had experienced before. Well, I had that sort of feeling from meeting Brannigan, from watching him work and hearing him talk. Suddenly I said to myself, "My God, this is a free and independent human being. Like those lovely fluttering pods spinning down from an autumn tree." For just a short time, while he was there at our home, I had that same feeling again, the way I'd felt watching the children on the lawn. Did you feel that at all?'

Afraid to risk an honest answer, Margaret smiled and said, 'No, I'm afraid not. I seem to have missed something.'

Two weeks after Brannigan's departure from Wiswell Towers, Margaret received a photograph of him enlarged to eight by ten inches. He was scowling as promised and over his head, by some dark-room magic, he had caused a halo to appear. On the back he had written:

I don't believe in sad farewells. So you'll hear from me again, whether you want to or not.

10

On the morning of Evan's last full day in London the postman brought him a letter from Sarah.

If you ever tell my mother I've written you this letter I will very definitely kill myself. I'm having quite enough trouble with her as it is. My feeble-minded brother, Trevor, thinks of you as his uncle. Did you know that? He knows very well that you are not a blood-relative of our family, at least he should, since I've told him often enough. But he persists, as he does in all his idiosyncrasies.

I certainly don't think of you as a relative, although I've known you all my life. Nor are you a friend precisely. You are just a very special person to me. I realize, however, that I must be a stranger to you since I've been away at school for these past few years, and when I'm not in school I'm often in Northumberland, or off in Brittany or Sestri Levante with my mother.

So you scarcely know me as a grown-up, which is what I am now. But I hope we'll be able to correct that when we see each other again.

I was very excited when I learned that you'd be going to California with Kincaid. I assumed that Sophie would go too, and take us with her. But then I was told that we would be spending the summer holiday in some dreary corner of Portugal where one has no friends and no freedom, and there's no excitement at all. I am absolutely unbearably keen to see California. I've read everything I could find about it here in the school library and I've sent off to the steamship lines for travel information. But now I find it isn't to be. Not this year. Or not ever perhaps, as long as my life is directed by other people. How tiresome that is.

I can't bear the thought of your being there in that gorgeous place and my being elsewhere. I know you're keen on sunbathing and sailing, and so am I. I had dreams of our sailing together on that lovely big ocean. I cried myself to sleep for two nights when I found out I couldn't go.

I know how busy you'll be, and I also know about your ten thousand lady friends, but *please* find time to write to me this summer. Mark the envelopes *personal* so Mum won't think they're for her to read. When you let me know your address out there, I promise I'll write you every day. Kincaid will tell you our address in Portugal.

I plan to sunbathe nude on the roof of Uncle Howard's house and get magnificently brown. And when I swim in the sea I'll wear an outrageous bathing-suit. Trevor will photograph me in it and I will send you a print. You will see that I am no longer the child you carried on your shoulders.

I will think about you all summer, and you must come to visit me at school as soon as you're back in England. Don't forget about me.

That same morning a note from Mary Cecil was delivered by messenger.

I must see you before you go. I have a mid-afternoon errand in Charterhouse Square. Can you meet me at a coffee-house called Micawber's in Cowcross Street? It's just east of the Farringdon tube station. I'll be there at four. I know it's short notice. If you can't come I'll understand.

The afternoon was unseasonably warm. He found her waiting in a tiny courtyard just behind the coffee-house. She was wearing a trim suit with a high-necked blouse and her hair was cut short. 'Am I a changed woman?'

'No,' he said. 'Only the hair is different.'

'Men always like long hair.'

'I think it looks smashing like this.'

'So do I. Suddenly I like myself.'

They ordered coffee then, and when the waiter walked away she said to Evan, 'So you're off to the colonies?'

He nodded. 'Tomorrow. Flying on the clipper.'

'What a splendid lark. I envy you.'

'Maybe you'll go yourself soon. It's a mecca out there for actors. Or so I'm told. Even Bingham may make the jump.'

'So Dorothy tells me. But she assures me he won't stay for long.'

'Neither will I.'

'That's what Madeleine Carroll said. And Leslie Howard.'

'But I mean it.'

After the waiter brought their coffee and cakes, she said, 'You weren't planning to tell me you were leaving, were you?'

'No. Last time we talked . . .'

'The night I called you in a fit of tears?'

Evan nodded. 'I decided you were telling me to keep away. Or to wait till I heard from you. It wasn't a clear message.'

'I didn't know what to say. Or what to think. I didn't know what Alec had said to you.'

'He seemed to think you and I were having a romance.'

'What did you say?'

'I told him we weren't.'

'But he didn't believe you?' she said.

'I'm not sure. He said it didn't matter in any case. He said the two of you have an "enlightened" marriage. I think that's the way he put it. He said fidelity was not a part of your relationship.'

'For him, it never has been. But I have different standards. I've never been unfaithful to him. Still he continues to think of me as a whore. Perhaps it makes him feel more free to do as he likes.'

'He also said you would never leave him.'

'I know. He tells me the same thing. When he looks at me, I think he still sees the sixteen-year-old girl I was when I met him. I worshipped him then. I adored him. I thought he was the greatest actor I'd ever seen, the most beautiful man. And the cruelty attracted me too. I hate to admit it but it's true. Then our daughter was born and

I had her to love, and I pretended not to notice how wrong I'd been about Alec. At last, there was nothing between us but the cruelty.'

'But you stayed with him.'

She nodded. 'There was our child. She loved him, as all females do. And then there was my work. As he pulled back from acting altogether, my career moved forward. We needed the money, so I found myself working all the time. In one repertory company after another and eventually in the West End. I took Angela with me as much as I could, along with Miss Joslyn, the lovely nanny I'd found. And when I couldn't have her with me, she stayed at home with Jossie and Alec. Oddly enough, he was a perfect father when she was little. Perhaps it's not so odd after all. He tries to make all women love him, so naturally Angela was no exception. She worshipped him, just as I had at the beginning. She still loves him, I suppose, but now she sees him through different eyes. She's a grown-up, and a wise one, and she realizes that Alec will always be a child. Spoiled and selfish and vindictive. You wonder why I've stayed with him? For all those years I did it for Angela. Since then . . . I don't know the answer to that. I think I felt as though we'd separated a long time ago. I hadn't left him but I wasn't with him either. Does that make sense?'

'Does he feel the same way?'

'I'm not sure how he feels. Alec has a strong sense of property. He doesn't like to give anything up. Perhaps he feels that way about me. I'm sure he doesn't really need me and he certainly concluded long since that I don't need him, but I suspect he wouldn't want someone else to have me.'

'Is that why he paid a visit to my flat?' Evan said.

'I expect so.'

'I think I persuaded him that there's nothing going on between you and me.'

'I'm sure he wasn't persuaded at all,' she said.

'Why do you think that?'

She smiled and brushed her hair away from her forehead. 'Because there is something going on between us. You know it and so do I. Why do you think we're sitting here like this? Why do you think I made an appointment to come see you at your flat? Why did I call you, weeping like a fool, in the middle of the night? There's something going on, all right. We just haven't admitted it to each other. It's a warm day but I'm shivering as I sit here looking at you. That's why I wore this suit. I knew what it would be like when I saw you.'

Evan smiled. 'I thought I was the only one who . . .'

'No, darling. Me too. For a long time now. Lying awake. Staring at the ceiling. Dreaming heavenly, naughty dreams when I finally go to sleep.'

'What terrible timing . . . I have to leave London tomorrow.'

'I just learned that yesterday,' she said. 'That's why we're sitting here now. I hadn't wanted to talk to you, didn't want to see you, till I'd cleaned up the rest of my life.'

Evan looked around him. All the tables were occupied now. Chatter of voices. 'Let's go somewhere else. Let's go home.'

'Please. Don't say that. I'll slump down on the floor like a cripple.'

'We can't just shake hands and say goodbye, can we?'

'How do you think I feel? I'd lie down in Kensington Gardens with you if you asked me.'

'We don't have to lie down in Kensington Gardens. We can . . .'

She reached across the table and put her hand on his

mouth. He put his hand over hers and held it there. 'Let me tell you what I want to do,' she said. 'If you don't agree with me, if it doesn't make sense to you, I'll get up from this table and go any place you want to take me. In a taxi, in your flat, in the hotel just next door to this coffee-house.'

'First let's get away from here.'

'No. First you have to listen to me.' She took her hand away from his mouth. 'I want things to be perfect for us. When I come to you I want to stay with you for as long as you want me. I want to be legally and publicly separated from Alec. I want the break to be clean and final. No dangling threads. No connections of any sort. I want to belong to you. In your eyes, in my eyes, in everyone's eyes. It's hell to have to wait for something you want so much but what kind of life could we have with Alec hovering over us at every turn? I have to end it with him. There must be no question in his mind that it's not over. And it won't take long, I promise you. I have no more patience than you do. If we walked out of here now and got into a taxi together, everything I've just said to you would go out of my head in an instant.'

They held hands as they walked towards the taxi rank in St John Street. She said, 'I'll ring up the Thornwood offices here to get your address in California. And don't be surprised if you see me there. Once we're together, I promise you won't be sorry we waited.'

· CHAPTER 11 ·

1

Soon after his arrival in California, Kincaid wrote a long letter to Sophie.

Here I am, well installed in a great stone pile on a hillside in Laurel Canyon. A staff to look after me, a driver to deliver me, and the world, it seems, in good working order. Evan's in a beach house in Malibu and is busy with the director, Tim Garrigus, working on a polished version of the script. Haven't seen much of him yet but will meet him tomorrow night for dinner. And once we begin shooting I'll see him every day.

I expect you're not eager to hear anything complimentary about California or the motion-picture business, but I can't pretend that I'm not impressed by what I've seen so far of the Thorne operation. Garrigus and Russ Tunstall, the cameraman, took me for a tour of the locations and the standing sets yesterday and I couldn't believe what I was seeing. They've actually recreated the bush country of Victoria and New South Wales. They had similar terrain to start with, of course, but the details they've added are the remarkable part. The outback buildings, the farm-shacks and barns, and the villages are exact replicas of photographs and engravings from 1880. The costumes and gear the same,

426

all worn and weathered as though they really had managed to survive since that time fifty years ago. Burt Deal, the production chief, and Iversen, the art director, tell me that these technical people, the crews behind the camera, are wizards. They can reproduce any building, any city, any weather conditions, any field or forest, or anything else that a writer or director can conjure up. 'They're the backbone of the business,' Iversen said. 'They can do what needs to be done, whatever it is.'

I'm being treated very well, as though I were someone other than who I actually am. The big signs with my picture on them are everywhere now. But they've added the title of the picture, *Bushranger*, in bold red letters. Everybody seems to be aware of what we're doing and there's a great deal of excitement about it, as you will see from the press-cutting I've enclosed. It's written by a woman named Gloria Westerfield, a powerful journalist out here. Everyone kisses her ring.

EXCITEMENT AT THORNWOOD

When Julian Thorne starts handing out a great deal of money you can be certain he expects to get back twenty times what he's spending. Many of the best actors in our British colony here are all smiles over *Bushranger*, Thornwood's new outdoor (is it a western?) epic that starts shooting in June. How's this for a cast? C. Aubrey Smith, Montague Love, Anthony Bushell, Donald Crisp, Ralph Forbes, John Loder, Reginald Denny, and Colin Clive. And among the ladies are Daisy Bishop, Cecile Cunningham, Elizabeth Patterson, and Beulah Bondi, all of them playing Australians. That's right, Thorne's new picture is set in Australia. And it will star a newcomer from down under named

427

Kincaid. If you haven't seen his picture on billboards around town the past few months, you haven't been awake.

Watch this space and we'll tell you more about Kincaid and *Bushranger*. Meanwhile, dear Julian looks like the cat who swallowed the canary. So perhaps we're all in for a treat.

2

Tim Garrigus had worked as an actor in a dozen western films before he became a director. 'Jack Hoxie and I kept the Majestic operation going. They had two cameras and two cowboy stars – Jack and me. Each of us made a sixty-minute picture in five days. If the whole shebang hadn't gone bust they could have had a hundred movies a year with just two half-sober ass-holes under contract. But they pissed it away. The front office always screws up. Either they're stupid or crooked. In this case, it was a little of both. Whatever the reason, I was working one Sunday and out of work on Monday.

'Then things took a good turn. Trem Carr had a director named Senesac who was so coked up he couldn't find his ass with both hands, so they called me up one morning at five o'clock and asked if I could finish a picture for them. As a director, I mean. Senesac was either in the hospital or in the clink, I don't remember which. So I did it. And then I did a couple Bob Steele pictures for them. Back to back. And the next thing I knew, Columbia called me in to see if I wanted to direct a McCoy picture.

Gentleman's work. A three-week schedule. Then I did a Buck Jones picture, and I kept sling-shotting back and forth between Jones and McCoy for six months or so. By then I'd decided I was better off behind the camera than I was in front of it. A lot of people out there think all directors are dumb bastards and in my case they're right. I just keep shooting till the actors finally get it right. Then we print that take and move on to the next set-up. This business is all on-the-job training. None of us knows anything when we start out. And some of us don't know much later on either.'

'That's not what Thorne thinks,' Kincaid said. 'He says good things about you.'

'I know he does. But Julian's no genius either. He's optimistic and he's lucky. He thinks every film he makes will be a winner. That's optimism. And at least half the time he's right. That's luck. Also, he's got an investment in me. I did a bunch of low-budget westerns for him after he brought me over from Columbia and now he wants to move me up in class. If I look good, he'll look good. It's not just money these studio heads are after. Mostly they want to look good. They want to be loved. Want people to say nice things about them. And most important they want to be creative. At least they want people to think they're creative. That's why so many pictures get ruined. Because some hot-shot studio boss decides to rewrite the script himself, or recut the picture after it's shot. It's all horse-shit. They don't let the guy who sells tickets at the ball-park come up to bat in the ninth inning with the bases loaded, do they? You know what I mean?'

Garrigus was in his late thirties. He was tall and trim, brown from the sun, and he wore western clothes. Tunstall, the cameraman, said to Kincaid, 'When a picture goes on a long location, and the actresses and the script girl and the make-up lady are picking out who they're going to sleep with, Tim's always first on everybody's list. Sometimes, if he's in the right frame of mind, the girls get to take turns.'

He also had a reputation as a brawler. 'Look at his wrists some time,' Tunstall said. 'They must be twelve inches around. When he was an actor they never wanted him to do his own fight scenes. A couple of times he accidentally popped somebody, one time an actor, a big bastard named Huntley, and another time a stuntman named Red Wallace. Wallace was cold-cocked for an hour and Huntley had to have his jaw wired together.'

One afternoon, not long after Kincaid arrived from London, Garrigus said to him. 'I've been sizing you up. What are you – about five eleven, a hundred fifty-five?'

'Five ten. A hundred and sixty.'

'You don't look that heavy. I'm six two, a hundred eighty-five. You think you could take me?'

'I never thought about it. I don't fight for fun.'

'I do. It's a lot of fun. What do you fight for?'

'I don't fight at all if I can help it. When I was a kid I fought because I had to. When I was a seaman I fought to stay alive. I guess the only reason I'd fight now is if I was mad enough to kill somebody. So that's what I'd try to do.'

Garrigus grinned. 'I guess I'd better not choose you. You might hurt me.'

'I don't think so,' Kincaid said. 'You wouldn't want to take me on anyway. It wouldn't be any fun. One punch and I'd be out.'

'You don't believe that for a minute, do you?'

'No,' Kincaid said. 'As a matter of fact, I don't.'

The day before shooting was scheduled to begin, the entire cast and crew was assembled on a sound stage at Thornwood studios. Garrigus spoke first.

'All of you people who signed on for this project had it explained to you that we have a tough row to hoe. Dust and dirt. Long hours. A lot of night-shooting. If it rains we'll shoot in the rain. Nothing neat or pretty. Comfort and convenience are out. Is there anybody here who didn't have all that explained to them?' He looked round the forty or fifty people standing in front of him, saw no hand raised, then went on.

'We're not trying to suffer or to make you suffer, but we've got a different kind of story here in a different atmosphere. That atmosphere is what we're after. All you actors will be playing Australians but most of the characters, or their parents, came from Ireland or England. We're not going to lean on Australian accents, or any accents, but we're sure as hell not making a Hoot Gibson western either. We're dealing with serious stuff. No fancy riding or twirling six-shooters. This is a picture about people doing mean things to each other. People get burned alive. Shot in the face. And some of them get hanged. It's a true story. It really happened. And when people watch what we're about to do in a movie-house in Oregon, or Ohio, or Mississippi, we want them to feel as if they're seeing it happen. We're going to show them something they haven't seen before. That's why we're going to be on location from start to finish. If your wife has a baby, we'll drive you into town to see her. If your mother dies you can go to the funeral. But apart from that we're all going to sweat it out together. We'll make ourselves believe we're in Australia. When we're finished we may not smell too good, some of us may not like each other much, but I think we'll have something in the can that we'll be proud of.'

When Thorne stepped forward he said, 'Tim said everything I was planning to say but he said it better. For my part, I just want to add that I feel we have something important here. We've tried to give you people all the tools you need to work with, and I assure you we will continue to be behind this production in every way. I've never made a greater effort to hire the best possible

431

person for every job and I've never been more optimistic about starting a film. Good luck to all of you.'

3

An odd creature, William Cranston, a grid of contradictions, each one of them uninteresting. His history seemed to identify him as a public man, group-oriented, a member of the regiment. But his comparative failure as a military officer had been specifically linked to his inability to function well in his group, either as leader or follower. It seemed that he was a private internal man attempting to function as a pack animal but finding himself unable to.

When his retirement relieved him of that life among the herd, however, it became quickly apparent that he had no inner resources whatsoever. He did not relate well to his wife, his daughter, his grandchildren, the staff, or himself. He seemed to have become emotionally cataleptic. No instinct for creature contacts, no ability to find some reward in solitude. He read nothing but military manuals, and those rarely; he almost never wrote or received letters. He was impatient with the household pets and he detested all kinds of music. The self-deception he practised about his work on his memoirs was like an admission to himself that he had no function, no recreation, and no joy. His security, the activities that never failed him, were snooker and his whisky decanters. But now, even those were not to be relied upon. His skill with the cue, which had never been remarkable, seemed to be deserting him. And whisky, for the first time in his life, began to affect him badly. Two drinks caused his vision to blur and his head to throb, and his long post-dinner sessions with port or brandy made him nauseous and unable to sleep. An eye-opener in the morning, which had been his accustomed cure-all, now brought on a whole new set of symptoms: clogged sinuses, leg pains, and trembling hands.

Travelling on the train to London, to his dreaded appointment with Margaret's solicitor, as Cranston sat alone in his compartment drinking coffee, he became as reflective and philosophical as he was able to be. He found himself actually *considering* various matters and ideas, seeing points of view other than his own, or, more accurately, defining his own points of view with uncharacteristic flexibility. He almost succeeded in making some connection between behaviour and reward. But this was altogether too abstract and unsettling for him to pursue. So he quickly turned his attention to the physical features and details of Wiswell Towers, the halls and reception-rooms and stairways, the walls lined with books, the portrait gallery, the parks and the gardens and the surrounding fields, the ponds, the oaks and firs and yew trees, his bedroom and sitting-room, his beloved billiard table and leather chair, the Chinese carpets, the urns and the armour, the silver and china and crystal, the massive carved staircases and polished corridors.

As he sat back, looked through the train window and listed all these splendours, it struck him suddenly – first as a warm sensation, like sinking into one's own tub, then like a sharp blow to the temple as the reality of this trip to London ricocheted back and forth in his brain – that these objects, these trappings and comforts, had become his only value system. They were indispensable. He could not, under any circumstances, give them up.

In Tremont's office the following morning, Cranston tried to bluster his way to the high ground and set up some position he could defend.

When Tremont greeted him and said, 'How are you

this morning?', Cranston said, 'Not well at all. To tell you the truth, I'm damned annoyed. It's a long bloody trip down here on the train and I prefer my bed at the Towers to those penitentiary cots at the Reform Club.'

Sir Charles Tremont was a tall and slender, white-haired gentleman, calm and quiet, visibly sure of himself, veteran of countless conflicts and tests of will. He sat down in the high-backed chair behind his desk and said, 'Of course all this is inconvenient for you and I apologize for that. I thought perhaps you might send your solicitor to this meeting so you wouldn't have to come down to London.'

'Certain matters I like to deal with myself.'

'I understand that. But there are always legal details that must be sorted out by the solicitors involved. Who is your solicitor, by the way?'

'Since I've come all the way down here we don't have to concern ourselves with that, do we?'

'Yes, I believe we do. It is my understanding after my talks with Mrs Cranston that you have begun a legal action for divorce on the grounds of adultery.'

'I've told her I've had enough humiliation. Told her I wouldn't stand for any more of it. And that's what I meant.'

'Your wife tells me she's received no legal notice of your suit. No communication from your solicitor.'

'I told her what I intend to do. In no uncertain terms. That's all the notice she needs.'

Tremont checked some notes on his desk. 'I believe that was several weeks ago.'

'That's correct. She's had some time to think it over. It gave her a bit of a shock. You can be sure of that. She thought I'd just sit back and smile like a library cat, no matter what. But I gave her a sharp surprise. She assumed

I'd signed on for the full hitch, no questions asked. Now she knows otherwise.'

'Let me be sure I've understood you. Are you saying that you threatened your wife with divorce some time ago but that you've actually done nothing to set the process in motion?'

'It's in motion, all right. Her head is spinning like a top. Thinking things over. Seeing William Cranston in a new light. Not quite so sure of herself now. Knows she's in for a fight.'

'Have you consulted a solicitor, Major Cranston?'

'No need for that. Not yet. But you can be damned sure I will when the time comes. Major-General Dale Ross Shannon, retired, the finest legal mind in England. And a bloody good soldier.'

After a moment Tremont said, 'Let me tell you what conclusions I'm drawing from what you've said, and you tell me if I'm correct. It seems to me that Mrs Cranston misunderstood you. What she thought was quite definite, seems now to be only a possibility.'

'What does that mean?'

'You seem to be saying that under certain conditions, if your wife made certain concessions, you might change your mind about a divorce.'

'Margaret and I have been married for a long time. I've been a good husband. I was trained in a hard profession, sir, but it didn't make me cruel. And I'm not vindictive. I have no desire to destroy my wife. I know how difficult it is for a woman to be on her own with no man to lean on. So, although I know I'd be doing the proper thing if I went forward with this divorce action, there's a possibility that I might reconsider if she made some adjustments in her own ideas. Margaret's not a fool. You can be sure of that. She has an independent streak, but when all's said and done, she's able to see where her best interests lie.

She'll come round. There's no doubt in my mind about that.'

'And if she doesn't?' Tremont said.

'She will. You can bank on it.'

'Let's be more specific, Major Cranston. The person you planned to name in your adultery charge is Arthur Tagg. Isn't that correct?'

'So she told you about him as well?'

'Of course. I needed to know the truth. She also said you insisted that Mr Tagg be dismissed.'

'Of course I did. A man has a right to protect his own home. What Tagg wants is good whipping. But I'll settle for having him sacked and off the premises.'

'And you believe your wife is willing to do that now?'

Cranston nodded. 'As I said, Margaret's no fool. She doesn't want me to leave her. And she's not a woman who wants to be known in her own county as an adulteress.'

'When did you discuss these matters last with your wife?'

'When I had your note.'

'Did you tell her what you've just told me, that under certain circumstances you'd be willing to reconsider the divorce question.'

'No, I didn't. As I said, I wanted to give her time to think.'

'Well, I believe she's had ample time to think. We spoke on the telephone last evening and she authorized me to tell you of our conversation. In the first place, she will not dismiss Arthur Tagg under any circumstances. Secondly, she has sworn to me that there is no adulterous relationship between herself and Tagg, and there never has been. She is perfectly willing to make that case in divorce court. And finally, as I indicated in my note to you, whatever you may decide about your own plans, she

436

has asked me to file papers for her requesting a divorce from you.'

'That's poppycock. There's no way she can divorce me and she knows it. She has no grounds.'

'She believes she does have grounds and so do I. Do you want to discuss that with me now or would you prefer to wait till you receive our papers?'

'By God, there's nothing to discuss. I've been a good husband to Margaret. Anyone will attest to that.'

'That remains to be seen. Her grounds are emotional cruelty and incompatibility.'

'What the hell does *that* mean?'

'It can mean many different things. In this case, your wife charges that the two of you have not lived together as man and wife, that you've had separate sleeping arrangements, for more than twenty years.'

'By God, I was a military man, sir, serving the Crown. My regiment was in India. My wife chose to be in England.'

Tremont referred to his folder again. 'My notes show that you returned to England twenty years ago and that you left the military service and came home to Northumberland in 1918. That's fifteen years ago.'

Cranston fidgeted in his chair. 'It's all a lie, Tremont. You're a man of the world. You know how women are about such matters. Proper and prissy. Never tell the truth.'

'Can you imagine why Mrs Cranston would make up such a story?'

'To have her way, I expect. To humiliate me. Make me look like a bloody fool.'

'Perhaps you're right,' Tremont said. 'Maybe she is lying. But if she is it will surely come out. She has authorized me to take depositions from your daughter, Sophie, from her friend Clara Causey, from her physician,

Dr Swope, and from her long-time personal maid, Rose Ball.'

'By God, I won't have it. I won't be gossiped about by strangers and paid staff people.'

'It won't be gossip, Major. These people will be under oath. I agree it's a nasty business but you must realize your adultery case would have been even more untidy.'

Tremont stood up behind his desk. 'I do appreciate your making the long trip to London. I think we've clarified the situation somewhat. If nothing else, I hope I've impressed upon you the need to appoint a solicitor for yourself. Your wife wants to move ahead with this as quickly as possible.'

4

In Portugal, Sophie received four or five letters from Kincaid before she mailed one to him. It was not a deliberate tactic on her part. Each morning, after break-fast, she sat on the terrace of her house looking out across the Gulf of Cadiz towards Morocco, pen in hand, a block of writing-paper on her lap. She never failed to begin a letter to him but she never got beyond the first page.

She had two impulses: one, to pour out the truth to him, to tell him how lonely she was and how desperately she missed him; the other to paint a lovely picture of her carefree days in Praia da Rocha. She was torn between the desire to tell him how much she needed and wanted him, and another desire – less a desire, perhaps, than a decision – to demonstrate to him that she had her own identity, her own survival system, that she had alternatives, that she was able to make choices of her own, that she need not be on the airship to California simply because he felt he had to go there.

At last she followed the first, and stronger, impulse. She went back to her bed one morning after breakfast, Kincaid's framed photograph on the table beside her, and simply told him the truth, as quickly as her hand could write.

God, what a frightful error I've made, thinking you could go off in one direction and I in another, believing I could be separated from you for all these weeks and months, and still survive. I am surviving, of course (I'm not a child), but only that. All the bright colours of the Algarve look grey to me. The harmless little birds look like predators. The house is huge and seems coldly cavernous, even with a family of servants padding about, and Trevor and Sarah shouting at each other. The meals, although they are indescribably delicious, and the excellent Portuguese wines don't appeal to me. I have no appetite, no desire for tennis or swimming, and I sleep badly. Some nights, when everyone else is in bed, I walk along the beach to the casino, drink a large cognac, and try to squander obscene amounts of money on the wheel. I bet recklessly but in my perverse frame of mind I still win more than I lose. They call me 'the lucky English', but I feel as though I have no luck at all.

All my life I've heard people sob and moan about their loneliness, and I sympathized, felt that I understood, felt that I had experienced it myself. But in the short time I've been here on the Algarve I've come to realize what loneliness really feels like. It's a void, Kincaid. Emptiness.

How I envy you. Busy every day. Seeing new things. Meeting new people. Working and learning and being excited about what you're doing. After all the bad things I've said about California, I can't tell you how delighted I would be if I were there now. Transported on a carpet, carried there somehow.

Since I love you and like you and adore you and care about you, it should be automatic that I would wish you well in what you're doing. But I can't do that, my darling. I can't feel good about anything that takes you away from me. I can't wish you success when a little voice inside me says our life together might well be changed, or diminished, or damaged by that success. What will become of us if you are continually being carried off somewhere, if we discover suddenly that you have two separate lives? One with me and one without me? Can we continue to be what we started out to be if that happens? I lie awake now, you see, trying to sort things through. At first I consoled myself by thinking you might not turn out to be as special as Julian Thorne believes, that as wonderful as you look, as wonderful as you are, those things might get lost somewhere inside the camera. I can't deny that I hoped that would happen. Such thoughts encouraged me as I sat here looking at the tile floors, sipping gin and lemon squash.

Now, however, I've come to believe that something bizarre and relentless has been set in motion that has very little to do with you, what you are, how you look how you move and speak. It's a kind of manufacturing process. First a public need is discovered and announced. Then everyone who believes they have such a need are told that a product is being offered that will fulfil it. Are you destined to be such a product? I'm afraid you are. The boy who delivers chops for the butcher can go into the movie theatre and discover role model, someone to envy, admire, and emulate. The girl who works in a milk-bar can sit in the same theatre and imagine herself in a cottage with the make believe man who moves so smoothly across the huge screen in front of her.

440

You must have had the same thoughts I'm having. As we wonder how this adventure of yours will turn out, it has already been decided. If Mr Thorne has his way, you will already have made another movie by the time *Bushranger* is seen in the theatres. You could become a familiar commodity before people have stopped to consider what you are, in fact, or who you are. You'll be recognized everywhere and you'll earn a great deal of money.

Fortunately for us, we already have an immeasurable amount of money, so we don't need that. And if you're to be followed and tormented by strangers wherever we choose to go, we certainly don't need that either, do we?

What I'm asking is this: if Mr Thorne's business fills up your life, if it occupies your time and your attention, and turns you into a public person, what will become of us, what will have happened to those two delirious people who ran off to a cottage in Brittany and swore to each other they never wanted to leave there?

I'm sure this is a depressing letter. It must be because I'm depressed. I'm not able to hide it and it seems to be infectious. The servants are slow and surly, Sarah screams at me every day that I've destroyed her life for ever by bringing her to what she refers to as 'the rotten Algarve'. She's swiftly moving from childhood to womanhood and in her own mind has already completed the process. The dreary news from England is that Margaret will not come here as planned. She will either come very late in summer or not at all. She has some obligation – an old school-friend or something – that seems to be pulling her to the Midi. So here I am, disgruntled and unloved. Even my darling son appears to avoid me. He prowls the beach with a pack of dangerous stray dogs who worship him, it seems, and he's been taken up also by an American painter named Quigley, who lives here year-round with his wife, Lenore.

As she read through what she'd written, Sophie began to weep. She slid down in the bed, pulled the coverlet up over her, and cried herself to sleep. When she woke up, she reread the letter, tore it up and threw it in the fireplace. She washed her face with cold water then, sat down at the table by the window, and wrote a second letter to Kincaid.

I've been naughty about writing and I'm very sorry. There's so much to do here and I've been busy every day with the children. They say this is the best summer holiday they've ever had. It is truly grand. I wish you could be here to share it with us. Such a lovely house on a cliff above the sea, a fine staff, and gorgeous weather. I'm delighted to hear the reports about your work. What a pleasure it must be to work with such good people. How nice it will be to hear all about it when we're both back in London in the autumn.

She wrote two more pages of light-hearted travel information, daily menus, wine lists, and adventures of Trevor and Sarah. Then . . .

How I wish you were here. I know you miss me as much as I miss you. But since we're both so busy, the time will pass quickly. Don't worry about me. All goes well and we'll be together soon.

Clara Causey was waiting at the west entrance of her home one summer morning when Margaret Cranston arrived. Standing beside her was her son, Hugh, wearing riding-boots and a leather jacket. 'My God, what a miracle,' Margaret said. 'I thought I'd surely seen the last of you. And your mother felt the same.'

Hugh put his arms around her and kissed her cheek. 'I'm not down here so often. Scotland has swallowed me up.'

'I thought you would have shot every stag in Sutherland by now and pulled every trout from the Oykell.'

'I'm afraid not, Maggie, my dear. They breed too fast for me. It looks as though I have a lifetime's work ahead of me.'

When she and Clara were alone in the morning-room, Margaret asked how long Hugh had been home.

'Today is the third day.'

'And how long will he be here?'

'No one knows the answer to that. There are no clocks or calendars in Hugh's life. He always appears unannounced, mostly to see his grandfather, I expect. He and Angus are enormously fond of each other. They drink and play billiards together. Then Hugh rides his stallion breakneck round the county to visit all the public houses. And just when one is convinced that he's settled in for a while, he's gone. Gypsy blood in him, I think. His father has always been perplexed by Hugh. If Hugh didn't have such strong Causey features, I expect Ned might have suspected me of dallying with a handsome stranger.'

'He loves Scotland, doesn't he?'

'It's hard to say. Hugh's feelings are a locked box. Instead of going after things he wants, he always seems to be fleeing from what he doesn't want.'

'My father used to tell me there's no problem to getting the things you want in life if you can avoid the things you don't want.'

'Maybe Hugh heard that somewhere. One thing is certain: he's always in flight. Constant movement. The only time he slows down is when he's drinking. And he drinks a lot.'

'He's awfully thin, isn't he?'

'Always was, of course. But it's a different look now. He doesn't eat, you see. Drinks great mugs of coffee laced with brandy. And whisky as well. And tankards of lager. And at dinner, of course, he drinks claret *sans arrêt* as he toys with his food. On the other hand, that slattern he lives with eats constantly from sun-up till bedtime, and often she takes a plate of food to bed with her. Or so her maid told me.'

'Are they married now or just . . .'

'I expect they've got married at last but one never knows for sure. She brought five children to him from her previous husband, so perhaps they have married for the sake of propriety. The Scots are a moral lot, aren't they?'

'Do you ever wonder what might have happened if he and Sophie had managed to . . .'

'If they'd stayed together? I've thought about that a thousand times. I love Sophie. You know that. In many ways I feel closer to her than I do to my own daughter. I think any man would be fortunate to have her for a wife. But I must say she's well rid of poor Hugh. There's some beast pursuing him and there always will be, I'm afraid. And no woman can live with that.' She smiled. 'That's not quite true, is it? You and I know that women are able to live with all sorts of things they never wished for. But all the same, it's not a life we'd wish on our daughters.' Then, 'Does Sophie ever talk about him?'

'Not really. She asks occasionally if I've seen him, or if

444

you've seen him, but nothing more. Sophie doesn't harbour bad feelings. She's able to put things behind her. Does Hugh mention her?'

Clara nodded. 'Asks about her whenever I see him. We talked about her yesterday as a matter of fact. I told him she was in Portugal with Sarah and Trevor. Hugh knows that area well. He had chums in Albufeira. Perhaps he still does. As you see, I'm not a reliable source of information about my son.'

Later, when they were having lunch together on the veranda, Margaret said, 'I was reading an article this past week by an eminent psychologist. A specialist in women's problems. His thesis was that Catholic women are often more trauma-free than the rest of us because of the confessional. Secrets eat us up, he says. Secret anxieties, secret hurts, secret hatreds and obsessions. He says every woman must have one friend to whom she can tell everything. It can be a man friend, he believes, but not a sexual partner. And most often and most successfully, it's another woman.'

'It makes sense, doesn't it?'

Margaret nodded. 'I've been thinking about it a great deal since I read his article. Dr Fenstermaker, I believe his name is, and I kept thinking you and I have always done that for each other since we were girls.'

'That's why we're so wonderfully sane.'

'I'm serious,' Margaret said. 'I think it's true.'

'And so do I. Ned would be shocked to hear this – men can't stand to be discussed by their wives – but I don't think I've ever kept anything from you.'

'Nor I from you.' She smiled. 'Until very recently.'

'Ah-ha,' Clara said. 'The contract is now broken.'

'No, it's not. Let's just call this a delayed report. I wasn't candid with you about Jack Brannigan. I did talk with him and he talked to me. We talked a great deal.'

'Wasn't I right about him?'

'Of course you were. But it stunned me to hear you talking about him, saying things I felt but could never have expressed so well. I thought, "My God, if Clara feels that way, then he must say the same things to everyone that he said to me." But then . . .' she sipped from her wine glass, 'I don't know how to put this. What I'm saying is that something's happening to me. Or perhaps it's already happened. I mean, Jack went away but he hasn't gone away. He's been writing letters to me ever since, two or three each week, and I've been answering. And it's not going to end there. He doesn't want it to and neither do I.'

'Well, you do have a secret, don't you? How is he able to write to you? Where does he send the letters?'

'He simply sends them to me at the Towers. Bold as brass. With his name and return address written in black ink on the back of the envelope.'

'Does the Major know about all this?'

'I don't know and I don't care. I can't begin to tell you how unconcerned I am about what William knows or does not know. I suspect that he doesn't know, but not because I've tried to keep it from him. Rose brings me my mail each morning as she always has, and that's all there is to it. In any case, William's mind can only handle a certain amount of material at any given time and at the moment he's preoccupied with his mental picture of me in Arthur Tagg's bed.'

'All of a sudden, you have an intricate existence, my dear.'

'It seems that way,' Margaret said. 'But in fact it's quite simple. I have something new in my life. So a great many things that have commanded my attention all these years suddenly look dreary and unimportant. Brannigan started my mind working again. I see now that I should have ended things with William years ago. I also see that as fond as I am of Arthur Tagg our friendship can never become anything but that. Poor Arthur has never learned to soar. I don't think he has ever surprised himself or anyone else.'

'Burning all our bridges, are we?'

'I don't think so. Just marking the difference between a bridge and a footpath.'

'Well put,' Clara said. 'But what if your wild Irishman turns out to be only wild and Irish and not reliable at all?'

'It doesn't matter. He hasn't promised me anything. I've never kissed him or touched his cheek with my hand. I have no future plans that include him. But I know now that I have no plans that include anyone else. I don't plan to go crazy and dance through the streets of London, like Isadora Duncan in gauzy trousers, but suddenly I find myself considering choices that had never entered my mind before.'

'Am I allowed to ask about those choices?'

Margaret smiled. 'I planned to tell you whether you asked or not. I'm going to southern France. To Frejus. Brannigan will be there before long and I'm going to spend some time with him.'

'Will the Major know about this?'

'Only that I'm going to France on holiday. He'll know all about it at the proper time but for now I don't want to complicate the divorce proceedings. Actually, no one knows precisely what I'm up to but you.'

'And no one will, my dear. I think it's the best news I've heard in years. Where is Frejus?'

'Between St Tropez and Cannes. Just by St Raphael. It's an old Roman town. I've read a great deal about it but I've never seen it. Now I'm going to.'

'Frejus. That's new to me. You're not likely to see anyone from Northumberland there.'

'Frankly, that doesn't concern me. I'm not hiding anything or avoiding anyone. I've just declared myself an independent contractor. From now on I will go where I like and do what I like.'

Clara made a small circular gesture in the air with her hand and said, 'I salute you.'

Later in the morning, as they were walking in the south garden, Margaret said, 'When I saw Hugh this morning he called me Maggie. I'd forgotten he always called me that. Now my new friend calls me Maggie.'

6

When Scott Fitzgerald was at Princeton, Ben Quigley was at Yale. While Scott waited in New York in his tailored uniform for an overseas assignment, Ben was an artillery lieutenant in France. After the war, when Fitzgerald was writing clever slogans and picture captions in an advertising agency, and trying to persuade Zelda to marry him, Ben had married Lenore Chester, from Baltimore and Palm Beach, had inherited a great deal of money from his grandfather, and was making final preparations for a showing of his paintings at the White-Barsky Gallery on Madison Avenue. The two men met, actually, at the vernissage.

Both of them had drunk a great deal of gin before their meeting that evening, but in spite of that, or perhaps because of it, they were immediately drawn to each other; they laughed and gossiped together, and discovered laudable qualities in each other. 'I secretly wanted to go to Princeton,' Quigley said, and Fitzgerald confessed that his first choice of school had been Yale. 'But they wouldn't have me.'

Scott also liked Lenore and she liked him, and when

Zelda came to New York for a visit all four of them celebrated outrageously the fact that they genuinely liked and admired each other so much.

No one was surprised by the success of Quigley's painting show. The fact that all the sales were made to his family members and their friends did not diminish the praise he received. The art critic for the *New York Sun* reported that 'Ben Quigley is an expressionist. And a good one. Potentially a great one. He has studied the works of good people: Manet, Gauguin, and Rouault. Although he works in that spirit, his paintings are not derivative. He has power, sensitivity, and sound technique. Rare equipment for such a young painter.'

After the success of Fitzgerald's first novel, he and Zelda, married at last, went to France. Ben and Lenore were already there. Ben's paintings had become monochromatic and non-objective by now, and Lenore, who had become the mother of two, was writing free verse and studying yoga. Quigley had learned the secrets of expatriate living in Paris and he passed them all on to the Fitzgeralds. He brought them to Gertrude Stein's. He introduced them to Hemingway, McAlmon, Man Ray, and Kiki. About Hemingway Quigley said, 'A promising writer but a chancy friend. A bit of a mean streak there. Has to win at all costs. Should have been an athlete. Or a performer perhaps. Very conscious of his image. Likes to be looked at. Likes to hold forth. Not great instincts for a man who's trying to be a serious artist.'

So the four of them laughed and frolicked and drank and caroused together, and got on famously. Lenore was one of the few women who genuinely liked Zelda. Lenore had a dancer's body and had studied ballet for years as a child. Zelda envied her skills but liked her nonetheless. They took their children to the Luxembourg Gardens or the Tuileries together, drank Sancerre in the shade of the trees, and flirted with the young gendarmes.

When the Quigleys went to the Alpes-Maritimes, the Fitzgeralds followed soon after. They took villas side by side, swam in the warm sea together and browned themselves on the sand. Indeed, there are those who say that Nicole and Dick Diver were in fact modelled after Lenore and Ben rather than Gerald and Sara Murphy.

When the Fitzgeralds returned to America, the Quigleys stayed on in France. After the calamity of 1929, when expatriates whose incomes had suddenly disappeared returned bewildered to Cincinnati and Atlanta and Pasadena, the Quigleys, whose holdings, because of cautious management, had come through the chaos undamaged, stayed on in France. So when the Fitzgeralds returned to Europe they were all together as before. But just as Zelda had lost contact with many other elements of her life, she now lost touch with Lenore. Trying to pursue a ballet career herself, she solicited Lenore's guidance but resented it when it came.

Scott, too, had become a problem. He was in transition. From being a professional writer who drank a lot, he had become a professional drinker who found it hard to write at all. And when he did manage to write, his stories about flappers and playboys and easy money found little acceptance in a climate of depression and social unrest.

They never conceded that their friendship had ended. And between Scott and Ben perhaps it had not. But the rhythm changed. By necessity. The Fitzgeralds could no longer afford the profligate life, either in France or America. Soon Zelda was in an institution painting disturbed water colours, and Scott was in California, bewildered and sick, trying to convince himself that just as his financial salvation seemed to be tied to an uncertain concept called Hollywood, so also was his artistic and

450

emotional salvation. Not only did he come to believe that a man named Thalberg, who supervised motion-picture production for Mayer, was a genius, he tried, pitifully, to use that notion as foundation for a serious novel. As further evidence of a decline that, in its way, matched Zelda's, he totally rewrote his best novel to conform to the asinine suggestions of various critics, and then persuaded his publishers to republish this twisted revision under the novel's original title.

For much of this period, however, Scott and Ben stayed in touch, wrote long letters to each other about Herbert Hoover and Ezra Pound and Al Capone and Thomas Mann. Scott never asked Ben for money unless he was desperate. Ben never hesitated to send him whatever he needed. But at last the letters from California stopped coming and there was no resentment, it seemed, from either party. The relationship, however it had started and whatever it had been, had run its course. The feast had been consumed. Circumstances had slowly closed the doors.

The Quigleys, although they were not held captive by outside events, had also changed course. Whatever flaws they found in themselves and each other they attributed to France, to its Gallic peculiarities, to their long stay there. There was also an unspoken suspicion that they would drink less if they lived elsewhere. It was unspoken because neither of them was willing to commence a programme of temperance. They seemed to feel that it would be beneficial if it happened but that it should not be formalized as an objective. Nature must be allowed to take its course.

Nature's course, as it turned out, once they were ensconced in their new home at Praia da Rocha, was to go along as before. They discovered that the wines of Portugal, as long as one doesn't try to ship them across the ocean, are as seductive and lovely, if not as varied, as those of France. They quickly stocked their cool cellar and proceeded to enjoy the contents. Ben had been particularly keen to get away from Cognac, Armagnac, and Calvados. And he succeeded in that. But he hadn't considered the truly incredible bottles of port that would be available to him from the wine merchant just down the road.

He continued to paint but his work, like that of Fitzgerald, had taken a downturn. His best impulse had always been towards post-impressionism and expression-ism but now, for reasons known only to himself, he turned from non-objective painting, which he had done badly, to *une espèce de réalisme.* Soft-edged, pastel-hued post-card scenes of banal subjects. Lenore, when she saw the first of these new efforts said, 'Why in the world are you painting like that?'

'I thought it would be valuable to go back to the beginning.'

'But that's no beginning. *C'est la fin.*'

For her part, with her children away in school in Switzerland, or in Maryland with their grandparents during school holidays, Lenore, once she was in Portugal, gave up automatic writing and neo-dadaism and became earth-mother to three dogs, half a dozen cats, and a great cage-full of tropical birds. Bright plumage of every colour, great beaks like hand-wrought weapons, and prehistoric calls and squawks at all hours.

It was because of her dogs, all mixed-breed mongrels, that Lenore first discovered Trevor. The dogs had come to know him before – he was attractive to all animals – when they were ranging the beach alone, so they ran towards him that day, as soon as they saw him, perched on a rock with his sketch-pad.

'Are you drawing the sea?' Lenore asked as she came up to him.

'No, I'm not. I don't copy. I make things up.'

'You think that's the best way?'

'It is for me. Picasso does it. Gauguin did it. Rousseau did it.'

'Those men are all quite different from each other.'

'It doesn't matter. They're all good.'

'What about Cézanne and Van Gogh,' she said, 'do you think they copied nature?'

'I don't think so. What do you think?'

'I'm not sure. My husband's a painter. Let's go ask him.'

Three hours later, when Trevor came home, he found his mother by the pool and told her about the Quigleys. 'We had a splendid time talking about painters. He's met Picasso and Utrillo and Braque and Miro and practically everyone else. He has paintings on his walls by all sorts of well-known painters. And hundreds of art books lying about. We had a fine time looking through those books and talking about painting. He knows a lot and so does she.'

'Where do they live?' Sophie asked.

'Just down the road from us. No more than a mile. Ben has a big studio with two or three easels. He says I can come there any time I want to and he'll show me some secrets about oil painting. So I said I'd come.'

That night, before he went upstairs to bed, Trevor said, 'I think I made some good friends today. They act as if they like me.'

The evening before Margaret was scheduled to leave for Frejus, Cranston rang her from the library. 'I'd like to have a talk with you. May I come up?'

'This is not a good time, William. Can't it wait?'

'It won't take long. But I do need to say a few things.'

'All right. I'll come down to the library then.'

Ten minutes later, when she came into the library, she said, 'I really am awfully busy this evening. I hope this won't be a long discussion.'

'I understand you're going off on holiday.'

'Yes, I am. But I assume that's not what you want to discuss.'

'No, it isn't, actually. I thought I should tell you about my meeting with your solicitor in London.'

'That's considerate of you, William, but I've talked on the telephone with him twice since then. I'm sure he passed on everything that was said.'

'Solicitors have their own point of view, you know. Not always dependable when it comes to getting the facts correct.'

'Charles Tremont is a stickler for facts. I trust him implicitly.' When Cranston didn't answer, she said. 'You're not ill, are you? Are you sure you feel well?'

'I'm all right, I suppose. Why do you ask?'

'For one thing, you're strangely subdued. For another thing, you don't have a drink in your hand.'

'Damned awkward business, all this. Doesn't put a man in a good frame of mind. I'm not accustomed to dealing with cold-blooded fellows like Tremont. Everything cut and trimmed. No allowance for the human equation.'

'The human equation?' She smiled. 'I must say that doesn't sound like your normal line of reasoning. I associate you with "sticking to the rules", and "punishment for the chaps who lag behind".'

He went on speaking then as though he hadn't heard her. 'You know my background. I don't make hasty decisions. It's my nature to be temperate, to consider all the options, to give the other man a fair shake. That's my way. Sandhurst training. Eliminates mistakes to a large degree. A cautious advance means there'll be no need for retreat. That's the way we learned it. I hate to make mistakes so I try damned hard not to do. But by God, when I make one, I'm man enough to admit it.'

Margaret looked at the great clock standing against the wall just to Cranston's left. 'I really do have a great deal to do, William.'

'Just hear me out. This is important to both of us.' He repositioned himself in his chair. 'I want to tell you that I've made an error and I'm admitting it. Do you understand what I'm saying?'

'I don't believe I do.'

'I mean I went off half-cocked on this divorce business. I was angry and I said things I shouldn't have said. We're not discussing whether I was right or wrong. I'm just saying I overstated my case. Too damned abrupt. Didn't handle myself as well as I should have. The punishment didn't fit the crime. I overreacted and then you overreacted.'

'I'm not sure I understand about the punishment and the crime. Can you explain that to me?'

Cranston nodded. 'The punishment was my telling you I wanted a divorce. You see, I've given it a great deal of thought and I'm willing to concede now that the crime I accused you of may not, in fact, have taken place. Or it might have taken place only in your mind. In any case, I've decided that divorce is too cruel. If you're innocent, I've misjudged you. If you're guilty, and I don't believe you are, but even if you are, I forgive you. We've had a wonderful life together, Margaret. That's what we should keep in mind.'

'Let me be sure I'm clear on what you're saying. No more divorce? No more adultery? No more insistence that Arthur must be sacked?'

'I'm right about Tagg, Margaret. Any fair-minded person would support me on that. But since you're loyal to him as a staff member, I'm willing to give a bit of ground there. I think we can allow him to stay on.'

'I see. You've had a total change of heart then?'

'I never wanted to end our marriage. I simply couldn't see how to avoid it.'

'But now you've found a way,' she said. 'Tell me what's changed. What turned you about?' When he didn't answer, she said, 'Nothing's changed, has it? Except your attitude. You simply decided to change your mind.'

'I misjudged you. I decided in the end that I could trust you.'

'No, you didn't. You decided your bluff wouldn't work. You thought if you threatened me with divorce, and a scandal as well, I would discharge Arthur. You'd have your way and all would be peaceful.'

'By God, I wasn't bluffing.'

'You weren't? All right. Let's find out. You said you thought I was having an affair with Arthur. Unless he left the premises you would divorce me, on grounds of adultery. Am I right so far?' He nodded and she went on. 'Now you've decided I did not have an affair with Arthur, so there'll be no divorce. And Arthur can continue to live here and work for us. Is that correct?'

'Those are my feelings.'

'I see. Now that we're being very open with each other, what if I told you you were right the first time? What if I said that Arthur and I did sleep together once? Just six months after he came to work here.'

'Is that what you're telling me?'

'I may be telling you that and I may not be. But what if I were?'

'If I knew you'd had an affair with him that lasted just one night, what would I do?'

'What would you do?'

'I'd forgive you,' he said.

'But it's adultery, isn't it? One night or a thousand nights.'

'Not to me. I'd forgive you.'

'And you'd allow Arthur to stay on?'

Cranston nodded. 'I'd forgive him too. I'm a soldier. Familiar with the soldier's life. I know such things can happen.'

'All right,' she said. 'Here's my second question. What if I told you I went to bed with Arthur three nights after he came to work here and we've been sleeping together ever since?'

'I'm not interested in these smutty games.'

'How do you know it's a game? What if I told you I made love to Arthur last night. And again this afternoon after lunch. Then what?'

'I'm ashamed of you. Talking like this.'

'Why be ashamed? You weren't ashamed of yourself when you accused me of adultery, were you? You had no evidence but you accused me anyway. Just because you used a nice legal word like adultery, did that make it easier for you? Let's try it another way. If I gave you undeniable evidence that Arthur was in my bed with me just this afternoon, would you divorce me then?'

'By God, I'd kill you. I'd kill you both.'

'No, you wouldn't. And you know it. You only shoot at targets and little birds. I'll answer the question for you.

You wouldn't shoot me and you wouldn't divorce me. But not because you care about me. Not that at all. You've just grown very comfortable in your billet here. You're like an officer who accepts any kind of duty that's handed him just so he won't be reassigned. It has never occurred to you to divorce me. You've never given it one serious thought. You're too damned comfortable to make the change. You simply decided to run a bluff, to play a little divorce game, to get what you want, to get rid of Arthur. Not because you're jealous of him, not because you think there's anything between him and me, but because you think he makes you look bad in front of your troops, because the staff defer to him, because they know he's in charge here and not you. It's true, isn't it? Isn't that the truth?'

'I'm the master here and everyone knows it.'

'No one knows it, including you. So you decided to set things right with your divorce threats, something you'd never thought of till you read those letters of mine.'

When he didn't answer she said, 'Now I'll tell you something else. We have not had a wonderful marriage, William. You know that as well as I do. And I'm willing to take my share of the blame. But all the same, in all the years we've been married it has never once occurred to me to divorce you. I never thought of it as an option. Never till now. When you forced it on me. Even then, I thought it was something we could get past. I didn't expect it to happen. Didn't want it to. And then you sent me that cruel, senseless note. Adultery. Naming poor Arthur as co-respondent. From that moment I stopped fighting the idea of divorce. From then on *I wanted it*. I still want it. More than ever, now. And it's going to happen, William. You tried to set an ugly trap for me and now you're caught in it. You've seen animals in traps. The more they struggle, the more they get hurt. You can

458

accept what's going to happen or you can struggle. Either way, the result will be the same.'

8

Riding on the train between Calais and Paris, Margaret sat silently in her private compartment and stared through the glass at the summer fields of Picardy. On the channel steamer from Dover she had stayed on deck through the short voyage, forward on the upper deck, a warm rug tucked round her, staring at the grey-green sea and the heavy sky, watching it grow lighter and clear at last as they approached the shore of France.

She was totally inside herself in a way she had often been as an adolescent girl, sewn inside a soft cocoon, sending no messages and receiving none. Since leaving Northumberland the day before, she had spoken only in monosyllables to railway conductors, taxi-drivers, hotel clerks, and room waiters. Once inside her suite at the Gresham she had not left it till it was time next morning to go to the boat train. She had not rung up Howard and Sybil, nor any of her friends in London. She'd had dinner by the fire in her sitting-room, had lingered there lazily, listening to a Stravinsky concert on the wireless, and had taken a warm bath then. Before ten o'clock she was asleep in her bed.

When the Paris train was just north of Amiens, Margaret turned away from the window at last and began writing a letter to Sophie.

How strange I feel today; how unfamiliar I am to myself. Don't be alarmed by that. It's not an uncomfortable feeling. Just new and strange. I forget sometimes how much I love to travel. And it suddenly occurred to me, just yesterday on the train to London, how seldom I've travelled by myself. I am a social creature, as you know, but one must admit that there are moments that are not improved by sharing. When the voice and the ears are fully occupied in conversation, the other senses seem turned off somehow. It makes one wonder why so many of us are panic-stricken by the prospect of being alone. Why do we insist that those who dine alone, or stroll in the gardens, or go to the theatre by themselves are pitiful souls? How pleasant it is to study a landscape in silence, to draw a solitary conclusion about the quality of your claret or your chop, to stand as long as you like before a Constable or a Vermeer. When I was a girl, solitude was a necessary and respected part of life. We did needlework and watercolours and read in our rooms. We walked in the fields and the gardens, or rode out across the moors on horseback. What a lovely silent world it was. How keen our senses were, how much better we spoke when we didn't chatter constantly. It was assumed that an admirable mind needed time for reflection and enlightenment. Conversely, constant chatter was always an indication that the person speaking had little to say.

How radically and quickly we've changed. Is it because of the wireless? It must be a factor. In the name of information or culture, one may now spend long indolent hours listening to absolute poppycock in whatever place one chooses. Also we have become tolerant of total nonsense at balls or dinner parties. The most mindless person on the guest list is often the centre of attention throughout the evening, for the simple reason that they take a conspicuous position in the hall and never stop talking till they claim their coat at evening's end and have their car brought round. I hope that Sarah and Trevor are not destined to live in a world of macaws and magpies whose intelligence will be measured in decibels.

Enough of that. Let's turn to more pleasant matters. Such as your parents' divorce. Solitude produces a macabre sense of humour, they say. So be it.

The die is cast, Sophie. The divorce is inevitable now. All voices have been heard, all points of view expressed, and the gears are turning. The Major, who insisted on the divorce, now has second thoughts. A cooler head. A forgiving heart. Or so he insists. My heart, on the other hand, has turned to stone. In case I live to be a hundred and six, I simply cannot spend the second half of my days as I have the first half, married to your father, being with your father, or living in the same house with your father. When I finally accepted all this, the guilt I had anticipated did not present itself. On the contrary, I felt as though someone had heard my tapping and the desperate scratching of my nails on stone, and had released me from the damp dark place where I've been kept, where I've kept myself, for longer than I like to remember.

She put the letter aside then, and finished it that evening, in her hotel on rue de Rivoli in Paris. The following morning, just before her car took her to the *gare* to board the Provence express, she gave the letter to the hotel concierge to post to Sophie.

At five that afternoon Brannigan met her in the terminal at St Raphael. 'Two pieces of luggage,' he said. 'At last I've met a woman who knows how to travel. Two small valises and a shoulder-bag. You're a treasure, Maggie.' He picked up her bags and they walked out to the street. 'I used to heft trunks and satchels at the boat terminal in Dun Laoghaire, where the Holyhead ferry

461

comes in from the Irish Sea. I was a scrawny little wharf-rat then, fresh down from Donegal, scrambling for every penny I could get hold of.'

When they reached the road leading down to the bay, he set her bags down, turned to face her, and put his arms round her. He kissed her on both cheeks, and said, 'Hello, Maggie.'

'Hello, Jack.'

'Welcome to Provence. The air is sweet, the wines are soft, and the nights are famously tender.'

They walked down an easy incline to the esplanade and sat on the wide terrace of a café that looked across the harbour to the sea. 'You'll have a goblet of wine with me,' he said as they sat down, 'and if we're lucky we'll not draw a sober breath all the time you're here. This is the only province in the world where the rosé wine is fit to drink. This lovely wine will enslave you.'

As she tasted the wine he said, 'How was your trip down here then?'

'Very nice. I took it by easy stages. From home to London. Overnight there. London to Paris the following day. And on to Provence this morning.'

'If you were truly eager to see me you could have made it here in two days instead of three.'

'If you were truly eager to see me you could have met me in Paris and we could have come down on the train together.'

'Ah-ha. I see I've met my match.'

Margaret smiled. 'Perhaps that's true but I doubt it.'

'How do I look to you then, after all these weeks? Would you have recognized me in a crowd?'

'I think so. But you're a bit thinner.'

'Indeed I am. A man of a certain age must watch his figure if he hopes to attract exceptional women.'

'And you're brown from the sun. You look healthy and very well indeed.'

'And so I am. Splendid genes on the Brannigan side. A sturdy lot. And a sense of fun from the Delancys. Music and verse and who gives a damn. Those are my mother's people.'

'Are you more Brannigan or more Delancy?'

'I'm proud to say I have the worst characteristics of both sides.'

They stayed there in the café for almost two hours, the sun dropping low and burning under the blue awnings as they sat on the west-facing terrace. 'I would like to sit here like this till the *patron* stops service and closes his doors for the night but now we must discuss your accomodations.'

'Don't judge me by Wiswell Towers,' she said. 'I don't try to duplicate my life at home when I'm on holiday.'

'Of course not. A woman who travels with two valises announces to the world that she is not a piece of fluff. All the same you are here as a guest of Jack Brannigan and it's my duty to see that you're well cared for.'

'So far, I've had four giant beakers of gorgeous wine. I feel immensely well cared for.'

'Ah, but where will you lay your head? That's a critical choice.'

'What choice do I have?'

'That's my point,' he said. 'You do have a choice. There is a lovely small hotel called the Var just down the esplanade from here. It is extremely clean, safe, and proper. Single women and widows stay there, and I'm told they feel quite secure. I've booked a room for you at the Var, with bath en suite, a view of the sea, and a single bed. That should be just right for you. On the other hand, so you would have a choice, you understand, I inquired at another hotel further along the esplanade. It's called

463

La Méditerranée. Since it was heavily booked I was not able to find a single room for you there. But I was able to reserve a suite. Larger than you'll want, perhaps. There's a good-sized balcony overlooking the sea, a sitting-room, a dressing-room with bath, and a lovely bedroom with blue walls and a white ceiling like a wedding-cake.'

'And a single bed?'

He made a face. 'I'm afraid not. The bed is unreasonably large. Out of proportion, I think. But it's pleasantly positioned. One can sit up in that extraordinary bed and look out across the terrace to the sea. But what good is that if the bed itself is not a proper size?'

When she didn't answer he said, 'What do you think?'

'I'm trying to decide. Since you say the Var caters to widows and maiden ladies, and since I fit neither of those categories, I'm afraid I'll have to settle for La Méditerranée.'

'I hope you won't be disappointed.'

When the attendant at the hotel took them upstairs to her suite, Margaret noticed at once that a man's robe was hanging in the *salle de bain*, there were shaving things by the sink, and several shirts in the *armoire*. She crossed the room to where he was standing by the open window and put her arms round him. 'What if I had chosen the spinster's room in the other hotel?'

'I would have taken you to a café and forced you to drink wine till you could neither stand nor speak. Then I would have carried you, unconscious, to this hotel and this excellent bed.'

She stayed with him for nine days. They drove to Antibes, Grasse, Vence, and Menton. They took the narrow-gauge railway through the mountains to Digne. They drove to Draguignan and Brignoles, and two days running, having lunch in an elegant restaurant in St Tropez, they delighted the chef by ordering double portions of Grand Marnier soufflé.

Three days before she was scheduled to leave, Margaret said, 'Couldn't we calm down and stay home a bit more? How does that sound to you?'

'Hard to say. It will probably be deadly dull but we'll have to make the best of it.'

They had many of their meals those last days on the terrace outside the bedroom. Late breakfasts with crois-sants and *pain au chocolat*, jam, eggs and ham, fresh fruit, *café au lait*, and always a cool bottle of *blanc* or *rosé* at hand. Their lunches were usually gathered up, mid-afternoon, at the charcuterie in the *impasse* behind the hotel. Pâté, salami, Roquefort and Port Salut, black olives, green olives, *radis au beurre*, hard-crusted bread, and giant frosty bottles of Strasbourg lager.

Dinner was a late proposition, sometimes as late as midnight, in the restaurant of the hotel on the *premier étage*. Great feasts. Senseless amounts of sea-food. Shrimp and lobster and random crustaceans, oysters and snails, and the grilled local catch of the day. And cham-pagne bubbling into their flute glasses and spilling over on the table.

'*Excess*,' Margaret said. 'Will you promise to have that word engraved on my headstone?'

'There are no headstones for those who over-indulge. They're allowed to live for ever to set an example to the careful, restricted, cautious and timid souls who go early to their graves as their reward for avoiding excess.'

'But I'll be the size of this hotel. When I board the train they'll load me into the baggage car.'

'If they do that, please tell them what I've taught you. *There can never be too much of a good thing*. And remember the words of Moses when he was questioned on this subject. He said, "When a comely woman toys with her food and leaves it all on her plate, when she takes small sips of her wine and is unwilling to finish even half a glass, then I swear to you, my children, there is something very wrong with that woman. And I don't mean with her stomach."'

On her last afternoon they took a long walk. To the Roman ruins in Frejus, then back to their hotel. As they sat in the café downstairs, she said, 'Where did you stay before I came here? Where did you sleep?'

'Where I normally sleep. In my caravan.'

'Where is it?'

'It's parked behind the cathedral just off the square in Frejus.'

'Can we go there tonight?'

He smiled. 'Not tonight or any night. That's a monastic cell on wheels. A punishing bed for failed Catholics like me.'

'Don't blarney me, Brannigan. I know you now. You can't get past me with that jam and sweet butter. If that's your home, and it surely is a great deal of the time, then I want to see it and spend the night there. Otherwise you'll think of me as a flower of the boulevard, a woman intended for great beds in hotel suites and then bustled on to the train for home.'

'You're starting to talk like me.'

'That's it Jack. I've learned all your secrets.'

They drove to Frejus in his car and had dinner in a

466

small bistro not far from the cathedral. When they finished eating he said, 'This may be the last time you see me. When I've taken you inside my caravan, when you sit there surrounded by clothing on hooks, stacks of books and papers, camera equipment and cooking pans, when you see for yourself that I live like an itinerant tinker from central Rumania, you'll say, "My God, the man's a clochard. I've been deluded and deceived, and I'll have no more of it."'

A few minutes later they were inside his caravan. It was very much as he had described it. She sat on the bed, which was attached to the long wall, and he sat on a stool at the foot.

'Wasn't I right?' he said. 'Aren't you ready to go back to La Méditerranée?'

'No, my dear, you were not right.' She took off her slippers and began to take off her stockings.

The next morning as they lay in the narrow bed together, she said, 'It's a strange feeling, waking up with someone and feeling as though you've been with them every morning of your life.'

'You have. You've been here nine days. You're nine days old.'

'You won't just drive off tomorrow and take this self-contained life of yours someplace where I can't find you – that's not the way it's going to be, is it?'

'It's not me who's going off. You're the one with train tickets in your handbag.'

'But I'm reliable. You know I am. I'm not so sure about you.'

'If you're not sure about me, you haven't been paying attention. Is that it, then? Have I failed to get your attention?'

'You've got my attention, all right.' She moved closer

467

to him, her head on his shoulder, her face against his. 'I just don't want to make a fool of myself.'

'Too late for that. We've both made fools of ourselves. We've proved to anyone who's been watching that we're drunken, oversexed fools. Two of a kind, they say. And that's what I say, too. Don't get the idea that I'll let you slip away. Fools like you are hard to find.'

· CHAPTER 12 ·

1

When *Bushranger* was still in the planning stage, weeks before Kincaid left London for California, in response to a query about the aborigines who'd been hired by the police to track down Ned Kelly, he wrote to Julian Thorne.

These men were brought down to Victoria from Queensland. The most skilful black trackers came from there. All in all, fifteen or twenty of them were used during the two-year search for Kelly and his friends. The police on the case, primarily men from Melbourne who knew nothing about the bush, blamed the trackers for their lack of success in tracking down the Kelly gang. But none of the people around Glenrowan, or Benalla, or Wangarotta were fooled. The trackers didn't want to find Kelly. They knew that he and his family and friends, and all the small farmers and selectors in the area, were fighting a losing battle against the big landowners and the police. So while they pretended to search for Kelly they made no real effort to locate him.

I know this point isn't made in the script, and it doesn't have to be made, but it's a fact to keep in mind when you pick the men who'll play those trackers'

469

roles. They're sympathetic fellows and your hunch is right: they should be the genuine article from Australia. They don't look like Africans, or American negroes, or Samoans. They look like themselves.

Here's the best way to proceed. I'm enclosing the mailing address of a man named Brig McBride. He's the manager of the Endicott cattle-run near Glenrowan, where I worked when I was a kid. He had a Queensland aborigine who looked after his horses. The man's name is Homer Tony. And he's still there. He'd be about forty years old now. He's smart as hell and he has a great face, but he can't talk. When he was six years old a couple of drifters robbed his father and shot him. Then they ruined Homer's tongue and his vocal cords so he couldn't tell anybody who they were. I know you're looking for authenticity. Believe me, this man is authentic. Have your people in Victoria tell him that Roy Kincaid wants him to come to California. He'll do it. If necessary I'll write to him, and he'll find four or five of his tribesmen who'll come along too.

The first time Evan met Homer Tony, at the Thousand Oaks location, he said to Kincaid, 'Jesus, what a face. That's the entire history of the world in those eyes.'

'When I showed up in Victoria he was the first friend I had. He knows all there is to know about horses. And a hell of a lot about people as well.'

'But the poor bastard can't talk.'

'That's right. But he knows how to listen. When I was a kid I used to talk to him for hours. He was the only one I had to talk to. But I haven't seen him now for a long time. We've got lots of ground to cover.'

'Then what?' Evan said.

'What do you mean?'

470

'What happens to him when the picture's shot? You just send him back to the bush?'

'I don't think so. Maybe he'll stay here.'

'To do what?'

'We'll see,' Kincaid said. 'I may have some plans for him.'

2

When *Bushranger* was half-way through its shooting schedule – cruel hot days in the desert and scrub forest north and west of Los Angeles – Julian Thorne came to visit Kincaid in his caravan one day during lunch-break. He wore a crisp linen suit and a Panama hat. When he sat down Kincaid said, 'You're the only clean human being I've seen in six or seven weeks. Is that the way people dress in the outside world?'

Thorne smiled and lit a cigarette. 'In Beverly Hills it's necessary to wear your wealth. Nobody wants to give you money unless they're absolutely convinced you don't need it.'

Kincaid sat down in a chair facing Thorne's. 'After that speech you made when we started the picture, I thought you'd be out here every day checking up on us.'

Thorne shook his head. 'Just because you haven't seen me doesn't mean I haven't seen you. I screen every foot of film Garrigus shoots. I think I told you once when we talked in London that our shooting schedule is usually determined by location and actors' contracts. Once we get on a set or in a particular location we shoot every scene that takes place there, no matter where that scene occurs in the script. But this time, because we're in the same general location all the time, we're shooting straight through the script from page one to the end. In sequence.'

471

'How about the last scene, where they hang me? We shot that first of all.'

'That's right. That was my insurance policy. That scene had to work or we'd have no picture.'

'Garrigus told me he liked it.'

'He loved it. And so did I. As soon as we ran that scene we knew we had something. We knew you could handle the part.'

Kincaid smiled. 'You told me a long time ago there was no question in your mind about that.'

'I know I did. And I meant it. But I've made mistakes before. I had to make sure I wasn't making one this time.'

'So we shot the last scene first.'

'Exactly,' Thorne said.

'And what if you hadn't liked it?'

'I'd have shut down the picture the next day and cut my losses. That doesn't surprise you, does it?'

'No, it doesn't.'

'Good. Now we can talk about some other matters. Present and future.' He snuffed out his cigarette, got up, and crossed to the couch. Sitting down there, he said, 'Our contract specifies that Thornwood Pictures owes you no money unless we release *Bushranger*. But if we release it we owe you a hundred thousand dollars.'

'That's right.'

Thorne took an envelope from the breast pocket of his jacket. 'Here's a cheque for that amount. There's no question that we'll be releasing the picture. A major release with full publicity and promotion. Since we're shooting in sequence we already have a rough cut of half the picture. And we love what we see. I guessed right about you, my friend. You have an important career ahead of you. So that brings me to the second part of our agreement. If I want to negotiate with you for a second picture I owe you another fifty thousand for this one.' He

472

handed Kincaid another envelope. 'Here's that cheque. I definitely want to go ahead with another project.'

'I can't promise, Julian.' Kincaid indicated the second envelope. 'You understand this doesn't bind me to anything.'

'Of course not. It's final payment for *Bushranger* and a good-faith assurance from me that I want to continue our relationship.'

Kincaid put the two envelopes on the table beside his chair. When he turned back to Thorne he said, 'Now that I know you're capable of shutting down a picture if you don't like the first day's shooting, I'll have to be paid in advance if we do another film together.'

'That doesn't surprise me,' Thorne said. 'If I were as hard-nosed as you are, I'd own this town.'

3

As she travelled by train from France to Portugal, Margaret decided that perhaps it would be wise to wait a bit before telling Sophie about Jack Brannigan. She was certain that her daughter would be as supportive as Clara Causey had been. But all the same, her sense of timing told her that the legal matters between herself and the Major should be settled first; that although she had plunged into a relationship with Jack without hesitation, it would be simpler if this visit to Praia da Rocha was not dominated by her revelation to Sophie of the sweet change that had taken place in her life. 'I will be a proper English lady on a summer visit to her daughter and grandchildren. Other matters can wait.'

For her part, as she awaited Margaret's arrival, Sophie resolved that she would not tell her that she had seen Hugh Causey. Since it had been an accidental encounter, or so it seemed, and since their meeting had consisted of a café luncheon near the street market in Portimão, she had nothing whatsoever to conceal from Margaret. But still, just as her mother had decided to keep to herself her visit to Frejus, Sophie concluded that her meeting with Hugh could be reported at some future date.

When they saw each other, however, when they were alone that first evening of Margaret's visit, after Sarah and Trevor had gone to their rooms, they spoke, first of all, of the matters they had planned to conceal. Sophie first, then Margaret.

'You'll never guess,' Sophie said, 'who showed up here suddenly, ten days or two weeks ago. Hugh Causey. I was strolling through the public market in Portimão one morning, I came round a corner, and there he was. I almost collapsed. I hadn't seen him since . . . God knows how long it's been . . . since before I married Toby.'

'Clara told me he had chums down this way. I saw him at Wingate not long ago.'

'Did you tell him I was here at Praia da Rocha?'

'No. But Clara may have. I can't remember.'

'He told me he'd heard I was in Portugal, but he wasn't sure where. He was staying in Albufeira and was on his way back there after an overnight stay in Lagos.'

'So it really was just a chance meeting?'

'I have no reason to think otherwise,' Sophie said. 'But with Hugh, one never knows. He's still like a character from an eighteenth-century novel. Sinister and elusive.'

'When I saw him he simply seemed wasted. Thin and used-up. Like someone who had squandered all his assets and wasn't quite sure what direction to take now.'

'Did you talk to him at all?'

Margaret shook her head. 'Pleasantries on the veranda. As I arrived, he was taking wing. Riding-boots and high energy. But it all seemed unreal to me. Like a ballet performed by ghosts.'

'There is something sad about him now. That was the first thing that struck me as we sat at lunch. He was always sardonic and sarcastic. A cruel sense of humour. And he's still that way. But it seems like a reprise now. A replay of things he thought and said when he was twenty. Nothing seems to have happened to him in all the years since I saw him last. Everything seems misty in his memory. When we sat down in the café and he began to drink the way he does – that part hasn't changed at all – I was afraid he was going to dissect everything that once happened between him and me, but not only did he not mention all that, it seemed as though he'd forgotten it. He talked to me like a sister or a spinster aunt. Recounting the misadventures of his early life: racing about on his horse, speeding through the county lanes in his roadster, punch-ups in the public houses, adventures with barmaids. All rattled off like a music-hall routine while I ate my lunch and he drank his.'

'Clara says he never eats. Coffee and whisky, she says.'

'No coffee when I saw him. But one tumbler of whisky after another. And it seemed to have no effect on him.'

'He knows you're married now, doesn't he?'

'I'm sure Clara must have told him but he made no mention of it. The monologue went on and on.' Sophie paused. 'Do you remember when Helen, Clara's niece from America, came over to England after the war?'

'Of course I do. She and Clara were very close. They still are.'

'Well, Hugh talked endlessly about her. Told me some things that even Clara doesn't know. Or so he says. If I told you what he said would you feel duty-bound to tell Clara?'

'Not if you ask me not to.'

'I wouldn't instruct you like that. But I think there would probably be no benefit in her knowing.'

'Then we shan't tell her,' Margaret said.

'Hugh was talking in great circles as usual but I got the strong feeling that something traumatic took place between him and Helen. Some disjointed story about her coming to his room in the middle of the night and a few days later she left to go back to America. Never spoke to him after the night they spent together. And not long after, he learned that she'd married someone in America. It seems he was terribly smitten with her. Perhaps he still is.'

Margaret smiled. 'Helen didn't know the local rules, apparently. No one was supposed to abandon Hugh. He was the one who always smiled sweetly and walked away.'

'Yes,' Sophie said. 'I seem to remember something like that happening to me.'

'Was it strange and painful seeing him after all these years?'

Sophie shook her head. 'I'm not the same person I was then. I remember, of course. I remember how shattered I was. But it's all as if it happened to another person. As I sat across the table from him, he seemed grey and two-dimensional to me. Like a snapshot from an old photo album. God knows, he's young and attractive still. And bubbling with sexual energy. But when I was driving home after lunch, I only felt sorry for him.'

'It seems odd,' Margaret said.

'What's that?'

'That Hugh should turn up suddenly after all these years. That the two of you should have an accidental meeting in a country far from England. And that he should tell you in detail about an affair that happened years ago, with a young woman who later married someone else. Perhaps it wasn't his cousin, Helen, he was talking about after all. Perhaps it was you.'

'A slim chance of that, I should think. After all, I was available for a long time after Toby died. If Hugh had been interested, he would have spoken up then.'

'Hugh has never behaved the way most of us do. His mother is quick to admit that. Perhaps he's only drawn to women he can't have.'

'If that's true,' Sophie said, 'then he's destined to love me for the rest of his life. Because I'm not available.'

When Margaret brought up Jack Brannigan she said, 'Perhaps you remember him. When the *Country Life* people came to our house he was the photographer.'

'Of course I remember him. God's gift to women.'

'Not all women,' Margaret said. 'Only to me, I hope.'

She told Sophie then about her trip to St Raphael and Frejus. When she finished she said, 'I have a feeling I would never have left him if I hadn't made plans to come here. I was only there for nine days, but by the time I left it was hard for me to remember where I'd lived before. You know how much I love the Towers. But for once in my life, for the first time I can remember, I have no desire to go back there. Can you see me sleeping in a caravan? Do you think I've gone quite mad?'

'Of course I do. If I hadn't gone quite mad myself in recent months, I would envy you. But what happens now? What are your plans? What will you do?'

'I don't know, actually. I'm trying to avoid too much planning ahead till your father and I can bring our chaos to some civilized conclusion.'

'Does he know about Brannigan?'

'Not yet. But he will. I'd love to tell him at once. Not to hurt his feelings but just to make it clear that there's no hope for us, that my future, however it may evolve, lies elsewhere. But at the same time, I think it's unwise to introduce a new element into the charade. Poor William

477

is still struggling to deal with what he imagines is my passionate involvement with Arthur.'

Margaret told her then about Cranston's seeming change of heart since his talk with Sir Charles Tremont. 'So I suspect the process will not be easy. William's obstinance is his most striking characteristic. I'm sure he will resist and obstruct in every way he can. He will lie about like Oblomov and agree to nothing. It will all have to be forced on him. And in the end it will be. But Lord knows how long it will take. It's hard to be patient but I will have to find a way.'

'And how about Brannigan? Will he be patient?'

Margaret smiled. 'He simply ignores worrisome details. And to him, William is only a worrisome detail. Jack's convinced that I belong to him and he belongs to me. He'd prefer me to be divorced but meanwhile life goes on. He knows if he rings me up from Donegal, or Oslo, or Bristol, and asks me to meet him there, I'll drop everything and go. If there was any possible way he could move in with me at the Towers, he'd do it in an instant. He doesn't care a damn what William thinks. Jack's a civilized man but he doesn't adjust the rhythm of his life to please whatever fool has got hold of the drum. He says, "I inhabit me own skin," and he does. That's all one has to know about him.'

They sat up very late, talking like schoolgirls. When they went to their rooms at last, Margaret fell asleep at once. But Sophie lay awake in her bed hearing the sound of her mother's voice. 'He knows if he rings me up and asks me to meet him, I'll drop everything and go.'

Late in the summer Evan Tagg received a cablegram from Mary Cecil:

MISERABLE AND FRIGHTENED. WANT TO COME CALIFORNIA.

As soon as he read her message he picked up the phone and called the cable office.

COME AT ONCE. CABLE ARRIVAL TIME.

The following day he had her answer.

FLYING CLIPPER
THURSDAY. ARRIVE LOS ANGELES 14 SEPTEMBER.

It was mid-afternoon when he met her at the Los Angeles airport. When she saw him waiting at the arrival gate she ran across the tarmac and put her arms round him. 'God, I missed you so,' she said.

'I missed you. I'm glad you're here.'

As they pulled away from the airport car park she said, 'What a strange and lovely land this is. I may never leave it.'

'Good. I hope you won't. Wait till you see the house I'm living in. Just at the edge of the sea. The waves crash under the house all night.'

'I thought you'd want me to stay in a hotel. Tony Quayle told me there's a morals clause in all the studio contracts here. All single people must sleep by themselves or they lose their jobs.'

'That doesn't apply to writers. Nobody cares what writers do. They assume we're all paunchy and pale and wear thick glasses.'

'But I'm an actress.'

'That's right. But you're not making a movie. Or are you?'

'No.'

'Then you don't have to move into a hotel unless you sign a studio contract. Besides, the morals clause wouldn't apply to us in any case. We're what's known as platonic friends.'

She put her hand on the back of his neck and said, 'That's true. So we have nothing to be concerned about.'

As he drove towards the coast road she said, 'Do we have to go straight home?'

'No. What would you like to do?'

'I'd like to have a nice drink, and sit across the table and look at you. You have a lovely profile but I need to look at you full-face. I want to watch your eyes and see your lips move.'

Evan found a café with an outdoor terrace and they sat in the sun with their drinks.

'It's bloody hot here just now,' he said. 'Scorching winds blowing in from the desert.'

'I love it. We've had a dreadful summer in London. All damp and rainy and suicidal. This weather's hypnotic. I plan to lie in the sun while you're working and turn my skin as brown as tobacco.'

'If you get sunburned I'll rub cocoa-butter on you.'

'I never burn, my darling. Even though I'm blonde and delicate the sun is kind to me. But all the same, I think I'd like it very much if you massaged me with cocoa-butter.'

She told him then about the situation with Alec Maple. 'I hope you weren't upset by my cablegram. But I was miserable and I was frightened and I needed to tell you.'

'The last time we talked just before I left London you thought you'd be able to deal with him.'

'I know I thought that. But what a fool I was. The sad truth is that one simply cannot deal with Alec. In all situations his instinct is to take the contrary view. If he's told to cross downstage left, he will cross upstage right. All his creative impulses are destructive. When he was a child, I expect he tortured his canary and set his cat's tail afire.'

'Did you tell him you plan to divorce him?'

'Of course. The day after you and I talked in London.'

'What did he say?'

'He displayed a full range of his dramatic talents. Disbelief, indignation, anger, and tears. But I think he was secretly delighted. Alec has no activity, you see, no interest really, apart from wenching and drinking. Much of the time he's painfully bored with himself. So when someone gives him a new role to play, as I've just done, he's suddenly reborn and fully energized. What I see as an emotional problem to be resolved between two grown-ups who once loved each other but no longer do is for him a challenge to his manhood, an attack on his authority. But most of all it's an opportunity for him to define himself. Since he left the theatre he's had very few such opportunities. Now I've given him one. An heroic role. And he will play it, one can be sure, in full voice. He will prove to me what a deadly adversary he can be.'

'You're saying he doesn't want the divorce and he intends to fight it. Is that it?'

She shook her head. 'Not exactly. Alec isn't wise but he's shrewd. Even if he could stop me from getting a divorce he knows he can't force me to live with him. He's on shaky ground, you see. Hospital records and doctor's bills have accumulated through the years. There's well-documented evidence that I've been physically abused. My solicitor is gathering all that material now. And he's taking depositions as well from people who know how

Alec has treated me. So the divorce is inevitable. It's simply a question of time. But Alec will delay matters as much as he can. Last time we spoke on the telephone he said he'd been offered a job in Capetown. As a commentator on the wireless. That was just before I cabled you telling you how miserable I felt.'

'Would he do that? Would he go off to South Africa just to postpone the divorce?'

'I don't think so. He can't leave London. He's unable to survive anywhere else. He develops all sorts of symptoms if he can't make pub rounds every day and boast to his mates about sexual triumphs. One day in Brighton or Bath and he develops a migraine. But on the other hand, he's a mercurial bastard. One can't be absolutely certain he wouldn't toddle off to Capetown if he thought it would annoy me. Or Vladivostok. Or the bloody South Pole.'

'You also said you were frightened.'

'Of course I am. There's always that. It's a part of Alec's structure. He simply strikes out without warning for no apparent reason. My doctor believes there's something oddly sexual about it. And I must say, whenever he's struck me he's seemed to derive a great deal of pleasure from it.'

'He's a nasty bastard,' Evan said. 'I'm surprised he hasn't taken a few blows himself.'

'Oh, but he has. He's been carried home bleeding many nights.'

'But it taught him nothing.'

'Nothing at all. I think he enjoyed that as well.'

The house Evan had rented was on a spit of land between Malibu and Trancas, sitting high on pilings with wide decks on three sides looking out on the ocean. They sat outside as the sky turned red and pink and orange. They ate sausage rolls and drank mugs of lager.

'I can't believe I'm here,' she said. 'Less than a week

ago I was dodging cabs in Oxford Street, ruining my best shoes in the rain. Now I've been dropped off in a tropical garden, watching little brown seals bathing in the sea. I'm quite intoxicated by it all. Am I allowed to become irresponsible and intoxicated?'

'Suit yourself,' Evan said. 'There are no restrictions whatsoever.'

They sat silent then for a long time, watching the sky begin to go deep blue and hearing the soft precision of the waves lapping against the mound of beach just in front of the house. At last Mary said, 'The theatre is a wicked place, you know, and the people who work there are reckless people. Particularly the actresses. At least these are the public perceptions. When an actor makes love on stage to a woman who's not his wife, it's easy to assume, since it's their profession to be convincing, that their stage relationship doesn't end when the curtain comes down. And when this same actress, in her next play in the West End, plays equally convincing love scenes with another actor, one suspects again what one suspected before. And it goes on like that until at last there's a sort of acceptance of her imagined life. Some tolerant theatre-goers come to expect it of her, to admire her, to envy her perhaps. When I was a very young performer it used to annoy me, to embarrass me, to see the expressions on people's faces when, at a dinner party, I was introduced as an actress. Almost without exception, a knowing look would appear in their eyes. And when people learned I was the wife of Alec Maple it truly stood them on their heads. When he was in his twenties and thirties Alec appeared more often in the tabloids than he did on stage. In a list of London rakes his name was often near the top. So, to be identified as his wife gave one a sort of bespoke reputation. Not one that I felt comfortable with. But oddly enough, I suppose it was a help to my career early on. If nothing else, it made people curious about me, keen to see me when they saw my name listed among the players in a new production. It titillated them even more, I suppose, because from my first London appearance I have always played virtuous women. Not prigs or professional virgins but women who were reliable, who stood for something, who seemed to live in terms of their own values. I'm sure they said to themselves, "Ah, that's what she seems to be. But if she's married to that Maple chap she must be something else indeed. Surely she's a bit spicier than she appears."'

'I have a feeling you're about to make some sort of confession to me,' Evan said. 'If you are, I'd prefer it if you didn't. It's not necessary.'

'You're wrong. For me, it is necessary. I don't want you to feel like a late arrival in my life. I want you to know me better than anyone does. And you will. Because I don't want to hold back anything from you.'

'I feel the same way. But that doesn't mean I have to be told everything you've ever done. I don't require a list of every man you've cared about, or who cared about you.'

She laughed. 'You see. That's what I mean. You've got it all twisted round. I don't intend to furnish you with a list of lovers. I'm trying to say, in my stumbling way, that there is no such list. I'm trying to tell you that if you think you've found a sophisticated woman of the world, then I've misrepresented myself. I'm not a courtesan, sweetheart. I know very little about all that. I've never been with any man except Alec. And after our daughter was born we were very seldom together. For more than eight years now we have never slept in the same bed. I know it's no longer fashionable to be a virgin, particularly if one is a 38-year-old woman, but I feel as though that's what I am. Does that frighten you?'

'No. Nothing about you frightens me.'

'Good. I'm glad to hear that.' She stood up and walked over to his chair. She leaned down and kissed him, then eased herself down on his lap. 'In London it must be three or four in the morning now. Don't you think I should be tucked up in bed?'

'Yes, I do.'

'So do I.' Then, 'Don't get up. You stay here. I bought something I think you'll like just before I left London. Let me put it on. Then I'll come back and show it to you.' She stood up. 'I'll just be a minute.'

After she went inside he sat with his feet up watching the sun drop down towards the horizon. When it disappeared at last there was still a broad red-gold band between the sky and the sea.

'Here I am,' she said. He turned and saw her standing in the doorway, lighted pink from the sunset. She was wearing a pale-blue nightgown as transparent as the rain. 'I didn't want to look like a boy with my short hair, so I've gained almost a stone since you left England.' She slipped the gown off over her head then and dropped it on the deck. 'I want you to like me,' she said.

5

On her way home to Northumberland from Portugal, Margaret stopped in London to see Sir Charles Tremont. They had lunch together at Prunier's. After telling him about her visit to Sophie and Sarah and Trevor, she said, 'Any word from Major Cranston or his solicitor?'

Tremont shook his head. 'Total silence on that front. It seems your husband has chosen inertia as his best weapon. It's frustrating but not uncommon. A person who makes no response comes to feel that he's invisible and therefore unassailable.'

485

'Can we deal with that?'

'Of course. We already have done. I've filed our papers with the proper authorities and explained the situation in detail. They will attempt to contact Major Cranston, and he will respond or fail to respond. We will then proceed accordingly. There will have to be some agreement about division of assets, but from the discussions you and I have had, that should be no problem. Wiswell Towers and its properties are held in trust for the Wiswells and their heirs, and you are asking no share of whatever assets Major Cranston has accumulated.'

'In any case,' Margaret said, 'if William feels that he will be pinched I am perfectly willing to guarantee him a reasonable annual stipend to supplement his pensions and income from shares.'

'I understand that. But I would advise you to withhold that generosity till we see if it's appropriate.'

'There is one other matter. And a potentially serious one. When I last spoke to William, he gave me the impression that he has no intention of leaving the Towers, even after I've been granted a divorce. Can he do that? Can he set up a fortress in the west wing and simply refuse to leave?'

Tremont smiled. 'I must say I have never encountered that problem in a divorce situation, but since my conversation with Major Cranston I can appreciate that he might make such a stand.'

'Most of his threats come to nothing but this one I think he might carry out. Can he do it?'

'He can do it. But he can't sustain it. Once you are divorced he has no legal right to be in residence at Wiswell Towers. There are two courses we can follow. We can file an action for trespass. That's a civil matter. We simply stipulate what I've just outlined for you. It's your property, he's no longer your husband, so he has no right to continue in residence there. This is the gentle way to proceed and it could take some time to have him removed. If he's completely intractable, if he insists on staying after the final decree, I would recommend the stronger course. We would ask the court for a protective order. This would come under the criminal code but wouldn't actually accuse him of a crime. You would simply attest that since you are no longer married you feel ill at ease having him there on your premises. You are allowed under the law to feel threatened even though there's no physical evidence of such a threat. I assume he has not threatened you. Am I correct?'

After a moment Margaret said, 'I didn't take it seriously at the time but he actually did threaten me. And Arthur Tagg as well. Although Arthur was not present when the threat was made.'

'Tell me what he said.'

'As you know this divorce proceeding originated with William. He accused me of adultery and said he would name Arthur as co-respondent. Later he decided that he'd been mistaken about Arthur and me. He told me this, the last time we discussed it. At that time I asked him what if his accusations had been true. He said if he knew for certain that we had been lovers he would kill me and kill Arthur.'

'Does he keep fire-arms in the house?'

'Oh, yes. A locked cabinet of rifles and shot-guns in his study. And two revolvers in a locker in his bedroom. I must tell you, however, that nobody knows about that threat but me. We were alone when he said it.'

'No matter. You heard it and he knows he said it. Here's what I'd like you to do. When you're back home send me a handwritten letter telling me what you've just told me today. I will keep that in your file in case we need it. Also, I'd like the exact date and approximate time it took place. Did you tell anyone else about this threat?'

'Yes. I told Clara Causey.'

'Fine. Mention that also in your letter to me.'

'Does this mean the constables will come one day and carry William out of the house?'

'That depends on Major Cranston. With the information you've just given me I think that won't be necessary. Once I explain to your husband what could happen, I think he will co-operate so it won't be necessary. But in any case I assure you it will be handled in a deliberate and civilized manner. You have certain rights, as all of us do. You mustn't feel guilty because you've asked me to protect those rights.'

6

Evan didn't stay at the location site with the actors and the crew, but since he drove out there every morning, up the coast road and across the Santa Monica mountains to Thousand Oaks, whatever mail came to him at Thornwood Studios was brought to the location the following morning.

One day in October, *Bushranger* only ten or so days away from its finish, one of the couriers from the studio handed him a letter during the lunch-break. Evan glanced at it, didn't recognize the handwriting, and put it in his jacket pocket. Later in the day, when he was leaving to go back to his house at the beach, he pulled the letter out as he was looking for his car keys. Sitting in his car in the parking zone, he tore open the envelope.

Dear Evan,
This is a hard letter for me to write and I'll probably make a bad job of it but I've been thinking about it

ever since I saw your name in the Los Angeles *Examiner*. Twenty times, I guess, I decided to write to you and just as many times I decided not to. I told myself there were probably a thousand Evan Taggs scattered around the country, so what was the use.

Then last week there was another piece about you in the paper and this time it said you were from England, and it gave your age, and there was a picture of you along with some movie director and that actor named Kincaid. Soon as I studied that photograph I knew it was you. There's something of Arthur in your face and a little bit of my own dad the way your eyes set in your head. But mostly I knew you from the Kodak snapshots we took of you when you were little. I've got a shoebox full of those pictures. I'm putting one in with this letter so you can see what you looked like when you were a little bugger and your dad had you hiked up on his shoulders. No pictures of me. People thought I was pretty when I was young and maybe I was but I never took a good picture. Still don't.

So you're a writer of some kind. Isn't that something? As you can see, I have some trouble just writing a decent letter. I heard a man on the radio say that pretty soon nobody will write letters any more. Just talk on the telephone, he said, and send messages by some photo system that doesn't make sense at all to me.

Don't get nervous that I'm getting all wound up to ask you for something. I don't need anything and I wouldn't ask you for it if I did. I'm able to look after myself. Always have been. Just so you'll know I mean what I say, I'm not even signing this letter. You know my name's Amy, unless you forgot, but my last name you've never heard. Also, you'll see by the postmark on the envelope that this letter was mailed in Santa Monica. But I don't live there. I'm taking the red car train out there later today just to post this letter. So you can see I'm not after anything. I'm making it so you can't look me up even if you wanted to. And why would you want to, anyway? That's what I ask myself. You can't have much of a warm spot for somebody who walked out on you when you were little, a person you wouldn't recognize if you bumped into her on the street.

So why am I writing to you then? I've got no good answer for that. I guess I'm doing it 'cause I can't help myself. I couldn't just look at your picture and say ho-hum and drop it in the trash can. Maybe somebody could do that but I can't. I just needed to say something to you. But as you can see, I don't hardly know what to say now that I'm doing it. Rambling on. That's all. I just want you to know that it's a funny feeling looking at a picture of a nice-looking grown-up guy in the paper and then saying to yourself, 'That's my kid.'

I just read over what I wrote and it's like a letter from a third-grader. So I'll sign off now. I've been living by myself for quite a few years so I guess I've forgotten lots of things I learned when I was younger.

I want you to know that just because I left you doesn't mean I forgot you or that I didn't care about you when I had you with me. I've suffered all my life for what I did to you and your dad. But it wasn't because I didn't love you that I ran off.

I hope you won't tell Arthur that I wrote you this letter. That wouldn't do anybody any good. I'm sure he found a nice wife over there in England and made a good life for himself.

There was no signature at the close of the letter.

490

The final scenes of *Bushranger* were shot in late October. The wrap party was held on a cavernous sound stage at Thornwood. Catered by Lucey's, music by Ted Weems' orchestra, and a guest list that included not only the cast and crew but all the other employees of Thornwood, a platoon of journalists, columnists, and photographers, twenty or thirty of the best-known actors and actresses in Hollywood, the mayor of Los Angeles, and the Australian consul-general, flown down from San Francisco for the occasion.

Wrap parties often wind down by ten in the evening when the egg rolls and potato crisps have all been consumed, and the gin and bourbon bottles are empty. The *Bushranger* party lasted till five o'clock the following morning.

Three days later Kincaid sat with Thorne in his office.

'How did you enjoy the party?' Thorne asked.

'Quite an affair. Interesting things going on as the evening progressed.'

'I understand you left early. So did I. But Garrigus tells me that everyone had a fine time. I'm delighted to hear it. When people work hard they deserve rewards.'

He lit a long slim cigar and settled himself comfortably in his high-back chair. 'Well, I promised you a great adventure. Do you feel as if you've had it?'

'Maybe I wouldn't use those exact words. But one thing I'm sure of. I've never seen a gang of people work harder to do something good, to get things right.'

Thorne nodded. 'That's our secret weapon. I think I told you this before we started shooting. All of us who head up studios like to think we're responsible when a picture turns out well, but the truth is we're at the mercy of the people who do the work. I can have the greatest concept, the best script, and the hottest actors and director in town, but if the people behind the camera don't handle the details, the ship won't sail. Ours is a business of details. My brother Sam says the slogan of the movie business should be "Everything matters." And he's right. When you watch our crews at work, you'd think that all of them owned a piece of the studio.' He puffed on his cigar. 'Evan tells me you're all set to run back to England.'

Kincaid nodded. 'I'm taking the train to New York on Friday. And the clipper from there to London.'

'We've checked all the footage and the sound-tracks and everything looks clean. If we need any wild lines from you, or any dubbing, we'll arrange to have it done in London. Garrigus would love a free trip to England. In any case, since we've been editing as we went along, we should have an answer print in no time. Korngold's done a great score for us, the editors are working overtime, and we're shooting for release prints by late November.'

'There's plenty of time, isn't there? Aren't you planning an Easter release?'

Thorne shook his head. 'We moved it up. We already have trailers in work for all the Thornwood theatres. We'll start to promote the film on Thanksgiving weekend and release it in five hundred theatres ten days before Christmas. We've got a big winner here, my friend. Everybody who's seen the rough cut agrees with me. Even my wife liked it and she hates motion pictures. She reads books and goes to concerts. But in that last scene, the death scene, when you said, "I suppose it had to come to this", she cried like a child.' Then, 'Now let's talk about where we go from here. I know I don't have a commitment from you for a second film but I'm confident I will have. When you see the work you've done in *Bushranger* and when you feel the public impact, I think you'll want to move ahead with your career. So let me tell you what I have in mind. Have you heard of a man named Dillinger?'

'I've read about him. And Evan told me he's writing a scenario about him.'

'Exactly. It's great material. And it's your picture if you want to do it. This man's another social outlaw like Kelly. But it's a whole different time and a different canvas. The story's happening now. Dillinger's in the paper every day. He's the most wanted man in the country but he has great support from poor people, especially in the Midwest. What do you think?'

'To tell you the truth, Julian, I don't want to think about it at all right now. I want to go home and see my wife. I want to sit in a chair and look out the window.'

'You don't have to give me an answer today. Just think it over and we'll talk about it next time I'm in London.'

Kincaid smiled. 'I might not be there. I may be off somewhere in India. Shooting tigers.'

'I'll find you. I'm good at that. To tell you the truth, I don't really want to pursue it further just now. I'd rather wait till you've sat in a dark theatre and watched yourself in *Bushranger*. Once that's happened you'll be on my side. You'll know what I've been talking about all these months since we met in London.'

'And then I'll fall off the tree like a ripe peach. Is that it?'

'Not exactly. But when a man finds something he's really cut out to do, it's hard to turn back. Men like you don't spend their lives looking out the window or shooting tigers. You're a killer at heart, Kincaid, and you've found your weapon. Whether you know it or not.'

'How's your love life?' Kincaid said. He and Evan were sitting in a café on the Malibu pier the day before Kincaid was to leave for New York.

'You're a cheeky bastard. Crude bloody ocker.'

'I see I've taught you a bit of the lingo. Soon you'll be bilingual.'

'Full of cheese now, aren't you? Accustomed to the hairdresser and the powder-puff. Somebody always at hand with a cup of coffee. Another bloke following behind you with your chair. Your name printed on the back in big letters.'

Kincaid smiled. 'I never could get accustomed to all that. It's damned silly, isn't it?'

'A sociologist named Hermann Osgood says that motion-picture actors are the royalty of America. Nostalgia for a king and all that.'

'If it's true, God help America.'

'And where America leads, the British will follow.'

'Did Osgood say that, too?'

'No. I say that.'

'Then God help the British too.' Kincaid emptied his glass. 'We need another lager, don't we?'

'Of course. It's a fine day for it.'

After he signalled the waiter Kincaid said, 'Let me try another question. How is your dear friend, Mary Cecil?'

'That's better. Mary Cecil is splendid. She is flawless and enchanting. And in answer to your original question, our love life is also splendid, flawless, and enchanting.'

The waiter came with their beer then. Kincaid lifted his glass and said, 'I salute you. She's a lovely woman.'

'She certainly is. And an excellent actress. Have you ever seen her work?'

Kincaid nodded. 'Sophie and I saw her last season. *Loyalties*. At the Garrick.'

'With James Bidwell.'

'Correct. She did a fine job.'

'She may have to go back soon. They want her for Novello's new play.'

'When are you going back?'

'Not till Christmas, I'm afraid. I promised Julian I'd get this script ready to shoot before I leave. He wants to be ready to go into production by the end of January.'

'That's the Dillinger story?'

Evan nodded. 'I see he's talked to you about it.'

'Very briefly. But I'm not ready to take on anything right now. I'm still in shock from *Bushranger*. I may never make another picture.'

'Does Thorne know that?'

'He knows it's a possibility. But I don't think he accepts it.'

'In any case, you're not coming back out here in January?'

'Not a chance,' Kincaid said. 'I want to look at the finished version of *Bushranger* and see how much of an ass I made of myself. Then I'll decide what I'm going to do and when I'm going to do it. Or if I'll do anything.'

When they left the café Kincaid said, 'You look like a man who knows how to keep a secret. Is that right?'

'That depends on what the secret is and who I'm supposed to keep it from.'

'The secret is that I have a surprise for Sophie. I don't want her to know about it till I can show it to her. But I want you to see it now.'

They left Evan's car parked near the pier and Kincaid drove up the highway towards Point Dume. 'It's not far from here,' he said. 'Ten minutes or so.'

A few minutes later they turned left off the highway

and into a smoothly paved narrow road, bordered by giant eucalyptus trees, angling off towards the ocean. Kincaid stopped the car, letting the engine idle, and half-turned in the seat towards Evan. 'I bought this land last spring when Sophie and I were out here together. It's heavily wooded but with great patches of meadow. A deep well with fine water and nearly a mile of ocean frontage. What do you think?'

Evan looked around him from the open car. 'Devon and Cornwall. A bit of each.'

'Exactly.' Kincaid put the car in gear and they moved ahead. 'This was a dirt road. I had it paved as soon as I bought the land.'

'It really does look like England. Stone walls and hedge. Sophie must have loved it.'

'Sophie doesn't love anything about California. And she doesn't know I bought the land.'

A second road curved away to the left and Kincaid followed it. It wound through a grove of oak and cypress, gradually turning towards the ocean-edge. Kincaid stopped the car again. 'Just ahead is the surprise. You're not going to believe what you're seeing.'

'Yes, I am. I've already guessed. You've built a fine California house for Sophie.'

'Not exactly.' Kincaid sped ahead then for five hundred yards, moved out of the trees into the sun, up a grassy knoll, and stopped.

'My God,' Evan said. 'I don't believe it.'

'That's the surprise.'

'It's Wiswell Towers.'

'Not exactly. But very close. Not so many rooms. Not as much square footage. But all the public rooms are identical in size and shape, and they'll be decorated exactly like the Towers. There'll be a dozen bedrooms and sixteen bathrooms and a coach-house for six cars.'

496

'How did you manage it?'

'I found an old architect, a gentleman from Carlisle, who was able to get hold of the original builder's plans for the Towers. Or maybe they were plans that an architectural society put together long after the building was finished. In any case, he was keen to do the job once he found out what I wanted. And he was also keen to go to America. So we struck a deal. Then later I was able to get him all the interior photographs that *Country Life* took. When he got here he located a retired art director, a man like Loren Iversen who's accustomed to big jobs on a tight schedule, building whole towns and sections of cities for motion pictures. So between the two of them, they're making good progress.'

'When will it be finished?'

'You can see by the trucks and cars parked here and there that we've got a good-sized crew on the job. They tell me it will be finished and ready to live in by the middle of March. That will include all the gardening and planting and linen on the beds.'

'And Sophie knows nothing at all about it?'

'Nothing. Nobody does. Except you. For the moment, the solicitor's name is on the deed representing John Doe. That's me.'

'Then Thorne doesn't know either?'

Kincaid shook his head. 'I wouldn't be in a very good negotiating position if he knew I was building a home here. That's another reason I've kept it a secret. The main reason, however, is Sophie.'

'I still can't believe it,' Evan said.

'Do you think she'll like it? I mean, you've known her all your life. What do you think?'

'I think you've done something extraordinary. I can't imagine that she wouldn't be delighted with it. She could spend months in this mansion you're building and never know she'd left England.'

'I think she'll like it,' Kincaid said.

'She'd better. If she doesn't, we'll nail her inside a crate and ship her back to London. Then you can invite Clara Bow to come live in your house.'

'That's a good idea. I'll remember that.'

9

In 1933, if one was paying attention, there were countless reasons for concern. Unemployment, hunger, and deprivation were to be seen worldwide. In Germany, Adolf Hitler had been appointed Chancellor. Soon after, the Enabling Law gave him dictatorial powers, and soon after that the first concentration camps were built. By 1945 ten million prisoners would have been interned there and half of them killed. Ninety-two per cent of the German electorate supported the Nazi Party. And Hitler met with Mussolini in Venice.

There were general strikes in the industrialized countries, Japan withdrew from the League of Nations, and Britain and the United States felt it necessary to pass new laws to help workers and farmers and people in depressed areas. Even in golden California, thousands of homeless people slept on the beaches or in parks, clashed with police, and staged raggle-taggle marches with banners. Authoritarian, ultra-conservative studio heads produced and released motion pictures about the benevolence of life in Russia. Also at this time, as if by grand design, the popular songs were *Stormy Weather, Boulevard of Broken Dreams*, and *Brother, Can You Spare a Dime*.

When Kincaid returned to London, however, he found

it remarkably unchanged. The people who suffered most were being told that poverty could have an ennobling effect and many of them accepted that wisdom. Since they had nothing but hope and the dole, they remained hopeful. A one-legged beggar who sat daily by the monument in Trafalgar Square had a sign beside him that read: 'I'm muddling through.'

In Sophie's family there seemed to be a sense of euphoria, as though they had been pounded by a great storm that had finally subsided. Everyone spoke of the coming holiday season as though some magic corner would be turned just at the close of the year, as though some watershed moment was at hand.

Sophie's daughter, Sarah, for example, although she was once again in residence at her dreaded school in Cobham, Kent, was filled with pride and purpose. The summer in Portugal, although it had been tedious for her, had allowed her to redefine herself. Using her discontent as a weapon, she had challenged her mother at every turn. She had wept and shouted and sulked, had refused to take part in any activities that included her brother, and had forced Sophie to deal with her as an adult.

Although she had moments of bad conscience about the turmoil and discomfort she had caused, Sarah believed the process had been absolutely necessary. Her responsibility to her own destiny demanded that she establish herself as an entity, as a person, as a woman. She told herself that Evan, when he came to the Towers for Christmas, would be instantly aware that this bosomy and long-legged creature, almost fifteen years old, was no longer a child.

Trevor's summer too had turned him round. His friendship with the Quigleys had been his first in-depth exposure to adults who were not relatives or schoolmasters. He was comfortably in love with both Ben and Lenore. But most important he had soaked himself in a sea of painting and he felt permanently changed by that experience. He had said to himself, 'I can do that', and in a few weeks he had proved he could. He had moved from proud astonishment that he was able to paint any sort of picture at all to a critical assessment of what he was doing and a determination to make himself better. Unlike Sarah, Trevor had no dissatisfaction with his relationship with his mother. Nor did he see Ben Quigley as a substitute father. But all the same he was warmly pleased to have a man he admired for a friend.

It seemed impossible that the battleground between Major Cranston and Margaret could be festooned with peace banners, but each of them, in fact, had found an area of truce. Or so it appeared. Cranston's was based, of course, as were most of his judgements, on self-delusion, but Margaret's was founded on self-confidence, warm memories of the recent past, and faith in the future. Cranston convinced himself that the storm would pass between himself and Margaret, that his indolent, aimless life would go on as it always had. Equal portions of arrogance, alcohol, and paranoia. And thoughtful fondling of his revolvers. For her part, Margaret simply resolved that no circumstances could prevent her from having whatever life she might choose for herself.

10

In their letters to each other Kincaid and Sophie had promised they would go off to Britanny together as soon as he returned from California. And they did. Two days after he got back. When they unlocked the cottage and carried their bags inside, she said, 'How long can we stay?'

'As long as you like. Till you get tired of me.'

'How about for ever? How does that sound?'

'Sounds good to me.'

They changed clothes at once and walked along the beach, chattering to each other like children who had just returned home from separate holidays. She told him about her mother's situation, about her own difficulties with Sarah, and all the events of her summer at Praia da Rocha. When she interrupted her story with questions about California, about Evan, and about the movie, he told her the details.

'So you're going to be a big success and all the women in the world will fall in love with you?' she said.

'That's what Thorne says but I don't believe him.'

'Do you mean to say you haven't seen any of the film? If I were you I'd be tortured by curiosity.'

'I was tortured by panic. I didn't want to see it.'

'But we'll see it when it's finished,' she said.

'I'm not looking forward to it but I expect we will.'

'And then Mr Thorne will be after you to come back to California and make another movie. Or is he after you already?'

'He has something in mind, I think.'

'Of course he does. What did you tell him?'

'I've never promised him anything beyond *Bushranger*.'

'What did you tell him exactly?'

'I told him I didn't want to talk about any project now. I said I was going back to England to see you, to sit in a chair by the window, and look out on Green Park. We'll see how *Bushranger* works out and then maybe we'll talk about something else later. *Maybe*, I said.'

'You mean you and Thorne will talk about it?'

'Yes. But I also meant that you and I would talk about it.'

'So I have a vote?' she asked.

501

'You have as many votes as you want.'

She stopped walking then, turned to him and kissed him. 'Maybe I should have all the votes. Perhaps I should be the queen and you should be my slave.'

'Why not? Do I get to sleep with the queen?'

'All the time. That's what slaves are for.'

Late that night, they lay on the couch in front of the fire, warm and tangled together, half asleep.

'Do you have any idea how awful it was for me,' she said. 'Do you know how rotten I felt, how miserable I was without you?'

He pulled her closer to him. 'It's all right now,' he said. 'I'm never going off without you again.'

'I'll never *let* you go off without me again.'

Because each of them misunderstood the other's reply, they were content. They closed their eyes and lay in each other's arms, dreaming their separate dreams about tomorrow.